SUPERB WRITING
TO FIRE THE IMAGINATION

Robin Jarvis writes: 'Whenever I am asked where I get my ideas for books and characters, I always wish I could come up with some weird and wonderful answer. "I dream them," for example, or, "I get inspired whenever there is a full moon." But, unfortunately, neither of these is true. Like many writers, I sometimes base my characters on real people (or parts of real people) and sometimes they are the complete product of my imagination. But they generally all start as a sketch or drawing and then take shape as a character is developed around them.

'I started making sketches of mice because they were the smallest things I could think of to draw. When I sent them to a publisher, I was asked if there was a story to go with the drawings. At the time there wasn't, but I sat down and thought of a project visually and drew a story board as though I were making a film. I had envisaged it as a picture book, but it became a 70,000 word manuscript and I've been writing ever since.

'I can't think of a better way to earn a living!'

THE DEPTFORD HISTORIES

BOOK ONE

The Alchymist's Cat

ROBIN JARVIS

Hodder
Children's
Books

a division of Hodder Headline

A Catalogue record for this book is available from
the British Library

ISBN 0 340 78865 8

Typeset by Avon Dataset Ltd, Bidford-on-Avon, Warks

Printed and bound in Great Britain by
Clays Ltd, St Ives plc

Hodder Children's Books
A Division of Hodder Headline Limited
338 Euston Road
London NW1 3BH

CONTENTS

THE BEGINNING

It was a fine night; the full moon edged the sleeping city with silver and the deep velvet dark of the sky was splashed with stars. A perfect night for a cat to roam.

The city of London was a marvellous playground to stalk in; with its narrow, dark alleys and open drains it held countless possibilities and there were hints of adventure round every corner. The squashed huddle of houses that shouldered together uncomfortably on either side of the shadowy street were blind to the night. Only in one window was a candle steadily burning but she took no heed of that.

There was a heady cocktail of scents on the air, a blissful mingling of twilight odours, and her sensitive whiskers searched hungrily through the breeze.

Beneath the dank, green reek of the river which always assaulted the nose, she detected the movement of many creatures; the night foragers were abroad. Mice were scratching in the walls of the wooden houses – raiding the pantries too, no doubt. A fearsome dog howled near the old bearpits and its plaintive wail floated over the ramshackle rooftops like a banshee. But no, there in the dim deeps, under the straw stacked against the gates of the brewer's yard was what she sought this night – rats.

As a spectral vapour she slunk from shadow to shadow, noiseless and determined as Death himself. Only her golden eyes glinting under the moon could betray her but she kept them half closed, leaving only slender slivers which floated over the cobbles like razors.

The thrill of the hunt was mounting as she lowered her head and padded after her prey. How strong the smell of rat was here, she could almost feel the heat of their blood burn in her nostrils. And then she waited; expert in the art of being still as stone, she held her breath – at one with the night.

The dirty straw rustled and a furry brown snout nosed the air suspiciously.

'I tells ya 'Arry,' muttered a nervous voice, 'there's summat not right in the air out there.'

'Tush Bert!' came an answering squeak. 'What's put ya in this un'appy 'umour. Y'aint been feelin proper fer days now.'

''Tain't that 'Arry,' replied Bert retracting his twitching snout. 'I swears by the Three thesselves I don't like the whiff of the wind.'

'Dullard!' snorted the other. 'I've a mind to dine off grain tonight and have my fill o' m'lord brewer's barley sacks. You stay 'ere 'an feed off dung an' beetles but I'm away.'

Harry shuffled out of the straw and shielded his tiny black eyes from the bright moon. What a glorious night for pilfering and eating your fill. The rat thrashed his tail gleefully and hopped on to the cobbles. He did not hear her spring.

'Aaaarrrgggghhh!' he bawled when he became aware of her hot breath on his neck and felt her strong claws squeeze round him.

'I'm dead, Bert!' he wailed. 'Flee, while you can . . .' and then he was silent.

The cat trotted away contented, with the dead,

juicy rat dangling from her mouth.

She wanted to enjoy this delicacy in peace and knew the very spot. On to a rain barrel she leapt and from there jumped to a window-sill. Then she sure-footedly walked around the side of the building using one of the decorative beams set into the wall as a ledge. And so up, to the sloping roof, where she stretched herself out on the cool tiles and devoured her supper.

In the full glare of the moon she was a gorgeous creature; her ginger fur almost seemed to glow under its baleful beams. Her features were fine and delicate, having a sharp chin and small pink nose – indeed she was considered a great beauty yet none of her countless suitors had claimed her.

From her vantage point she surveyed London like an empress with a supreme look of disdain upon her proud face. The streets were quiet now, even the dog had ceased its howling; all was calm. Yet she was wise enough to know that it was on such nights as these that the most gruesome murders were committed or the direst tragedies could occur. Death and disaster were always eager visitors when they were least expected.

A man trailed through the streets below with a lantern in his hand. With her glittering eyes she watched his progress and saw him pause on every corner where he called out, 'Eleven of the clock on a fine October night and all's well.'

She hated mankind, they were ugly, stupid and cruel beasts – yet she had the wit to use them on occasion. There were at least seven houses in the city where she was known and where a spot of milk or table scraps could be had in return for a measure of play acting. A smile spread over her face as she thought how easy it was to mew prettily and press her head against their shambling legs in a mock display of affection.

'Verily, I am yours,' was the expression she always wore for the gullible fools. What simpletons they were to think they owned her, she who could hunt when there was no moon – by scent alone. She was totally a creature of the wild, untameable and ravishing as darkness itself.

Beneath the tiles she heard the muted voices of bats whispering their prophecies to each other; she had never tasted bat before and idly wondered what they were like.

The moon rose higher in the clear sky and she dozed happily with her head in her paws but even in sleep she was alert.

Her ears flicked in agitation as the nightwatchman returned. She heard the squeak of the rusty lantern chain as it swung slowly and the breath of the fat oaf wheezing out of his lungs as he prepared to call out once again. Why were people so ridiculous? her drowsy mind speculated. Why could they not feel the thrill of the hunt and prowl at night? She would probably never know.

'Midnight on a fine October even' and all's well,' came the voice of the man.

'Fine and well indeed,' said a different voice nearby.

She leapt to her feet at once, angry that she had missed the newcomer's approach. She peered into the shade beneath one of the chimney stacks and

The Beginning

quested the air to get a scent, but try as she might the identity of the stranger eluded her.

'And what a fine lady we have here,' it said from the gloom. The voice was rich and silky, oozing with charm and fascination.

Her eyes glared at the shadows and a warning rumble began in her throat.

'There's fire in the dame too,' purred the voice with undisguised delight. 'Excellent! You please me more and more, my dove.'

'Tib?' she ventured uncertainly. 'If that's you lurking there come out, or by the gods I shall swipe at thee!' Effortlessly her needle-like claws slid out and she scraped one against the tiles making a piercing sound like the screech of a stuck pig.

Soft laughter drifted over the rooftops. 'I come not to fight my sweet,' the stranger told her gently, 'but to woo thee and win thy heart – oh lucky heart to beat in thy breast, would it were beating for me.'

She spat her rejection and looked away; she was getting bored of this. How many times had she heard the same old thing from the mouths of all the toms from Highgate to Lambeth?

'Stay a while my treasure,' called the voice urgently. 'I shall leave my cover if 'twill win thy favour.'

She turned, curious to see who had been making a fool of himself this time.

From the black shadow pits two eyes appeared and they were the most stunning she had ever beheld. Like twin emeralds they were, yet they possessed a spark, nay, a sacred fire blazed in them, the sight of which quickened her breath and set a flame of her own coursing through her blood.

'Here am I to claim thee,' said the voice and the sound of it was like music to her now.

Out of the dark he came, a slender, handsome cat, the finest she had yet seen. Like a piece of the wild night he melted from the shade, with an easy, confident gait he approached and his noble head was held high. Into the moonlight he glided and she saw with hungry eyes that his fur was sable from ear tip to tail end.

He studied her carefully for a moment and put the power of his eyes on her.

'Tell me sir,' she murmured breathlessly as she gazed at him, 'from whence do you come? I have not heard of such a one as you in all my nights abroad.'

The black cat sat down beside her and his tail twined with hers and she, being too overcome by the heat of his glance, did not even notice. 'This night is the first I have seen with these eyes,' he said mysteriously.

She dragged her own away and stared at the carved wooden sign which marked the fish shop opposite. Her breaths eased yet still she was aware of him and his influence; the touch of his fur next to hers was like a wound that ached to be healed.

'How are you called, my maid?' he asked.

'I have many names,' she answered with a weak laugh. 'Younder am I known as Mewler; to the grocer – China I am after the oranges that he do sell; in the merchant's – Silky; and to the fat landlord of The Old Swan – Mouser. Tell me, Master Midnight,' she said teasingly, 'which of these is mine own?'

He shook his head wisely. 'You play with me, my

maid,' he replied with mock hurt. 'To none of those vulgar callings would you answer. Too elegant and shapely are you and too sharp-witted also to suffer thus at man's clumsy hands. May I not know the truth?'

She was accustomed to flattery, the local toms had often poured treacly words on her and all to no effect, but this one was different. She smiled and acknowledged his superiority over them all. 'I am Imelza,' she replied courteously.

'Imelza,' he repeated trying the name out on his own tongue, 'it does suit you well.'

She faced him coolly and inquired, 'Now you know, My Lord, will you not return the gesture? What shall I call you?'

'Two names you have already give me, my pretty Imelza,' he laughed. 'First, "Master Midnight" and now "My Lord". I like them both well enough.' The mirth subsided and he said to himself, 'And how apt they prove to be.'

'But this is most unfair,' she countered, 'that you should know my true self yet you would withhold yours from me.'

The black cat turned his green fires on her. 'As to that,' he purred, 'if it pleases you – call me Imp, that should suffice. Yet I have many true names, more than you could guess.'

'Imp,' she muttered. 'I like "My Lord" better.'

'Then let it be so.'

The moon shone down on them and that night they were as one, and so the seed of terror was sown.

1

Childhood Forsaken

'Nothing is what it seems,' Will whispered to himself, repeating a favourite saying of his father's. The boy stared up at the sky. 'Is it the usual ill-humour of November that falls – or is God weeping for them?'

Grey rain drizzled down and the small, sodden group of mourners shivered uncomfortably. A large dew drop dangled from the pale minister's nose as he read from the New Prayer Book and his droning voice filled the drab churchyard. The downpour continued, the puddles grew and the drenched garments of those assembled became spattered with mud. Will lowered his eyes, the tears on his face lost amid the rain.

1664 was drawing to an end. The nation was revelling in the Restoration. Charles II had been on the throne for four years and the wounds of the Civil

War were slowly healing. But the peace would not last for much longer. Already there were rumblings of a war with the Dutch and sweet England was about to enter into one of the most terrifying and grimmest times it had yet witnessed.

Such events however seemed a world away from that dismal ceremony in an Oxfordshire churchyard where the rain beat down.

Daniel Godwin had been well respected by those in the village of Adcombe, he had never given his neighbours cause to complain and he was a fair master to those few he employed. If it had been a lesser man who was being laid to rest then this filthy weather would have kept them all away.

Daniel had been a yeoman who worked behind the plough all his life, but the soil that he tilled and watered with sweat was his own. The titles to the land which he furrowed and nearly broke his back for belonged to him alone and not a day had passed by without his grateful thanks being offered up to the Lord. But now he was dead – the smallpox was not in the pay of the Almighty and the righteous it claimed as eagerly as the sinful.

In all, the tally of dead on the Godwin estate amounted to five; these being Daniel, his wife Sarah, Beth and Anne – their two daughters – and a man called Shackle who was one of the labourers on the farm.

The waiting grave was deep and Will stood upon its mud-slithering brink, gazing steadily down into the blackness below. He felt as empty as it would soon be full. Master William Godwin was a slim youth. The hair which hung about his shoulders was chestnut in colour – a perfect match to his hazel eyes – and, fortunately, his lean face had been spared the usual marks which the smallpox leaves in its wake. Yet today that face was devoid of expression.

One by one the coffins were lowered. How strange to think that the mortal remains of all those he had loved were now sealed into them. He choked back a sob as the smallest of those horrible caskets descended to join the others. Anne had only been six years old.

A comforting hand patted the boy on the shoulder. 'Shows them yer respects Will lad,' said a voice, 'cast in some earth.'

Will blinked and turned round. A fat, heavily jowled man with a red, bulbous nose and whiskers like a badger was looking at him squarely. 'There is no soil,' the boy muttered, 'just mud. Look – see how it pours over the edge. Already the . . .' he faltered, not able to say the correct word, '. . . boxes are covered.'

Mr Balker, the miller, gripped the boy's shoulder more tightly with his podgy hand whilst he reached into the pocket of his great coat with his other. 'Now don't you fret on so lad,' he told him bringing out a small bag. 'I had no likin' for the sunset yesterday – an' afeared as I was that the day would be a wettun I got me some earth from the sexton.' He handed the bag to Will who received it gratefully. 'Don't get me wrong now,' the miller added with haste, 'weren't no special trip up 'ere that I made, I were only passin' an' the notion took me, 'ats all.'

'I thank you, Mr Balker,' nodded Will. He understood – the miller enjoyed a sour reputation and was anxious that no one should see this chink of humanity in his calloused armour.

The boy took the dry soil from the bag and slowly sprinkled it into the grave. 'Goodbye,' he said.

'Now let's get you indoors,' coughed Mr Balker gruffly. 'The Millhouse is yonder an' you'll be needin' summat warm in yer belly, I'll warrant.'

Will hesitated. It was his duty to thank the minister but the black-gowned figure was already hurrying towards the church. The other mourners were scurrying off also, hastening to their crackling hearths – they had shown their respect for the departed and now their thoughts were for themselves.

'Come you, lad,' urged the miller, 'you don't want to join yer folks just yet.'

Will took a last look at the deluged grave and pulled the collar of his cloak tightly under his chin. He was on his own now.

'Would you just look at the state of you both!' the bustling woman cried, throwing her arms up in distress. Muddy pools spread over the stone-flagged floor as the two squelching arrivals stamped and removed their outdoor clothes. 'John Balker, take them boots off at once!' she scolded. 'Never was there a more slovenly wretch.'

The miller muttered under his breath but his sister pretended not to hear. Instead she rushed to Will's side and helped him off with his things. 'Bless you Master William if you aren't raw with the cold,' she tutted. 'It's the Devil's own weather today. You'll be lucky not to catch a distemper, I swear!'

Hannah Balker was, in appearance, very much like her brother. She was plump and rosy with small

piggish eyes, but there the similarities ended. Whereas the miller was inclined to be crude and rather too fond of the ale jug, she was the opposite. Mistress Balker was a devout soul who possessed all the religious zeal of a Puritan. Her impious brother caused her much anxiety and she prayed for him almost constantly. With her hands fluttering over her black, woollen skirt and up to the white cap which covered her silvering hair she ushered him and Will into the small parlour where a fire had been lit in readiness for their return.

The miller grunted with pleasure as he toasted his tingling palms before the flames. Will sat in one of the large wooden chairs and watched Hannah scurry in and out of the kitchen with a large jug of beer and two tankards. She set them down on a low table, poured the brown, foaming brew then nudged her brother out of the way.

'Always underfoot,' she clucked. 'Sit you down, John Balker, and let me fetch that poker from the fire.'

Stubbornly the miller remained standing so she squirmed past him and reached down to the hearth. From the leaping flames she took a long iron poker by its blackened wooden handle and flourished it over her head. 'I told you to sit,' she told him sternly. 'Do so or I'll brand thee as surely as if you were a Jesuit.'

Mr Balker opened his mouth to protest but he took one look at the glowing tip of the poker and sat down at once.

His sister stared at him for a moment then went over to the table. The poker squealed and steam hissed up as she plunged it into one tankard after another. 'There you are Master William,' she said kindly handing Will the warm ale, 'that'll put the colour back in you. It's spiced with ginger, nutmeg, cinnamon and cloves – the way your dear father liked it.'

The boy thanked her and sipped it thoughtfully.

The miller eyed his sister as she left the room and hurried back to the kitchen, the keys which hung from her waist jingling like bells.

'Fuss, fuss, fuss,' he grumbled pulling himself from the chair to resume his position before the fire. 'If she's not fussin' she's frettin' about popish plots.' Several minutes passed in which he warmed his posterior and took great swigs from his tankard. During this time he regarded Will most keenly. Mr Balker had a great liking for the Godwin family; he remembered how kind Mistress Sarah had been to him after he had lost his own wife. Until Hannah had arrived to take him and the Millhouse in hand he had eaten all his meals at the Godwins' farm.

'How old be you now, Will?' he asked breaking the silence.

The boy stirred from the mellowing effects of the spiced ale and replied, 'I shall be twelve years old come next July.'

John Balker wiped the froth moustache which had appeared on his lip. 'Well, I know 'taint easy, lad, but you'll have to become a man quicker 'n most. You've got responsibilities now – land that needs working, servants with wages to pay and that big house to run. Won't be time fer malarkin' about and tomfoolin', you'm got to put all that behind you – boyhood's over. Think you're ready fer all that?'

Will lifted his face and gazed steadily into the miller's eyes. 'I've thought about this, sir,' he answered soberly, 'thought about little else since . . .

since *they've* been gone like.' He put the beer down on the table then said, 'Yes, it'll be difficult but I think I can manage the estate. I saw how my father ran things, I shall try to continue in the way he would wish.'

A great and hearty roar issued from the miller. 'Bless me but you've some surprises in you!' he laughed. 'Why, that might have been Daniel himself speakin'.' He gave a throaty chuckle and raised his tankard but it was empty. 'Where's that sister of mine with the jug?' he grumbled. 'A man could die of thirst with her around.' He called her name loudly, then sat on the chair again. 'Don't you get frettin',' he told Will, wagging a thick, chilblained finger. 'I'm always here if'n you want advice or assistance. Bound to be tough goin' at the start and that's what I'm here fer – to give you a helpin' hand.'

Will finished his ale and pulled a stray clove from his mouth. There was something he had been meaning to ask the miller and it had been nagging at him to mention it. 'Mr Balker,' he ventured.

'Now that's enough of that talk,' chided his host, 'it's plain John I'll be to you from here on. We're neighbours now an' I ain't no better'n you. Mind,' he added leaning his portly frame forward, 'I'm not sayin' as there aren't those round 'ere I am better'n.'

'John, then,' the boy continued. 'What I said just now still holds true, I mean to be the man my father was but . . .' he lowered his eyes and looked into the fire, 'but I have something to confess which shames me.'

The miller raised his eyebrows. 'Oh yes?' he began with interest.

Will pressed his lips together until they went white before he managed to spit it out. 'I cannot read!' he said bitterly.

The fat man's face broke into a wide grin. 'Bless us all!' he rumbled. 'Why there's nowt shameful in not knowin' yer letters, Will; you can learn if'n you've a mind to. Hannah can do the house accounts fer you till then, there's a quick little mind in that Puritan head of hers.' The mention of his sister's name reminded him of something else and he shouted for the jug once more.

Will looked relieved; that was a great weight off his mind and he turned to another matter which had been worrying him since that morning. 'Mr . . . John,' he began, taking a folded sheet of paper from the inside of his shirt where it had been spared the ravages of the weather. The miller looked at it in puzzlement. 'It's a letter,' the lad explained, 'it arrived at daybreak, only I don't know what it says – could you read it for me?'

Mr Balker took it and bent towards the fire in order to see more clearly. The flickering yellow light danced over his round features as the expression which he reserved for business crept on to his face and his lips mouthed the words on the page. 'Well bless us all!' he exclaimed with surprise. 'After all them years.' He sat up straight and peered at Will down his strawberry blob of a nose. 'Ever heard mention of an Uncle Samuel?' he asked.

Will frowned and shook his head.

The miller slapped the letter with the back of his hand. 'That's who this be from,' he said. 'I recall that yer father once talked about a brother. But I had to coax it out and it was the only time he ever referred to him.'

'Are you sure?' asked Will. 'He never said anything about him to me or my sisters – of that I'm certain.'

Mr Balker stroked his whiskers as he strained to remember. 'Seems there was bad blood 'tween them,' he said, 'and I think I'm right in sayin that uncle of yours was a lot older than your father. A might too clever for his own good was how Daniel put it when I pressed him. Well, well, fancy him sendin' you this, an' all the way from London too.'

'London?'

'That's where the letter's from and that's where Samuel Godwin lives now it seems.'

'So what does it say?'

The miller shifted uncomfortably in the chair and, for an instant, seemed reluctant to tell the lad. 'Your uncle's heard about your sad loss,' he eventually began, 'though bless us I can't think how – it being a day's hard ride to London from here.' He shivered as though something cold had touched his heart before continuing. 'Says he knows how you must be feelin' an' invites you to stay at his lodgings until you've a mind to return as there is a matter of the most import which cannot wait to be settled. 'Parently there's some business of a financial nature which he needs must discuss with you. He ends by askin' you to respond swiftly as the roads will worsen as the winter sets in.' Mr Balker passed the letter back and Will wondered at the troubled expression that had stolen over his face.

'If'n you want my advice,' he said, 'this be a matter best left alone – if your father never talked about him then your uncle can't be worth much.'

Will turned the paper over in his fingers, he was not sure what to do and yet a curious feeling began to grow inside him. To be honest he was greatly excited by this invitation; a mysterious uncle he had never heard of before and the chance to see the wondrous city of London thrilled him.

'I would like to go,' he said softly, 'I need only be gone two weeks – I could leave instructions for the management of the farm while I'm away.' He looked across at the miller who was studying him in silence. 'You don't think I should, do you?' he murmured.

'That I don't,' returned Mr Balker. 'I've been to London, lad, I know what it's really like. The river is as stinkful as anything on the Lord's earth and the city's as sinful as the Devil's bedchamber. Folks are bad there. I know – I've seen 'em.' He paused and looked at the floor, but his gaze penetrated beyond the rush matting and for a moment he was lost in some dreadful memory. Just as quickly the mood left him and he glanced back towards Will. 'But it's not just that vile place I'm warnin' you of,' he told him, 'there's summat not right about that letter. Just what sort of business is he referrin' to? I know Daniel never 'ad no dealin's wi' 'im. If that piece o' paper were mine I'd cast it into the fire.'

Will was startled by the miller's earnestness but he had already made up his mind. 'Just now you told me that I must leave behind me my boyhood,' he said. 'This then is my first decision as a man. The memories here are too painful for the present, I am loath to stay with the ghostly faces of my family staring out of every corner. A journey to London may well be the cure I need to shake off the melancholy which has been creeping upon me, and who is to say that my uncle's motives are not what he says them to be? Perhaps he knows about some inheritance of which I am unaware?'

Mr Balker realised that he would not be able to weaken the boy's resolve; he had seen the same determination in Will's father. 'Then I shall help you all I can,' he said at last. 'We must answer swiftly as the letter instructs. Stay here, I shall fetch quill and paper.'

So the reply was written, but the hand which scrawled the spidery words trembled, and not from the cold.

Soon all the arrangements had been made. Another letter had come from Samuel Godwin making it clear that he would expect Will on the fifteenth of November and would meet him at the Sickle Moon tavern in Bow Lane. He also enclosed six shillings to cover any expense that Will's journey might incur. Will's excitement mounted as the days crept by and his spirits were lifted even more by Mr Balker's announcement that he would travel with him to the city as he had business there of his own.

'Now's as good a time as any to see to it,' the miller had said briskly, 'and I've let it lie for far too long. I'll ride with you into the city and see you safe within its walls.'

A bleak dawn saw Will clamber into the saddle. Mace was rather too large for him; she had been his father's horse and the boy sat uneasily on her back. Still, she was a good-natured animal and what he lacked in horsemanship she was experienced enough to make up for. With a light heart he waved farewell to the servants who had gathered to see him off and turned the mare to leave.

The first hint of winter was in the chill air and a white frost covered the ground. Will was glad of the gauntlets made of soft leather which his mother had given him on his last birthday – no icy wind would nip his fingers. As he rode the short mile between his farm and the Millhouse his mind was filled with the journey ahead and who he would meet at the end of it. There were so many questions still left unanswered; the second letter had still not specified the exact nature of the business and the boy's head was filled with fanciful ideas. But rising over all of these was the mysterious character of his uncle. What would he be like and what would he have to say to the nephew he had never seen? All these thoughts were running through his mind when he came across the stream which fed the millpond and Mace followed it obediently. The low roofs of the Millhouse came into view and he discerned two figures standing in the yard.

Mr Balker was already in his cart and shooing his sister indoors out of the damp morning mist that rose off the pond. As Will approached, he heard their never-ending squabbling and he smiled to himself. For as long as he could remember the Balkers had been at odds – yet he knew they would be lost without one another. He was too young to remember the miller's wife; she had died before he was born but his father had told him how deeply it had affected the man.

'Get you in, woman!' bellowed the miller. 'I'll not

be governed by an old spinster like yerself.'

'You're a fool, John Balker,' Hannah ranted lifting her skirts off the damp ground. 'Let the past stay in the past. There's nothing you can do to mend matters now. She's gone from you and won't never come back.'

'You'll cut yourself on that sharp tongue of yours,' he spat bitterly. 'People change – I've changed and it's time to find out if'n she has also.' At that moment they became aware of Will and the argument lapsed into the more usual bickering.

'Well just you mind to keep out of them inns, John Balker. A sot's an easy target for the Devil's arrows.'

'Mornin', Will,' hailed the miller, sweeping off his hat in greeting.

'A good morning to you, John,' returned the boy cheerily, 'and to you Mistress Balker.'

Hannah smoothed her starched white collar and beamed up at him. 'Oh can't you talk sense into my foolish brother, Master William?' she pleaded. 'Make him stay here. He's too old and too addled to go all that way, and London's an evil place I've heard.'

Before he could answer, the miller screamed back at her, 'Peace, Hannah! I will not be gainsaid in this! Now get you indoors!'

There was such an edge to his voice that his sister stepped back in alarm and bowed her head meekly. 'I bid you farewell then, brother,' she muttered, 'and a safe and pleasant journey to you, young master.'

The door to the Millhouse closed behind her and Will stared at it in surprise. He had never heard the miller take that tone with her before and he wondered at it.

Mr Balker shuffled on the board of the cart and avoided the boy's eyes. 'Won't never get to London if we idle here,' he said clicking his tongue and twitching the reins. The old, dappled carthorse pulled back its head and began to plod out of the yard. Will urged Mace to follow and, at a leisurely pace, she trotted after.

For the rest of the day they rode side by side, the rattling of the cartwheels filling their ears until they forgot what silence was. The miller soon shook off his ill temper and the talk became less strained. They chatted freely about all manner of things until the nature of the roads forced them to concentrate solely on the journey. Many times the wheels of the cart struck unseen stones, and once the mud was so thick that it threatened to hold them firm. They met little other traffic on those rutted roads; several waggoners, a vagrant who begged for passage, two milkmaids balancing wooden pails upon their heads who giggled when they saw Will on his father's horse, and a drover taking cattle to market.

They spent that night at a small and friendly inn where the miller restrained himself and drank only the penny ale which was weaker than the tuppenny and had little effect upon his massive bulk. Will staggered to his room with his eyelids almost closed. He had never felt so tired; his legs and backside ached from the saddle and he quickly dragged his clothes off and threw himself on to the bed. Within moments he was fast asleep, dreaming of what he would see tomorrow.

The miller's loud voice woke him the next morning. The sun was just edging into the sky and its delicate beams slowly stole into the room. 'Up you get, Will,' he boomed, 'there's a tidy bit of ground to cover till we make London.'

After a good breakfast of bread, butter and a selection of cold meats they paid the bill and went to the stables.

'When shall we get to London?' asked Will once they had left the inn behind them.

Mr Balker yawned and picked his teeth with a splinter of wood. 'Soon enough,' he replied. 'At the rate we're goin', I fancy we'll see it at noon an' be there early this evenin'.'

The bright morning continued and they travelled on with the countryside opening up around them. From the woods and forests on either side of the road trails of smoke drifted up and, although Will knew that it was only the fires of the charcoal burners, the miller told him stories of robbers and wild men who dwelt in the trees. He was full of entertaining and thrilling tales and the boy loved to hear them. Even the call of a fox was woven into the story, becoming the shriek of some unearthly creature that brave men had perished trying to slay.

And as the sun rose to its highest in the clear wintry sky, they found themselves looking down into the Thames Valley and there, in the distance, was a vast blue blur.

'There she is,' breathed Mr Balker almost reverently. 'London – city of cities. Where dreams and nightmares mingle and come as one.'

Will stared at her in awe; he had never beheld anything like it in his life. 'She's beautiful,' he gasped.

'So was Grandmother Eve,' commented the miller,

drily, 'and that's how she seduced Adam and damned us all. It's the same down there, lad. London might seem fair and lovely from here but the closer you get to her the more you'll be able to discern the truth of it. First the smell'll get yer and then you'll see just how unlovely she really be. All them tiny houses that look so pretty from here are wretched slums an' the streets are filled wi' rottenness of every sort. My sister would tell you that the Devil himself stalks through those streets and I would'na decry her in that. If ever there was proof that the Antichrist was at work on this earth then London is it. Everything you never wanted to know is taught and practised in yon ravishing vision – even under the shadow of those steeples you can see pricking through the haze.' He turned to look at Will and his face was drained of colour. 'It's a terrible place,' he uttered. 'Are you still set on entering there?'

But the majesty of the city, whether it was an illusion or not, had overwhelmed the boy and he nodded fiercely. 'I'll not turn back now,' he said.

'So be it then, but I'll warn you one last time, William Godwin. Don't you go looking to find any of your father in that uncle. I've a notion they were from different moulds – if not different makers.' And with that Mr Balker clicked his tongue, the wheels of the cart turned once more and, still mesmerised, Will followed.

2

'Where Dreams and Nightmares Mingle'

The narrow streets closed about them and the ramshackle houses on either side jostled and fought with each other for space. Will had never seen so many squalid and cramped dwellings. Most of them were constructed around timber frames and many leaned or lurched at peculiar angles out over the bustling thoroughfare. Dominating all this, however, was St Paul's Cathedral. It was the grand dame of all buildings; soaring almost into the clouds, it dwarfed churches and palaces for miles around. Even without its spire, which had collapsed some time ago, the central tower was the tallest thing Will had ever beheld. Surely God lived there, he thought to himself and he humbly lowered his eyes.

In the streets, the sights were strange: street traders advertised their wares in loud and harsh voices; dogs barked at the piemen and growled at the horses; an old dancing bear shambled round in a circle for the bored onlookers who had seen it all before and who poked the unfortunate beast with sharp sticks to make the performance more exciting. Children with no shoes on their feet but sly looks on their faces ran in and out of the crowd pulling at the merchants' clothes and stealing from the stalls. A pock-marked woman with long, lank hair leaned out of an upstairs window and emptied a slop bucket on to the crowd below. In the ensuing uproar fists were raised and oaths spat out but the woman simply threw back her head and laughed – toothlessly.

Will drank all this in with wide and ogling eyes. Since he and the miller had passed through the old, high walls of the medieval city he had encountered a thousand new things. One of the most ghastly was to be found upon the walls themselves; upon those lofty ramparts there were the limbs of villains and traitors. Heads, legs and arms had been stuck on great spikes for all the populace to see and Will could not stop himself from staring at these grisly totems. A tingling thrill was coursing through his veins; seizing him like a fever it took absolute control. He was besotted with it all – fascinated beyond measure by this wealth of experience unfolding before him.

They came to a butcher's shop and he coughed into the handkerchief which he held to his nose – the miller had been right about one thing, London stank! But it wasn't just the stench of the dubious meat which hung from the huge hooks outside the butcher's shop, *everything* smelled atrociously. The fish market filled the air with a reek that had to be experienced to be believed, and to make matters worse, if such a thing was possible, an open sewer ran down each and every street. Yet even this could not bring the boy to his senses.

Mr Balker shifted in his seat and called, 'What think you of London now, Will lad? Is she as dainty a lady as you once thought?'

He only laughed in reply then asked, 'How much further is this tavern?'

'The Sickle Moon? Oh, 'tain't too far,' the miller told him. 'To tell you the truth, I'll be glad of a tankard this night. The road's been a dusty one this day.'

Through the overshadowed lanes they rode and the sun sank low behind the tiled rooftops, its pale red fire dancing in the countless diamond panes of the leaded windows all around. To Will they were like jewels and whilst they dazzled him he failed to see that the glass in which the light burned was smothered in dirt. London had cast her spell with great success, never was there a more willing victim to her charms. Yet the magic never lasted for long; she would tantalise and tease, then just as you were enslaved you were cruelly abandoned and she sought for other insects to entice into her web.

The Sickle Moon tavern was situated on the corner of Bow Lane and Cheapside. From all outward appearances it seemed to be a cheerless, almost forbidding place. It was the only building on the street which was untouched by the soft rays of the failing sun. No smoke issued from its crooked chimneys and weeds cascaded from the eaves. As soon as Will saw it he shuddered, taking an instant dislike to the shabby establishment.

'Be dark soon,' observed Mr Balker as he dismounted from the cart. 'Best get indoors. Looks like the stables are through that archway. Come on, lad.'

But Will hung back reluctantly. 'I don't like this place, John,' he said. 'Can't we go somewhere else?'

'Not if you want to meet yer uncle,' the miller answered flatly before leading his horse away. He didn't care what the tavern looked like – if the ale was good then that was enough for him.

In one of the second-floor rooms a lamp was lit and Will glanced nervously at the ruddy glow which glinted from the narrow window. An unreasoning fear stole over him. It was as if the building had awoken. 'It knows I'm here,' he whispered to himself. 'It's watching me.' The voice of Mr Balker called to him from the stable yard and the boy gave a sigh of resignation. For the first time since his arrival Will wished he had not come.

Even when the horses had been stabled Will was far from happy; the straw there was filthy and the stable-lad a foul-mouthed youth who glanced covetously at Mace and ran his fingers through her mane with a wide, sneering grin on his face.

Will felt as though he were coming out of a fair dream, the enchantment which had possessed him and burned so fiercely in his blood disappeared and the scales of glamour fell from his eyes. Everything now seemed unfriendly and as the shadows lengthened in the stable yard they seemed to reach inside and a chill touched his heart. He dragged his heels behind the miller with an uncomfortable sense of dread and apprehension mounting in him.

Mr Balker pushed open the heavy, studded door and stepped inside the tavern.

The interior of the Sickle Moon was poky and small. Oak beams supported the bulging ceiling which had been blackened by the flames of a thousand candles. On one side there was a large fireplace where some logs were now burning. But the wood was wet and the flames spluttered, filling the room with smoke and the smell of damp. Sawdust was strewn on the floor and seated upon the plain benches and low stools was a collection of villainous-looking men. The dregs of London must have been there that night.

Around one of the tables sat three old soldiers fallen on hard times. Once they had served under Cromwell in the New Model Army. At Naseby one of them had lost an arm but by the end of the war all three had lost their livings. Begging and thievery was their calling now and they pursued it as vigorously as their previous careers. A gang of drunken street traders huddled together by the fire and told each other evil and bawdy stories which were interspersed from time to time by horrible guffaws. A strange-looking man with bulging eyes, tufts of red hair and a wide, slobbering mouth dribbled into his drink by the door and picked distractedly at the frayed rips in his shirt, whilst in the furthest corner two cloaked and stony-faced men stared before them not saying a word to each other – as though waiting for something to happen.

As soon as Will and the miller entered, nineteen pairs of squinting, suspicious eyes swivelled round in their direction. The buzz of talk stopped at once. Curious and aggressive faces scrutinised the strangers with undisguised interest. Will felt very uncomfortable. It was obviously a very dangerous place. Surely they had come to the wrong tavern; there must be two Sickle Moons hereabouts. He edged closer to Mr Balker to voice this opinion, but the miller hissed him into silence then clapped his hands together and waved a greeting to them all.

'Pray don't let us stop your tippling, gentlemen,' he told them merrily. 'We are but travellers who want nothing more than a bite to eat and to sample the London ale.' Gradually the crowd returned their attentions to the mugs in their hands and, little by little, the conversations began again.

'Have a care,' the miller said to Will through a fixed smile. 'Don't look so jumpy. Won't do no good to let these folk see ye're nervous. There's a seat by the window over there, let's make ourselves comfortable – that cart has shook my bones all day.'

Mr Balker sprawled on the bench and drew up a stool to rest his feet on. Will sat opposite and began gazing around him.

'Keep yer eyeballs looking this way, lad,' the miller whispered anxiously, 'or you might just lose them! This is no place for the curious.' He scratched his chin and muttered under his breath, 'This is plain madness, what's yer uncle thinkin' of invitin' you here? He'd best come soon, that's all I can say.'

'You don't think he's already here?'

'No, unless it's that carrot-topped fellow with the face of a frog over there. He seems to be the only one of any note – oh I know he's nothing now but them rags on his back were fine once and his lily white

23

hands ain't never seen hard work. Mebbe yer uncle's down on his luck.'

Will sneaked a glance at the pop-eyed man and grimaced. 'I hope it isn't him,' he whispered, 'he isn't at all what I was expecting.'

'You never know, there are many strange paths a man might take in his life – who's to tell what Samuel Godwin has been up to these last thirty years. I don't think your father even knew . . . hush now.'

'Evenin' sirs,' cried a strange, thin voice at Will's shoulder. 'What's yer pleasure?'

The boy shifted on the stool to see who had spoken.

A vulgar woman of middle age was standing behind him. Once upon a time she may have been handsome but the years and the rigours of life had robbed her. Peggy Blister had lost her looks but she spent many hours in front of the glass trying to reclaim them. Sadly, the more years that passed the longer this process took. Will was so startled by her appearance that he nearly fell to the floor. She looked like a hideously painted doll and so thickly were the pastes and rouges applied that she was forced to keep her face very still in case the garish mask cracked and flaked away. Consequently she spoke very strangely as she had to keep her teeth clenched together.

The miller pretended not to notice and kicked Will under the table to mind his manners.

'A jug of your finest ale, mistress, if it pleases you,' he asked politely.

'Oooh hark at him,' came the tight lipped response. 'Peg ain't had no fancy talk like that in a month o' Sundays. You can come 'ere again, sweetheart.' And she swaggered off to fetch the drinks, avoiding the

table where the red-haired man was sitting.

Will giggled. 'She looks like Mr Swales the blacksmith,' he said unkindly. 'Remember when he did that mummers' play and had to get dressed up in ribbons and his wife's clothes?'

But the miller did not share his mirth. 'Hold yer tongue Will,' he said. 'She'm can't help it.'

The boy opened his mouth to argue but before he could say anything Peg had returned.

'Here we are, my gallants,' she murmured. 'I done brought you the Humming Ale, that'll slake yer thirst and more besides – Dragon's Milk my reg'lars call it.'

'Bless you,' nodded the miller, 'this looks to be a fine brew – and so prettily presented.'

Peg shrieked with delight then leaned over and tickled the miller's whiskered jowls. 'My but yer a proper charmer, a girl has to be on her guard round you.'

Will was astonished, he had never seen this side of Mr Balker before. He knew that his weakness was the ale jug but never dreamt that he dallied with serving wenches. The boy wondered what the miller's pious sister would say if she were here. The ridiculous-looking pair continued to laugh and joke with one another before Peg went to fetch something for them to eat.

'What are you doing?' Will asked when she was out of earshot.

The miller raised his tankard before answering. 'Ah,' he breathed smacking his lips, '' tain't a bad little brew after all.' He studied the boy's face and leaned across the table. 'Listen to me, young master,' he said. 'I know what I'm about, so just you stay quiet.' The portly man took another drink then raised his head to catch a further glimpse of Peg. Strangely enough it wasn't desire that Will saw in his eyes but an expression of overwhelming sorrow and compassion.

A sudden commotion broke out behind him. Peg was on the way back but had passed too near to the frog-like man, who, with a delirious shout of joy, made a grab for her. 'EEE!' she squealed, 'Get away you 'orrid little demon!' There followed a loud 'CRACK' as she struck his head with one of the wooden dishes she was carrying. Food flew everywhere and the man let go of her to nurse his bleeding nose. The rest of the customers laughed and she sauntered over to the miller and Will as though nothing had happened.

'Sorry luvs,' she told them. ' 'Fraid half yer supper's on the floor.'

'Dear lady, you are unharmed I hope?' Mr Balker inquired.

'Oooh listen to 'im,' cooed Peg, gripping his podgy cheeks and wobbling them between her fingers. 'What a dove you are. But don't you worry none, I've nought to fear from the likes o' that over there. He's just a barmy old loon – Verney the Adamite he is, harmless but he do tend to tear yer clothes given half the chance. Now you sink yer teeth into this my darlin' an I'll fetch some more.'

When she had gone Mr Balker raised his eyebrows. 'So he's not yer uncle then,' he murmured. 'I wonder where Samuel Godwin can be?'

'Do you mean that you were playing up to her just to find out who that man was?' asked Will impressed by the miller's cunning. 'And I thought you were . . .'

'I know what you were thinkin',' the man scowled, 'an' p'raps it weren't all play actin'. I feel sorry for the Pegs o' this world – 'tain't easy bein' a single girl in London.'

Will said nothing – he thought that it was a long time since Peg had been a girl. Instead he tucked into the bread and cheese.

For two hours they sat there, waiting for Samuel Godwin to arrive, but the only newcomer was an old beggar woman who pestered the customers for money until Peg harshly threw her outside. Mr Balker drank more of the Humming Ale. He finished off the jug and called for another. Gradually a silly smile began to spread over his face and Will realised that the brew was so named because of the effect it had on your head. This tuppenny beer was far stronger than anything he was used to and after the first tankard he drank no more. Another hour dragged by with no sign of his uncle and Mr Balker's eyes glazed over beneath their drooping lids. Will began to get very worried indeed.

'Hah ha!' tittered the miller, tipping the jug and finding it empty. 'More ale,' he shouted across to Peg. 'Go milk that dragon of yours.'

'Please don't have any more,' the boy implored. 'That's two flagons you've had already, John.'

Mr Balker drew himself up in his seat and tried to appear dignified. 'What fer you deny . . . denyin' me my beer lad?' he slurred. 'Ain't a man got the right to partake of a liddle beer when the fanshy takesh 'im?'

'Of course he has but I think you've had enough.'

'Enough!' scoffed the miller loudly. 'If'n I'd had

enough I wouldn't be wantin' more now would I, Master Clever Britches?' and he slapped the table moodily. 'Folk'll think I ain't got no coin the way yer carryin' on. Well I has see. I got me a purse stuffed wi' clinky, chinky money.' To Will's horror he stood up, swaying from side to side, and fished a leather bag from beneath his riding cloak. 'Don't you worry, Peg!' he cried over the heads of the other drinkers. 'I got me plenty in 'ere to pay my way,' and he shook the purse until the coins jingled inside it.

Will dragged him back to his seat, 'Are you mad?' he hissed. 'What do you think you're doing? This place is full of cut-purses and cut-throats. They'd kill for far less than what you've got there.' Mr Balker sulkily put his money away and Will glanced round to see if anyone was staring. Everything seemed normal, perhaps nobody had been taking any notice. No – there in the furthest corner, those two men who had not uttered a single word all evening were looking straight at him. Quickly the boy turned away, they were a fearful pair; one had a great scar down his cheek and the other was blind in one eye. Wildly Will wondered what he should do. If only the miller had not got himself drunk, as if things weren't bad enough – this was becoming a nightmare.

' 'Ere's another jug, my duck,' said Peg. 'I see it's put a fine shine on that nose of yours.'

'Oh there'sh a luvverly lady for yer,' beamed Mr Balker. 'Such a pretty, kind creature – oh Margaret won't you come back wi' me?'

'Margaret?' she frowned putting her hands on her hips. 'I ain't your Margaret!' Peg slapped Will on the shoulder. 'What's he rattlin' on about?' she asked.

But the boy had absolutely no idea. 'I don't know,' he told her. 'I've never heard him mention a Margaret before.'

A large tear rolled down the miller's purple nose and dripped into his ale. 'Oh she won't never come back to me now,' he blubbed. 'My darling Margaret – can you ever forgive me? What'sh my poor liddle baby doin' thish night?'

Peg sniffed haughtily and the heavy black lines of her eyebrows arched with indignation. 'Got another doxy has he?' she said coldly.

Will shook his head. 'I . . . I don't think so,' he stammered, 'but perhaps he's had too much of your Dragon's Milk.'

Peg snapped her fingers at him and the humour died on her scarlet lips. 'Oh you reckon do you, my little man?' she sneered unpleasantly. 'He'll have had too much when his money's run out. So long as he can pay I'll pour it down his oafish throat.' Then she tossed back her hair and walked huffily away.

Will knew that it was time for them to leave. It didn't look as though Samuel Godwin was going to show up at all. He pulled the tankard from Mr Balker's hands to grab his attention. 'John,' he began, 'do you know where my uncle's lodgings are?' Slowly the man nodded. 'Good, then we shall have to go there – we should have made for them straight away instead of stopping here.' He pushed the beer to the far end of the table and said with more confidence than he actually felt, 'I do not like the way he has used us this night and I will tell him so.'

With difficulty he managed to hoist the large man from the bench. The miller threw an arm about the boy's neck and in a slow drawl blubbered, 'You'm a good lad, Will. Yer father taught you right, that he did. A good man Daniel was to his family – if only I had been so kind to mine.'

Will took no notice as he was too busy trying to get him to walk to the door. Twice they stumbled into tables and sent stools rolling across the sawdust. One of the old soldiers glared at them threateningly. 'Douse him in the horse trough!' he spat at Will.

'Come on John,' pleaded the boy, 'we must get out, the night air will do you good.'

'I knew a lass from Gloucestershire!' piped up the miller bursting into song.

'Not far now John, that's right – one foot after another.'

' 'Ere!' squawked Peg just as they reached the heavy oak door. 'Where you two wretches off to? You ain't paid!' The garish woman strode purposefully towards them brandishing a heavy stick in her hands.

Frantically Will rummaged through his pockets to find his money and as he did so Mr Balker slid down and sprawled on the floor. 'What's the reckoning?' the boy asked in a panic.

Peg pursed her painted lips, her face cracking a little. 'That'll be five shillings,' she demanded.

'Five shillings!' exclaimed Will. 'We don't owe you that much!'

From his position on the floor the miller broke in, 'Oh I got me plenty of money – ha ha. Anyway, about thish lass from Gloucestershire.'

'There we are,' snarled Peg with menace in her voice, 'your friend says he's got plenty of money. Your tally's five shillings.'

Will knew that the situation was getting treacherous. Fumbling, he drew some coins from his pocket. 'Here,' he said, 'there's two shillings and that's still robbery.'

Peg's hand snaked out and caught hold of his arm. 'Oh no you don't my little manny,' she growled. 'I said five and I means it. Your friend's caused me great heartache he has, said he loved me truly and promised to marry me he did—'

'No he never!'

'Oh yes he did, and there's plenty in 'ere who'll swear to it. Them street traders'll do aught fer me. Does I have to call 'em over to take it from you? They're a 'orrible lot they are – kill their grannies fer a free drink they would.' She cackled and revealed for the first time her mottled brown teeth. Will could only stand there and watch as she slid her other hand into the pocket of his jerkin.

Suddenly Peg screeched and was yanked backwards. The goggle-eyed man with the red hair had seized her once more and dragged her on to his knee.

Will took his chance. As Peg yelled for assistance and kicked Verney the Adamite, he heaved the miller to his feet and they staggered out of the door.

It was a still night. No wind stirred the smoke which rose from London's chimneys and the columns climbed steadily into the sky, forming a great dark canopy high above the rooftops. This thick layer of sooty cloud blanketed the heavens and obliterated the stars, and far below, the narrow streets and lanes were filled with shadow. An air of anticipation enveloped the city, its waiting calm an unnerving contrast to the chaos inside the Sickle Moon.

Into this silence came Will and the miller. Flustered and cursing, the boy propelled his drunken friend into the yard where he leant him against a post. 'Just you stay there, whilst I get the horses,' he told him sternly. Mr Balker grunted and passed a sweating palm over his forehead – he was becoming drowsy.

Will peered into the blackness of the stables – they were empty. 'The horses are gone!' he cried in disbelief. 'They've stolen the horses!' He looked round madly. What were they to do now?

'Don't you . . . don't you get a f . . . fre . . . frettin',' hiccuped the miller in a sleepy voice. 'We . . . we can walk to bad ol' Sam . . . Sammy's – not far, not far.'

'Yes,' agreed Will trying to think straight, 'that's the only thing we can do now – my uncle can settle this. He will know where to find a Justice.' Will eyed Mr Balker doubtfully. 'Maybe I should douse you in the horse trough – are you sure you can lead us?'

The miller tapped his nose then took a deep breath followed by a long and purposeful stride. 'John Balker always w . . . walks a true path,' he proclaimed. 'Come, young Master Godwin.' With his legs wobbling beneath him he tottered out of the yard.

Will shook his head; since they had arrived everything had been a disaster, surely nothing else could go wrong. He ran under the arch after the miller and so did not see the light spill into the yard as the door to the tavern swung open to let out two figures.

The cobbles rang under Mr Balker's heavy boots as he made his meandering way along Cheapside. Will caught up with him, glancing for a moment at the immense midnight bulk of St Paul's rising behind them. Silhouetted against the dark sky even that holy place appeared to be a fortress of dread and despair – more a home for the Devil than the Almighty.

The miller was humming softly to himself, his eyes fixed on the empty street ahead. 'A might . . . mighty fine night,' he said to Will. 'Who could have woes at such a time as this?' The boy said nothing; he was thinking of the churchyard that now contained his family and in his alcoholic stupor the miller guessed his thoughts. 'Aah, Will lad,' he sighed, 'look not to the past and what's gone. They're books bes . . . best left aside, their pages are too bitter for you or I to look on. It's tomorrow we have to consider now. Let's make that a page worth rea . . . reading.' He tutted to himself and the sound reminded him of his sister. 'Oh Hannah,' he breathed, 'I should have listened to you. You were right, I'll not seek her out. She'd have come back long ago if she'd a mind to. You've a wise little head on yer shoulders, Hannah Balker, and as large a heart as any I've met – though I'll deny sayin' that if you tell her, lad.'

Will smiled; even after all that had happened the miller could lift his spirits. The large man might be brusque and foolish at times but he was a good soul. 'I'll not tell her,' Will said. 'I like the Millhouse just as it is; if harmony were to settle there it wouldn't be the same.'

'Ha! That's true enough – never was there a truer word spoken. It's ever been a place of discord, and that's a truly grievous fact.' Mr Balker paused on a corner of the street and a large grin split his face. 'Listen to us,' he laughed, 'clucking on like two old hens. If that's what London grog does, then I'll not touch the infernal brew again and it'll be a long time afore I set foot in the city after tonight. Come now boy, yer uncle's not far.'

'Too far fer you!' hissed a foul voice.

The miller halted in surprise and peered into the shadows on either side of them – there didn't seem to be anything there. He shook his head to try and shrug off the effects of the drink then stared into the gloom once more. 'Who's there?' he ventured.

Will stood by his side and whispered nervously, 'I heard it too. Let's leave it alone, whatever it is.'

But Mr Balker was curious. If they had come across one of the devils which his sister was always ranting on about then he wanted to see it. 'Come out!' he demanded.

'As you wish,' returned the dreadful voice and from the darkness emerged two figures. There was nothing supernatural about them, they were just men – yet the miller's heart quailed when he saw the look in their eyes.

'Run, Will!' he shouted.

But it was too late. Before either of them could move their attackers pounced.

One of them lunged at the boy and hurled him to the ground. Strong hands shoved his head back and it struck the cobbles with a horrible thud. The man pinned his arms down then sat on his chest. Will could not move, the back of his head ached and he knew it was bleeding. His eyes closed – as if sparing him the sight of the hate-filled face above.

Mr Balker staggered to and fro, the other rogue clinging to his back in an attempt to throttle him. But the miller's neck was thick and all those years of carrying flour sacks had made him strong. With his face turning purple, he cast off his assailant like a dog shaking off a flea. The startled man sailed through the air and with a splash landed in the gutter. He wiped the stinking water from his face and wailed when he saw the fat miller charging at him like an angry bull.

The sound of the brawl echoed through the deserted streets and drummed into Will's pounding head.

'Now, my young master,' snarled the man on his chest, 'you'd best keep quiet if you want to keep yer tongue. It's just yer money I'm after.' Will shuddered as he felt bony fingers search through his pockets. 'Aha!' sniggered the evil voice. 'Here we are – what's this then? Three shillin's! Is that it? 'Ere Jessel,' he called to his partner, 'thissun's only got three lousy shillin's.' But the other man was too busy trying to fend off the miller to answer. 'Curse it!' growled the voice above Will. 'I'll 'ave summat to say to *him* that's fer sure.'

In the upstairs window of a nearby house a lantern was lit, the noise below having drawn the attention of the owner. As the sudden light slanted down into the street, Will's eyes fluttered open and in the yellow glare of the lantern he saw his attacker's face.

It was large and ugly, with a great scar running across the broken nose and down the cheek, but the eyes were black as coal and brimming with malice. Will recognised him at once. 'You were in the Sickle Moon,' he said.

The man punched him in the ribs. 'You'll be sorry for that, lad,' he spat. 'I'm not gonna leave you alive to bear witness against me.' From his belt he swiftly drew a long knife and pressed it against the boy's throat. 'I don't care what *he* told us, Jack Carver won't dance at the gallows for the likes o' you.'

Will held his breath. The cold blade snicked into his neck and a hideous chuckle gurgled over him.

'Leave him be!' boomed Mr Balker suddenly. The miller bounded up towards Will, seized hold of the man's shoulders and snatched him away just as the knife broke the skin. Three drops of blood flew in the air as the blade flashed in the light of the lantern and sliced a gleaming arc through the shadows.

With a clatter the weapon spun to the ground. Mr Balker made a grab for it but Will's attacker was too quick and he kicked it from his grasp. 'Let's see how you deal with two of us!' he snapped. 'Jessel – hold him.'

The one called Jessel darted forward and launched himself at the miller once more. 'I got 'im, Jack,' he cried. 'Take 'is purse an' let's scarper.'

Bony fingers closed about the handle of the knife and the man with the scar stepped into the pool of light. On the ground nearby, Will propped himself up on his elbows and saw him advance towards the miller. 'Watch out, John!' he called.

Mr Balker could see the blade glinting before him. He struggled to get free of Jessel's grasp but his strength was spent and he cursed the madness which had made him drink so much. 'Quickly, get away from this place!' he shouted to Will in despair.

'Stay where you are, whelp!' commanded Carver. 'Or your pig-faced friend gets it in the gut.'

Will stared up at the lit window where a frightened

face peeked down at the scene below. 'Help!' the boy shouted. 'Help us please!'

Jessel glanced up at the troubled face. ' 'Urry up,' he urged his partner, ' 'im up there'll have the nightwatchman down on our necks!'

'Not if 'e wants to stay alive 'e won't,' snarled Jack lifting his sparkling, black eyes menacingly. The face withdrew from the window and the light was extinguished.

He waved the knife before the miller. 'Now then, fat one,' he said in a deadly tone, 'gimme yer purse.'

Mr Balker took the bag of money from his pocket and handed it over. The scar-faced man shook it and the coins jingled inside.

'Listen to that,' burbled Jessel gleefully, 'there must be a few golden crowns in there.'

Jack Carver nodded. 'I fancy there is,' he replied quietly, 'and I can't let this gentleman go without giving him something in return now can I?'

'I don't want nothin' ' said Mr Balker.

'Now that ain't true!' Jack told him. 'A minute ago you wanted this 'ere knife – well now I'm givin' it to yer!'

In one swift movement the deed was done. John Balker clutched his stomach and fell to his knees. 'Margaret,' he whispered hoarsely, and then he died.

Jessel stared at the body of the miller. A dark pool of blood was oozing over the cobbles. 'You killed 'im,' he stammered. 'What you do that fer? You 'ad his money.' He looked nervously down the street. Others had been roused from sleep by the fight and candles shone in many windows. 'Yer mad Carver!' he cried rounding on his partner. 'Look, folk are stirrin' themselves – the nightwatchman'll come – we're hung fer sure!'

Only now did the horrific scene before him sink into Will's mind. Mr Balker was dead. The boy threw back his head and screamed. Then he picked himself off the ground and ran into the night.

Jack whirled round and cursed. 'We're not crow bait yet,' he told Jessel, 'but we'll not be safe with that lad runnin' free.' With murderous thoughts now burning in both their brains they leapt over the miller's corpse and gave chase.

Will had no idea where he was going. He charged through the streets and lanes like one gone mad. The sight of Mr Balker falling to his knees danced before his eyes and no matter where he ran he could not escape that terrible image.

Blindly he charged down an alley, tears of shock and fear streaming down his face. He had to run – he had to get away from this mad city and if he had to race all the way home on foot then he would do so. With sewer water splashing round his ankles he pelted into the shadows. He could hear the men coming after him but he was younger than them and he knew that not even the Devil himself could catch him tonight. It was fear that guided his feet and fear it was that drove him on, faster and faster.

Then he saw it, a great wall rearing above him, rising from the darkness of the shaded alley like a wave of doom, mocking his efforts to flee. He had run into a dead end.

An icy pain gripped Will's insides as he realised there was nowhere else to go. He spun round but two silhouetted figures were already creeping down the alley towards him. The boy looked up at the sheer wall and flung himself against it. Frantically he tried to climb, vainly groping with his fingers for something to hold on to. But it was no use, the mason had been too great a craftsman, for there was no gap or niche anywhere between the bricks. Will slithered down, his fingers cut and bleeding. Sinister laughter floated on the chill air and the sound cut right through him – this was it, he told himself, his life was over.

'Poor little mite,' sniggered Carver wickedly, 'gone an' got hisself trapped – you can always tell a foreigner. They don't know this city like what we do.'

Will pressed himself against the bricks and watched with mounting terror as the figures approached. It was too dark to see their faces, but the blade of the knife in Jack's hand gleamed with a cold light of its own, as if it lusted for more blood.

'I'm gonna slice 'im up so good that his own mother wouldn't recognise him!' the evil man hissed.

'Keep quiet, Carver,' snapped Jessel. 'Just do it and have done. Listen, they've found that fool of a miller back there, won't be long till they track us down! This job's been naught but trouble from the start.'

'Mebbe,' returned Jack, 'but I'm here to make an end to it now.' He raised the knife and Will shivered anticipating the deadly blow. But the strike never came.

'ENOUGH!' boomed a forceful voice.

Carver and Jessel whirled round, and from a narrow doorway stepped a man cloaked in black with a hood covering his face.

'Keep out o' this whoever you are,' warned Jack fiercely, 'or I'll cut you too.'

'Let the boy be,' commanded the stranger. 'He is mine. Go now if you value your necks.'

For a moment Will thought he was saved, but when he saw that the man was unarmed his relief turned to doubt. The boy wondered who the man was – he must be insane to challenge those two cut-throats. Obviously Jack thought so too for he let loose a horrible laugh.

The cloaked figure was not intimidated. Instead he sailed towards Will and placed himself between him and his attackers. Calmly he told Jack, 'Assuredly, you loathsome creature, there is little cause for merriment on your part, for at this moment your very soul is in peril. The more you linger here the closer you come to being thrown into the pits of Hell itself. The boy belongs to me.' His tone was insistent and there was a disturbing quality about it which unsettled Jessel and made him take a step backwards.

'Leave it, Jack!' he told his friend. 'There's summink foul about that one.'

'He don't frighten me!' Carver spat viciously. 'I got the knife – it's him what's gonna see Hell first.'

'So be it,' said the stranger. A hand appeared from the folds of the cloak and pointed an accusing finger at both of the men. 'I consign your miserable skins to the nightmare of perdition!' he cried flinging his arms open.

A terrific roar shook the alley. Orange flames leapt from the ground and a cloud of noxious yellow smoke exploded all around them.

That was enough for Jessel. 'It's Old Nick himself!' he howled and he fled out of the unnatural, choking fog like lead from a musket.

'Jessel!' called Jack, terrified at being left behind. 'Wait fer me!' He threw down the knife and ran wailing, 'Spare me, Lord – spare me!' at the top of his voice.

Will coughed; the smoke smelt like bad eggs and it stung his eyes. He squinted through the haze at the hooded figure who stood before him and felt afraid once more. What kind of creature was this? What black powers were his to command? Will almost wished Jack had knifed him – better a quick death than to be tormented by demons for eternity.

The stranger made sure the men were gone before catching hold of the boy's arm and dragging him to the doorway he had come from. 'In there,' he told him. Will was thrust inside the building and he stumbled down the unseen steps beyond the threshold. It was a large unlit room, with a wide leaded window that faced the alley outside. He moved forward but in the darkness knocked a jar off a shelf which fell with a crash on the floor.

'Keep quiet!' he was told. 'The mob are coming, they are hot on the trail of those knaves.'

Will held his breath and listened; from the street outside he heard the tramp of many feet and outraged cries of 'Murder! Murder!' And high amongst those voices came the shrill shrieks of Peggy Blister. Unconsciously Will withdrew into the blackest corner and crouched down.

The cloaked figure left the doorway and darted back into the alley. A great crowd of people were streaming towards him with lanterns and flaming torches held high above their heads.

'Hold,' shouted the hooded stranger.

The thronging mass halted, holding out their torches to try and glimpse the face beneath the cowl. 'A most heinous act has been committed,' a bewigged man piped up. 'There has been murder!'

'Let me through!' screeched Peggy Blister, pushing others out of the way. She squeezed to the front and in the flickering torchlight her painted face looked even more startling. With her hands on her hips she eyed the black figure with suspicion. 'Who's that?' she demanded. 'Get out of our way! There's killers on the loose an' we'll not rest till we've strung 'em up. They done butchered my childhood sweetheart, they did.' For this shameful lie she received much sympathy and she basked in it like a dog in the sunshine.

'I fancy you are wrong, mistress,' issued the silken voice from the hood, 'for I myself witnessed this evil deed.'

A murmur of surprise rippled through the mob. 'I hope you ain't callin' me a liar!' shouted Peg indignantly.

'I would not presume to,' came the softly spoken reply. 'What I say concerns the murderer, not your romantic mythology – I cannot call it history.' Before she had time to understand the slight and rally with a coarse answer he went on. 'There was indeed only one murderer abroad this night,' he said, 'for I saw this jolly miller quarrel with him in the distance as I walked to my lodgings.'

Within the nearby building Will heard this and he looked up curiously. The light of the torches fell into the room, curving round countless bottles, jars, pots and bowls. Gingerly he got to his feet and crept closer to the window.

'Who was it then?' called the crowd excitedly.

The figure pointed at the ground where Jack Carver's knife still lay, smeared with blood. 'I will tell you what I saw,' he said, 'even though I despise the thought of it. The murderer of that poor man was a mere boy.'

The mob gasped as one. Peg looked stunned. 'It's that thieving little brat what owes me three shillin's!' she snarled venomously.

'Yes, good friends,' the man continued, 'a child has committed this foulness – he pushed by me three minutes since, out in Cheapside. What horrors are we breeding now? I beg of you to find this monster.'

Will could not believe his ears; that man was practically condemning him to death. If they discovered him he would be swinging from the nearest gibbet. He rushed at the door to protest his innocence but a shadow fell on the steps. The figure had returned and barred his exit. 'If I were you I would not set foot out there,' he said.

'How dare you, sir!' raged Will furiously. 'Why have you done this – why did you lie so? John Balker was my friend, I must get by and tell them that or I shall be a fugitive forever.'

A strong hand shoved him back into the room. 'Indeed, that was the intention. Wait, the rabble is leaving – soon the whole of London will be searching for you. I do believe that the only safe place is here.' He slammed the door and sent the bolt rattling home.

'Out of my way!' Will shouted. 'Let me out of this dank little hole!'

The figure ignored him and took a candle from one of the shelves. 'Tut, tut,' he muttered, 'I can see I shall have to tame that tongue of yours. I can't have you speaking in that tone to your elders and betters. This may not be the palace of Westminster but it is not a dank hole. Here is where wonders are made, where dreams are spun and lives saved. Alone in this teeming city this place stands proud – a beacon of wisdom and knowledge that shines through the murky pits of ignorance.'

Will remembered the weird explosion in the alley and his anger died down. 'I thought it was just some kind of shop,' he murmured.

'Some kind of shop?' repeated the man in annoyance. 'This is an apothecary!'

'Well that's a shop, isn't it?' Will muttered stubbornly. 'Who are you anyway?'

Suddenly the candle spluttered into life and in the circle of pale light the figure cast back his hood.

He was an old man with a large, hooked nose and deep-set eyes. The fine white hair which sparsely covered his high, domed head contrasted sharply with his frowning, beetle-black brows. The full lips parted into a cruel smile. 'I am a doctor!' he proclaimed grandly. 'Doctor Elias Theophrastus Spittle! And you are now my servant.'

3

The Apothecary

Will almost laughed. 'I am no one's servant,' he told the apothecary haughtily, 'my father was a yeoman—'

'I have no interest in your life before this,' Doctor Spittle interrupted, 'and you would do well to forget it yourself.' He moved away from the door and set the candle down on a counter. 'There, if you wish to leave you may, but harken to my words – step outside this place now and the mob will surely string you up. There'll be a new puppet dangling at Tyburn before the dawn.'

Will moved towards the door but he knew that the man was right. The night was filled with the angry clamour of the mob as they hunted for him. There was no way he could escape from the city without being captured. He turned back to the apothecary who was smiling conceitedly. 'What is it you wish me to do?' Will asked.

Doctor Spittle waved a hand at the jars and bottles all around. 'I am a very busy man,' he told the boy. 'The needs of my clients use up a very great proportion of my valuable time. There are herbs to collect, substances to grind, compounds to make and pills to stamp. I have found myself woefully stretched of late – that is why you are here. You shall be my dogsbody. All those tedious and loathsome chores will now be yours and I can be left to pursue my other work. Think of it as an apprenticeship if you like – unpaid of course. Whilst you consent to perform these simple and menial tasks I shall shelter you from the cruelty of English justice. So long as you serve me then your neck will be spared the noose.' He sighed contentedly and chuckled to himself. 'I find this a most agreeable arrangement and I promise that you will learn a great deal.'

Will remained silent. His mind raced over the alternatives; it was impossible to find his uncle now for the address was on the miller's body. It was maddening to think that Samuel Godwin might be living next door and he would be none the wiser. He could only agree to the apothecary's terms, but just until the murder had been forgotten. Perhaps after a week had gone by, and there was some new sensation to distract the attention of the city, he would be able to slip away unnoticed. With his mind made up he looked at Doctor Spittle. 'So be it,' he said. 'I agree to work for you.'

The man nodded, 'Indeed you are a wise child. What a wondrous miracle it is that has brought us two together. I would thank the Lord for this happy chance – if I believed He existed. Pray be not alarmed; I am a man of science, not a heretic.' He took up the candle once more and pointed to a dim corner of the shop where the floor was covered by empty sacks and straw. 'There is your resting place, boy,' he told him. 'From now on that shall be your bed. Sleep well.'

Will stared at the dirty sacks. 'I can't sleep on those,' he protested.

The change in Doctor Spittle was immediate. A mad light flared in his dark eyes and he bared his teeth like a ravening wolf. His free hand shot out and struck Will savagely on the cheek. The boy staggered backwards from the force of the blow, his face stinging. 'You will obey me!' the man bellowed.

'You must remember that now you are my servant you must live like a servant! I want none of your airs, boy! Your life is in my hands. Would you rather have the rope biting at your neck this night? The choice is simple – wooden boards or the gallows, which is it to be?'

Silently Will sat on the floor, but he stared at the apothecary mutinously.

'You had better get used to this if you are to survive in the city,' breathed Doctor Spittle as he calmed down. 'The life of a servant here is no better than that of a dog. If your yeoman manners show themselves once more I shall beat them out of you. Now I must retire to my chamber upstairs. The night air is bad for me. My health is a fragile thing which requires much consideration.' He moved to the back of the shop where a small door led to a steep flight of stairs. Before climbing them the doctor glanced back. 'Rest easy, dog,' he said. 'I assure you there is nothing to fear here.' And then he was gone.

Will heard the wooden steps creak as the old man ascended. The room was now dark, the glow from the candle diminishing gradually as further up the stairs it went. There came the sound of a door closing and it was swallowed completely.

On his uncomfortable bed Will reflected on the past harrowing hours. Suddenly his old life seemed an age away – as though that childhood in Adcombe had belonged to someone else. Nothing was left of his previous existence and for the present it looked as though he would be forced to remain in this harsh new world.

He cast himself on to the sacks and relived those last, dreadful moments with the miller. Somewhere in the city those two murderers were free, and though the blood of Mr Balker stained their hands, Will was the one accused. With the horrific image of his dead friend haunting him, he fell into an unpleasant, fitful sleep and tears streaked down his face. The hollow night engulfed London and no one heard the boy's forlorn whimpers.

'Up, young dog!' shouted Doctor Spittle, kicking Will awake. 'There are matters to attend to before we open shop.'

Will rubbed his head and tried to rise but his back was stiff from the floor and the draughts which had played over it. Yawning, he watched as the apothecary, still in a grubby nightgown, pattered to one of the shelves and returned brandishing a large pair of scissors.

'Can't be found harbouring a fugitive,' the man told him. 'One of my customers might come in and recognise you from last night – that wench from the Sickle Moon is often here looking for new paints with which to daub her ugly face.'

Roughly he seized hold of Will's long hair and pulled it till he yelped. 'What a lush growth you do have,' the apothecary said almost enviously. 'A shame it has to be cut. But no servant has the locks of a gentleman.'

'Let go!' cried Will as the man's long, yellow nails tangled themselves in his hair and pulled viciously. He was dragged to his feet and the bump he had received the previous night began to bleed again.

'Be still,' barked Doctor Spittle, 'or you'll lose an ear.'

In the dreary light of the new day, Will's shoulder-length hair was snipped and hacked from his head. A soft heap lay about his feet when the apothecary was finished. Gingerly he drew his fingers through what was left. It was very stubbly and short. He ran to the window to see his reflection in one of the diamond panes but hardly recognised the face that stared back at him. 'I look like a beggar's brat,' he murmured.

'Not quite,' the apothecary said critically. 'But get some soot from the hearth and rub it well in – that ought to finish it.'

Will bit his tongue, knowing that if he refused then he would be whipped. So, shaking the hair from his shoulders, he knelt by the fireplace and wiped his hand over the blackened bricks.

'A proper little urchin you are now,' sniggered Doctor Spittle when the boy had smeared dirt on to his face. 'What does it feel like, dog, to stand on the other side of the fence?' He rubbed his hands together then took hold of the boy's arm and dragged him away from the hearth. 'Now does your apprenticeship begin,' he said importantly. 'Behold my apothecary shop in the light of the morning – one day you shall know the virtues of all the herbs and plants on those shelves. What a fortunate young dog you are to have so wise a master.'

The shop was one long room, crammed from floor to ceiling with pots and vessels of all sizes. There were drug jars with diamond patterns in the glaze and covered with lids of parchment; one glass bottle contained slimy black leeches, another some dark liquid – the smell of which made Will want to retch; there were oils and spices, different coloured powders, bunches of dried leaves, numerous shrivelled objects pickled in alcohol and an assortment of lotions and preserves.

Proudly Doctor Spittle showed all these strange things to Will. 'This,' he said picking up a ceramic tile shaped like a shield, 'is my pill slab. On this you will roll out the pastes which I have carefully prepared and stamp out the pills for my customers. Do you see the coat of arms here? This shows that I am a licensed member of the London Pharmacopoeia. With every pill you stamp it shall remind you of my superior intelligence.' He placed the tile on the counter then took a fist-sized ball from one of the shelves. 'Here is a Goa stone,' he said. 'With this I can cure complaints of the stomach. It is made from musk and calomel in the Far East. And this,' he chuckled, rattling a bottle containing yellow lumps of earth, 'is what I chased your assailants away with last night. Sulphur is a most useful element; it can put the fear of the Devil in the ignorant.'

He crossed to the doorway and drew the bolt back. 'I have talked too much,' he muttered, 'time is wasting – I should have opened already.' The apothecary then realised that he was still dressed in only his nightgown. With a look of scandalised horror he dashed upstairs shouting, 'Idiot! Why did you not tell me I was still arrayed thus. I have important clients who would never come here again if I appeared to them so rudely. You have a lot to learn, young dog! And get that mess of hair cleared away before I come down.'

Will stared up at the ceiling; he could hear the old man stumbling about as he hastily pulled on his clothes. Doctor Spittle alternated between extreme arrogance one minute and ludicrous behaviour the next. It was difficult to judge which mood he would swing into and that in itself was frightening as you could never be sure what he was going to say or do. But Will did not have time to speculate further for he heard the upstairs door slam shut and he hurriedly searched for a broom to sweep the floor with.

Soon all the clippings of hair had been cast into the street. There was no longer any noise coming from the room above, so he peered through the doorway which led to the steep flight of stairs. There he found another door. This led to the yard at the back of the building in which a tall yew tree stood, and against the far wall there was a small border for growing herbs. But the apothecary was nowhere to be seen.

'Spittle!' cried a voice from the shop. 'Where is the

poxy man? Does he think I have all day to waste here? I have appointments! Spittle!'

Will drew back into the shadows of the stairwell nervously. What if the customer were to recognise him somehow? The impatient call came again – he had to attend to the man. Taking a deep breath he stepped into the shop once more. 'A good morning to you, sir,' he began politely. 'Can I be of assistance?'

The man looked at him in surprise and Will returned the curious gaze. The customer was richly dressed in turquoise silks and gold brocade; upon his dainty shoes there were bows to match and in his hand he carried a long walking cane tipped with silver. His face was oval shaped, with dewy eyes and a thin mouth. All this was framed by the thickest and longest hair Will had ever seen on a man; he did not realise that the fashion at court was to wear periwigs.

'Who – or what – are you?' asked the stranger, fluttering his lace collar between his hands.

Will was about to tell him when he checked himself just in time. 'I . . . I work for the doctor,' he said simply.

The man regarded him as though he were something he had trodden in. 'Do you indeed?' he murmured. 'Well he would do well to teach you some manners, you impudent knave. Servants never stare at their betters. Now go and fetch your master – *tout de suite*. I dislike your squalid company.'

Reluctantly the boy gave a bow, then went in search of the apothecary.

Up the stairs he went, cursing the customer with each step. By the time he came to a small landing his face was burning with indignation. Will raised his hand to knock on the apothecary's bedroom door.

There was no answer so he knocked again. Still nothing. Will tried the handle and looked inside.

It was a small room with an unmade bed in one corner and a large wardrobe dominating the furthest wall. Books were strewn on the floor amongst piles of old clothes and the grease of candles formed frozen drips down the sides of the low bedtable.

Will was puzzled, but behind him, on the landing, he saw yet more steps leading upwards. These ended at a door which was painted a dark crimson. For some reason the sight of it made him catch his breath and butterflies fluttered in his stomach. The paint was the colour of blood and the memory of the miller's murder flashed before him once more. A sweet and sickly smell floated down from the room beyond. It was a nauseating stench which turned the boy's skin to gooseflesh. Something evil lay through that door, he told himself. Yet Doctor Spittle must also be there and Will forced his legs to move forward and climb.

The stairs here were narrow and the wood rotten in places. There was no window on the landing so it was filled with gloom and Will had to strain his eyes to find his way.

'What are you doing up here?' cried Doctor Spittle suddenly appearing before him.

So intently had Will been staring at the steps that he had not seen the crimson door open and the sound of the apothecary's voice startled him.

'This place is forbidden to you!' raged the old man. 'Do you understand? Never come up here!'

Will nodded quickly then cried, 'There's a customer downstairs. He wants to see you most urgently.'

Doctor Spittle swore under his breath and brought

a large key from a pocket in his coat. 'Why did you not say so at once?' he shrieked, locking the door behind him. 'Describe him.'

'Lots of silk, walking cane, pasty face and big hair.'

The apothecary pushed him aside and tore down the rickety steps with his hands in the air. 'Lord of Death!' he wailed. 'That is Sir Francis Lingley! My wealthiest and most influential client. Why did you not call me sooner?' And he disappeared down to the shop faster than Will had thought possible.

Alone on the narrow staircase the boy turned to look at the glistening red door. It really did look as though the whole thing had been freshly steeped in gore. With a wavering hand he reached out and touched it with his fingertips. He was expecting it to be wet and sticky, but it was dry as a bone. What secrets lay beyond this, he wondered? What foulness was kept inside to make such a howling stink that it rivalled that of the city itself? Cautiously he tried the handle; the lock rattled loudly but held firm. From within the sealed room there came a muffled screeching and scratching.

Will backed away in fear. There was something in there! Was the door locked to stop him entering or to prevent something escaping? Quickly he jumped down the steps and ran after the apothecary.

In the shop Doctor Spittle breezed towards his customer with his arms flung open in apology. 'I crave your pardon, My Lord,' he grovelled.

Sir Francis sniffed. 'I do not come here to idle away my time conversing with kitchen boys, Spittle,' he said huffily.

'Of course not, My Lord,' squirmed the apothecary. 'And what may your needs be today?'

The nobleman lowered his voice. 'Warts,' he whispered. 'There is a rash of warts on the back of my neck. *Je suis très malade* – have you a salve or a lotion which will rid me of the infernal things?'

Doctor Spittle nodded discreetly. 'I shall prepare something for you, My Lord – a most uncomfortable ailment to suffer from. I shall set to work at once. If you return in an hour's time all will be ready.'

'It had better be,' Sir Francis snapped. 'If the wretched things are not dealt with soon I believe they shall spread.' He shuddered at the thought of it. 'Can you imagine if they were to afflict my face?' he cried. 'I would never be able to appear at court again.'

The apothecary bowed. 'Rest assured,' he said confidently, 'the ointment I shall prepare will not fail.'

'If that is true then you will not find me ungenerous. I go now to the coffee house to hear the news – I shall return in one hour. *Adieu*.' With that Sir Francis tossed his head and flounced out of the shop.

Doctor Spittle waved farewell to him through the window and when he was out of sight he scowled. 'Yes sire, no sire,' the old man grumbled. 'Well, my little Sir Peacock, there you go, strutting through the city in all your finery with your head held high, full of your own importance.' He paused, then a mischievous grin lit his face. 'If only you knew that your affliction was a present from me in the first place.' He turned from the window and the mirth vanished, for there was Will standing by the counter.

'Did you really give him the warts?' the boy asked. The apothecary hesitated for a moment, then tittered. 'I did indeed,' he told him. 'I have to keep myself supplied with customers, so when they are cured of one ailment I ensure they return to me with another. In My Lord Francis's case I merely added a little poison from the skin of a large toad to the last ointment I made for him. I'm surprised the warts are only on the back of his neck. I was hoping for something a little more dramatic – I shall just have to squeeze the toad a little harder next time.'

Will was appalled. 'That's vile,' he said.

'I call it shrewd business sense,' shrugged the apothecary, 'and that popinjay really deserves a blemish or two. Did you see his garments? Only the best for Sir Francis.' He looked down at his own clothes and pulled a sad expression for they were threadbare and grimy. 'Alas I have not the means,' he sighed. 'I am forced to purchase my gowns from the raghouse. No silks or velvets for Elias Theophrastus Spittle. No lace to wear at his throat, no ribbons to adorn his shoes and no merry periwig to conceal his baldness.' He passed a hand over his sparsely covered scalp and murmured, 'Would you believe that once I had a full head of hair? Red as copper it was – like a lion from the Africas I appeared in my youth.'

Will doubted that and he thought ruefully of his own hair. Was that really why the old man had cut it off? Was he jealous of anyone who had something he did not? Surely no one could be that petty and envious? He watched thoughtfully as the apothecary reached up to take bottles and jars from the shelves – the more he found out about him the less he understood.

'We must hurry, dog,' Doctor Spittle told him

brusquely. 'A cure for warts is what we need. Hah!' He passed to Will a mortar and pestle instructing him to grind up the ingredients which he would measure out.

And so Will's new life as the servant of the apothecary began. That first morning passed by without any further incident. When Sir Francis returned the ointment was ready for him and Doctor Spittle fawned and scraped before the nobleman in a revolting manner. Other customers came and went and the old man made sure that he was there to greet them all with sickening humility. Only when they had gone would he sneer and deride them. At noon he threw Will a crust of stale bread and some old cheese whilst he sank his teeth into an eel pie. For the rest of the day he kept the boy working hard, fetching, carrying and sweating over a boiling pot in which he made his infusions. When the afternoon was drawing to a close and the daylight began to fail, the old man bolted the door and told Will to sweep up and go to bed, giving him the last of the hard cheese for his supper.

Will ate the frugal meal hungrily. Tonight he was glad of the sacking and straw on the floor. He knew that he would sleep extremely well and he threw himself down, thankful that the day was over. As sleep crept upon him he stared at the ceiling and wondered at the silence above – Doctor Spittle must have gone to the attic.

'What can he be doing up there?' he murmured drowsily to himself. 'Still, I won't be here for much longer – I'll give it a week . . .' And the boy fell fast asleep.

The following days went by much as the first and during this time not once did either of them venture outside. Poor Will hated working there; the windows were kept shut and the only fresh air that entered his lungs came in through the door with the customers.

In that short amount of time he became accustomed to the old man's strange habits. Despite his dishevelled and threadbare appearance, the apothecary continually preened himself. Will discovered that he was terribly vain and caught him gazing at his reflection many times. He also had a very sweet tooth and devoured great quantities of marzipan and spicecakes which he kept for himself and shared not a crumb with Will. Another of Doctor Spittle's weaknesses was his passion for gossip and he listened to the scandal of the court with his tongue almost hanging out of his mouth. From Sir Francis and a few other clients he would hear of the marvellous parties thrown by the King and he gurgled with delight if they told him in detail of the feasts that had been prepared at the palace. Yet even these tales of exquisite desserts could not sweeten his nature, for after the customers had departed he would grumble about them and hurl insults their way. It was at times like these that Will had learnt to keep his head down and get on with his work, for the old man invariably found fault with him and gave vent to his envy and malice with cruelty directed at the boy. Several times Will went hungry because some customer had told of a magnificent syllabub or an apple mousse of surpassing excellence.

'Curse their tongues!' Doctor Spittle would shriek jealously. 'If I can't afford to savour such things then why should you taste my bread and cheese? Dogs eat scraps in the street, you should do the same! Here am I forced to eat biscuits to appease my cravings when there's folk like that plaguey Lingley stuffing his gullet with pear tarts or delicious cubes of jellied milk.' And so Will would get no dinner that day and the apothecary would storm upstairs to the attic room where the boy was forbidden to go.

Doctor Spittle spent all his spare time locked behind the crimson door. In that secret room he spent most of the night and Will wondered if the old man ever slept. The mysterious attic began to dominate the boy's thoughts. When he was not thinking of how he could escape from the city he found himself pondering on this mystery. While he toiled in the shop his mind turned increasingly to that subject. It became an obsession with him and once, when the apothecary was busy with a customer, he slipped upstairs to see if it was unlocked. Once more he heard the faint scratchings from within but the door would not open and he darted downstairs before he had been missed. Now he was more determined than ever to find out Doctor Spittle's secret and any fear he had at first felt was overcome by this driving curiosity.

A whole week passed by and Will was still stamping out pills and mixing lotions. The chance to return home had not yet presented itself, and besides the talk on everyone's lips was still of the dead miller. Peggy Blister had invented such a tragic story of thwarted lovers who were separated in their youth then briefly reunited until a wicked child murdered the hero that someone had printed a broadsheet about it. Just about everyone knew the tale now and Will's description was at the forefront of everybody's thoughts whenever they saw a street urchin dash by. It became so bad that when customers came into the shop the boy was forced to skulk in the corner to avoid prying eyes.

Another week slid by and before Will realised, it was December. The nights became colder and he moved his sack bedding closer to the hearth, warming his hands by the fire's embers. He really did look like a beggar's brat now and he smelled like one as well. He hadn't had a wash since his arrival in London and on the odd occasion he had to stir some herbs or essences into a potion, the hands that came dripping out of the perfumed water were so white compared to the rest of him that it looked as though he was wearing gloves.

It was the thirteenth of December and Will was on his hands and knees scrubbing the floor. Doctor Spittle was absorbed in filling a large Delftware jar with preserves, but his attention seemed to be somewhere else. He kept pausing and gazing out of the window at the sky, as if wishing for the night to come.

The door to the shop opened and when Will chanced to look up he saw a pretty young woman standing there. She was a truly lovely creature and though her striped dress was not made of silk she carried herself as though she were a countess. Her golden hair was curled upon her forehead and cascaded softly about her bare shoulders. She waved the fan in her hand at the apothecary who looked up from the jar and chuckled to himself.

'Missed me, you old rogue?' she asked with a laugh.

'Molly, my dear,' he welcomed smarmily. 'It's been a while since you visited me last. I thought you had become dissatisfied with my humble shop.'

'Get away, you old devil!' she giggled. 'Save that fancy talk for the gallants and the fainting ladies that come in here. You an' I ought to know each other well enough by now. You haven't seen me of late because I ain't been here – I been away on *business*.' And she gave the apothecary a meaningful wink. 'Still, that's all done with now. Molly's been dumped again but she ain't complainin'.'

Her voice was light and sweet as a bell. Will thought she was the most beautiful thing on God's earth and in that dingy place she seemed like an angel to him. He gawped at her and it was then that she became aware of him.

'What's this?' she laughed teasingly. 'Don't tell me you're taking in strays now, Spittle? I had you marked down as a rascally old skinflint – please don't tell me I was wrong.'

The apothecary assumed a dignified air and replied, 'I have taken on an apprentice.'

'Pooh!' snorted Molly irreverently. 'I'll believe that the day I turn Quaker.' She curtsied to Will and gave him a warm smile. The boy stood up and bowed shyly in return. 'Treatin' you bad is he?' she asked, cocking her head at the old man. 'You want to watch him you know. Not to be trusted is old Spittle.'

'You're the loveliest thing I've ever seen,' Will piped up.

The young woman stared at him in surprise then laughed once more, but it was not done in mockery. 'Well bless us all,' she cried, 'this lad's got better manners'n most I could mention.'

Doctor Spittle frowned; the woman was too frivolous. 'Get back to work!' he told Will. The boy knelt down obediently and resumed scrubbing the floor.

Molly sighed. 'You are a villain,' she scolded the old man, 'I bet you work that poor lad till he's spent.'

'If you please,' the apothecary began, 'have you come just to annoy me and distract my apprentice or will you purchase anything?'

The woman did not answer; instead she wandered over to a shelf and peered at the bottles there. 'Do you have any rue, camphor or henbane?' she asked eventually.

'What tricks are you up to now, Molly?' inquired Doctor Spittle.

'Same as before,' she answered sweetly, 'taking care of my friends – there's no one else who will and shame on them for it.' The woman picked up a jar and shook it. 'These ginger roots are past their best,' she commented.

The apothecary muttered an oath and hurried forward. 'Enough!' he said. 'I shall not stand for your tampering, I have told you this before. I am the apothecary, not you!'

He speedily brought out the things she had asked for and as she paid him an insolent smile curled on her face. Turning to Will she said, 'Have a care, young apprentice, old Spittle doesn't like to think anyone is as wise as he. If you learn too much of his trade then feign ignorance for the sake of his moth-eaten pride.' With that she gave an impudent laugh and trotted out of the shop.

From the window Doctor Spittle watched her step jauntily down the alley. 'Devil take her,' he grumbled. 'Too smart for her own good is Molly – it'll be the undoing of her one day. Well, she might think she knows a thing or three about physic but nothing she's got stuffed in that pretty little head of hers is a match for my brains.'

He raised his eyes to the ceiling and a quick grin lit his face. 'Night will fall soon,' he whispered excitedly. The apothecary stuffed his hand into the pocket of his coat and brought out a large bunch of keys. 'Call me if anyone comes in,' he told Will, 'but I doubt if we shall have any more custom tonight.'

But even as the words were spoken a small figure burst into the shop. 'Apothecary!' the man wailed. 'Come quick, my master needs you! He lies ill of fever and the physician is nowhere to be found.'

Doctor Spittle wavered. He hated visiting the sick – he was always afraid that he might catch their illnesses. Usually he refrained from making such calls but this man was known to him; he was the servant of a rich merchant whose cook was renowned for her splendid confections. He stole a glance up the stairs and decided that his other work would have to wait that night. This was a job that would undoubtedly pay well, unless the patient died, of course, and he might even get the chance to taste a syllabub.

Licking his lips he hastened to the counter and pulled his seldom-used apothecary box from beneath it. 'Take me to him,' he told the anxious man and in a moment they were both gone.

Will scratched his head. It wasn't like Doctor Spittle to venture near a sickbed. He put down the scrubbing brush and stretched. That was enough; the floor had never looked so clean. The boy sat on the counter and wondered when the old man would return – if he put the leeches on the patient then he might not be back for hours. He stared about him in a bored sort of way until his wandering gaze rested upon something which made him jump off the counter with amazement. Beside him was a large bunch of keys.

Will picked them up in disbelief. In his fluster Doctor Spittle had forgotten to take them with him.

In a trice the boy dashed up the stairs – this was his chance to discover the apothecary's secret. Breathlessly he stood outside the blood-red door and placed one of the keys into the lock. It turned with a smooth click and Will gulped as he tried the handle. Already he could hear the scratching sound from within. Gingerly he opened the door and looked inside. With his mouth open in amazement Will looked around him.

The attic was a tiny place, made even smaller by the equipment the apothecary kept there.

A vast number of ancient leather-bound books and parchment scrolls covered the walls and reached up to the sloping ceiling. The skull of some large animal grinned down from a high ornate shelf and its macabre stare was mirrored in a silvered ball of glass which hung from the rafters, next to which was the shrivelled body of a puppy and two wooden cages. There were scientific instruments of gleaming brass with which to study the heavens, bunches of strange plants that the boy had not seen in the shop below, bottles of acid with skulls painted on them and small bags, which to his disgust he found contained human teeth. A chart depicting a five-pointed star was pinned to a rare space on the wall and a long telescope pointed out of the window. In the small fireplace a black pot bubbled, giving off bright green smoke that trailed and curled up the chimney.

Will coughed. So *that* was where the dreadful smell originated! He covered his nose and tried to find out where the scratching noise was coming from. There over his head! He stood on tiptoe and peered into the two wooden cages he had assumed were empty. Inside each was the furry body of a rat: one was brown, the other black. They had been frantically scratching at the floor of their cage but now they stared at him in surprise.

The boy laughed, so there was no monster up here after all, this was just Doctor Spittle's study where he read his books and examined the stars. But a doubtful voice at the back of his mind whispered to him, 'Are you certain? Look again.' A coldness suddenly washed over Will – this was no ordinary place. He looked once more at the magical symbols on the wall, at the bottles containing eyeballs and the esoteric patterns gouged into the sill of the window. Now he understood. Only a magician would keep such things. Doctor Spittle was a sorcerer!

The boy shuddered. Everyone knew that magicians were in league with the Devil. The imagined fear he had felt before now congealed into a very real terror. Of all the horrors in the world, Will was most afraid of witches and wizards – yet here he was living under the same roof as one. Doctor Spittle's apothecary shop was just a cover for his real, evil work. It was too much. Will would rather take his chances in the city than remain here one more night. It was well known that wizards used the blood of children in their spells. Will put his hand to his throat and strangled the cry of panic that was welling up.

'I've got to get out! I've got to get out!' he squeaked in fear. Spinning on his heel the boy rushed to the door, but it was too late. There within its crimson frame stood Doctor Spittle.

The old man's black brows bristled with fury and a deadly glint flashed in his dark eyes. He ground his teeth together and growled, 'Dog! Why have you dared to defy me?'

Will could only stammer and gabble in reply. 'I won't tell anyone,' he cried. 'I promise. Let me go, please!'

'Only my eyes have ever beheld this secret chamber!' stormed the apothecary wildly. He drew himself up to his full height and his shadow stretched menacingly up behind him, reaching over the rafters and towering above the boy's head. The fire in the grate crackled and the flames blazed more fiercely than before. From the pot the green smoke billowed into the room and wound about the old man's legs, spiralling up to his chest until he was wreathed in a glowing mist.

Will cowered. Doctor Spittle had become a nightmare. Sparks leapt from his eyes and a chill breeze stirred the folds of his coat. A hellish light lit his face from below. 'Now pay the price for your inquisitiveness, boy!' he raged. 'You have outlived your usefulness!'

A terrible howl issued from the chimney and a savage wind tore into the attic. Will staggered before its violence and stumbled into the window pane. The rats in the cages screamed as their wooden prisons rocked and were nearly plucked from their hooks. Books and parchments were seized in the gale and flapped about the boy's head like birds caught in a storm. 'Stop!' he yelled. 'I can help you still! Wait!'

Unseen hands pulled at the window's latch and it flew open, cracking several of the diamond panes. Will was lifted into the air as the unnatural tempest thrust him on to the sill. But before it could hurl him outside he caught hold of the frame and held on for dear life. Far below him he saw the street and he snapped his eyes tight shut.

'Peace!' called the apothecary abruptly.

A still calm descended on the room, papers and books fluttered to rest on the floor and when Will scrambled away from the window he found the old man studying him with fresh interest.

'An interesting notion, young dog,' he said. 'There are indeed certain . . . items I need for my experiments which prove impossible for me to collect myself.' He reached up to stop the cages swinging and poked a yellow fingernail at one of the rats inside.

'You . . . you're a wizard, aren't you?' gasped Will catching his breath.

Doctor Spittle steadied the mirrored globe before answering. 'There are many things I have . . . studied,' he began slowly. 'It is true that I have had considerable success with my forays into the black arts but that is too narrow a field of study.' He ran his fingers over the books which had remained on the shelves. 'Magic is an easy art to master,' he said dismissively. 'Something all cheap-jack scholars

can learn – providing they are willing to sacrifice something in return. No, I do not call myself a magician – my true dreams and desires lie in another direction.'

'What direction is that?' ventured Will.

Doctor Spittle made a sign of humility. 'I am an alchemist,' he whispered. 'The science of the ancients is my particular and especial interest. For most of my life I have pursued my goal and at times I have been close to achieving it.' With a sigh he sadly shook his head. 'But always there was something missing. Continually at the end of my experiment I would be thwarted and the Stone would elude me once more.'

'Stone?'

A far-off smile spread over the old man's face. 'The Philosopher's Stone, boy,' he uttered as though speaking of something holy. 'That is what I seek; that perfect element which transmutates base metals into gold. The ancients knew of it, and down the ages I believe others have discovered it, but alas, as yet, I have not. The Stone is always just out of my reach, but one day, one day I shall attain it and then the world shall see. The star of Elias Theophrastus Spittle will rise and I shall have more riches than the King himself. We shall see who will bow and scrape then, oh yes. All my life I have been forced to serve others; when I possess the Stone all that will change.'

Will's breath was less laboured now, but he was still uneasy. He had bought his life with rash promises that he had no intention of keeping. There was definitely no doubt about it – Doctor Spittle may be a magician but he was also out of his mind. Even he knew that nothing could change base metals into gold – if that was possible then there would be hordes of wealthy witches swanning about. He eyed the door as the apothecary stepped aside but the old man caught his glance and chuckled.

'Thank you for reminding me,' Doctor Spittle said. He took the key from the floor where it had fallen and turned it in the lock. 'Now you can stop wasting your time plotting an escape,' he told him. 'I have too many little jobs in store for you to let you go now. Even if you do manage to slip out of my net, rest assured, boy, that I will find you. There are many methods I can employ in the search and many agencies at my command to fetch you back. If you thought your work hard before, then you were never more wrong. That will seem like a May revel compared to what awaits you.'

He moved to the open window and squinted at the sky. The night had fallen and the earliest stars were pricking through the heavens. 'But first things first,' he admonished himself. 'I have been waiting all day for this moment.' He rummaged through a great pile of papers and unravelled a rolled-up chart. On it was marked all the stars of the heavens with their names written in a flowing script beside them. Doctor Spittle yelped with glee as he traced a line with his grimy fingernail and pulled the large telescope closer to the window.

Will watched in silence as the old man put his eye to one end of the brass cylinder and carefully adjusted the focus with hands that trembled with excitement.

'A perfect night,' he drooled, 'absolutely perfect. No clouds in the way – in fact you could even get a clear view without this apparatus, but for a closer inspec . . .

aha!' His whole frame tensed as he peered through the lens. 'Magnificent,' he said joyously. 'Undoubtedly the best sighting so far.'

Will leaned forward and looked up to where the telescope was trained. There in the twinkling night was a comet. It shone brighter than any star and its tail pointed over the rooftops like a wintry dagger. The boy had never seen one before and he marvelled at it.

Doctor Spittle pushed himself away from the eyepiece, then hunted in his astrological charts. 'It is a sign!' he proclaimed. 'Nothing traverses the heavens without due reason. Such celestial omens can herald the birth of a Messiah or announce terrible disasters. Something is afoot as surely as fish have scales and I mean to discover what.' In a fever of excitement he pored over the chart, linking one mystic symbol with another. Then he froze and sat bolt upright.

'Hah!' he screeched, slapping his hands on the window-sill. 'You see that comet, dog?' he cried, grabbing hold of Will's arm and pointing upwards. 'That is a harbinger of doom!' And he threw back his head to let loose a high, wicked laugh. 'A terrible calamity is about to befall this miserable world.'

4

A Hideous Task

The church of St Anne at Blackfriars was a plain, stone building. At this late hour its stained glass windows were dark and all was quiet within its cold walls. High in the belfry bats were whispering to one another, nodding sagely and repeating their ancient prophecies. They knew what was to happen this night.

A grim silence lay over the churchyard. It was an untidy, creepy place. The upkeep of the cemetery had been too much for the last minister – what with the war and all the problems that it had brought. He had died a troubled man and now his bones lay in the very soil he had neglected. The subsequent minister had not attempted to tame the jungle either, he was more concerned with saving souls than reclaiming old tombstones from the wild tangle outside. It was Nature herself who now ruled the churchyard. Inside St Anne's the gospels were preached but beyond its walls the dangerous realm of the old goddess flourished.

A sharp frost laced the night airs. Imelza pulled herself further into the bramble thicket, yet the keen fingers of early winter continued to chill her and she shivered uncontrollably. A large, forgotten headstone was at the heart of the thorny bush and she crawled over to it for shelter. There, beneath the granite scales of a twisting dragon, the ginger cat looked down at her swollen belly and knew the time was near.

'Where is that midwife?' she cried in distress. 'The word should have spread through the chain by now!'

The Widow Mogs ambled through the narrow streets. She was a fat old tabby, whose fur was brindled and moth-eaten with age. Her face was framed by folds of flab and her eyes were almost hidden beneath the abundance of skin that surrounded them. She was a slow, dirty animal but her importance in the feline hierarchy could not be denied.

In the entire city of London there were only two cat midwives – the Widow Mogs and Old Ma Wackette. These ugly and miserable creatures were in constant demand to deliver the kittens to first-time mothers. Over the years they had attended innumerable births, yet these two old cats had never clapped eyes on each other. Each had her own territory and woe betide the foolish feline who requested the services of the wrong one. London was thus divided into two camps: those delivered by Widow Mogs and those by Old Ma Wackette. It was a strange loyalty that lasted throughout a cat's life: if they had been a Mogs' kitten then so would their children and the same was true for a Wackette's.

The tower of St Anne's now reared above the Widow Mogs and she blinked her tiny emerald eyes at its tall black shape. 'Stupid ruddy place to choose, isn't it, Peachy?' she said scornfully. 'What silly little bint 'ave we got tonight then, my old chuck? They don't learn, do they? These young know-it-all missies are all the same. We seen each an' every one, ain't we, Peachy?'

Widow Mogs always talked like this. Peachy had been the pet name for her husband who had perished long ago. But from the day he died she had continued to chat to him. It was a harmless habit of hers and nobody minded so long as she continued to do her work properly – besides, Old Ma Wackette was supposed to be even battier than she was.

Muttering in this fashion to her long-dead mate, the midwife entered the churchyard and passed through the deep shadows of the brambles and headstones. 'Mogs is here!' she cried. 'Where are you, my petal? Mogs can't help you if she can't find you! Mew up, my sweet.'

Imelza flicked her ears and raised her head. 'Here!' she called. 'Over here!'

'Fine place for a litter, we don't think – do we Peachy?' grumbled the Widow Mogs pushing through the thorns. 'What's wrong with a nice dry attic or stable loft, that's what we'd like to know. Never heard of such a thing, out in the cold an' with winter settin' in as well. Shame on the little madam. Oooh, there you are, chucky.'

At last the midwife had found Imelza. She plopped

her bottom on the cold ground and eyed the beautiful ginger cat with a professional glance.

'Seems the chain was right for once then,' she said drily. 'Makes a change that, doesn't it, Peachy? You are near ain'tcha, darlin'?' She stretched out a paw and touched Imelza's large stomach. 'Them's ready to pop right out,' she clucked knowingly. 'We got 'ere just in time. Now don't you worry none, I know what I'm doin'. Just get comfy and breathe easy.'

Imelza felt better now that she was not alone. She lay her head down and did as she was told.

'Wait a bit, wait a bit!' the midwife said in an agitated manner. 'I don't do nothing fer free, you know. Before I starts I wants payin'. You know the conditions, dearie – Mogs always dines before she delivers. I don't want to appear callous but what if something should go wrong and you snuff it my love? I'll have come all this way fer nothin'. Fair's fair as my Peachy always says.'

Imelza clutched her stomach as the pains increased. A loud miaow issued from her throat but she struggled to control the agony for a moment. 'Here,' she began haltingly, 'see, I keep my . . . my part of the bargain.' Carefully she rolled over and dragged a dead sparrow from under her. It was the only thing she had caught in days and to part with it was a terrible wrench, yet she knew she must.

The midwife's eyes shone as she snatched it from her. 'Ooh look at that, Peachy,' she cackled. 'Nice birdy – your favourite, remember.' The fat old cat spent the next few minutes crunching and chewing on this delicacy, whilst Imelza groaned and cried beside her.

'There now,' said the Widow Mogs as she pulled a feather from her lips, 'I'll see to you my little one. Put your trust in me. I've been seein' to kit-kits since before you were born.'

The minutes ticked by as the midwife assisted Imelza. 'Won't be much longer now,' she said soothingly, 'and then you'll have a lovely little family all yer own.'

Many times the ginger cat threw back her head and screamed with the pain. Her teeth ground together and her eyes rolled in the sockets as she snatched in her breath. She had never imagined it would be like this and at one point thought she would faint away. Then, as she strained and pushed, her golden eyes stared up at the night sky and beheld the comet swinging over the city. Its fierce white light was mirrored in her eyes and curved over them, blazing and dazzling into her mind. Suddenly all her pain vanished. All she was aware of was that cold radiance above and nothing else seemed to matter.

'Lovely!' chirruped the Widow Mogs gleefully. 'Look, my dear you've a fine little lad – a stronger little tyke I ain't never seen in all my years of wifferin'. He's a beauty, with your very own colour.' Holding up the tiny bundle she began licking it clean. The kitten wriggled and squirmed at the touch of her rough tongue and before she could finish the job he leapt from her grasp and nuzzled against his mother.

Imelza stirred from her trance-like state and shook the memory of the comet from her mind. A great smile split her face when she saw her fine young son rubbing his chin against her.

'Ooh,' called the midwife excitedly, 'here's another,

my dear. Why, 'tis a little girl. My but she's a darlin' honey – turn many a head she will when the time comes.' This kitten she clutched tightly to herself and would not let go till every inch had been cleaned.

She was a lovely creature whose fur was a subtle tortoiseshell and when she opened her tiny mouth to mew it was the sweetest voice ever heard in that dreary churchyard.

The Widow Mogs placed the newborn next to her brother and congratulated Imelza. 'There now, 'tweren't so difficult was it, my pretty? You'll make a fine mother I'm sure. What a perfect little family you got, makes my old eyes glad to see it does. Well now you're bedded down I'll leave you in peace, but you make sure you find some shelter and soon.'

Imelza purred contentedly as she gently turned her children over with her nose. They were indeed a beautiful pair of kittens and she felt herself truly blessed. Suddenly her eyes widened and she gasped as a new pain seized her. 'It is not over yet!' she cried. 'I feel one more inside!'

The midwife frowned. 'Ooh Peachy,' she whispered, 'did you hear that? It don't sound good that don't. Let me see, Mogs'll help yer.'

Imelza screeched and her claws ripped up the soil around her as she gulped the air down. With a concerned look on her face the midwife stared at the kitten which was emerging. One more squeal from Imelza and it was through.

A feeble lump of skin and bone lay motionless on the ground. Widow Mogs sniffed at it and sneered with disdain. 'Runt,' she muttered scornfully.

'Let me see,' begged Imelza.

'Don't you worry yourself over it, petal,' the midwife told her sternly. 'Such things do happen. The nasty thing has no place in the wild world. You've two lovelies already there, pay no heed to thissun – it won't last long. The sooner it perishes the better for all.'

Imelza was horrified. 'Give me my child!' she yelled.

The Widow Mogs blinked at her in surprise. 'It won't do you any good, dearie,' she told her flatly. 'Sickly little things like this are best left to die. No use bringing weaklings into the world now, is there?' She leaned forward and whispered casually, 'If you wish, I could take it away with me, save upsetting yerself. I knows how to get rid of rubbish like this.'

The ginger cat stared at her; she knew exactly what this vile old creature would do with her baby. 'Get away from me!' she screamed. 'Get you gone, you hideous old bloodsucker! Go find some other prey before I sharpen my claws on your face!'

The midwife scuttled out of the thicket fearing for her life. She had never been spoken to like that before. Why was the mother taking such offence? Everyone knew the privileges that came with wifferin'. Once she was safely out in the churchyard she stuck her tail haughtily into the air and strolled away with all the dignity she could muster.

Imelza pulled the runt towards her and gazed at it. The trembling kitten was another boy, only his fur was black as sable. She smiled ruefully; he had his father's colouring and that endeared him to her. Tenderly she licked him and his thin voice bleated up at her. 'Seems your brother got all your strength,' she sighed, 'and your sister all the good looks. Well, I'll not see you die, little one.'

With her three children tucked round her, Imelza gave thought to the weeks ahead. She had to find shelter, yet how could she leave them to do so?

Will looked warily about him; the dark streets did little to ease the dread which filled his heart. Strange how this, the first time he had been allowed out of the apothecary's shop, should terrify him so. But the errand he had been sent on would make the strongest shiver in his boots. He tried not to think of it but the grisly thoughts were impossible to shake off.

Over a week had passed since the comet had faded from the sky and during that time Doctor Spittle had been true to his word. Will had been made to work even harder than before. His duties now included helping the alchemist with his unnatural experiments and he spent many a sleepless night watching the noxious mixtures bubble and boil. His eyes smarted from the fumes and his throat was sore from the endless clouds of coloured smoke.

He had been practically useless in the shop lately and on one occasion actually fell asleep whilst grinding some herbs. Grey circles ringed his bloodshot eyes and he seemed a shadow of his former self. The only person who had noticed this and cared enough to mention it was the young woman, Molly.

She had visited the shop twice since he had first seen her and on both these occasions she had exhibited a great knowledge of all the things on the shelves. Molly had taken one look at Will and immediately upbraided Doctor Spittle for overworking him.

'You'll slave him straight into the grave, you old demon!' she had stormed. 'Look at the poor lad, he's almost done in. Give him food and let him rest.'

Her words may have had some effect on the alchemist for he became more generous with Will's meals and the nocturnal vigils grew fewer. Will liked Molly enormously; she was the one bright ray that entered the dismal shop. Once, when Doctor Spittle was engrossed in the attic room, she and Will had spent half an hour chatting amiably. It was marvellous how she managed to put him at ease and he almost blurted out all his tragic history without realising. Luckily they were interrupted by another customer, yet for a long time afterwards Will found himself wondering if he could have trusted her. With so much treachery and deceit in the city it was odd that there should be someone like Molly. Perhaps next time he would tell her something of his past.

His footsteps echoed through the grim gloom. It was not far now. What a ghastly mission to be on. It was past midnight, all godly folk were in bed and only a few windows were still aglow. Along Paternoster Row he trailed, then down Warwick Lane until the high walls surrounding Ludgate came in view. Here he stopped, daunted by the gruesome and disgusting task that lay ahead. If only he could run, all he had to do was keep going through that gateway and not turn back. But the face of the alchemist flitted before his eyes and the words he had spoken before despatching the lad hissed in his ears once more.

'Should you decide to seize this chance and escape me, know that I shall not rest till all the devils of Hell have tormented you and fetched you back here.'

Will's stomach turned over. He had to do this horrible thing and he bitterly regretted those hasty words he had spoken to Doctor Spittle that evening in the attic room. Yes, he could certainly go places the old man could not, but he had no idea that those rash promises would lead him down this dark and damning road. Quietly he prayed to God for courage and strength.

Ludgate prison was silent at this late hour. The narrow, barred windows were blind to both the night and the boy who ventured into the courtyard before them. Stealthily he tiptoed nearer, his attention fixed on that which had drawn him. There it was, the terrible structure which had taken the lives of so many men, women and children – the gallows!

Starkly it rose before the impregnable walls, an ugly black scaffold. It was a frightening and imposing threshold to death and there, swinging gently from the cross beam, was its most recent victim.

Will thanked the Lord that the moon was clouded this night, for if he had seen the face of that unfortunate man he would have surely died himself.

With his heart in his mouth he crept up, mounting the wooden stairs to the platform, until the fearsome apparition was within reach. The dark silhouette suspended above him cast a horror over his soul and he could not believe that he had actually come this far. The dead man's feet were level with his chest and Will noticed with disgust that someone had stolen the corpse's boots. He cursed the unknown thief then realised that he was no better. Doctor Spittle's orders were clear and the boy knew what he must do. The alchemist had sent him out to fetch the hair from a hanged man's head.

Shuddering, Will crossed to one of the main support beams and began to climb. Up he went, splinters from the rough wood jabbing into his palms and spiking his cheek, until he was high enough. From here he could reach out and . . . a trembling hand delved into his pocket and pulled out a pair of scissors.

'Forgive me, Lord,' he murmured, 'I do not wish to harry the dead.' His shaking hand stretched towards the downcast head and the scissor blades opened. 'Please sir,' he said, 'do not haunt me for what I am about to do.'

Snip.

A lock of lank hair fell into his palm but at that moment the clouds drew away from the moon and the ghostly light fell directly upon the dead man's face.

It was a terrifying mask of death: the tongue lolled from the bloodless lips and the skin was ashen grey. Yet what petrified Will the most were the man's eyes. They bulged out of their sockets and were turned straight towards him in an accusing stare.

The boy screamed and fell from the beam, landing with a crash on the platform. The rope which held the man creaked and the shadows that danced over the hideous face made it look as though he were laughing. Will screamed again and in an instant lamps were lit in the windows of the prison.

'Who's that out there?' called a guard.

'There's someone messin' about at the gallows – look!'

'Call the nightwatchman!'

'Catch the miserable little fiend!'

An answering call came from the other side of the courtyard as the alerted nightwatchman came running, wielding a stout cudgel in his fist.

Will scrambled from the stage but Arnold Strogget, the nightwatchman, had seen him. 'Stop, in the name of the King!' he bawled. The boy took no notice and fled into the street. 'Come back here you devil!' snarled Master Strogget and he chased after for all he was worth.

Down the narrow lanes Will ran and behind him he heard the grunts and fierce shrieks of the nightwatchman. A desperate terror was on the boy and he spurred himself on. But the conditions he had been forced to endure soon took their toll. He was tired, undernourished and his legs were weak. Realising that his strength was failing he searched for somewhere to hide. But the moonlight flooded every corner of the street, banishing the shadows and denying him refuge. With the blood thumping in his temples he turned a corner and saw his salvation.

There was the church of St Anne – but Will had eyes only for its graveyard. Into the wild forest of bushes and brambles he tore, leaping over tombs and diving under branches. Feverishly he wriggled into a dense clump of gorse then curled himself into a ball and held his breath.

He could hear the nightwatchman panting up the road. With any luck he would continue right past and not think to search the cemetery. But fortune was not smiling on Will that night, for as the man slowed down to catch his breath he gave thought to the cover the churchyard might give. He peered up the street just to make sure, then smiled. If the boy was still running he would surely be able to hear him. There was only one place he could be now. Arnold Strogget tapped his cudgel expectantly against the church wall and entered.

From his hiding place Will could hear him stride through the grass. He dared not move for he would give his position away and before he had crawled out of the gorse bush the man would be upon him. He was in a terrible state and with the shock of what he had just done still reeling in his head, the sweat which streamed down his face was icy cold.

A dreadful crashing sound made him cower even further into the gorse. The nightwatchman was sweeping his cudgel through the bushes as he advanced. Will sobbed from fear. Soon he would be discovered and dragged away to join that poor man on the gallows. His fingers closed about his own throat as if he could already feel the rope tighten round his neck. Still Master Strogget advanced, drawing nearer with every swipe and thrust.

Master Arnold liked to give felons a good bashing and he put all his might behind the swings of the cudgel. The thickets bowed before him and he grinned with pleasure – that perishing little ghoul deserved all he got. 'Disturb the dead would yer?' he shouted at the undergrowth. 'I'll learn yer not to thieve. Break yer fingers for it I will.' And he lashed out even more viciously as if to demonstrate.

'AAAEEEOOOWWW!'

The nightwatchman froze. He had never heard a sound like that before. It was a horrid, shrill cry that screeched round the churchyard and curdled his blood.

'What was that?' he muttered.

'AAAEEEOOOWWW!!'

'Save us!' he stammered glancing nervously about him. 'That does sound like nothing from this world.' Perhaps what he was chasing was not a person after all. What if some undead horror had wormed out of its cold grave to visit the living? 'Steady Arnold,' he told himself, 'don't let your brain get overheated. Things like that don't happen.' But he was woefully ill at ease and his flesh crawled. The graveyard now appeared sinister and full of deep shadows where anything might be lurking. A breeze swayed the branches of a gnarled oak tree and the bushes all around began to rustle. The man clutched his cudgel with both hands. 'Where are yer wits?' he asked himself. ' 'S only the wind, nought to be sceered of . . .'

'AAAEEEOOOWWW!'

That was it. With a final shriek Arnold Strogget leapt into the air and hurtled from the churchyard.

Still in his hiding place Will bit his lip – he wanted to get away too. The sound was nightmarish. Was it one of Doctor Spittle's demons come to torment him? Bravely he waited till he was sure the nightwatchman had gone, then squirmed out of the gorse bush.

The high-pitched wail was sent up again and Will staggered through the thorns to escape the unseen monster. And then the cry changed. This time it was sorrowful and forlorn, sounding like an animal in pain.

Will halted. Should he find out what it was? If there was indeed some poor creature lying there in agony he could hardly ignore it. Hesitating, he moved

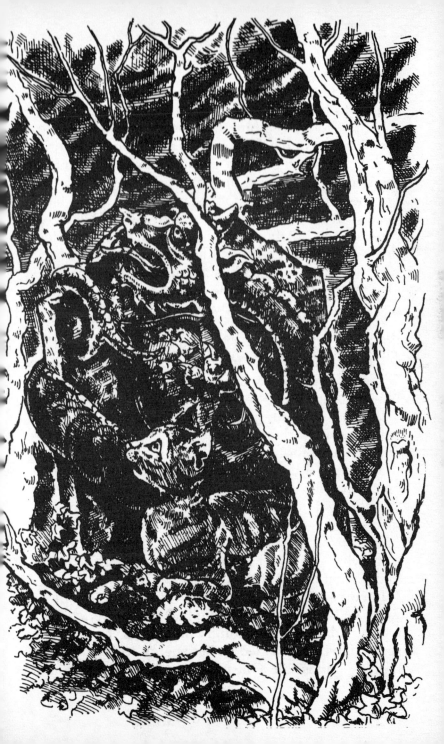

towards the sound, hoping it was not a devil playing a trick to lure him into its den. One more plaintive whimper convinced him that it was not and he made for a great bramble thicket at the rear of the cemetery.

Kneeling on the damp ground he stared through the knotted twigs and his heart was moved to pity. For there, by an ornate tombstone, was Imelza – half dead with the cold and starvation. Alongside her were three kittens, but they looked as though the midwinter death had already claimed them. The ginger cat lifted her once lovely face and gazed unsteadily at the boy. One feeble mew was all she could manage before her head slumped on to her chest and her eyes closed.

'Poor puss,' Will tutted, 'all alone with your little ones.' Glumly he sat back and for several minutes stared at the pathetic little group in silence. Then, before he realised what he was doing, he found himself dragging the brambles out of the way.

It was a difficult, painful task and his fingers bled from the sharp thorns. But at last a space was made wide enough for him to reach in. Holding the kittens in his cupped hands Will breathed his warm breath on them. They were all still alive – but only by the slenderest of threads. Gently he popped each one into his pockets then took the mother in his arms.

'Don't you worry now,' he told her. 'I can take you somewhere dry and warm tonight, though I don't know what old Spittle will say.'

Imelza snuggled into the crook of his arm. The past week had been the worst she had ever experienced. Never had she been so hungry or so weak. The kittens seemed to have drained all her energy and she found hunting impossible. One puny mouse was all she had eaten in the last fortnight and no longer was she the fairest cat this side of the river. Now her once beautiful, well-defined features were pinched and careworn and her ribs showed through the fur.

She had finally given up all hope and was about to surrender herself to 'He that walks in darkness' – that terrible presence which waits in the shadows and whom every cat knows it will meet one day. It was to this grim spirit that Imelza was calling, submitting her life to him, acknowledging his claim to her at last. This unearthly invitation was what the nightwatchman and Will had heard. But when Imelza had looked up to see the face of the dreaded one, she had beheld only that of a human child.

Sighing, she thanked whatever chance had brought him to her – people did have their uses after all.

Will stroked her softly and made his way out of the churchyard. Ludgate was buzzing like a stirred up wasps' nest so he avoided the area and skirted round St Paul's on his way back to the apothecary shop. All he had to do now was persuade the alchemist to let them stay.

The face of Doctor Spittle was pressed up against the window when Will arrived. It looked like a comical gargoyle but wisely Will did not laugh. The old man blinked when he saw the boy and scowled at the bundle in his arms. Hastily the face withdrew and he rushed to open the door and drag him inside.

'Where've you been?' he roared. 'It's taken you an age. Did you get it? What's that you have there?'

Will answered the questions all at once in a rush of explanation. 'I was chased by the nightwatchman, I had to hide, yes I've got it though I didn't like doing it and this is a cat.'

'Well get rid of it!' snapped the old man. 'Let me have the lock of hair.'

The boy placed Imelza on the sacking in front of the dying fire and, one by one, took the kittens from his pockets.

'More of the vermin?' squealed the alchemist, agitated to distraction. 'Take them out of my shop at once!'

When all the kittens had been placed round their mother Will gave Doctor Spittle the hair he had cut from the dead man's head. The old man snatched it greedily and gave it a tentative sniff. 'You sure he didn't have the smallpox?' he asked with a sudden suspicion. Will nodded and the alchemist almost skipped with glee.

'I want to keep them,' the boy said daringly. Doctor Spittle glared at him but quickly he carried on. 'They're cold and starving; they would have perished if they'd stayed outside one more night.'

'Better that than come in here stealing heat from my fire. Let them die. Put them in a sack and drown them in the Fleet.'

'I will not!'

The old man stepped forward, his eyes gleaming. 'Defiance is it, my young dog? Well, we know what happens if you don't obey me – don't we?'

'But I thought you would be pleased,' Will cried.

Doctor Spittle stared at him confused. 'Pleased? Why should I be pleased to have flea-bitten animals brought under my roof?'

'You're a magician, aren't you?'

A Hideous Task

'Alchemist – I've told you before.'

'Well, don't they have familiars?'

There was a pause and the old man ran his fingers over his bald patch. 'Here's a notion,' he mumbled. 'A familiar. Yes, all the greats possessed familiars – why not I? Interesting, I wonder if anyone has ever measured the intelligence of the feline. It would be fascinating to see how far I could train one.' He took a fresh look at the kittens and stooped to examine them. 'This female won't do, and as for the runt, I find his ugliness distasteful. I could never work with it – the nasty little leech. What have we here though? A fine specimen this is – see how much stronger the ginger kitten is? Yes I like him. There is some blue milk upstairs – they can have that. They will not sleep down here. I don't want my customers tripping over them in the morning. They shall remain in the attic – I have my experiments to continue with tonight so I can keep an eye on them up there.' With that he scooped up the cats and ascended the staircase.

When he was alone Will sighed with relief. He understood the whims and vanities of Doctor Spittle enough by now to know how to get round him. At least the cats would be warm and fed tonight – he just hoped the old man wouldn't get bored with them. What would happen when he realised a cat could not be trained in the magic arts? Yawning, he decided that this was a problem which he would have to solve some other time. At the moment he was far too tired to think any more. It had been an exhausting and perilous night for him and, as soon as he curled up on the sacking, the boy fell into a disturbed and fitful sleep.

5

A Dragon in the Rags

The dawn was grey and cold; its dismal light poked through the diamond panes of the attic window and fanned across the cluttered room. Imelza opened one eye and took in her surroundings. She and her kittens lay by the hearth, where a pot bubbled over the fire and sent peculiar blue smoke up the chimney. For a while she was content merely to gaze at the cheering flames and be glad they were all still alive.

'So, you're with us at last, madam,' came a voice behind her.

Imelza turned her head. Amid the bizarre clutter of the room she saw an old man and then she remembered, it was he who had fed her the previous night. The cat did not like the look of him. She had known enough humans to be able to tell which of them were trustworthy – this one appeared cruel and shifty. Warily she watched as he cackled and addressed her once more.

'I hope you spent a pleasant night in my attic,' he said, 'I have grand plans for that fine son of yours. He could be of the greatest use to me.' Doctor Spittle crouched beside her and reached down to stroke the ginger kitten.

Imelza eyed him with caution and her claws slid out in readiness. Her son struggled uncomfortably at the touch of the old man's hand but he picked him up anyway. Imelza's ears flattened against her skull and she hissed at the human to return her child.

'Tush, tush,' Doctor Spittle muttered, 'I won't harm him.' He stared at the kitten in his grubby hands then gave him back to his mother. 'A remarkable youngster you have there, madam,' he told her, 'but I must give him a name. A familiar must be called something dignified and noble. A character from legend perhaps, Zeus or Hermes? No, I always preferred the Roman gods – they were more vengeful and merciless.' A wide and toothy grin cracked his face as he clapped his hands together. 'Aha!' he shrieked. 'Henceforth your son shall be known as Jupiter! A fine and glorious name indeed.'

Imelza licked her son's face and he raised his tawny eyes to her. She thought 'Jupiter' sounded ridiculous. Still it was not up to her to name her children. Cats are peculiar creatures, they never name their young. It is their belief that a kitten should choose its own when the time is right. They can go through life with a thousand titles but having only one true name. Gently Imelza purred into the small ginger ear which rubbed against her chin. 'Jupiter will do for the present,' she whispered. 'Take it to please the human, so that he will give us food. When the winter is over we shall leave this place.'

Doctor Spittle studied them keenly, wondering what thoughts, if any, trickled through a cat's mind. He congratulated himself on his choice of familiar – that one would grow up to be the strongest of the litter. The smile faded from his lips however when an ugly, black face reared over Imelza's side. There was that puny little runt. Its head was too large for its sickly body to support, so it wavered and wobbled like some poisonous plant bending in the breeze. The alchemist pulled an unpleasant expression – it really should have been drowned or had its scrawny neck wrung.

'Look at it,' he spat. 'See how it gazes round. I hate the wretched, loathsome thing. 'Tis more of a slug than a cat! Leech is the name I give to thee!'

Imelza put a paw round her weak child and comforted him. 'Fear not, my dear one,' she purred. 'I shall let no harm come to you.' The runt blinked, then his livid green eyes slid slyly towards the alchemist. Something spiteful and malevolent was kindled in those emerald depths but quickly he buried his face in his mother's fur.

The sound of footsteps came pattering up the stairs and the crimson door of the attic slowly opened. Will peeped in and was obviously relieved to find them all still alive. Doctor Spittle lifted his eyebrows and looked at the boy questioningly. 'What is it, dog?' he grumbled. 'Have you not got enough to occupy yourself?'

'I was just . . . wondering how the cats were,' he replied.

The old man sneered. 'Wondering if I'd killed them, you mean,' he chuckled nastily. 'Well I've been too preoccupied with my work to do that.' He dragged his hand wearily over his eyes and waved at the pot over the fire. 'Another failure. For my very life I can see no way forward in this; my experiments have come to nought. It would seem that the Philosopher's Stone will be eternally out of my reach.'

He pointed at Imelza and said, 'At any rate, madam there has been fed and so have her young. You can see they are all hale and hearty. The ginger one I shall train as my familiar. Jupiter is his name now, after the Roman supreme ruler of Heaven – Jovis Pater. Oh yes, and the runt is called Leech.'

'What about the other?'

Doctor Spittle turned his attention to the girl kitten. 'The markings of the tortoiseshell are very beautiful,' he grudgingly admitted. 'The subtle dabs and splashes of cinnamon on her lustrous coat are quite magnificent. And yet I have no interest in her. Jupiter I named because it is only proper for a familiar. Leech was a different matter. I hate the vile abomination – and you cannot curse what has no name.'

He leaned back in his chair and took up a faded manuscript mumbling, 'If you wish, you may name the girl yourself. I must pore over my work to see where my research has gone astray – perhaps there was something I overlooked.'

The boy knelt beside Imelza and scratched behind her ear. She liked that and pushed against his hand for more. This human was better, she told herself.

Doctor Spittle grunted to himself as he studied the scrolls before him. He was so engrossed that he was oblivious to everything, in fact he had forgotten they were there at all.

Will patted the tortoiseshell's head then tickled her under the chin. 'I think because of your markings I'll call you Dab,' he said.

From the shop below there came an impatient cry. A customer had arrived. Both Will and Doctor Spittle ran out of the attic and rushed downstairs.

Imelza breathed deeply; it was good to be alone at last with her children.

'Hoy!' squeaked a voice from above.

Imelza started and looked up at once. There was so much hanging from the sloping rafters that it was some time before she found where the voice had come from.

'Hoy! You! Tigerstripe!'

'Sshh!' urged another.

At last her gleaming eyes fell upon the two cages and poking out of one of them was the furry face of a black rat. At once Imelza's hunting instinct tingled through her. It was kind of the humans to provide her with live food. She rose and stretched herself before prowling beneath the cages.

'Flesh,' she purred hungrily. 'Flesh that dangles from above – most tantalising. I desire to prick it with my claws and let the blood spurt out.'

'Hah!' scoffed the rat fearlessly. 'You tigers always after Heliodorus's bones. Well he not let you have them see, not never. I tell you now to keep well clear of him. He have long teeth to nip off your nosey.'

'Why don't you hush up, you daft 'ead?' came the cry from the other cage.

'Pah!' snorted the black rat. 'You cringey coward – I not afraid not never.'

Heliodorus was a proud black rat. He spoke with a thick accent, picked up from all the characters he had met throughout his life. Before the alchemist had captured him he had been a nomad – one of those solitary individuals who make no place their home and who travel endlessly. There was nothing he liked better than starting a new journey, climbing the mooring rope of a great ship and scurrying into the dark hold. His bright, beady eyes had seen strange exotic sights and his ears had been scorched by tropical suns. Yes, Heliodorus could tell tales of the mysterious East and of the monstrous creatures that live in the boundless seas. But now he was a prisoner, trapped in a tiny cage.

Imelza laughed at his threats and paced restlessly beneath him. Her muscles tensed and she leapt into the air. The cage lurched and tipped as her sharp claws hooked round the bars. The ginger cat dangled precariously from it, but the thrill of the kill was burning in her now. It had been too long since her last hunt.

'Prepare for death,' Imelza gurgled.

Heliodorus stood back as the large ginger head reared into view. The golden eyes flashed maliciously at him, but to her consternation he seemed unafraid. She glanced at the other cage and saw there a fat brown rodent who was visibly shaking with terror. That was more like it – she'd teach this foolish one that that was the proper way to behave.

Imelza pushed her nose through the bars and bared her fangs. The black rat did a strange, brazen sort of dance then lashed out with his claws, slapping her nostrils and roaring with laughter. 'Away, foul Tigerstripe!' he boomed. 'You not chew on me today!'

The cat let out a startled squawk at this assault to her nose and lost her grip on the bars. With a wail she tumbled backwards and fell to the floor.

Heliodorus crowed with glee and blew a loud raspberry. Imelza glared up. She had never met with such impudence before.

The rat turned to the other cage and chattered to its occupant. 'There!' he proclaimed. 'That is the way to face the enemy. I snap my fingers in its face and defy it! Heliodorus knows – he strong. Tigerstripe not eat of him. He not be in cat belch – not never!'

Imelza curled up before the hearth with her children. One day, she promised herself, she would grind that rat's bones.

Days and weeks slid by and the calendar moved into January. During the day the apothecary shop was very busy. All manner of folk streamed in to find cures for colds or agues brought on by the bitter weather. Whilst in the dead of night, the only window illuminated in the whole of London was that of the attic room. There Doctor Spittle pursued his alchemical dreams, but all to no avail. Experiment after experiment ended in failure and his disgraceful language was hot enough to melt the frost on the windows.

Will witnessed a gradual change in him as time went by. He became more desperate and despairing as each attempt to find the Philosopher's Stone resulted in disaster. His black tempers became more frequent and sometimes the boy would awake in the middle of the night to hear the old man crashing round the attic room screaming at the top of his voice. Then he would hear the screech of a cat as it was kicked from corner to corner. There was nothing he could do to prevent this, for he knew better than to go against Doctor Spittle when he was in such a mood. Instead he would block up his ears and try to think of something else, some fairer time when his parents were still alive and he had never heard of London.

All this while the kittens grew and flourished, but they learned to mistrust the old man who brewed his formulae over the fire. Except perhaps Jupiter – the alchemist was kinder to him than to the others. As he measured out the ingredients for his doomed quest he would talk to the ginger kitten, explaining what he was doing. And Jupiter would sit on the table beside him listening, fascinated and intrigued by the great knowledge the human possessed. He wished with all his heart that he could know only half as much.

Imelza was not sure if she liked her son taking such an interest in human affairs but she said nothing while the winter was still upon them. Dab was content, like her mother, to sit before the hearth and bide her time. She was already becoming a graceful and beautiful creature and her lustrous coat grew more lovely every day. Doctor Spittle left her alone so she had no strong dislike for him. Leech, however, despised the old man with every waking moment. He often bore the brunt of a failed experiment and came to fear the alchemist's slippered feet. Never was a kitten more afraid of its master, yet a further shadow was beginning to blacken the runt's heart. Leech was jealous of the way Jupiter was being instructed and he began to harbour a bitter grudge against his brother.

Then, one day, fate stepped in and events began to take a more ghastly turn.

It was a bright wintry morning in the apothecary's shop. Will was just sealing a large jar of preserves when Sir Francis Lingley sauntered in. He was dressed more richly than usual, having had good fortune of late and rising higher in the esteem of the King. His silks that morning were the colour of daffodils and his velvet cloak a luxuriant wine red.

When Doctor Spittle hastened to assist him Sir Francis stepped back in disgust. '*Mon Dieu!*' he cried. 'Look at you, man! *Vous avez l'air d'un mendiant*. Are your finances so bad that you needs must dress so shabbily?' With his forefinger daintily extended, he pointed at the alchemist's grimy clothes. They were stained with chemicals and burned by acids. '*Vous êtes une disgrâce!*' he laughed scornfully. 'I might just take my custom elsewhere – it is not fitting for someone in my position to be seen dealing with the likes of you. *Bonjour!*' He turned on his heel, took a sniff at a lace handkerchief as if dispelling the memory of so odious a confrontation, then left.

Doctor Spittle's face was terrible to behold. His lips were drawn back in a hideous snarl and his cheeks flushed a dark purple. Will thought he was going to burst. As soon as Sir Francis passed out of sight the alchemist bellowed and the force behind his voice made the very pots on the shelves shake and clink together.

'How dare he!' he stormed. 'How dare that poxy Jack-a-Dandy come in here and ridicule me with his simpering French phrases!' He coursed through the shop, kicking over jars and bottles until one smashed and a quantity of black syrup oozed over the floor.

'I'll give him something to worry about! It'll take more than a toad squeezing to fix him this time. I'll have to think up something truly uncomfortable for him to suffer from.' The old man shook his fist at the door then paused as he caught sight of his frayed sleeve. 'Alas,' he moaned, 'my garments are indeed the worse for wear. Too long have I been absorbed in my work.'

A smile quickly lit his face as though he had come to a sudden decision. 'Yes, that would do it – better than a thousand warts. But I shall have to be patient.' He crossed to the door which led upstairs. 'Clean this mess!' he ordered Will before rushing up to his bedchamber.

Will could hear him dragging all his clothes from the wardrobe and flinging them around, screaming at the top of his voice. 'Tat!' he bawled. 'Nothing but threadbare rags – that's all I ever wear! I'd burn the lot if the flames would deign to take it. Hang the Lingleys of this world! One day I'll have money enough to buy more silks and frills than his miniscule mind has ever imagined.'

The boy knelt down and busied himself cleaning the floor. He did not hear the door open, so when the friendly voice said, 'A merry morning to you,' he jumped and fell flat on his face, right into the sticky syrup.

'Oh forgive me!' Molly apologised helping the boy

to his feet. Will groaned; treacly, black goo covered his face and dripped from his nose. With a shiver he felt it slide under his collar and down the back of his neck. The young woman gasped at the state he was in; but gradually a grin appeared which in turn was replaced by a titter, then a giggle, until she was laughing and holding her sides.

Will glared at her indignantly but then he too collapsed in a fit of laughter. All the tension and strain vanished during that mad moment and for a short time he felt like a young boy again. He was seized by that carefree joy which he had not felt since the day he had assumed the mantle of adulthood in Mr Balker's parlour. Molly's laughter was infectious and every time she caught a glimpse of his glistening, syrupy face a fresh, uncontrollable fit took hold of her.

Their mirth was suddenly curtailed when Doctor Spittle raged downstairs. 'What – you again?' he yelled at Molly. 'Have you no better occupation than pestering my apprentice?'

The giggles subsided and Will hid his smiling face in case the old man thought they were making fun of him.

But the alchemist was too preoccupied to notice as he hurried to the door with a look of grim determination. 'See to this customer then send her on her way, dog!' he said with a scowl. 'Only take care she pays for what she takes!' Then he strode out of the shop and hurried down the alley.

'Nice to see you too!' Molly called after him. 'What's rattled him this day? I ain't seen 'im in such a hot temper for a year or more.'

'He's feeling sorry for himself,' Will explained.

'Sir Francis Lingley was in before.'

'Oh that one,' she tutted.

'Do you know him then?'

'I did once,' she replied and the smile faded from her lips. 'When I first came to London he was . . . a friend of mine.' She fell silent and stared out of the window, remembering those days as a wide-eyed girl seeing the great city for the first time. A lot of things had happened since then; her heart had been broken three times by men who had deceived her, and those beautiful eyes of hers had cried themselves raw on many occasions. Molly finally knew the cruel ways of the city and how to deal with the harshness of life. She had been forced to learn the hard way, yet somehow had managed to survive. She was wiser now, and a little older. No man would take her for a fool any more and her fractured heart was impervious to honeyed words and a dashing smile.

The young woman stirred and shook her blonde hair, banishing those painful times with one quick movement. 'Still, that was an age ago,' she told Will, 'and I'm right glad of that. Thought more of his own looks than he ever did of mine. He ain't no proper gentleman either – meaning he ain't got no land nor nothin'. All he owns is a chest full of fancy clothes and a couple of rooms near Whitehall. That's how the court works see – you gets all these hangers-on who flatter and fawn till they get noticed by the King who shows his pleasure by givin' 'em titles and whatnot. No, that Frank is no better than you or I – worse most like, seein' as how he was born the son of a Stepney innkeeper.'

'Stepney?' Will echoed. 'But I thought he was French – the way he talks . . .'

'French! Him?' gurgled Molly. 'If he's French then I'm the Queen of Spain! Bless you Will, that's just a fashion at court. The King lived in France for some time you see, whilst old Crommel was still alive. So His Majesty likes things to be Frenchified. Frank might spout a few easy phrases here an' there but he couldn't hold a proper conversation with a true Frenchy. Nothing is what it seems, Will lad – that's a lesson you ought to learn if you work for old Spittle.'

A cold shudder passed through the boy. 'Nothing is what it seems,' – that was what his father used to say. It unnerved him hearing it now in that dank shop.

His reaction was not lost on Molly. She put her hand on his and asked gently, 'You all right? Did I say summat I shouldn't? I'm not saying' old Spittle's a saint but he wouldn't hurt you I'm sure. Don't fret now.'

Will wiped the syrup from his face. 'It wasn't that,' he said. 'I was just thinking of my family.'

She wrinkled her pretty nose at him. 'Ahh, won't that old skinflint let you go an' see them? I knowed you were here at Christmas – couldn't he have spared you even then? I'll bet your mother misses you something dreadful. Whereabouts do your folks live then?'

The boy coughed back a sob and hastily dragged his sleeve over his eyes. 'I come from a village called Adcombe,' he mumbled.

There was a pause; for the briefest of moments Molly seemed taken aback. Then she collected herself and breathed, 'Adcombe – sounds a small enough place. I'll wager nothing much happens there.'

'All my family are dead.'

Molly stared at him. 'Oh Will,' she sighed, 'I'm sorry. It's not easy when you're alone, is it? Here, let me get the rest of that stuff off you.' She took a cloth from the counter and dipped it in some water. Then, very gently, she began to clean his face.

Will gazed levelly at the young woman and decided to tell her all about the tragic circumstances which brought him here. 'Can I trust you?' he asked abruptly. 'Trust you not to tell another living soul what I'm about to say?'

'Course you can,' Molly replied. She was surprised by his earnestness but could see that he was desperate to tell her something. 'I cross my heart and hope the Devil gets me if I break a confidence.'

Will stared at the treacly floor. 'You know that story about the miller?' he began.

'What, the one where he gets done in by that wicked lad? Oh yes, that's a favourite of mine that is – gruesome little tale ain't it? I've no liking for millers, they're always fat and richer than they ought to be. I liked the way this one got . . .' Her voice faltered as she saw Will turn a deathly pallor. 'What is it?' she asked.

'The boy in it was me!' he sobbed. 'But it wasn't like it says. I never killed him. It was those two men. They did him in.'

Molly frowned. 'What do you mean, Will? Are you saying that story was about you?'

He nodded fiercely, the choking sobs racking his body. 'It was months ago now,' he confided miserably, 'but that first night in London was awful.

First the horses were stolen and then the miller was murdered. There was nothing I could do and now I'm trapped here and Mr Balker's dead!'

Molly pulled herself away and the face she turned on Will was paler than his own. 'This Mr Balker,' she began in a thin, bleak voice, 'was he from Adcombe too?'

'Yes, he was my friend. He travelled with me to London.'

The young woman knelt on the floor and tightly gripped his hands. 'Listen to me!' she began sternly, 'I want you to tell me everything – from the very beginning. Do you understand?'

Will looked at her doubtfully – there was a dangerous light shining in her eyes and it scared him. He had never seen her like this before and the change was frightening. Her hands were hurting his wrists and though he struggled he could not get loose. Was she going to take him to the magistrate? 'You promised not to tell anyone!' he cried. 'You swore!'

'Just do as I say!' she shouted furiously. 'Or it'll be the worse for you!'

It was a busy day in the city; horse drawn coaches laboured between the countless, stubborn traders who thronged together. As the carriages ploughed by, the pedlars jostled with each other to reach the window and raised their wares for the occupant to inspect. Very often the milk-white hand of some great lady would throw them a coin or stop the coach altogether whilst she purchased some trinket or other. The narrow lanes were dreadfully congested and the going was slow for both horse and human traffic.

A Dragon in the Rags

Doctor Spittle pushed his way down the crowded streets. He was like a great black thundercloud charging across the summer sky. Without a care for anyone else, he barged and shoved, kicking those who were not swift enough to get out of his path. Several angry street vendors whirled round when the toe of his boot struck their heels but on seeing his face they leapt aside and let him pass.

'Call me a beggar will he!' the old man fumed. 'One day he'll rue those words.' Scowling with an expression that would curdle cream he left Cheapside, marched up Ironmonger's Lane and made for Throgmorton Street. After a brief walk, made the briefer by his impatient long strides, the building he sought came into view.

It was a ramshackle, dilapidated hovel, situated on the sharp corner of the road. Long ago it had been daubed a brash, bright blue but now the paint was peeling and cracking from its walls – it was the raghouse.

This was where all the second-hand clothes, curtains, bed linen, wall hangings, handkerchiefs, hats, sacks, carpets, wigs and slippers found their way. Anything remotely useful or even useless could be found within that scruffy little dwelling – but you needed a strong stomach to hunt through its flea-ridden glory.

Doctor Spittle had such a stomach – so long as it was cheap then he would wear it. He had discovered a number of bargains over the years and been the proud new owner of many a hardly used nightgown found in that establishment. Practically all the garments he was wearing that day were originally from there. He had a nose for finding just what he needed and would hunt through the grimy rag heaps like a pig snouting after truffles.

Eagerly he pushed open the faded blue door, stooped under the low lintel and stepped inside.

The old man blinked and waited for his eyes to adjust to the darkness. It was always dim and gloomy in the raghouse; bundles of dirty material were piled up against the broken windows and blotted out the light, as if in sympathy for the moths that fluttered endlessly around. In this perpetually twilight world the alchemist gazed about him. On every side huge pinnacles of cloth soared up and touched the oak-beamed ceiling. They were great islands of rag, looming out of a tattered, filthy sea of shreds. Not one inch was left uncovered, even the beams had garments dangling from them, and strung from corner to corner, like the web of an immense spider, was a network of twine which in turn supported the weight of a thousand pieces of grubby linen. It was a bizarre spectacle, like the ghostly banners of some ancient coronation or perhaps the washing lines of a hundred witches. Doctor Spittle had often reflected with a wry smile that this place made his own cluttered attic look positively spartan. There was nowhere in London, or probably the world, to compare with this mass of neglected lumber.

He wiped his nose and ducked under one of the grotesque washing lines. The air was stale in here and it stank of rancid fat. On the rare occasion his feet came in contact with the bare floor, it was found to be sticky with the innumerable years of accumulated grease that smeared the endless supply of clothes. Doctor

Spittle was used to this, however, and he merely wiped his sole on a nearby stack.

After venturing a little further into the ragged forest he put his hands to his mouth and called out, 'Gobtrot?'

Instantly he heard a scuffling, followed by a series of excited barks. The alchemist peered into the gloom ahead and from the shadows there emerged a panting whirlwind of a terrier. It raced over the bundles, scattering handkerchiefs and old ribbons in the rush. Doctor Spittle backed away in alarm, this was not what he was expecting.

The dog flew at him, leaping up as high as it could, his little jaws snapping and trying to bite the old man's fingers. Once it must have been white in colour but its wiry fur was now grey with dust and dirt.

'Down!' wailed the alchemist raising his arms to avoid those needle-like teeth. The terrier yapped and barked at him, dancing on its hind legs to see where the fingers had disappeared to. Doctor Spittle would have run back to the door there and then if his hands had not become tangled up in the twine above and brought a smelly curtain down on his head. The dog loved this and he seized a corner of the cloth with his teeth then shook it ferociously.

'Bunter!' came a voice. 'Stop that at once!'

The terrier took no notice and gave the curtain a terrific yank. The rotted fibres tore and the dog rolled head over heels into a pile of rags. A tatty heap crouched down and picked up the wriggling imp. 'Just you behave now,' it said crossly.

Doctor Spittle dragged the curtain from his head and saw the walking bundle shamble towards him.

'Ah – Gobtrot,' he wheezed. 'I did think you would not arrive in time. That little cur attacked me!'

From the summit of the unwholesome mass of cloth a face appeared through a tear in the material. The proprietor of the raghouse was a small, fat man. His many wrinkles were clogged with grime like the gutters of a tumbledown house and his pale eyes watered constantly. Wisps of fine, grey hair poked through the hood which covered his head and stiff bristles spiked out of his blobby nose.

'Why, Apothecary Spittle!' he exclaimed, bowing politely. ' 'T'as been a tidy while since you honoured us with a visit. Don't worry none about Bunter. He just has a neat little way of welcoming customers he does. But what am I thinking of? I must fetch Mistress Gobtrot and smartish – she'll be awful glad to see you again.' The exceptional-looking man bowed for a second time, then, with the terrier under his arm, he picked his way between the mountains of jumble that reared around him to an unseen part of the shop.

While he waited, Doctor Spittle fell upon the nearest pile and ferreted through it greedily. Over his shoulder flew all manner of garments as he frantically searched for something suitable. But the only interesting items that his rooting brought to light were several old bones. These he cast distastefully away.

'Ooh, I see Bunter has been up to his little tricks,' came a frail voice. 'He's a treasure really and keeps the rats down something wonderful.' The alchemist turned and there was Mistress Gobtrot.

She was dressed very like her husband, wrapped in the same shabby cloth that made them both resemble supernatural troll creatures from some darkling wood. From these filthy bindings only her head and hands ever appeared. She even looked like Mr Gobtrot, right down to the bristling nose. The only major differences between them were that she was very much thinner, and had also taken to wearing a wig recently. It was a large, wild rook's nest of a creation that slipped over her eyes if she moved too suddenly. To prevent this happening Mistress Gobtrot had developed a habit of leaning her head back. But this artifice made her look as though she had either broken her neck or was gazing at something fantastically interesting on the ceiling.

Doctor Spittle staggered to greet her. 'Madam,' he declared, 'how good it is to see you once more. You are a definite tonic to this weary old man.'

She fluttered her dirty hands coyly before her face and lowered her eyes demurely. Immediately the wig slithered down and obscured her vision.

Her husband laughed beside her; this was the way Doctor Spittle always greeted his wife. He had heard it countless times but it never ceased to amuse him. 'What's this?' he chuckled. 'Enough of your polished talk, sir. You'll turn her pretty little head.'

The woman moved the wig back into position and continued the conversation, her grimy face cocked at an awkward angle to prevent further landslides. 'Anyways, sir,' she addressed the ceiling, 'what was it you wanted this day?'

'A spotless nightgown perhaps?' suggested Mr Gobtrot.

'Sheets maybe?'

'No, no, no!' Doctor Spittle told them, making a grand gesture with his arms. The terrier's ears perked

up as the alchemist's sleeve brushed past. Doctor Spittle eyed the dog cautiously to make certain it was secure before he carried on. 'I'm sick and tired of my mundane wardrobe,' he complained to the Gobtrots. 'I want something special. Give me silks – or velvet if you have it.'

'Ooh,' remarked Mistress Gobtrot, clasping her mucky hands in front of her as she pictured the spectacle in her mind. 'You'll look a real diamond in that.' She enthused, 'We've got a trove of velvet, ain't we? Just you stay here a moment, Apothecary.' Eager to please, the woman hitched up her grimy skirts and clambered over the tall heaps nearby.

The Gobtrots knew the exact location of everything in the raghouse – nothing existed in that place without their being aware of it. So in tune with their environment were they that they could find the smallest button within five minutes of its being asked for – even if they had not seen it for a year or so. As trees and rivers possess in-dwelling spirits so the Gobtrots were surely the genii of that establishment.

She knelt upon one of the great piles and began dredging into it like a demented rabbit digging a burrow. 'Here we are,' she piped up, 'lovely green curtains. No? Well here's a delicious purple cloak – look.' She held it up for the alchemist to see.

'What is that gash down the side?' he inquired.

' 'Tis only where a sword stuck into the previous owner, sir,' she replied brightly. 'I could easily sew that up for you and I should think those blood stains would come out.'

Doctor Spittle declined the offer.

'What about this then?' she asked holding up a coat of royal blue. 'Still got most of its buttons too.'

'That seems to be adequate,' agreed the alchemist.

The woman threw it over to her husband and Doctor Spittle inspected it. The coat was just what he wanted – he would certainly cut a dash in that. Mind you, it did give off a very strong and pungent odour. He shot an accusing glance at the terrier but the little dog wagged its tail innocently.

'Nevertheless, I suppose beggars can't be choosers,' he told himself and, sighing with resignation, he thrust his arms into the sleeves. 'Devil take it!' he bawled. 'The wretched thing is far too small – do you think I am a dwarf?'

'Don't you worry now,' assured Mr Gobtrot respectfully, 'we'll scour the shop from top to bottom to supply you with your needs.'

His wife resumed her delving. 'There's an opulent red piece here – oh sorry, it's a dress. Here's another cloak – a black one this time.'

As she lifted it up a vast cloud of moths flew from the folds. They were the fattest the alchemist had ever seen and had obviously gorged themselves on the proffered cloak. All that was left of it was a series of tattered strips. 'Ooh my!' exclaimed Mistress Gobtrot falling backwards and losing her wig altogether. 'They've had a good nibble of this.' She rummaged further down and wailed. 'They must have been a chomping for years, there's nothing but scraps under here now.'

'Don't throw anything away, wife!' called her husband anxiously. 'You never know when a certain bit might be wanted.'

'Have you nothing else?' asked Doctor Spittle, swatting the bloated insects which flitted overhead.

'I'm afraid not, sir,' returned Mr Gobtrot glumly. 'That were all the quality stuff we had in that pile. We'll be clean out of velvet now. Them moths know a good thing when they bite it.'

'Hang your horses, husband!' called Mistress Gobtrot as she retrieved her rook's nest and waded back to them. 'You're forgetting that load what came in yesterday. We haven't shown the apothecary that yet.'

'Well strike me down for being a dullard!' he cried, slapping his temples. 'I pure forgot about that. Come with us, sir, we've not given up yet.'

So the three of them, not forgetting the terrier, wound their way deep into the heart of the ragged landscape.

Through a range of squalid mountains they trailed, until they came upon a small open space which served as the Gobtrots' living quarters. It was covered by a canopy of rat-chewed silk that hung from the ceiling. This bizarre awning gave the impression of some windswept tent, pitched in a high, craggy pass. Beneath it there were two stools, a threadbare rug and very little else. The Gobtrots had no bed, for they slept each night upon a different cloth heap. Their wants were simple and few and this way of life suited them admirably.

In the manner of one proudly showing another his home the proprietor showed the alchemist theirs. Then he pulled a heavy metal chest from beneath some sacking and prised the lid open. 'Now, sir,' he said, 'I'll not embarrass the gentleman what brought this to us by telling you whence it came. Just take a peep at this.'

Doctor Spittle looked down into the open chest. A mass of dark red velvet met his eyes. Drooling, he caught it up and hastily tried it on.

It was a magnificent long robe and, although it was rather old-fashioned in style, the quality was superb. Swirling arabesques of fruit and flowers were sewn on to the shoulders, twining about the scaled body of a long dragon whose eyes were set with shining stones. Even the lining was richly decorated, being silk and heavily embroidered with a curious pattern. The glorious effect was further enhanced by a trimming of silver lace which edged the wide sleeves and ran all around the hem. Doctor Spittle felt marvellous. He stroked the soft velvet and almost wept with the unbearable bliss of it.

'An immaculate fit, sir,' applauded Mr Gobtrot.

'Why it could have been made for you,' agreed his wife. 'Makes you look positively royal it does. A proper prince indeed.'

'I must view myself!' gabbled the alchemist. 'Quickly, have you a looking glass?'

'I have the very thing,' nodded Mr Gobtrot wandering off for a moment. With Bunter still under one arm, he returned carrying a large oval mirror in a damaged gilt frame. 'Now then, sir,' he breathed, 'gaze and be amazed.'

Doctor Spittle stared at his reflection and let out a squeal of delight – it was true – he looked magnificent. Striking noble postures he regarded his mirrored self and adored what he beheld. Flushed with conceit he turned to one side and admired the effect from a different angle. He was breathtaking. Craning his neck he gauged the rear view and was satisfied that that too was gorgeous. He was beside himself with glee and gave little hops as he preened and pouted.

It was then that he noticed his thinning hair and he scowled at the looking glass. 'Why must age rob you of your finest features?' he cried. The Gobtrots looked at him sympathetically. 'It really was thick and plentiful once, you know,' he informed them, 'and a fierce, fiery red too.'

'How about a periwig, sir?' suggested the woman cheerfully. 'I could always run and have a look for you. Bunter's been playing with them of late so they're a bit scattered but I could quickly find them.'

'No,' he replied with consumate sadness. 'I have a very sensitive scalp – I do not think I could wear one all the day.'

'Pity,' she clucked, unconsciously scratching her own, 'they make them so well these days too. No one would know you was wearing one.'

Doctor Spittle said nothing but drew his fingers through his white locks. Then he peered more closely at the mirror and his face assumed an awful aspect.

'Whatever is it, sir?' asked Mr Gobtrot. 'Have you been taken ill?'

The alchemist certainly did not look well. For a while he remained in exactly the same position, then he moved and pointed at his reflection. 'See there!' he hissed out of the corner of his mouth. The Gobtrots stared in the direction he was pointing, but all they could see was the lining of the robe. 'Do you not realise?' he cried. 'Look! Can you not see the writing? There in the embroidery!'

They looked again and to their surprise the old man was right. Hidden amongst the fancy sewing that spread over the lining there were indeed words. They were cunningly placed in and around the decorated vines but they were there sure enough. 'Why so there is,' admitted Mr Gobtrot. 'Why didn't we notice that afore?'

'Because it can only be read in a mirror,' Doctor Spittle muttered. 'It's been painstakingly done in mirror writing – but why and by whom?'

He swept the robe off his shoulders and exposed the rest of the lining to study it more keenly. Very slowly he began to read.

'I Magnus Augustus Zachaire, by divine grace and everlasting mercy, herenow set down the true and actual definition of that which is called The Tincture of the Philosophers in all other wise known as the Philosopher's Stone . . .'

His voice failed as he grasped the significance of what he had discovered. With his hands quivering he read on. The passage purported to be a translation of a medieval manuscript which gave the exact formula for making the Philosopher's Stone. Doctor Spittle choked back a cry. He had in his hands the solution to all his problems. The dreams he had dared to crave were now within his reach. If what this said was true then nothing could stop him becoming fabulously wealthy.

Trembling with excitement he turned to Mr Gobtrot. 'Where did you get this?' he cried.

'Hah now, sir,' the man answered with a wink, 'you knows I can't divulge that. As I said before, I'll not embarrass my sources. Why I'd not get any new stock if folk didn't trust me to hold a confidence. So I'll just keep mum if you please.'

'I demand to know!' shouted Doctor Spittle.

'Ho ho, that I'll not tell,' chortled the man. The terrier under his arm growled and bared its teeth. It didn't like anyone shouting at its master.

The alchemist grabbed Mr Gobtrot's filthy clothes and shook him violently. Bunter yapped and wriggled forward, his jaws straining to bite. Doctor Spittle spat at the dog contemptuously then mumbled a string of Latin words under his breath. At once the terrier began to shake and its tail drooped. With a yelp it fell to the floor and scampered under a stool where it buried its snout in its paws.

'You will tell me, you imbecile!' stormed the alchemist furiously.

'You let Mr Gobtrot alone!' squeaked his wife in outrage. 'I'll tell it – you black-hearted villain! That hoard came from a big house in the city.'

'Which house?' pressed Doctor Spittle turning on her. 'Was there any more to be had there?'

The woman shrugged. 'Don't know which house and that's definitely all there was to be had. We don't ask too many questions of our suppliers – it's rude to be over-inquisitive,' she said pointedly.

'You must know something!'

'Only that it had been empty and shuttered up for many years. No one had wanted to buy the place see. Not with the memory of him what lived there still fresh in memory.'

'Who – Magnus Zachaire?'

'Mm, a wizard or witch he was, so they say. I doesn't believe in such things myself. We haven't never seen anything out of the ordinary, have we Mr Gobtrot?'

'That we never have, wife.'

Doctor Spittle rubbed his chin thoughtfully. It was obvious that she knew nothing more. He took a deep breath then his manner changed and he was wreathed in smiles. 'Pray forgive me if, in the urgency of my asking, I forced you to surrender any informations which you were unwilling to part with. I humbly apologise and crave your pardon, kind sir and most gracious lady. Now, I should like to purchase this handsome garment. What is the price?'

'One shilling,' said the woman.

The alchemist counted out the money and bowed when he gave it to her. Then he courteously made his farewells and found his own way through the labyrinth of rag heaps.

When he heard the door close, Bunter sidled out of his hiding place and gave a tentative bark. Then, when he was sure the stranger had indeed gone, he charged round the tattered mountains and yapped to his heart's content. After that he methodically marked out his territory once more.

The Gobtrots looked at each other.

'He's an odd one that apothecary,' he observed.

'Yes, but what a precious way he has with words,' she sighed dreamily twisting the hair of her wig between her fingers.

'I can see I shall have to keep my eye on you, Mistress Gobtrot,' he chuckled. 'You're too pretty to be left on your own – I don't want someone stealing you away, do I?' And he put his arm round her shoulder and lovingly kissed her dirty cheek.

Doctor Spittle burst into the apothecary shop and charged up the stairs. He did not see Will sitting unhappily by the counter. Into the attic the alchemist barged, cats scattering before him. He threw the robe over the back of a chair then disappeared down to his bedchamber from where he dragged a long looking glass. This he positioned against one of the walls so that he could read what was written on the robe's lining and hunted for a quill and paper.

Imelza sniffed at this interruption and resumed her position before the hearth, gathering her daughter to her once more. Dab gave the old man a curious stare but settled down with her mother. 'Why is he so cross all the time?' she asked.

'He is human,' Imelza explained.

Leech prowled round the room, slinking from one corner to the other, not daring to show himself in case he was kicked once more. From the shadows he watched as his brother padded towards the alchemist and began clambering on to the table he was working at.

Jupiter crawled over the edge of the table top and gave a small miaow.

Doctor Spittle was busily copying down the cryptic message but he glanced up and cackled to his familiar. 'I have it,' he crowed. 'At last the secret is mine.'

Jupiter put his head questioningly on one side and twitched his whiskers.

An hour ticked by at the end of which the alchemist threw down the quill and clapped his hands together. 'Here it is!' he gurgled, clutching the paper delightedly. 'My life's work is almost ended.' So pleased and happy was he that he patted Jupiter's head. 'I knew I had heard the name of Magnus Zachaire before; he was a noted mystic and conjuror of the last century and immensely wealthy. Unfortunately his reputation as a dabbler in the black arts was too great, for he frightened the London mob and one morning they dragged him out of bed and drowned him in the River Fleet. What a tragic waste of all that wisdom and knowledge. Still, at least he had the foresight to create this robe – and now it has come to me.'

He studied his own copy of the instructions and nodded enthusiastically. 'It has been written in code,' he told the attentive kitten. 'Such was the practice of the ancient wise men; they would veil the true meaning of their work in case of discovery. Should the wrong person get hold of their formulae all was safe because they would never be able to decode the complicated ciphers that had been used.' He slapped himself on the chest confidently then coughed. 'However,' he cried, 'I have studied the intricacies of this art for the whole of my life – it should prove no problem for Elias Theophrastus Spittle.'

The alchemist leaned over to the row of shelves and snatched down every volume that touched upon the subject. By the time he was finished the table groaned under the weight of them.

'Now,' he mumbled, glancing at the paper, 'I already know most of the terms described here. The dragon we all recognise as mercury. Then there is the king, his son, the grey wolf, the black crow, the lion, the unicorn and the royal marriage. Yes, those I am already familiar with – but these others: the withered tree, the divided circle, the halt-footed mare and all the ones that follow I am not aware of.'

He took the first book from the pile and eagerly turned the pages. Jupiter watched him, absorbing every word and every action. All afternoon Doctor Spittle pored over his books, making notes and consulting his manuscripts – but, little by little, his confidence began to wane. At one point he shrieked, 'Listen to this meaningless drivel! "When the crowned king marries the red daughter beware the leper that rides upon the lion's back." Just what in thunder is that supposed to signify?'

The hours rolled by and the pile of books grew less, but behind him discarded volumes littered the floor. He was no closer to solving this nauseating little riddle and the truth of it galled him. That he could be confounded by the cunning of someone who had lived in the last century was almost more than he could bear. How could such a thing be possible? He had devoted most of his life to studying this very subject – it was infuriating to be thwarted when success was a hair's breadth away. Doctor Spittle pulled at his own thinning hair and thumped the table despairingly.

Creeping out of the shadows, Leech summoned up all his courage and approached one of the books. The esoteric symbols intrigued him and, with his sickly green eyes opened wide, he stared at the pages. But the writing was meaningless to him and he could not guess what it all signified. Enviously he glared up at his brother and wished it was he sitting there. 'Why can I not be trained also?' he whispered to himself.

In the shop below, Will sat before the fire and gazed at the glowing embers. The evening was drawing in and he had already locked up. He did not hear the ranting and raving of the alchemist upstairs – he was too wrapped up in his own thoughts.

That morning he had told Molly everything, from the time he and Mr Balker had left Adcombe to that night in the street where the miller had met his end. She had listened to everything with a cold and impassive face, making no comment and offering him no comfort. Only once did she interrupt him and make him repeat a portion of the tale, and that was the description of the two murderers. Then, without saying a word she had left the shop and he had not seen her since.

For a while Will wondered if she had believed him. He was half expecting the Justice to turn up to arrest him but the remainder of the day had passed uneventfully. Perhaps she did not want to be associated with someone suspected of murder, even if he was innocent. Whatever the reason, he had seen a side of her today that he did not like and found himself wondering if he actually wanted to see her again. The expression on her face when he told her about the miller's death was something he could never forget and the memory of it made him shiver.

The fire fell in upon itself and Will stirred. It was dark outside now and even darker in the apothecary shop. He foraged for a candle and lit it by the dying fire.

'Damn it down to the depths of perdition!' bawled the voice of Doctor Spittle from above. The attic door slammed, followed by the sound of something being thrown down the stairs, then the heavy footfalls of the old man stomped into his bedchamber.

Will could hear his curses and wondered what had gone wrong this time; he had not given the alchemist much thought all day. An unpleasant idea started to creep up on him. What had been hurled down the stairs? He prayed it was not one of the cats. Taking the candle, he went to see.

The stairwell was pitch dark when he ventured to look and the candle flame sent a host of tall and severe shadows towering over the boy's head. Will walked up to the steps and glanced at the mysterious thing that the alchemist had cast down.

The robe of Magnus Zachaire lay sprawled over the steps. Will picked it up and brought the candle closer so he could inspect it. The splendid arabesques on the shoulders caught his attention and he marvelled at the detail. With his finger he traced the scaled spine of the dragon that twisted in and out of the stitched foliage, then he held his breath.

The shining stones of the dragon's eyes threw back the guttering candlelight so that they seemed almost alive. Will moved the flame to and fro and the stones blazed back at him, sparkling and dazzling. It was a terrific game and he would have continued, only – he looked at the shape of the dragon once more. Why did it remind him of something?

A figure moved through the darkness beyond the circle of light, descending from above.

Will racked his brains. Somewhere he had seen this same dragon before – but where?

The face of Doctor Spittle floated into the circle of light. His glowering eyes were fixed upon the boy, wondering what he was doing.

'Where have I seen this?' Will said aloud.

The alchemist flew down the remaining steps in one leap. He fell upon the boy, grabbing his arms and shoving him against the wall.

Will was too startled to resist; hot wax splashed over Doctor's Spittle's face as the candle fell from the boy's grasp. The old man snarled at him and Will found himself staring into his mad eyes.

'What do you mean, you've seen this before?' demanded the alchemist.

'I . . . I don't understand.'

Doctor Spittle shook the robe under the boy's nose and squeezed him by the throat. 'Tell me where you have seen this before, dog!' he commanded.

'I can't remember!'

The alchemist screeched with rage, 'Then I shall make you!' He flung back his arm and made a fist ready to strike him.

Will closed his eyes anticipating the blow. The fingers about his throat tightened as the alchemist tensed in readiness – he had imagined such a sensation before – then it came back to him.

'Stop!' he shouted, ducking and flinching. 'I remember!' The fist was lowered but the throttling grip around his throat remained. The black brows of the old man raised expectantly. 'It was in the churchyard where I found the cats,' Will told him gasping for breath. 'This dragon was carved on a gravestone there.'

Doctor Spittle released his vice-like grip. Digesting this news he rubbed his hands together as he considered what to do. As if seeking divine inspiration he raised his eyes and stared up into the darkness of the stairwell, then a horrible smile lit his face. The old man took up the robe and slipped his arms into the sleeves. Then, dressed in a fashion that was a hundred years out of date, he rushed up the stairs to the attic.

Will slid to the floor and rubbed his neck where the imprints of the alchemist's fingers were already turning to bruises. Why was he so interested in that dragon anyway? 'He must have gone completely mad,' he whispered croakily.

'Mad!' hissed Doctor Spittle returning down the stairs. He was laden with bags and sacks and in the crook of one arm carried a bewildered Jupiter. 'Oh no, my young dog,' he sniggered wickedly. 'Far from it. Here, take this.' He thrust the bag into Will's hands and snapped his fingers. 'Come,' he urged, 'this cannot wait.'

'What can't?' asked Will. 'Where are we going at this time of night?'

Doctor Spittle grinned unpleasantly. 'You are going to take me to this churchyard,' he muttered. 'The time has come for me to call on Magnus Augustus Zachaire.' Then he gave a hideous laugh and extinguished the candle.

6

Necromancy

Jupiter purred with excitement as the sumptuous and mysterious scents of the moonless night tantalised his nose and whiskers. Like little lamps shone his eyes as he peered out from the arms of Doctor Spittle. The deeply shaded streets were intriguing for he could sense the teeming life which crawled through the darkness and heard the pit-a-pat of innumerable tiny hearts. The ginger kitten longed to stalk through the secret lanes and savour the delicacies that the night brings forth; but there were other, more urgent matters to attend to.

Jupiter was learning a great deal – his knowledge was increasing with each passing day. He took in everything his master told him and thirsted for more. He gazed up at the alchemist and pressed his head into the velvet of his robe.

The old man's face was grim – he was deep in thought, running over ancient rhymes and incantations in his mind. There was much to do this night and he prayed that before dawn he would have the answer. A twinge of fear thrilled through him for a second but he shook himself crossly and banished the sensation. Such emotions were for the ignorant and foolish – he was neither of these. No, there was nothing to shiver at; so long as he did the thing properly and did not balk at the crucial moment all would be well. He stared at the boy in front of him and his black brows knitted together: *there* was the only weak link in tonight's drama – he would have to keep a close watch on him.

Will walked ahead with the bags slung over his shoulder and a dark lantern in his hand. It was not far to the churchyard now. He had no idea what the alchemist was going to do but he was wise enough to be afraid. Looking cautiously about them the boy hoped they would not meet anyone for the hour was late and they were a suspicious sight. A nightwatchman would ask questions and these would be very difficult to answer.

Soon the tower of St Anne's church rose above the trees. Will steeled himself for whatever ordeal lay ahead and slowly approached the gates.

Pausing on the threshold of the graveyard, Doctor Spittle surveyed the rambling jungle beyond. 'Interesting,' he mused, scratching Jupiter's ear, 'that there should be such an untamed corner in the heart of the city. Can you feel it my familiar – can you sense the wildness which reigns within? Almost as if some power older than man has reclaimed this once hallowed plot of land.'

Jupiter stirred in his arms as he recognised his birthplace. He had no liking for that knotted tangle of tombstone and briar. The memory of hunger and suffering was still fresh and his tail twitched in agitation. What was his master bringing him back for? Had he done something to anger him – was he going to be left here?

'Let us enter,' the alchemist said. 'Show me the headstone.'

Will nodded and they passed inside.

The cemetery was quiet and still. There was no breeze tonight to stir the branches and no moonlight to shimmer over the brambles, yet a restless and brooding atmosphere charged the air. The instant Will crossed into that country of the dead he was aware of it. It was as though the churchyard knew he would return and had been waiting. This was an unpleasant idea and he quickly applied himself to the task of finding where the kittens had been born.

Doctor Spittle glanced round with a surly fascination for everything. 'A most curious location,' he muttered. 'I do not profess to have a scientific explanation for the disquiet which I feel. There are many forces abroad in this world Jupiter, few of which we understand. Science is still a very young flame, as yet it has only illuminated a fraction of the great mysteries. But so long as men are driven to discovery then they shall feed that feeble fire until it shines into the darkness like a beacon.' He smiled at the kitten and said softly, 'Until then the likes of you and I will be forced to use whatever methods are at our disposal to pursue our goals.' He glowered at the bags

Will was carrying and sighed, 'Even if we stray occasionally from the straight path of science and revert to cruder but equally effective routes.'

'Here it is,' Will hissed quickly. He drew back the brambles and there was the ornate tombstone he had briefly glimpsed once before.

Doctor Spittle moved forward and uncovered the lantern. Its yellow beam spilled out over the grave, chasing the shadows which fled into the thorny depths of the bushes nearby. The soft light curved over the twisting body of the dragon that twined about the headstone, picking out the weathered detail of the scales and the black hollows of its eyes. The alchemist grunted; it was indeed identical to the one on the robe. 'Clear more of the thorns away dog,' he commanded. 'I must be certain Magnus Zachaire is buried here.'

Will did as he was ordered and the suspicion that had been growing now seemed to be confirmed. 'God's mercy,' he whispered to himself, 'let my fears be unfounded. Surely the old devil isn't going to dig him up. I may have taken a dead man's hair but I shall not rob a grave.'

When enough of a parting had been made in the thicket the alchemist put Jupiter on the ground then knelt down. Bringing the lantern closer to the stone he passed his hand over the carvings. 'There is an inscription here,' he murmured, squinting at a moss-covered patch. 'Some of the letters have worn and crumbled, the others are clogged with soil.' He fell silent as he clawed the grime of nearly a hundred years away with his fingernails. 'There,' he muttered, 'that ought to be . . . aaah, yes. Listen to this.

*'Under me lie the mortal bones
of Magnus Augustus Zachaire.
May the Grace of God Almighty
give mercy to his blackened soul.'*

Doctor Spittle gave a small chuckle of satisfaction then struggled to his feet. 'All is well,' he announced to Will. 'Now that I am certain, we can begin.'

'Do you mean to . . . to dig him up?' asked Will nervously.

The old man regarded him with some surprise. 'And what use would that be pray?' he cried. 'Do you think he was interred with his secret written on the lid of his coffin? I should think that highly unlikely – I am more than fortunate to have found his resting place. The mob might have left him in the Fleet to drift out to the open sea. No, there will be no use digging up old bones – I have another plan in mind.'

Will felt cold; it was obvious that the alchemist would definitely have made him dig if he thought there was anything to gain by it. Was there nothing this wicked old villain would stop at? The boy looked down at the kitten and wondered why it had been brought – was Doctor Spittle really attempting to train it as a familiar?

'Give me the bag!' the alchemist said abruptly. 'It is now well past midnight and we have much to do before sunrise.' He took the bag from Will and foraged inside. 'Book, candles – one, two, three, four – chalk, string, banishing bell, knife, powders, containing vessel, wand. Yes, I think we can begin.' He took out a large book, bound in battered old leather, and flipped through the vellum pages. When he had found the desired place, he lay the volume on the grass and brought the lantern a little closer.

Will peered at the open pages; there were no words there – only intricate patterns. The old man looked up and saw the puzzlement on his face. 'I believe I told you of my intentions this night,' he began.

'You said you were going to call on Magnus Zachaire.'

'That is still my aim.'

'But he's been dead for years and years!'

The alchemist grinned and nodded slowly. 'Even death is no barrier to one who has studied as I have done.'

'I don't understand,' breathed Will although the truth was beginning to dawn on him.

'I told you it was no use digging up old bones,' cackled Doctor Spittle. 'Far better to speak to the man himself. Do you not agree my young dog?'

Will gasped, 'That's impossible!'

'For you and the rest of the rabble in this stinking rat hole of a city perhaps,' returned the old man pompously, 'but not for Elias Theophrastus Spittle!' Taking a knife and a small pouch from the bag he rose and, with a dramatic sweep of his arm, wrapped the robe about him. 'Enough talk!' he roared. 'We must commence.'

Brandishing the knife over his head the alchemist called out, 'Bless this blade O Illuminati, guide my hand that it may cut straight and true.' From the sack he pulled out a quantity of black cloth; it resembled the habit worn by monks and he folded this, then lay it upon the ground before the headstone. Around the garment he proceeded to inscribe a large triangle in the soil with the knife and declared, 'Let this be the appointed gateway.'

With the hairs rising on the back of his neck, Will watched as Doctor Spittle delved into the pouch and sprinkled some grey powders into the narrow furrows. 'What is that?' he ventured.

'Simply a mixture of charcoal and salt,' the other replied, 'harmless to us but effective against – other forces.'

'What forces?' the boy asked with a sick feeling in his stomach.

Doctor Spittle turned a grim face on him. 'I am going to summon up the spirit of Magnus Zachaire,' he whispered. 'Now be silent! I shall need all my wits about me for the next procedure.' He took another look at the book and studied the designs on the page. 'Should I make one mistake in marking out the field of force then we are doomed. Stand here and bring Jupiter with you. Now take hold of this.' He passed one end of a long piece of string to Will and tied the other around the handle of the knife. 'Keep it pressed firmly to the ground,' he instructed. 'On no account leave go or your very soul shall pay the consequence.'

Carefully he drew a large circle with the blade, making sure that the line was unbroken. Then he wound some of the cord around the handle so that the next circle he traced was smaller. With great pains Doctor Spittle gouged esoteric marks and symbols in the space between the two rings, scrutinising his work keenly to be certain all was perfect.

'Now heed my words,' he told Will. 'You must not move outside these markings until I give you leave. Do you understand?'

The boy swallowed nervously and nodded.

'Very well, and be sure to keep my familiar with you – if even he breaks the circle all is lost.' Will took Jupiter in his arms and held him tightly. The alchemist then poured the powders into the grooves he had laboriously etched into the soil.

Will shuddered – this was worse than digging up a grave. He had heard about conjurors and necromancy but he had never thought to meet one let alone participate in such a frightening ceremony. He was afraid to stay, yet even more afraid to run.

Now Doctor Spittle placed the four candles around the outer circle and lit them from the lantern. In this eerie ring of light he took up a slim wand and said to Will, 'How strong is your courage, dog?'

'I am not certain, sir,' the boy replied warily. 'I used to think I could meet any peril that this world might fling at me but . . .'

'Just so,' hissed the old man. 'You are wise to make the distinction. What you may see tonight will require a steady nerve for you must remain silent throughout. Do nothing to distract me once the ritual has begun and on no account cross the outer circle.'

Doctor Spittle then stroked Jupiter. 'And you my little familiar, you must also remain where you are. Your task tonight is to watch and learn – see how your master achieves his goals.' The kitten purred back at him, its golden eyes following his every movement.

The alchemist held up the wand and began the incantation. 'Here me O lords of the Underworld!' he shouted. 'Elias Theophrastus Spittle invokes thee! All you sufferers of good and creators of evil listen now to my words!' He called out several Latin phrases then pointed the wand at the candles. The flames spluttered and sparked. Spitting white fire they grew taller and tapered high into the dark heavens.

Will shrank to the ground, his lip trembling with dread. He bowed his head and prayed to be spared this night. 'Mercy on us,' he breathed.

Doctor Spittle flung his arms out and with a commanding voice boomed, 'Magnus Augustus Zachaire! I call you from the cold earth. Escape the bonds of Death and come forth. By the great names of power I summon you. Enter the Sign of Fire and appear before me!'

Abruptly the trees and bushes began to sway as a strong wind rushed through them. It gusted around the churchyard and tore between the tombstones.

'APPEAR!' Doctor Spittle commanded forcefully.

The very ground trembled at the sound of his voice; the candles began to shake and their flames dwindled down to their normal size. The alchemist held his breath and stared intently at the triangle in front of him.

Within that simple shape a faint mist began to form. At first it curled up out of the ground, softly hissing from the soil, gathering into a thick carpet of grey fog. Yet it remained within the allotted space, forming a perfect triangle; and although it bubbled and billowed upwards it could not cross those lines drawn by the blade. Gradually it stole over the black gown that had been placed there. Fine wisps of smoke pulled at the cloth and then, very slowly, the garment began to move. The grey mist engulfed the material, smothering and oozing through its folds until it soaked into the fibres.

Will watched in disbelief as the habit rose off the ground and was lifted into the air. The pale mist wreathed itself about it and, by degrees, the shape filled out. It was as though some invisible figure had pulled the gown over its head. But beneath the hood there was no face – the unearthly vapour swirled where the head should have been and between the hem of the gown and the grass below there was only empty air.

Doctor Spittle surveyed the faceless spectre appreciatively. With a pleased smile on his lips he lowered his outstretched arms and asked, 'Is this in truth the shape of Magnus Zachaire that stands before me?'

From the darkness under the hood there came a soft, sibilant answer, 'In truth it is.' The voice was hollow and echoed as though calling from a long way off. Goose-pimples pricked out over Will's skin for that sound chilled him to the marrow – it was like hearing a snake speak in a human voice.

'Do you know why I have called you from the grave?' asked Doctor Spittle.

'I do.'

'Then tell me the solution to the riddling message. Reveal unto me the secret of the Philosopher's Stone.'

'Verily it shall be done,' said the apparition. 'Rivers of gold shall flow under thy hand. Thou shalt be blessed with wealth undreamt of by mortal men. The treasuries of all the kingdoms in the world will be as nothing compared to thine. The key to the ultimate fortune is the prize I offer to thee.'

'Yes! Yes!' drooled the old man feverishly. 'What is the answer to the riddles?'

'Give me a parchment and the means to write and the secret shall be thine.'

The alchemist rubbed his hands together and gave a greedy chuckle. Crouching down he snatched up the book and tore out one of the end pages.

A sleeve of the habit reached out and a ghostly hand formed at the end of it. The long fingers extended and groped the air impatiently. 'Give it to me,' the disembodied voice told him.

Doctor Spittle was still hunting for a chalk in his pockets. 'Beyond the dreams of avarice,' he sniggered to himself.

Will was terrified, yet his eyes were transfixed upon the supernatural figure which beckoned the old man forward. In the boy's arms Jupiter wormed and struggled to get free. Then, with one great kick of his hind legs, the kitten darted out of his grasp and before Will could stop him, ran between the alchemist's legs.

'All the wealth of the world,' Doctor Spittle chuckled. 'Here good spirit, yield thy knowledge to me.' He moved towards the phantom figure when suddenly a fierce squeal stopped him in his tracks.

The old man glanced down, startled out of his all-consuming greed. There was his familiar – he had trodden on his tail. Doctor Spittle growled angrily at the cat for getting underfoot, then he choked. Only now did he realise the enormity of his folly. The perimeter of the outer circle was only a fraction away from the toe of his boot. He had been about to step over the line!

Quivering with alarm he dragged himself back into the safety of the inner circle and Jupiter hurried after him. The alchemist stared at the kitten with overwhelming gratitude then glared at the wraith that still waited with its hand outstretched.

'Trickster!' he bawled. 'Thou evil fiend, begone from this world – I did not summon thee. Thy time is over, return to the Pit from whence thou camest.'

Foul laughter issued from beneath the hood and the figure leaped into the air. 'I am not so easy to dispel, puny mortal!' crowed the wailing voice.

The mist flowed out from the gown and beneath the hood two points of light glimmered into existence. The voice continued to laugh, only the sound was clearer now and grew louder with every passing moment. Plumes of thick, black smoke shot up from the candles as they crackled and the flames became red as blood.

With the infernal glow glinting in his ginger fur Jupiter snarled and arched his back. His hackles stood on end and he prowled around the inside of the circle pawing the air with his claws as the apparition took on its true form.

With a rush of blistering heat, fierce flames shot out of the soil and blazed within the triangle. The reek of sulphur flooded the churchyard and the gowned creature stamped its hoofs on the baking ground, revelling in all its evil splendour. Then, at last it threw back the hood and fixed its gleaming eyes upon the fools who had summoned it.

Will's scream pierced the night itself as he fell to the ground and hid his face. Doctor Spittle cowered back from the awful sight of the fiend before him. All his strength drained away as the horror he had released unfurled great wings of darkness and towered over him. In a panic he stumbled backwards, tripping over the bag in his haste. A dull ring sounded as his boot struck something metal. The alchemist hesitated, staring down at the thing which rolled out by his foot. As the shadow deepened about him and as the vile, nameless creature beat its wings, the old man raised his head and a defiant grin lit his face.

'Begone!' he shouted. 'Avaunt from my sight!'

Only cruel, mocking laughter answered him and the hellish fires burned more furiously than ever.

Doctor Spittle snatched the object from the ground and waved it over his head. At the touch of the cold metal his old confidence returned. It was a brass hand bell that he held aloft and in a steady voice he said. 'Now do I banish thee!' And he rang the bell with all his might.

The clanging noise had an immediate effect upon the nightmare that confronted them. It covered its ears and shrieked with pain and then, it was gone. An empty black gown dropped to the ground.

The cemetery was as quiet and still as if nothing had happened.

Doctor Spittle dragged his hands over his eyes and let out a relieved and thankful sigh. 'It is over,' he told Will. 'You may look about you. Our unwelcome visitor has departed.'

Will lifted his head and peeped through his fingers. The candle flames were back to normal once again and there was not a trace of that eerie mist or the awful stench of sulphur. But the earth inside the triangle was black and scorched.

'What was that thing?' he stammered.

The alchemist cleared his throat. 'That, my young

dog, was only one of the minor demons. They are forever artful and always try to deceive. I fear that I am too credulous; for a moment I was deluded. If I had stepped outside the circle then ... well I won't make myself ill by dwelling on that.' He bent down and picked up his familiar. 'How fortuitous that Jupiter was more vigilant than I. A happy chance it was that joined the separate threads of our lives. I bless the night you brought this little fellow to my shop. Do you realise that he saved both our souls? Well done my fine furry friend.'

Jupiter purred and rubbed his chin against the old man's hooked nose.

Will hugged his knees; it was colder than ever now. 'Can we return to the shop?' he asked.

'Return to the shop?' cried Doctor Spittle. 'Have you forgot our task, dog?'

'But you're not going to continue?'

'I most certainly am,' he sniffed. 'One mischievous demon isn't going to put me off. Besides, we shall see no more of those tonight. This entrance is closed to them now – they cannot abide the sound of bells you know.' The old man pulled the robe about him to keep out the chill, then brandished the wand again.

Chanting the same incantations he made curious signs in the air and roared, 'Magnus Augustus Zachaire – come forth! I grow weary of this charade but am prepared to continue till judgement-day if need be!' And he stamped his foot petulantly.

The blackened earth of the triangle groaned and a small crack appeared along the breadth of it. Out of this fissure a shimmering blue shape emerged. It was not mist this time, more like the surface of a river when the moonlight strikes it. Tiny stars of sapphire drifted up through the ground and zoomed in the air like angry fireflies.

Will gaped as this new manifestation crept out of the cindered soil. Who would believe the horrors he had witnessed this night? he thought to himself. He had come a long way since he left the peaceful village of Adcombe, and the road had been a dark and forbidding one. With every desperate turn the path of his life seemed to get grimmer, although he doubted if he would ever again be as afraid as he had been this night.

A glimmering cloud now hung in the air. The stars within it pulsed and flashed, their soft radiance falling upon the boy's face.

'Who is it that calls Magnus Zachaire?' came a weary voice.

'Elias Theophrastus Spittle.'

The stars dimmed. 'I do not recognise that name. Did I know thee in life?'

'I was not even born when you were of the body.'

'What year is this?'

'1665.'

The shapeless cloud stirred. 'Hath it indeed been that long?' came the distressed and sorrowful voice. 'Why dost thou wrench me from my rest? Who art thou to disturb me so?'

Doctor Spittle folded his arms. 'I have come to discover your secrets,' he declared, 'if you are in truth who you claim to be.'

At the centre of the glowing vapour the light welled up as the stars melted into one another. From this brightness a face appeared, as clear as blue glass, yet with all the features well defined. It was the face of a man.

He was lean, with a large Roman nose and piercing eyes. A neat little beard covered his sharp chin and the dark hair was swept far back above his forehead. About his neck there was a ruffed collar, of the type worn many years ago when Elizabeth was England's monarch. The cloud dissolved into a damasked doublet that was slashed at the sleeves to show the silk underneath. This vision floated above the ground, flickering from time to time, fading then shining.

'Verily I am Magnus Zachaire,' it snorted, 'or rather *was*.'

'Excellent,' murmured Doctor Spittle, 'then you shall tell me—'

'Hold!' interrupted the spirit. The deep blue eyes glittered as they regarded the alchemist. 'That robe you wear – is that not mine own?'

Doctor Spittle was a little put out by this interruption. 'It was,' he blustered, 'but has since passed on to me. I have read the message you left and wish to—'

'Thief!' denounced the spirit angrily. 'Thou knave! Thou iniquitous rogue! Your robe holdeth a secret thou canst not imagine.'

'Oh but I can,' smirked the alchemist. 'Tell me Magnus, when did you discover the Philosopher's Stone?'

The spirit stared back at him then smiled. 'So, thou dost understand a little,' it said, 'but not all or I should still be sleeping.'

'Tell me the meaning of the riddling words,' demanded Doctor Spittle. 'I need to know more so that I may recreate your work.'

'My work,' repeated the shade and there was a bitterness in its tone. 'Money is not the answer. Leave this path thou hast chosen Elias Theophrastus Spittle! The golden idol is a severe taskmaster – serve it not. True rejoicing is to be found in thyself alone, look not elsewhere for happiness. The heart that be enslaved by greed is a dead heart.'

The old man tapped his fingers with irritation. 'What say you?' he cried indignantly. 'Speak no pious words to me. In life were you not a covetous miser? Did gold aplenty not fill your coffers?'

The blue light failed. 'I learned too late,' it said with regret. 'I have learned much on the other side. Heed my words.'

'Spare me your concern,' scorned the alchemist, 'and unlock the secret.'

'For thine own sake I cannot.'

Will had been listening to all this with great interest. He felt sorry for the spirit; it was so sad and melancholy. As Doctor Spittle shouted and shook his fist at it, a distant sound drew the boy's attention. He shifted on his haunches and turned away from the developing quarrel. The noise had come from outside the churchyard, some way down the street beyond. He strained his ears and peered steadily through the branches of the trees and thickets. The heavy tramp of boots on cobbles was coming nearer and a dim light swung to and fro. It was the nightwatchman.

Will whirled round to Doctor Spittle and tugged at the robe. An annoyed hand slapped him away. 'Do not bother me, dog!' snapped the old man. 'Can you not see I am occupied?'

'But—'

'Silence!' shrieked the alchemist. He gave the boy a warning growl then turned back to the phantom.

'I shall never tell thee what thou desirest to know,' said the spirit. 'Release me at once – let me have peace once more.'

'Never!' yelled Doctor Spittle. 'You shall surrender the secret to me!'

'I refuse.'

'You cannot!'

'But I have.'

'Doctor Spittle, please!' Will pulled at the robe a second time.

'In Heaven's name, dog, why do you plague me so?'

'A nightwatchman!' Will explained hurriedly. 'He's coming this way.'

The alchemist stared over the cemetery wall and saw the lantern of Arnold Strogget slowly swing as the burly man swaggered down the street. As yet he had not seen the bizarre group in the churchyard for he was plodding like a drudge and gazing stupidly at his feet.

'Hah!' scoffed the spirit. 'Unless the laws have changed much in sweet England since I passed on, thou wilt have to flee, alchemist – conjuration is punishable by death. Either that or thou shalt be ducked as was I, which amounts to the same in the end. A sorry dilemma it is, and just as we were getting acquainted with one another. Now thou wilt have to release me.'

But Doctor Spittle was not finished yet. He took one more glance at the approaching nightwatchman and reckoned that he had time enough before they were spotted. 'So pleased you were enjoying our exchange,' he said treacherously to the spirit. 'I too would like to further acquaint myself with a fellow scholar such as yourself.'

'A pity it is,' Magnus chuckled, 'yet the briefest of meetings are oft the most memorable.'

'I see no reason for it to be curtailed so soon,' the old man cackled. He rummaged inside the bag and brought out a small bottle of smoky glass.

A tinge of doubt crept into the spirit's voice when it saw the vessel in his hands. 'Release me this instant!' it demanded. 'Thy time runs out – the nightwatchman yonder is almost here. Should I call out, the buffoon will surely hear me."

'Then I must see to it that you keep silent,' Doctor Spittle told him. He uncorked the bottle and placed it upside down on the ground. Then with one eye on the street and the other on his work he hastily inscribed a small circle by his feet and cast the charcoal and salt over it.

'What mischief is this?' cried the spirit, but there was no reply. The alchemist had closed his eyes and was muttering strange words under his breath.

Will looked from one to the other. The spectre appeared frightened whilst his master seemed triumphant. Steadily the blue light began to diminish and with a horrified look on his ghostly face, Magnus realised what the other was up to.

'Nooo!' he begged. 'Thou canst not imprison me in . . . AAAGGHH!'

Screaming like a banshee, the shade of Magnus Zachaire was sucked down into the scorched soil once more. With curses on his lips he struggled to escape the powerful forces which dragged at him – but it was no use. Presently the last of his shimmering vapour disappeared down into the cracked ground and his protests were swallowed by the earth.

Doctor Spittle sniggered and pointed the wand at the small circle by his feet.

Will leaned forward. Bright points of light streamed out of the grass and flew up the neck of the small bottle. The glimmering essence of Magnus Zachaire filled the glass vessel until it contained all of him and shone like a fragment of the summer sky.

At once the alchemist was on his knees. He grabbed the bottle and, before the spirit could escape, rammed the cork back into the bottle's neck.

'Snuff out the candles, dog!' he told Will quickly. 'We must be silent now and let the nightwatchman pass.'

Will obeyed and just as Arnold Strogget peered over the cemetery wall he remembered to cover the lantern.

'Two of the clock on a cold January night and all's well,' came the cry.

They waited for the footsteps to disappear down the street before daring to speak.

Doctor Spittle held up the glass bottle and shook it gleefully like a cruel child tormenting a captured wasp. 'See what I have here,' he chortled. 'How gratifying to rescue a trophy from tonight's work.'

The angry face of Magnus's spirit pressed against the dark glass and his fury kindled the light inside. 'Release me!' the muffled voice demanded.

The alchemist tutted churlishly and tapped the

bottle with his fingernail. The brilliance of the soul within welled up through the skin of his hand. 'You must learn to speak with more respect,' he said. 'Would it not be pleasant to conduct this interview in a more agreeable and relaxed atmosphere? I suggest we return to my apothecary shop forthwith.'

With the enraged spirit hurling abuse at him, Doctor Spittle popped the bottle into his pocket. 'I believe it will be safe to leave the circle,' he told Will. 'Collect everything and return it all to the bag. It is time to return home. After these last few hours I believe I could sleep for a week; never have I felt so drained.' He patted the pocket which held the bottle and gave a forced laugh. 'I do not think our new friend is going anywhere for the time being. I must have a fresh mind if I am to pursue the Philosopher's Stone.'

Stooping, he picked up his familiar and gathered the robe tightly about him. 'Come along!' he urged. 'Jupiter and I need our rest.' Doctor Spittle did not wait for Will. He strode through the graveyard and left the boy to follow when he was ready.

Will shoved the last candlestick into the bag. The only thing left to pack was the black gown that the demon had worn. Cautiously he prodded it with his finger, just to make sure there was nothing of that nightmare still lurking within the folds. Fortunately, no claw reached out to grab him and no mist poured from the cloth. With great speed Will pushed it into the sack and heaved it all over his shoulder.

As he trailed between the tombstones he glanced back at the magical signs still visible in the ground. What, he asked himself, had he done to deserve this dangerous and deadly life? Wandering back through the dark London streets the boy had no idea that the worst was still to come.

7

Playing with Fire

Imelza stretched out lazily. The logs in the grate had turned to ash and those embers still aglow would soon be consumed. She rolled on to her side and basked in the cherry-red warmth, blinking and idly tapping the tip of her tail on the floor.

A speckled bundle uncurled at her side and Dab yawned widely. 'Are you still awake, Mother?' she asked rubbing the drowse from her eyes. 'Can you not sleep?'

'The hours of darkness are not for sleeping, my daughter,' Imelza told her. 'The night is the hunter's country – we ought to be out there, not cooped inside this stinking attic. But have no fear, for soon the time will come when we can leave this place and I shall teach you the ways of the wild.' Imelza raised her head and stared into the remains of the fire, yet the light which sparkled in her eyes was no reflection. 'The day blinds most creatures with its vainglorious show,' she whispered, 'yet the night cloaks all in mystery. The scents and sounds of the velvet dark can strike a fire in the blood and set your mind reeling.' She shuddered as a delicious tingle washed over her. 'To be one with that all-encompassing gloom is the only reason to live. Hours uncounted have I remained still as stone, melting into the shadows, waiting for my prey.'

Dab listened with growing discomfort, not sure if she liked this sort of talk. As yet she had never had to kill to eat and the thought that one day she might made her queasy inside. The tortoiseshell doubted if she would ever find murder as easy as her mother described. However, she disguised the revulsion which was creeping upon her and tried to make herself look attentive.

Imelza was smacking her lips, remembering all the dainty bodies she had savoured throughout her life. That was the rightful meat to feast on – not the woeful scraps served here. How she longed for the delight of sweet flesh between her teeth once again. 'Oh daughter mine,' she breathed, 'how I tire of this place.'

'Hoy, you, Tigerstripe!'

She glared up; it was that insolent black rat again. She had grown to hate the jeering wretch. It was agonising to have live bait constantly dangling from above and not be able to satiate her blood-craving. It had taken great self-control but Imelza had learned to ignore the disrespectful rodent – if only he would leave her alone.

Heliodorus scoffed irreverently. Teasing the tigers down below had become his favourite pastime of late. He turned to the occupant of the second cage which hung from the rafters and called, 'You join Heliodorus in happy jesting – yes?'

The podgy brown rat opposite shook its head fearfully. Beckett was a timid animal; he was frightened of everything – even the moths which fluttered in through the bars alarmed him and he would cringe in a corner until they flew out again. 'Don't 'ee wind 'er up so,' he gibbered across the gulf between the two cages. 'Yee knowed it fustigates 'er into a wicked temper.'

'Tigerstripe not get Heliodorus, not never!' the black rat shouted down. 'Ho, ho – she sad sight most certainly. Oh yes, poor M'Lady she have no sharpy claw no more! Where her backbone got to eh?'

Imelza gritted her teeth and flicked her ears. Was she to be tormented like this every night, she asked herself. With the scornful voice of Heliodorus screeching through her she turned back to Dab. 'And where is Leech, thy brother?' she asked, keeping her voice level as though nothing was bothering her.

Her daughter was gazing upwards. She rather liked the black rat. She thought he was funny, although she would never dare to voice this opinion. When Imelza addressed her she had to swiftly collect her wits. 'Why, I know not,' she answered distractedly. 'He was here when the old human took Jupiter away with him. I recall that Leech was most upset afterwards. Where he might be now I cannot guess; he is always slinking off on his own.'

Imelza glanced round the attic. It was in a worse

mess than usual for in his frustration the alchemist had flung books everywhere. The ginger cat narrowed her tawny eyes into slits and pierced the shadowy recesses of the room. 'I see him,' she uttered in an unhappy voice. 'My son lies asleep in yon corner. It grieves me that he keeps so much to himself.'

Dab pouted in agreement. 'My poor brother feels most the anger of the human; he loves him not at all.'

'And yet Jupiter is doted on,' mused Imelza sorrowfully. She looked steadily at Dab. 'Promise me,' she began, 'that should I ever be taken from you, you shall watch over your brothers. My heart forewarns me that some terrible wedge shall come between them. Swear that you will do all in your power to heal whatever hurts they inflict upon each other.'

'I promise Mother,' stammered the tortoiseshell, startled by the earnestness of the request.

Heliodorus chose that moment to emit a long and raucous raspberry. Both felines looked up and there was the rude creature, squeezing his bottom between the bars and wiggling it to show his contempt.

As he hooted and collapsed helplessly on to the floor of his cage Imelza twitched angrily – these gibes were really beginning to get to her. Dab hastily turned away, for she did not want her mother to see the great smile that had lit her face.

The shop door rattled far below and all knew that the alchemist had returned. Heliodorus ceased his mirth and listened as footsteps clumped up the staircase. Imelza and Dab shifted uncomfortably, wondering what kind of mood the old man would be in, and in his dark corner Leech was roused from sleep as the key clicked in the lock.

The attic door was hurriedly opened and Doctor Spittle breezed inside. He was in the lightest of humours, cradling Jupiter in his arms; he even chuckled when he saw the state of his workroom. ''Twould seem a tempest has rampaged through here,' he laughed. 'I can see there is much to do on the morrow.' Raising his familiar to his lips he startled the kitten by giving it a kiss. Then he placed it on the floor next to Imelza. 'There you are, madam,' he cried, 'the prodigal has returned safe and sound. I begin to marvel that I ever managed without his aid.'

Imelza sniffed her son; the night still clung to him and she envied his excursion. In the corner, Leech pressed himself against the wall and as the alchemist pattered closer, he eyed the old man's boots warily and looked for an escape route. But the kicks he was expecting never came.

Doctor Spittle reached into his pocket and drew out the small bottle. At once the cold blue light filled the room. The old man lifted it over his head and danced around as though drunk. 'What a pretty bauble,' he declared proudly.

The frail and anguished voice of Magnus Zachaire called out to him, 'Release me thou blackheart!'

'Not yet my shining one,' came the tittered reply. 'You know the conditions of your freedom – meet them and on my oath I shall let you go.'

The pale face against the glass was twisted in despair; the spirit longed to return to its peaceful rest – every moment in the living world was a torment to it. Magnus's glittering eyes glared balefully at his captor but the intense gleam dimmed as he slowly realised there was no choice. Through the smooth walls of his prison he viewed the attic, recognising much of the equipment and all of the wall charts. A terrible regret tore through his being; memories were already flooding back, instants he would rather lose in the eternal sleep of oblivion. He could not bear it. Images of his unhappy life invaded his thoughts, relentlessly taunting him unto the edge of madness.

'I submit,' he moaned, 'the secret is thine, just consign me to the grave once more – deliver me from this accursed torture.'

Doctor Spittle grinned callously. 'I shall,' he said in a superior tone, 'but not at this late hour. I need my rest – the morning is a proper time for the unravelling of coded messages.' Still smiling at his own cleverness this night, he placed the bottle on to one of the low shelves, amongst the other jars and vessels.

'Stay!' cried Magnus piteously. 'I cannot abide another hour of this agony. Stay I beg of thee!' But the crimson door had already closed and the alchemist's footsteps trotted down to his bedchamber.

The spirit wept softly to himself, penitent beyond measure for all his sins – but it was too late to spare him the pain of remembrance. The blue light faded as he brooded in his melancholy and the attic returned to darkness once more.

Imelza gave the bottle a curious look then dismissed it. 'Jupiter, my son,' she began, 'are you unhurt? Did the human treat you well?'

'Mother!' he exclaimed. 'You would scarce believe what I have seen this night. Truly my master is well versed in secret arts. You should have seen how—'

'Master?' snapped Imelza angrily. 'Why for do you call him so?' A growl rumbled in her throat and in her eyes a furious gleam shone. 'Have I not taught you the Hunter's Creed?'

Jupiter looked down abashed.

'What is the way of things?' she demanded.

'Trust no one,' he mumbled shamefully.

'And?'

'Beware of the one that waits in the darkness . . .'

'But of the most important teaching?'

Jupiter groped for the answer – it was on the tip of his tongue. It was difficult with his mother's reproachful eyes trained upon him. The seconds dragged by as he sought for the correct words, fearing what she might do to him if he failed.

Imelza was incredibly stern – this was extremely serious. A cat must know these important lessons; they had been handed down through innumerable generations from when the world was young. Never had they been flouted and her child was not going to be the first to do so. The threatening noise in her throat grew louder and her eyes became slits – she would claw it into her son if need be.

Jupiter trembled, knowing the trouble he was in. Wildly he glanced over at his sister. Dab too was afraid. Violence terrified her and to see her mother snarling at Jupiter brought her close to tears. Hastily she stole a nervous look at Imelza then mouthed the answer to her brother.

'A true hunter would rather be dead than tamed!' he shouted hurriedly. 'Tooth and claw is the only discipline!'

Imelza's eyes widened and she purred with

satisfaction. 'You would do well to take those teachings to heart,' she warned. 'Do not forget who and what you are, my son. A hunter you shall always be – that is the rightful destiny for us all, not to dance and perform at the human's pleasure.'

But Jupiter made no reply for he knew she was wrong. There was another path open to him.

Imelza licked herself and cleaned her whiskers. It was time for rest; the wild night would have to do without her yet again. Now that they were reconciled she smiled at Jupiter and bedded down to sleep.

Jupiter waited until he heard the softest of snores and beckoned Dab over. The tortoiseshell tiptoed across to him with a look of reproof on her face. He did not wait for her to scold him. 'Bless you Dab,' he thanked her the moment she stood at his side, 'you saved me a vicious beating back then.'

'Perhaps it was unwise of me,' she teased. 'Your pride could do with a few knocks, brother mine.'

He laughed at that then turned to check on their mother. 'Follow me,' he told his sister, 'I must tell you of tonight's adventure.'

So, the two kittens padded over to the far wall where they hoped their talk would not disturb Imelza.

'Was it really beautiful outside?' Dab asked. 'I can't remember the time before we were here. I should like to see the outside world.'

Jupiter nodded eagerly. 'Oh Dab!' he enthused. 'The city is a fantastic place, there are so many distractions that my head swam. I wanted so much to rush off into the shadows but my master constrained me.'

'Hush!' cried Dab appalled that he should use the word again.

'I care not!' he hissed defiantly. 'Mother does not know everything – I want to be more than what she wishes. Oh Dab, there are such secrets to be learned, far more important than the Hunter's Creed. Do you know what I have discovered already?' His sister shook her head, not sure if she really wanted to know. 'Magic!' he declared. 'I am beginning to understand some of that hidden craft. Why I believe that even the squiggles in my master's books are becoming clear to me!'

'No!' Dab breathed in horror.

'Yes,' he assured her, 'whilst I sit beside him he traces what he reads with his finger and speaks the words out loud. I have watched and I have learned until I too can recognise some of what is written.'

'But what use will this awful knowledge be?' she asked. 'No good can come of it surely?'

'Let me tell you what happened tonight and you will see what I shall be able to do one day.'

And so Jupiter related all that had happened in the churchyard that night. Dab listened in amazement and her eyes were soon large and goggling. From the shadowy corner Leech strained his ears to catch what was said. If only *he* had been there, if only *he* could read the human's writing. Silently he crawled out of the darkness and crept ever closer to his brother and sister.

When Jupiter had come to the end of his tale Dab tutted. 'As I said, no good can come of that. There is no kindness in disturbing the natural order – you should leave well alone, brother.'

'Pish!' he retorted. 'Watch this. I'll show you what I am capable of.' He stared intently at the ashes in the dimly glowing grate and began to chant peculiar words. His whiskers quivered as magical forces channelled through his small body and his golden eyes blazed with force.

The cold ashes stirred over the dying embers. Jupiter squeezed his eyes shut and concentrated hard, his ears flattened on to his skull and his voice became strained.

With a deafening whoosh, fierce tongues of flame burst from the grate and roared up the chimney. The fire which volcanoed there was blinding. It filled the attic with its brilliance and the heat beat from it as though it were a furnace.

Before the hearth Imelza sprang to her feet, claws ready. The clamour of the blaze had startled her from sleep and the blistering waves of flame almost scorched her. She leapt backwards, away from this confusing and fearsome enemy. Fires were meant to bring comfort not frazzle the fur off your back.

From the cages above there came wailing. Beckett shrieked in panic as the temperature in the attic galloped and soared to a degree that was stifling. A pot by the fireplace began to smoke ominously and then 'CRACK!' it exploded into a thousand pieces. Heliodorus peered down and fanned himself with his tail. On his travels he had been used to hot climates but never had they been this severe.

By the far wall the three kittens watched aghast. Jupiter had no idea the powers he had unleashed would be so mighty. Speechless, he gawped at the torrent of flame blasting from the grate. Even at this distance the heat was unbearable and to his consternation he saw that the books strewn on the floor were beginning to smoulder.

'Make it stop!' yelled his sister.

Leech stared about him in astonishment. That all this should come about simply by the use of a few words bewildered him. He sneaked a look at his brother; he had never guessed that Jupiter was capable of such a magnificent feat and a jealousy which burned more ferociously than the magical fire consumed him.

Jupiter closed his eyes again and recited the correct words.

Immediately the roasting fire disappeared. The attic was plunged into darkness and swallowed by the gloom.

'What has happened?' cried Imelza fearfully as she came to join her children. 'What devilry is this?'

Nobody answered her. Jupiter was too afraid and Dab did not want to get him into trouble. Leech, however, saw an opportunity here for spite. 'If you please, Mother,' he piped up, 'it was Jupiter who did this. He was showing off what his lord and master has taught him.' His brother shot him a despising glance.

'What mischief have you been up to, my son?' Imelza asked. 'Was this in truth your work?'

Jupiter nodded. 'I intended no harm, Mother,' he told her, 'the spell was stronger than I expected. I did not mean to wake you.'

If he was expecting his mother to scold him he was surprised. Imelza merely gave him a blank look for she did not know what to say. Magic spells were beyond her experience. All she could eventually manage was a stammering, 'Take more care next time.'

Jupiter stared at her hopefully. 'Does that mean you no longer have any objections to my being taught by the human?'

'I deem that would be pointless,' she replied with weary resignation. 'Perhaps I was indeed misguided. Maybe there is a higher calling for you, my child.'

Leech snorted with disgust. He had hoped Jupiter would be soundly punished. This he saw as a definite reward for his brother's irresponsible actions. With venomous thoughts seeping through his mind, he slunk away from the group and made for the fireplace.

The embers were almost cool now. Sitting back on the still steaming floor he recalled the sight of those tremendous flames, bitterly coveting the power Jupiter had shown. Slyly Leech turned his ugly head and his eyes swivelled round so that he could keep a watch on his brother.

Dab was laughing nervously. 'I could have died!' she gasped. 'I thought we would sizzle for certain. You are clever Jupiter.'

A smug smile twitched over her brother's face. 'Indeed I am,' he boasted, 'but that was only my first essay into the secret ways. The more I endeavour to learn, the greater I shall become.'

'And the larger shall your head swell,' observed his mother.

Jupiter would have laughed, but just then he caught the eye of Leech. Quickly the runt averted his face but Jupiter remembered that here was a debt which needed repaying.

'Try to get me into trouble would you?' he whispered. 'Very well, I think I shall use my gifts a second time this night.' Under his breath he began to utter another simple spell. When it was done he turned to his mother and sister. 'An unguarded fire is surely a danger to the unwary,' he said. They looked at him curiously, not understanding his meaning. But Jupiter merely raised his eyebrows and nodded towards Leech.

The runt was sitting with his back to them when suddenly a great commotion erupted in the grate. Leech made ready to run in case the fire returned – but it did not. The ashes spluttered and with a loud popping noise a large, red-hot spark whistled from the fireplace and flew towards him.

Leech squealed in fright. Turning tail he scuttled away as fast as he could. But the fizzing cinder shot after him like a guided comet. It bounced on the floor, cutting bright arcs into the gloom, and homed in unerringly on the terrified kitten. Pots and scrolls clattered down as Leech dived on to one of the shelves to escape this tenacious and fiery hornet but it was no use. The spark sailed straight and true and zoomed right down on to his tail.

The poor runt's howls were dreadful to hear. In his bedchamber, Doctor Spittle, who had been oblivious to all else, turned over in his messy bed and grumbled into the pillow. 'Curse those minor demons, will they never leave me in peace?'

Jupiter giggled helplessly, but Dab was not laughing. She could see now what her mother had meant. It would certainly be difficult to keep her brothers on friendly terms at this rate. If the quarrels continued they would be at each other's throats before long.

Imelza looked over at the shelf where Leech wept and nursed his smoking tail. 'Come child,' she called, 'let me see . . .'

'I won't! I won't!' he bawled back at her. 'It's not fair! Why do I always have to suffer?' And he buried himself under a pile of parchments where he sobbed great tears of self-pity.

Imelza sighed, 'Perhaps we should let him alone; he needs time to himself.' Then she chided her other son. 'You should not bully your brother,' she told Jupiter crossly. 'He is not as strong as you. It is no easy task to be the runt; could you not show him more kindness?'

'Me, be kind to him?' cried Jupiter in disbelief. 'Believe me when I say I've tried, Mother, yet every time I'm nice he does something vile in return. Leech is horrible!'

'Then you must try harder,' she said.

Jupiter only laughed.

Dab watched them wander over to the hearth where they prepared to go to sleep. As she pattered over to join them at the fireside, her pretty little head was full of misgivings. Some terrible strife lay ahead for her brothers and she knew the outcome would be an evil one.

The tortoiseshell lay on her side and peered across at the shelf where her brother had hidden himself. 'Good-night Leech,' she called softly. There was no response and Dab settled down to a troubled night's sleep.

It was black as pitch under the sheaves of

parchment. Leech preferred the dark; no one could see him there and no one could see how ugly he was. The only times he was remotely happy were those rare occasions when he was alone. During these isolated periods he could imagine anything he desired, he could be anyone he wanted. His ugliness did not matter when he was estranged from the world and he pretended that he was handsome like his brother. Unfortunately these moments did not last long – there was always some rude awakening from his daydreams and there would be his mother gazing at him with pity in her eyes. He knew she was sorry he had ever been born. She had never said as much but he knew it all the same. This had saddened him at first, but it did not matter any more. At that moment he hated everything in the world and resentful tears streamed down his nose.

' 'Tain't fair,' he repeated, quietly snivelling into his paw. 'I must have been born under a sorry star indeed. Why does Jupiter get all the attention and all the indulgences? Why doesn't anyone like me – 'tain't my fault I'm the runt – I never asked for it to be so.'

Wallowing in his dejection, Leech blew on the tip of his singed tail – it was still smarting. Miserably he muttered, 'How I loathe my brother; it's always Jupiter this, Jupiter that. Why must he be the one to have all the power and get all the praise?' He lifted his odd, angular face at the memory of that marvellous spell. How the fire had rushed up the chimney! In spite of his grievances Leech grinned – undoubtedly that had been a grand spectacle. The joy of it was extinguished however when he recalled that it was Jupiter who had contrived it. For several minutes he sat sullen and wretched until a fantastic idea came to him. If Jupiter could do it then why couldn't he?

Leech poked his head out of the parchments and stared at the dead fire. He had been careful to memorise exactly what his brother had said and surely it was only a matter of concentration?

He closed his eyes and recited the words his keen ears had heard. Bracing himself for the magic to course through him he gripped the shelf tightly and waited.

Nothing happened.

Leech opened one eye. Perhaps he had overlooked something. Taking a deep breath he tried again. His forehead crinkled and the frowns hooded his eyes completely. The words rasped from his mouth as he ground his teeth together, putting all his strength into the spell.

Still nothing happened.

The runt paused for breath and found that his head was pounding with the strain.

'Ho, ho,' came a soft voice behind him.

Leech whirled round as though stung by another cinder. 'Who is there?' he asked timidly.

'Thou wastest thy time and effort,' the voice said.

The kitten sniffed the air; he could not detect anyone. Only the musty scent of mouldering parchment and the withered scent of dried herbs met his nose. Perhaps the acrid smell of his own burnt fur had dulled his senses. Who then had spoken?

Could one of those impudent rats have escaped and sneaked down here to mock him? If that was the case then the foolish creature had to be hiding behind those bottles and jars. Leech was sick and tired of being the butt of so many jokes. It was bad enough when Jupiter laughed at him but to have a rat do the same was nothing short of degrading. Even now it was probably laughing till its ribs ached. He felt like catching that cruel rodent and teaching it some manners.

A wicked expression settled over the kitten; there were better things to do with rats he remembered, and he realised that he would enjoy being a hunter. Better to silence those jeers forever with one snap of his jaws, he told himself.

Assuming the correct stance, he prowled forward. 'Little ratty, little ratty,' he purred with menace, 'speak to me, speak to Leech that I might know where you are.'

'Dolt! I am no rodent!'

Leech stopped in his tracks and nearly toppled from the shelf. To his dismay one of the bottles was glowing and there in the midst of the swirling radiance a ghostly face had appeared.

The spirit of Magnus Zachaire drew close to the glass. Those sparkling eyes stared out at the runt and a curious look glittered in them. 'I fear thou shalt never be a hunter,' it said with some amusement. 'The din thou makest is enough to waken the—' He broke into sudden laughter as he realised what he was about to say. 'Well here I am to prove it!' he chuckled.

Leech fidgeted uncomfortably. Bottles that spoke were a new wonder to him and he was not sure if he trusted it. Suspiciously he turned to see if this was another trick of his brother's. No, Jupiter was still fast asleep by the hearth.

'Have no fear,' the spirit said, 'I cannot harm thee. I

can do naught. See – I am imprisoned.'

The kitten moved a little nearer then reached out a paw to touch the glass. It was true: whatever that shining creature was, it could not escape. This boosted his confidence. He pulled a fierce expression and spat.

Magnus scowled at that and the light flared abruptly. Startled, Leech cringed backwards. 'I suffer that from no one!' the phantom bellowed angrily.

'Forgive me!' the kitten pleaded as he hastily wiped the offensive matter from the glass. The glare dimmed and the luminous face accepted the apology. 'What are you?' Leech inquired, meekly bowing his head.

'In life I was Magnus Zachaire,' returned the shade wincing at the memory, 'a man of much learning. Or so it amused me to think.'

'Human!' exclaimed the kitten. 'But you understand my speech. How is this possible?'

'I have been in the pathless void,' Magnus replied darkly. 'Mine eyes and ears both see and hear many things beyond the range of mortal men. To converse with thee is a small matter, yet it drives away the pain. While we talk I am spared the agony of enduring recollection.' He passed a transparent hand over his brow and there was something of relief in his tone when he next spoke. 'Tell me,' he began, 'why art thou named Leech? Who gave thee so uncharitable a title?'

The kitten gazed at the floor. 'Is it not obvious?' he mumbled. 'The old human called me thus because I am ugly and the runt of my mother's womb.'

'Elias Theophrastus Spittle is cruel indeed,' remarked the spirit. 'There is naught shameful in being the runt, for weaklings grow and can achieve greatness.'

'Not I,' came the sour response. 'All mock me – there are times I wish I was dead.'

Magnus's floating head reared at that. 'Jest not about the grave,' he said solemnly, 'thou knowest not what death means. It is a cold emptiness that ever gnaws at thee, rush not into its chilling embrace before thy time.'

Leech shrugged, 'What do I care? At least I would escape my brother.'

'Thy brother? Ah yes!' The face stared through the glass at the slumbering group before the fireplace. 'I was witness to his display,' he said admiringly. 'Never have I seen the like. Yonder kitten shall grow to be exceedingly strong and powerful, his strength increaseth daily. I foresee a time when even Elias Theophrastus Spittle will not be able to hold him in check.'

Leech snorted unhappily and tossed his head. 'You are like the others,' he whined, 'they too praise my brother – well, not me. I hate him!'

A mild chuckle issued from the bottle. 'Poor, wretched Leech,' Magnus said sadly, 'take the counsel I give to thee. Leave this black road of jealousy and loathing which thou hast begun to tread. Disaster and tragedy shall surely come of it.'

'What care I? Is it right that Jupiter has everything? Why should he be the only one to understand the human's writing? Why can't I work the spells also?'

Magnus smiled. 'Hmm, I saw thy attempts afore,' he said. 'Did I not say then that it was a wasted effort?'

'Why do you say that? Have I not just as much right to work magic as my sainted brother?'

'You have no right whatsoever.'

Leech pulled himself up sharply; there was a definite ring in the voice. 'Why?' he asked.

The spirit wagged a spectral finger at the kitten. 'Dost thou not understand the laws governing magic?' he sighed. 'In any family, large or small, it is possible for only one member to practise the secret arts. Jupiter has taken the choice from thee, Leech. He sought to wield enchantments before you did and thus the right has passed to him. He is the one selected from your house, you cannot compete against him. The rules cannot be broken, they have held true since creation and thou must accept that.'

'Then am I doomed to a life of servitude under my brother?'

'Perhaps,' Magnus admitted. His hands drifted up to his face and a strange look passed over him. 'There is much to learn on the other side,' he muttered, 'many things, past, present and yet to come, are revealed unto you. I gaze now on some distant time, when science does strangle the world and life reaches for the stars.' He hesitated as the vision unfurled and his voice trembled with amazement. 'If the present path is followed unswervingly then from the darkness deep beneath the earth a living god will rise and he shall be named Jupiter – Lord of All.'

'No!' hissed Leech furiously.

The eyes of Magnus Zachaire wrenched themselves back to the present and focused on the kitten before him. 'This is written,' he said, 'if circumstances remain constant – thy brother shall indeed become a god.'

A hideous sneer stole over Leech. 'But what if my brother were to meet with some accident?' he whispered.

'Then the power that was his would pass to thee,' answered the spirit.

Leech grinned as malice filled his thoughts and the smouldering hatred he bore for Jupiter burst now into unquenchable flames. With his tail flicking in agitation he stared across at the sleeping figure of his brother. 'I shall have to see what can be contrived,' he breathed.

8

Adieu

Doctor Spittle slept long and deeply; the past few weeks had taken their toll on him. This was the first complete rest he had allowed himself for a very long time and he was reluctant to stir from it. Through dreams that ran with rivers of molten gold he pranced, flitting like an old, fat butterfly from one heap of treasure to another. The gleam of his fortune dazzled him and as he raised his hands to shield his eyes from the glare he realised that he had awoken at last. The bright light was in truth the rays of the wintry sun which was already climbing the sky. The alchemist blinked, grumpily squinting as the delightful dreams swiftly dissolved and the grey reality of the world greeted him.

Mumbling, the old man forced himself out of bed, but when his bare feet met the cold floor he whistled through his teeth and hopped back on to the mattress. Standing there in his threadbare nightshirt, Doctor Spittle stretched and his crooked back clicked with surprise. As he scrabbled through the messy heaps of clothes which surrounded the bed he chuckled merrily at the thought of what today might yield.

'With Zachaire's assistance,' he said, 'the Stone shall indeed be mine.'

The alchemist dressed hurriedly and ran like an excited child to the door of his bedchamber, so eager was he to commence the work. But on the small landing he paused as a familiar voice drifted up from the shop below.

'*Vite*, boy – *vite*! Fetch that rascally ragamuffin of an apothecary!'

Normally Doctor Spittle would have scowled at this insulting remark but nothing could mar his happiness this morning – not even Sir Francis Lingley. With his head set at a regal tilt he descended the stairs, his face wrapped around with a very large smile.

He met Will at the bottom of the staircase and waved him back into the shop.

This morning Sir Francis was dressed in an outfit of emerald silk. A hilarious but expensive broad-brimmed hat trimmed with feathers and silver tinsel sat atop the oval head and this finery drew the alchemist's attention at once. His smile failed as he realised that he had neglected to put on his new robe that morning, but he rallied and welcomed the dandified customer with a warmth that made Will look up sharply.

'A good day to you, My Lord!' he exclaimed.

'How good it is to see you in my humble shop once more. What service may I offer to you this chill morning?'

Even Sir Francis was taken aback by the profuse greeting. After his rude treatment of the apothecary yesterday he was expecting at least some coldness. He fingered the yellow lace which festooned his throat; how pleasant it was to be thought of so highly by the common sort. He was glad that Doctor Spittle was still well disposed towards him – it would make his request a trifle easier. Expertly he pointed a ribboned toe and gave a polite bow.

'You do me much honour, Apothecary,' he said coolly, 'yet it is not your knowledge of herbs and simples which has brought me hither this day.'

The alchemist raised a bushy eyebrow. 'Then what indeed has taken you from the court and led you here?' he inquired.

Will looked from one man to the other – he could sense that each was up to something. As he was considering what this might be, Sir Francis became aware of his curious stare.

'If we might be permitted to speak in private,' he whispered to the old man, nodding at Will to show his meaning.

Doctor Spittle turned to the boy and clapped his hands. 'See to my workroom,' he instructed. Will left the shop and trailed up the stairs.

When he was sure they would not be overheard Sir Francis came to the point at once. 'The King is giving a banquet next week,' he cried. 'It is certain to be the most splendid event of the year. A childhood friend of His Majesty sails this very day

from France and it is in his honour that the feast is given.

'A most perfect opportunity for advancement,' mused the alchemist perceptively.

Sir Francis gaped at him for a moment – this apothecary was a mite too sharp at times. 'Exactly so,' he agreed, briskly covering his hesitation. 'One who is friends with the Comte de Foybleau would also find high favour with the King.' He lowered his voice and flicked the curls of his periwig over his shoulders as he continued. 'I have it on good authority that the Comte speaks little or no English and looks kindly on those with wit enough to use his native tongue when addressing him.'

'Then your future is assured,' Doctor Spittle returned mildly and the ghost of a mocking smile flickered at the corners of his mouth, 'for do you not have the mastery of that language?'

Sir Francis gave him a withering stare. 'You know full well I do not!' he snapped. 'Was it not you who furnished me with what scraps of French I already possess?'

'It may have been,' admitted the alchemist slowly, 'but you have surpassed those few words I first taught you.' He lowered his eyes and brushed an imaginary crumb from his grubby jerkin. 'I do not recall including the word "*mendiant*" in that original list – it means "beggar", does it not?'

Sir Francis loosened his lace cravat to ease his discomfort and strained to keep calm. 'As to that,' he mumbled, 'and my tone of yesterday, there does appear to be an apology owing. But, the fact remains that I, and much of the court, know very little true

French. What I do understand is merely a jumble of fragments that I have garnered from the chatter of others.'

'A most unkind chatter it must be to contain so many insults,' Doctor Spittle drily commented. 'What a foul crew you must throng with, My Lord.'

The smile froze on the other man's face; the apothecary was not making this easy. It galled Sir Francis to ask anything of this untidy wretch and his fingers twitched in their frilled cuffs, anxious to strike the impudent fellow. After a moment's careful thought, however, the smile widened and Sir Francis was laughing nervously – this was too important a chance to let slip. He dabbed at his sweating forehead; better to let the man have his fun than miss this marvellous opportunity. 'You are, are you not, a learned soul?' he asked. 'A scholar even?'

Doctor Spittle gazed at him with a steady eye. 'It is true, I do indeed understand more than most,' he answered archly.

Sir Francis let that one pass, but it set his teeth on edge to do so. When this banquet was over and he was close to the King, then he would deal with this insolent rogue in a fitting manner. For the present he would have to suffer these barbed words and he turned to speak once again. 'Then furnish me with more than the ridiculous phrases that I and everyone else bandy about the court,' he begged. 'String together sentences which one would ask a native of France.'

'But if the Comte were to speak with you, you would be unable to comprehend him.'

'No matter,' Sir Francis said confidently. 'I can tell

by tone of voice whether a nod or tut is needed. Just give me the rags of a conversation and I shall tailor them to suit my needs.' He looked keenly into the old man's face then added, 'I should be eternally grateful.'

Doctor Spittle bowed. 'Return here on the day of the banquet and what you desire will be ready.'

'The day of the banquet?' the other spluttered. 'But I must commit it to memory. How shall I do so in such little time?'

'That is a problem for you to overcome,' replied the alchemist. 'Alas I can do the work no swifter.'

Sir Francis snorted impatiently then nodded as he accepted this. 'So be it,' he said, 'only be sure 'tis done, for I will be knocking on your door at first light that day.' With a flourish of his feathered hat he marched from the shop.

Doctor Spittle rubbed his hands together. 'At last,' he cackled, 'that beribboned maypole has entered my web and is in my power.' With a spring in his step he almost skipped upstairs.

Dab pushed her cheek against the boy's palm and purred. Will stroked her head then scratched under her chin. The kitten rolled on to her side and closed her beautiful amber eyes as she yawned. From her place before the hearth, Imelza came forward. She gave the boy a wary look then sat beside her daughter.

'Stop that at once,' she hissed, 'it is most unseemly – you are not tame, child.'

Shyly Dab looked up at the boy then remembered the proprieties. 'Forgive me, Mother,' she said, 'I forgot myself.'

'A hunter never forgets,' admonished Imelza. 'The life here is too easy, that is the problem. Your instincts grow dull. When the weather turns we shall escape.'

Dab said nothing, but her mind revolted at the thought of leaving the attic. Of course she wanted to see the outside world, but not stay there and have to kill for survival.

Will watched the cats and laughed; anyone would think they were talking to one another. He gave Dab one last pat on the head and Doctor Spittle entered.

'The time has come,' he cried excitedly as he rushed over to one of the shelves. A flurry of parchments was thrown over his shoulder as he rooted amongst the jars and pots. A terrified screech issued from the shelf as a small black shape darted out and raced behind a cupboard. 'Cursed slug!' roared the alchemist. 'Why is it always underfoot? Aha!' He brought out the small bottle which contained Magnus Zachaire and set it spinning on the table.

A prolonged whine echoed from within and the blue light pulsed in fright. 'Enough!' pleaded the spirit. 'Dost thou reckon my suffering too small that thou wouldst seek to compound it?'

Promptly the old man slapped his hand upon the bottle and put a stop to its revolutions. 'Good morrow, Magnus,' he uttered. 'I trust you are ready to unravel the conundrums you have set?'

'I am.'

Doctor Spittle took the robe and spread it out upon the table with the embroidered lining uppermost. 'Then let us begin,' he said.

The ethereal face appeared in the bottle; a fierce

glint crept into the eyes as they surveyed the velvet gown and a strange smile formed upon the lips.

'What has amused you?' rapped out the alchemist sharply. 'Is there a matter here to cause merriment?'

The smile disappeared and the spirit shook its head. ' 'Twere only old memories which haunted me,' it said quickly.

'Well, we don't want any of that to bore the breeches off us,' sniffed the old man tapping the table in irritation. 'Kindly get on with the task set.'

Magnus turned his attention back to the message embroidered on the lining. 'He who wouldst seek the Philosopher's Stone must know this,' he began.

Doctor Spittle nodded eagerly and reached for his notes as the spirit continued.

'This most wondrous element is a stone yet not a stone, it is of God yet not of God, it is flesh yet mineral also, it is secret but known to all.'

'Yes, yes, we are all aware of that tired chestnut, but of the formula? Explain the symbols you have used!'

'So be it,' returned the spirit.

For the rest of the morning they worked together. With grudging reluctance Magnus Zachaire translated the meaning of his riddling code and Doctor Spittle gleefully annotated his notes, declaring from time to time, 'Of course' or 'Surely not'. By the middle of the afternoon all was explained and the alchemist happily puffed out his chest.

'Now fulfil thine end of the bargain,' demanded the spirit.

The old man glanced up from his sheaf of paper and smirked. 'My dearest colleague,' he said, 'that would be most unwise of me. How am I to know this is the true formula? I must experiment with it first before I can be sure. No, I think you will have to be patient a little longer.'

The light inside the bottle turned almost white with rage. 'Thou reneging knave!' Magnus boomed. 'Hast thou no honour?'

But the alchemist only laughed.

The rest of the week was taken up with the collecting of the necessary ingredients and once he was sure he had them all, Doctor Spittle locked himself away and set to work. Throughout the daytime Will saw to the shop and attended to the needs of the customers. By now he knew what went into most of the cures and philtres the apothecary sold and coped with accomplished ease.

The fourth day saw the beginning of February and the boy grimly reflected that he had been in London for nearly three months. He tried never to think of his previous life now – dwelling on that time only brought home the misery of his present situation. Adcombe now seemed to be a far-off dreamworld and the boy who had idled away his childhood afternoons there was a separate person from the one who now slaved for the alchemist.

Doctor Spittle was certainly busy during this time – Will hardly saw him as the great experiment neared fruition. Occasionally a wisp of green smoke stole down the stairs to remind him that the work was still in progress, or an evil smell enveloped the whole building and was enough to keep the customers away.

On the night of the fifth day, Will was roused from

sleep by the sound of laughter. In his bedchamber above the shop Doctor Spittle was enjoying some fine joke but the noise was horrible, not the carefree, glad sound of true mirth; this was tinged with hate and wickedness. Will pulled the sackcloth over his head and immersed himself in sleep once more.

A harsh knocking awoke him the next day. He rubbed his eyes. The light was still dim and he doubted if the morning cock had yet crowed. Peering through the gloom he perceived a tall figure hammering on the shop door. Immediately Will hurried over to see who this could be. A delicate and beringed hand shoved him out of the way. This was followed by the velvet-cloaked Sir Francis Lingley, resplendent in orange satin and white frills.

'The apothecary!' he demanded. 'Fetch him. I have no time to dally this day for there is much to do before the court bestirs itself – and I have an appointment with my tailor who refuses to be kept waiting, bothersome fellow. I shall be at costs of twenty pounds for the coat he is making for me to dazzle them with tonight. I hope it will prove a wise investment.'

Will ran up to wake Doctor Spittle who for some reason seemed almost benign and pleased to hear of Sir Francis's early arrival.

'You are well come, My Lord,' the old man said some minutes later. This time he sported the robe for the other to see and he swished about in it pretending to examine an earthenware vessel on a high shelf.

Sir Francis eyed the gown with some surprise and his expression was almost envious when he saw the shining stones and silver lace. But he consoled himself with the fact that such a thing was not really fashionable and brought himself to the matter in question. 'Do you have what you promised?' he asked bluntly.

The alchemist took a roll of paper from beneath the robe, allowing him a glimpse of the fine embroidery within. 'I have indeed,' he returned with a bow.

Sir Francis had the scroll from his hand in a trice and hastily unfurled it. Doctor Spittle had been true to his word; in one column there were a score of possible topics of conversation. These included 'I trust the weather was clement for your journey from France?' and, 'London is a sweeter place for the arrival of you and your delightful wife' or 'I have heard that you have three charming children, I pray the Lord keeps them well whilst you are from them'. The opposing column contained the French translation of these worthy sentiments and it was clear that Sir Francis was overjoyed.

'Precisely what I needed!' he exclaimed. 'I am ever in your debt Apothecary. I shall have a word with the cook tonight and see if there is aught he can spare for you. Some delightful dessert perhaps – a syllabub or pear tart?'

'Most gratifying I'm sure,' replied the alchemist with little sincerity. 'You will see, My Lord, that I have also included several compliments which you may like to pay to the Comtesse: "What lovely shoes"; "You look radiant tonight"; that sort of thing. Oh yes, there is also something which you might care to say to the King, commenting on his noble choice of friends.'

Sir Francis squeaked with anticipation. 'I cannot bear to wait,' he cried. 'Oh, how I shall impress the court with my effortless grasp of the French tongue. The Lingley star will rise very high tonight, Spittle. Now I must be off and learn these divine morsels by heart.' With a rustle of orange satin and a wave of his frills he was gone.

Doctor Spittle's lips broke into a wide grin and he went laughing up the stairs.

Alone in the shop Will scratched his head. 'Now what was that all about?' he asked himself. 'And why is old Spittle so happy?'

A bitter smell met the alchemist's nostrils when he entered his workroom. The air was thick with an acrid mix of noxious chemical vapours and a crucible glowed red hot over the fire. Taking a long pair of tongs he prodded the liquid metal within. It bubbled and blew out a hideous stench.

'How much longer?' he cackled.

'At midnight tonight the Stone shall be thine,' answered the spirit.

'Midnight tonight!' echoed the old man.

'Verily, and shouldst thou add merely a few grains of it to any base metal it shall surely transmute into gold.'

'Never have I come this close to achieving my life's work!' gasped Doctor Spittle, slumping into his seat. 'I must take care; it would do me no good to over-excite myself and suffer a seizure just as the Stone is within reach.' He stared round at his cluttered attic as though it was the last time he would set eyes on it. 'Gladly shall I exchange this poky place for a palace,' he chuckled. 'What say you, Jupiter?'

The familiar had leaped on to his master's lap and the alchemist stroked him fondly. 'Soon you shall dine off a gold plate,' he said. 'I can scarce believe it myself – after all these years of scrimping and hardship to purchase the necessary equipment, the time has come.' A big, joyful tear trickled down the hooked nose and splashed on to Jupiter's head.

The remaining hours of daylight were painfully slow and Doctor Spittle remained glued to his chair, watching the bubbling substance in the crucible give off streams of foul fumes. When the evening came he was still there, his eyes fixed on the strange liquid. It had become transparent now and tiny crystals were beginning to form around the edges.

The light died outside the small attic window but the alchemist was insensible to the growing dark. Only the fire and what simmered there existed to him; it filled his vision and his mind. The night crept by and as midnight drew closer the cats became restless.

Imelza prowled around, anxious to escape this stinkful prison. Dab watched her timidly. Her mother was growing more agitated with every passing day – the tortoiseshell felt sure that if they were cooped up much longer then something disastrous would happen. Imelza's yearning to roam abroad unsettled her and she crouched by the hearth, dejected and heavy of heart.

Jupiter had moved from the old man's lap and was engrossed in one of the open books which still littered the floor. From one of the topmost shelves Leech spied on them all. Slyly he observed his brother and watched as the material in the crucible gelled and become almost solid. It had turned white and looked like a thick, salty paste, yet green smoke continued to fly out of its gurgling centre. Leech peered out of the window and knew it was nearly midnight.

'Not much longer,' breathed the alchemist in a hallowed tone.

'No indeed,' said Magnus quietly. ' 'Twould appear thou hast succeeded, Spittle. That is a rare feat to accomplish. Once I was in possession of the correct formula it took seven years to find the Stone. The Almighty hath looked kindly upon thee.'

'Rubbish!' hissed the old man. 'It was my skill that blended the ingredients and my eyes that watched over the chemicals – no heavenly agency was at work. Man is the true lord of Nature, there is nothing he cannot achieve.'

BANG!

'Lord of Death!' cried Doctor Spittle jumping from the chair. 'What was that?'

BANG! BANG! BANG!

' 'Twould seem that someone is most desperate to enter thy shop,' said the spirit.

'Sounds like the Devil himself.'

'I assume thou speakest from experience,' returned Magnus.

The alchemist ignored him, and leaned over to the window where he peered down at the street below. A broad hat smothered in white feathers and gold lace obscured the figure hammering on the shop door. Doctor Spittle let out a hearty laugh when he realised who it was. 'Ha, ha!' he hooted. 'A dishevelled Lingley has come to call! Now what has fetched him from that toothsome banquet, I wonder?'

At the sound of his voice the man tossed back his head and glared upwards. 'Spittle!' he screamed. 'I'll see you hang for this!' The old, guffawing head withdrew from the window and Sir Francis was left fuming on the step. He pounded on the door again and the worried face of Will peered through the glass to see who it was.

'Open!' screeched the man. 'In the name of all that is holy, unboit this door or I shall break it down!'

The boy quickly obeyed and was thrust aside as the man barged into the shop. 'Sir!' Will exclaimed. 'What is the meaning of this? The hour is late—'

'Silence, lad, if you value your head!' Sir Francis stormed. He threw up his arms and shouted until he turned a violent shade of beetroot. 'Come down Spittle, let me face the fiend who has ruined me this night!'

'I am here,' said a soft voice.

The man whirled round and there, with a candle in his hand, stood the alchemist. A triumphant gleam shone in his eyes and he studied Sir Francis keenly. 'Well, well, My Lord,' he whispered quietly, 'pray tell me the reason for this riotous disruption. See, you have woken my apprentice and I myself was immersed in important work which should not be left unattended.'

'My Lord?' spat Sir Francis contemptuously. 'Oh yes, you black villain, you know full well that I am disgraced and no longer bear that title!'

Doctor Spittle pretended to look shocked but he could not prevent a smirk stealing over his face. 'Why, my dearest sir,' he began with just the hint of a snigger, 'what can you mean – what unhappy event has occurred to rob you of your nobility?'

Sir Francis – or rather plain Francis Lingley as he was now – took off his hat and threw it at the old man with all his strength. '*You* occurred, you deceitful felon!' he shrieked. 'I curse the day I ever set eyes on this hole of a shop! It is you who have brought this calamity upon me! I should kill you where you stand!'

Doctor Spittle tittered to see the man so distraught but this only made the poor fellow worse and he tore off his periwig and stamped it into the dusty floor.

Will was astonished and confounded. 'What has happened?' he asked. 'What has he done that is so terrible?'

Francis rounded on him and waved a piece of paper under the boy's nose. '*This*,' he hissed through clenched teeth, 'is what brought about my doom! These "conversational" sentences have consigned me to the life of a pauper! I am utterly destroyed!'

'I don't understand . . .' Will stammered glancing at the giggling alchemist. 'How could they?'

'Because he has cheated and lied to me!' snarled the man. 'Oh yes, the banquet began well enough. The guest of honour, the Comte de Foybleau, arrived with His Majesty and we were all there ready to greet him. All day I have drummed these hateful French sentences into my head so that I would be word-perfect tonight – my God, how I shudder now to think of it, that I should have played such a determined role in my own downfall!' He paused for breath then continued, 'When the feasting was complete we rose to dance and the Comte was introduced to those of note. I pushed myself forward and gave my most gracious and becoming bow. The Comte had by him a manservant versed in both French and English. This person informed me that His Lordship expressed a delight in my attire. I saw this as my chance and hastened to compliment the Comte and his charming wife in their own tongue. This I managed adroitly; they were both well pleased and wished to speak at greater length. With my pride soaring I began to use the sentences you had furnished me with, but to my consternation they both stared at me in puzzlement.'

'Why?' asked Will. 'What was wrong?'

Francis snorted and pointed accusingly at the alchemist. 'Only later did I discover that I was not actually flattering them but was in fact uttering the most odious insults.'

Doctor Spittle burst out with a great horse-laugh.

'Yet that was not the end of my disgrace,' Francis persisted. 'The more I tried to retrieve the situation the more I dishonoured myself.' He wiped the beads of sweat from his brow and tears sprang to his eyes. 'In my madness I apparently told the Comte that his wife had the face of a barnacle goose and the figure of a butchered sow and if his children took after her then they must be hideous beyond imagining.'

Will drew his breath. This was terrible – greater men had lost their heads for less. His sympathy went out to the once proud and haughty lord – no one deserved such humiliation. He hardly dared to ask what happened next but Francis needed no prompting.

'Their horrified expressions told me that I had made some nightmarish mistake, yet in my stupidity I thought I had mispronounced some word or other – never did I dream that what I said was one long list of rudeness. Like some moon-kissed buffoon I gabbled on until the Comte slapped me with his glove and his wife spat at me. The whole court was listening by this time and the King himself came over to see what the commotion was.'

'Ha!' exulted Doctor Spittle. 'So you uttered that last sentence, did you not?'

'Just so!'

'Hee hee! And did you compliment him on his noble choice of friends?'

'Pouvez-vous remettre un bouton à ce veston?' screeched Francis, the veins on his temples throbbing with rage. 'What possessed me to trust you? Vile, loathsome creature that you are! Only then did I realise I had been betrayed! If those sentences had been provided earlier I should have had time to work out what they actually meant. Idiot though I was, I actually put my faith in you!'

The alchemist leaned against the counter for support. He was so helpless with laughter that he shook uncontrollably, making one of the pots on the table jiggle off the edge and smash to the floor.

Francis's face was awful to look on; his lips were white and his nostrils were flaring like those of a mad horse. 'You think it is funny?' he bawled. 'You think that my asking the King if he can sew a button on my coat is a great jest, do you?' His hand flew to his belt and in an instant produced a small, deadly dagger.

The laughter died in the alchemist's throat when he saw the blade advance. He glared at the man wielding it and snarled, 'Sheathe your dagger, Lingley. Would you make a fool of yourself twice in one night?'

'I will be avenged!' the other declared fiercely.

The alchemist smiled. 'Very well,' he said calmly. 'Come and gut me.'

Francis ran at him and the dagger was raised.

Not knowing who to help, Will rushed forward. If this man killed Doctor Spittle he could escape and his heart leapt at that – he could return to Adcombe with no fear of pursuing demons hunting after him. For a vital second he wavered as the delicious idea took hold; he would finally be free to till the land on the Godwin estate and run it as his father had done till the day he died. What a heavenly release from this cruel and grim city.

Will recoiled suddenly – had he really become so callous? Could he in truth stand by and let Francis commit murder?

As he was struggling within himself a cry of anguish and fear resounded through the shop. The knife clattered to the ground and Francis fell back in terror.

'His eyes!' he spluttered. 'Look at his eyes!'

Will turned to see. Doctor Spittle was cackling and an orange glow now illumined the room. It was brighter than the light of the candle and with a shiver the boy saw where it came from. The alchemist's eyes were blazing with flame; they were like two burning coals and they glared at Francis with evil intent.

'You dare to raise your hand against me?' the alchemist cried, seeming to grow in stature. 'Begone, before my anger consumes you!' He held out his hand and the tips of his fingers dripped yellow flames.

'Aaiieee!' wailed Francis. 'You're a demon!' And he hurried out of the door as fast as his feet could take him.

Doctor Spittle chuckled and crossed the shop to close the door. He was his usual self again. 'I do not think we shall ever see him in here after tonight,' he said mildly, 'not now he is *déclassé*. I wouldn't be surprised if His Majesty hounds him out of the kingdom altogether.' He stopped abruptly when he saw Will's astonishment. 'Fear not, young dog,' he assured him. 'That was only a party trick – nothing more – but it put the wind up our Francis, did it not?'

Will nodded feebly; this horrible old man frightened him more and more.

'Now get you back to rest,' the alchemist instructed. 'I have my work to return to.' And he left Will staring after him.

With a light heart Doctor Spittle entered the attic; from now on nobody would deride him. He had suffered the scorn of others for too long; tomorrow he would be richer than all of them and he hummed a merry ditty at the notion.

Locking the door behind him he turned to the crucible over the fire and looked blankly down. It was empty.

'The Stone!' he murmured. 'Where is the Stone?'

'The clock has struck midnight,' said the voice of Magnus Zachaire. 'The Stone was here then, but thou wert not.'

'I . . . I do not understand,' the old man said slowly. 'Then where has it gone?'

The spirit laughed. 'The heats took it,' he crowed. 'Did I not warn thee of the dangers involved? The Stone must be removed from the fire at the precise moment or it withers and is no more. All that work was for nought – thou wert too busy seeking vengeance to heed thine own ambition. Thy malice blinded thee to all else.'

'Then I shall begin again!' Doctor Spittle growled

defiantly. 'I have accomplished it once, a second time will be easier still.'

The spirit said nothing but as the face faded within the bottle an odd glitter stabbed from his dark eyes.

9

'Lord Have Mercy on Us'

Days and weeks passed by, until March settled in, bringing with it warm winds and fair weather. The spring came with an abundance of lush green growth and perfumed blossom rained down from the trees which grew in the courtyards and small gardens of the city. The winter had been an extremely mild one and many thanked the Lord for His leniency. A lazy, contented air lay over London and the gentry delighted in taking strolls around Hyde Park where they studied the latest fashions and talked of the recent scandals. The horrendous spectacle that Sir Francis Lingley had made of himself was all but forgotten and, as no one knew where he had taken himself off to, he was old news and the court tongues wagged to different tunes.

The war with the Dutch continued, but to the

common folk it was only a rumour which had little effect on their lives. Only when the ships came to port and the haggard sailors rampaged drunkenly from one tavern to the next did they become aware of it.

Under the blue, hazy shadow of St Paul's, March turned to April and the clement weather continued. Soon those who had thanked the Almighty for the temperate winter were muttering against Him. In the warm sun the smells of the city gradually worsened; the meat in the butchers' shops went rotten more quickly and the sludge of the open drains flowed thick and slow in the heat. It was the ideal breeding ground – for vermin of all kinds. Rats multiplied in their thousands and armies of ants invaded houses, crawling into kitchens and marching into pantries. Hosts of large, black flies swarmed through the cramped lanes and everyone closed their windows against them.

Will was bored. He stared out of the leaded panes and fanned his face with a sheet of paper; the air inside the apothecary shop was sticky and close. It had been a quiet morning for customers – only two had come in and of those only one had purchased something. A cloud of insects buzzed past the glass and instinctively he stepped back.

'If only Molly would come,' he sighed wistfully. The pretty young woman had not set foot inside the shop since that morning in January. Will missed her cheerful and irreverent manner; a visit from her would certainly brighten his day. 'I wonder what can have happened to her?' he murmured.

A thunderous noise crashed overhead but the boy took no notice. 'He's at it again,' he simply muttered.

There followed a quick succession of sounds: bottles smashed, heavy footsteps stamped up and down and a high screech cut through the stifling atmosphere. Will had been expecting the latter but he winced anyway. 'I don't know how that poor cat stays alive.'

Since that night when he had brought about the ruin of Sir Francis Lingley, Doctor Spittle had been trying to recreate his experiment. At first his confidence was overwhelming but as each attempt ended in failure he became increasingly impatient and frustrated. This had a disastrous effect upon his work: his concentration would fail at a crucial moment and the entire procedure would have to begin again. Even the arrival of a new comet in the sky failed to grab his attention and it was left to other astrologers to suppose what this would portend.

From the spirit of Magnus Zachaire Doctor Spittle had little help; it merely repeated what he already knew and on occasion the alchemist was driven to distraction by the unnecessary remarks it made about his competence.

Will kept out of his way as much as possible, for the old man's temper boiled as viciously as the chemicals in his experiments.

A door slammed and the boy glanced upwards; quickly he made a grab for the broom and when the alchemist entered he was busily sweeping the floor.

The old man looked drawn and the bags beneath his eyes were grey from the sleepless nights he forced himself to endure. He glowered at Will and crossed to one of the shelves. From this he took down a large jar and emptied the contents on the ground. 'Be sure and clean that also,' he said curtly.

At that moment the door to the shop opened and a large ox of a man squeezed inside. His face was round as a cannon ball and purple with the heat. The tufts of black hair which sprouted on the top of his head lay flat against his scalp, plastered down by the sweat which constantly cascaded over his corpulent features like salty waterfalls. A fly that had followed the stranger into the shop landed on his dripping brow and crawled down his heavy jowls. The man squashed it with an expert thumb and flicked the dead insect off his streaming skin. It landed directly at the feet of Doctor Spittle.

The alchemist regarded it peevishly then raised his eyebrows at the fat intruder.

The man coughed and blinked his pale blue eyes. Then he held up a dumpy little hand and saluted. 'Be you the apothecary?' he asked in a squeaky high-pitched voice that contrasted starkly with his bulk.

Doctor Spittle pulled a face; he itched to get back to work. 'I might very well be,' he answered tersely. 'Whatever it is you require my apprentice can attend to it.' With the empty jar in his grasp he turned to leave.

But the stranger was not to be put off so easily. 'Is the lad skilled enough to prepare a remedy that can protect against the plague?' he demanded.

The alchemist stopped in his tracks and whirled round. 'What say you?' he shrieked.

'Plague!' gasped Will.

'Aye!' the man replied. 'That's what it's feared to be. 'Tis said it has already claimed some poor soul – one Margaret Ponteous. She fell into the fever and never came out of it. This very hour I have passed a house outside the city walls that is shut up with the sickness. It was a wretched slum of a place and I crossed the street to be as far from it as possible.' He stared grimly at Will then turned back to the alchemist. 'That is why I am here, in case the contagion of that house has in some way touched me.'

Doctor Spittle let out a squawk and staggered backwards. 'Get out!' he gibbered. 'Take your filthy person away from my shop – I have no wish to die a raving death.'

'But you are an apothecary, are you not?' squeaked the man in surprise. 'I have come seeking help, surely you would not deny me aid?'

'That I most certainly would!' the old man declared. 'And I shall!' In an effort to shield himself he put his arm over his mouth and snatched the broom from Will, then he shooed and prodded the large man out of the door and threw the bolt home.

Leaning against it he put his hand over his chest where his heart fluttered in alarm. There was nothing Doctor Spittle feared more than illness and disease and he took great precautions to avoid them wherever possible. 'We are closed for the rest of the day,' he told Will with a trembling voice.

'Shouldn't we have done something to help him?' asked the boy.

The alchemist's face was pale as he steadied himself and wandered across the room. 'Certainly not!' he said with a shudder. 'You do not understand the nature of the sickness, boy, or you would never suggest such a thing. Now, I must retire. I do not feel up to resuming my work this afternoon. Remain here and see to it that no one enters.'

'As you wish,' Will answered.

And so the Great Plague began. Death, in all his guises, was a frequent visitor to the squalid homes of the capital. Smallpox, cholera, and countless other fevers were common enough, so, at first, the tales of one more sickness frightened few. But nobody could possibly imagine just how many would succumb to this sinister new arrival.

Like some ghastly angel of Death the plague spread its dark wings over the city, moving stealthily from house to house. Nothing could stop the insidious flow of this silent assassin. It stalked the darkened streets and searched for the living, touching them with fatal caresses and breathing oblivion into their faces. No one was safe; it cut down the destitute and the noble with equal zeal and left only misery and emptiness in its wake.

The pestilence struck as suddenly and unexpectedly as a lightning bolt – so swift a gatherer of souls that a strong man could wake up hale in the morning and be dead by nightfall.

All quaked in fear lest it chose to call on them next. More and more buildings were sealed and boarded up, with red crosses painted on the doorways along with the words, 'Lord have mercy on us'. Weekly mortality bills were posted and to everyone's dismay the number of dead rose steadily. Church bells tolled with increasing frequency and the desolate sound was echoed throughout the land.

In the apothecary shop, Doctor Spittle anxiously sat in his attic, fearing a visitation. He all but abandoned the great experiment and spent entire days worrying himself into a nervous frenzy. It would be just like fate to cut the thread of his life when he was on the verge of fulfilling his dreams. Not once did he step outside and walk through the streets in case the sickness was waiting to pounce. He entrusted to Will the management of the shop and, at times of particular anxiety, the alchemist would shout his instructions down to him so as to avoid contact completely.

Will became increasingly concerned about the old man. It was not natural for even him to spend so long locked away. Entire days passed by without a sound coming out of that room, and with everyone he met talking of nothing but Death the boy's spirits sank very low.

Doctor Spittle swilled two chemicals around in a jar and examined the result. But it was only a half-hearted attempt to get back to work – he really wanted to take his mind off the plague, but that seemed impossible.

Somewhere in the night-cloaked city a death bell rang out – another life had sweated and shivered its way to judgement. The alchemist set the jar down and clasped his shaking hands together.

'What is it thou fearest, Spittle?' came a low voice. 'Is it in truth Death – or what awaits thee on the other side?'

The alchemist glanced at the bottle on the table and scowled at the spirit's face. 'I am not afraid,' he lied unconvincingly. 'Death shall not gather me just yet, I have too much to live for to surrender to that gentleman.'

'Ah yes,' Magnus chuckled, 'gold – but where is thy fortune?'

'Enough!' snapped the old man and he stuffed the

bottle on to one of the shelves, hiding it behind some books. Rattled, he sat back in his seat. At once Jupiter came to him and the cat's presence calmed his jangled nerves.

The kittens were nearly adults now. Dab was almost as large as her mother but surpassed her by far in beauty. Leech was still scrawny and awkward-looking; any hopes Imelza might have had of him being an ugly duckling were grossly unfounded. Jupiter, however, was nearly twice the size of his mother; he was strong in both mind and body and Imelza felt that she no longer had any control over her wilful son.

Doctor Spittle stroked his familiar's head. 'The pestilence will never invade our little territory, will it?' he muttered. 'No, not whilst I am vigilant.' Jupiter mewed back at him and the old man managed a faint smile. 'Are you hungry, my trusty assistant? Yes, it is late and you have not eaten – come.'

He rose and took from a cupboard some strips of salted fish. He had no appetite for them himself so he doled them out to the cats who purred round him the instant the supper was produced. Only Leech hung back, watching warily from a corner. His stomach growled at the sight and smell of food but he would rather go hungry than suffer another vicious blow from those boots.

'We must not forget our rodent friends,' said the alchemist as Jupiter stood on his hind legs to take the last morsels. Doctor Spittle reached up, tossing the scraps into the two cages, and the rats leaped on them.

Heliodorus chewed hurriedly but without pleasure.

'Eeuch!' he grumbled. 'I has munched better victuals than this.'

'Oh, I doesn't know,' Beckett meekly replied, 'it do seem quite a tasty bit of nosh.'

'You Englishers got no taste for finer things,' commented the black rat, 'not never.'

Dab padded over to the corner where Leech cringed in the shadows. 'Here,' she said kindly, 'I saved some of my supper for you.' And she passed a piece of the dried fish to her brother.

The runt snatched at it and gobbled it down, bones and all. 'You're the only one with any kindness,' he said with his mouth full. 'If it wasn't for you I'd starve to death.'

The tortoiseshell shook her head. 'It would never come to that,' she told him. 'Mother wouldn't let it happen – nor would Jupiter.'

At this Leech snorted. 'Yes he would,' he spat resentfully, 'our darling brother cares for no one but himself and that evil old human.'

'Well, I think you're wrong,' Dab insisted.

Leech narrowed his eyes and gazed over her shoulder. 'Really?' he asked. 'Look at him now. There he sits on the lap of our gaoler, basking in the praise and the affection which gets poured upon him. It makes me sick!'

Dab made no answer. Jupiter really was spending an awful amount of time with the old man – he hardly ever talked to them now. It troubled her and in silence she returned to their mother.

Another distant knell proclaimed the passing of one more poor soul. Doctor Spittle's agitation returned and he drummed his fingers distractedly on the table.

'Dost thou hear it?' called a muffled voice.

'Keep quiet!' the alchemist shouted at the pile of books on the shelf.

But the spirit laughed back at him. 'Listen to the sounds of Death, Elias,' it taunted. 'The bells that ring compass thee round. Thou art enclosed within a circle of disease; how much longer before it tightens and closes upon thee? When will thy bell ring?'

The alchemist thumped the table and demanded peace.

Magnus's response to that was simple. 'Why should I permit thee what thou withholdest from myself?' he uttered.

But Doctor Spittle was not listening. A new sound had reached his ears. Horses' hooves were slowly clopping down the street outside the alley and a loud rumbling of cart wheels as they bumped over the cobbles followed behind.

A blue light shone out from behind the books and Magnus's voice was soft and tormenting. 'Hark!' he whispered. 'There go the pest-waggons, taking the dead to be buried. How many bodies are carried tonight, Elias? Two – three? How much longer before more waggons are needed? How much longer before one of their number comes for thy boil-covered corpse?'

The alchemist peered out of the window to see if he could spot the grim vehicle as it passed by. Immediately he dragged himself back and stumbled over the chair.

Down in the shadows of the alley something moved; it was too dark to tell for sure, but for an

instant he thought he saw the figure of a man step backwards into the gloom.

'Someone is out there!' he spluttered. 'In the alley below, a figure wrapped in black – he was staring up at me!'

'Perhaps the gentleman thou dreadest hath arrived at last,' suggested the spirit.

Doctor Spittle swallowed nervously and edged towards the window once more. 'Nonsense!' he said. ''Twas only a trick of the dark, nothing else – my fancies are sending shapes to delude me.' Yet his lips were quivering when he squinted down again.

The alley below was empty. 'There,' he reassured himself, 'the product of my addled and overheated genius, that's all it was.' But the alchemist had no sleep that night.

Time dragged on. Only on the third of June were the minds of the populace briefly diverted from their woes. The distant report of guns boomed out over the River Thames; somewhere the English fleet was doing battle with the Dutch and prayers were, for once, concerned with matters other than the pestilence.

Will heard the far-off explosions and looked up from the spices in his hands. He envied those mariners; out there on the open sea there was no plague – only adventure and excitement and a freedom he could not begin to imagine. The noise grew fainter and he continued with his work.

Out of necessity, he was kept busy preparing nosegays from sweet-smelling herbs and dried flowers. They did nothing to ward off the sickness but when walking through the streets they were a vital relief from the reek of the pest-houses. A flourishing trade of dubious cures and phoney preventatives was springing up everywhere. Some of the other apothecaries and even a few physicians preyed on the fears of the gullible and desperate by selling these fraudulent concoctions. Most were alcohol-based, so even though they were of no use against the disease, people invariably felt better for taking them.

Doctor Spittle, however, was too preoccupied to apply for a licence to sell these mixtures. He was being watched.

That first glimpse he had had of the figure in the alley had only been the beginning. He was convinced that someone lurked in the shadows each night, spying on him. On many occasions since, he had caught a movement in the corner of his eye. But every time he turned to confront it, the figure had melted into the darkness. It was most alarming and the words of Magnus Zachaire constantly came back to haunt him and strike terror into his heart. What if it really was Death himself?

The old man became obsessed; he had to find out who or what it was and he began to lie in wait. For hours he would crouch under the window-sill until his back complained and all the feeling disappeared from his legs. Then he would pop up like a Jack-in-the-box and glare down expectantly.

It was on one of these uncomfortable nights of vigil that his patience was finally rewarded.

The hour was very late. Doctor Spittle was hunched under the window, hugging his knees and keeping his ears alert for any footsteps on the cobbles outside. Imelza was prowling about the room as she usually did and getting on the alchemist's nerves.

'Why can't the poxy creature settle?' he bawled throwing a book at her.

'She is a creature of the night,' came the answer from the shelf. The bottle which contained the spirit was now permanently tucked out of sight, for Doctor Spittle could not bear the insufferably smug face of that wretched spectre. 'The essence of darkness calls to her,' Magnus continued, 'it sings in her blood and beckons her to roam through the shadows.'

'Well she isn't going anywhere!' retorted the alchemist. 'Once out she'll only want to come back in and I won't have her bringing the contagion to me.'

'Elias,' said the spirit abruptly.

'What is it now?' he grunted.

'Thy friend hath arrived; I sense a presence outside.'

The old man sprang to his feet and held a lantern over his head. The light fell on to the alley and there it was.

'Lord of Death!' he cried.

A nightmarish figure stared back at him. It was dressed from head to toe in a long black coat. Heavy boots were on the feet and leather gauntlets covered the hands. The old man uttered a little cry of dismay when the lamplight fell upon the mysterious man's face – it was not human.

A long, sharp beak pointed up at him from the centre of the head and the eyes that shone in the yellow beam were large and round like those of some monstrous fish. The figure made no attempt to hide itself, but stayed in the open, regarding the attic window and the alchemist framed within it with a horrible, glassy stare.

Doctor Spittle found this more disconcerting than when it hid in the shadows. He squealed and fell to his knees.

'He has come!' he cried. 'Death is here!'

So loud were his shrieks that he woke Will in the shop below and the boy hurried up the stairs to see what had happened.

'Are you well, sir?' he called through the door.

The alchemist rushed forward and put his full weight against it. 'Who's there?' he gibbered.

'It's me, sir – Will.'

'The young dog,' Doctor Spittle breathed with relief. He turned the key in the lock and opened the door a crack. 'Out there,' he explained, 'in the alley, someone watches me.'

Will stared at him doubtfully; the old man looked terrible. With his wisps of thinning hair standing on end he appeared mad. 'Shall I go and see who it is?' the boy suggested in an attempt to humour him.

'Yes!' the other agreed. 'No! It might get in! But if it is Death then a mere door would be no barrier. Yes, go out and discover what it is.'

Will hurried down to the shop and ran to the entrance. For a moment he hesitated and searched for something to use as a weapon in case there really was some villain out there. Seizing the broom he unlatched the door and crept out.

The alley was dark and deserted.

'Come out, wherever you are,' Will piped up brandishing the broom as though it were a sword.

There was no reply; only the plague-ridden wind moved through the darkness and brushed against him.

Shivering, in spite of the warm night, he returned to the shop.

Doctor Spittle heard the returning footsteps and he pressed his eye to the keyhole. 'Dog,' he hissed, 'did you see him?'

'There was no one out there, sir.'

The door was flung open and the boy dragged inside.

'What say you?' demanded the alchemist. 'Are you lying to me, boy?'

Will tried to shake his head but the old man had him by his hair. 'No, sir, I swear,' he cried, 'when I got outside whoever it was had gone.'

Doctor Spittle released him and dashed back to the window. 'Umm,' he muttered, 'the creature has departed.'

'Creature?' repeated Will. 'What do you mean?'

The alchemist sat down and passed his hand wearily over his face. 'It was terrible,' he said. 'Some frightful demon has come for me, or perhaps it is the pestilence clothing itself in human form. A great beak it had and large round eyes that gleamed at me. What manner of body did it hide under that great coat, I wonder, and what talons were concealed by the gauntlets?'

To his annoyance the boy in front of him grinned. 'That's no demon,' Will told him, 'it sounds to me like one of the plague doctors. I don't blame you for being afraid, I was the first time one came to the shop. They're the only ones who can enter the pesthouses – they wear those garments to protect themselves, but I reckon they're frightening enough to scare any disease away. I shouldn't like to meet such an outlandish figure on a dark night.'

Doctor Spittle looked at him blankly, then a frown crossed his brow. 'And what was one of them doing in my shop?' he roared.

'He wanted herbs to put in the beak,' said Will. 'They need it to keep the smell away.'

'Idiot dog!' bawled the old man. 'How dare you allow someone who has been into one of those disease-infested places into my home! Are you so feeble that you thought nothing of it?' He lashed out and gave Will a mighty crack with the back of his hand.

The blow caught the boy across the mouth and he yelped at the force of it. A trickle of blood oozed from his lip and he glared at the alchemist with hatred blazing in his eyes.

'Get out,' Doctor Spittle commanded. 'Must I do everything? It seems if I am to outlive this sickness I must take a greater interest in the affairs of the shop once more.'

Will closed the door behind him. He wished the old man *would* catch the plague – it would serve him right.

'Striking the lad will not aid thee, Elias,' chided Magnus softly.

The alchemist whirled round. 'Silence!' he told the pile of books that screened the bottle. 'When I desire your opinion I shall seek it.'

The spirit gave a quick laugh. 'Then explain why a plague doctor watcheth thee,' he said.

Doctor Spittle stammered and wrung his hands. 'I don't know,' he burbled lamely.

'Surely no one bears thee such malice?'

'No, I am a respected apothecary. Why should anyone waste their time hounding me thus?'

'Then mayhap I was right after all,' chortled Magnus. 'It is an omen, Elias, a sign of thy impending death.'

The alchemist was close to tears. He strode up and down biting his fingernails. Suddenly he stamped his foot. 'Wait!' he announced. 'There is one who hates me and would stop at nothing to torment me to my grave.' He straightened his back and swept his fine white hair over his bald patch. 'Francis Lingley!' he declared. 'He must still be in London. Can the King do nothing right? That fop of a man ought to have been clapped in the Tower – or exiled at the very least. Well, I have nothing to dread from the likes of him. The next time fancy Francis comes sniffing at my door in this pathetic attempt at revenge, I shall put an end to his pestering for good.'

The following day the alchemist was in a jovial mood. Now that he was certain no supernatural agency was hounding him he was almost back to his usual self. He pottered about the shop for the first time in ages, tutting at the decline in stock and scrutinising the contents of the pots.

Will's lip still stung. A yellow bruise had formed at the side of his mouth and he went about his chores sullenly. Now that the old man was back downstairs he loathed it and wondered that he had ever been concerned for the vile wretch.

A tap at the window and the sound of a woman's laughing voice made him look up hopefully. But the boy groaned in disappointment. It was not Molly who passed by and entered the shop, but an older and uglier customer – Peggy Blister.

She often came into the apothecary to purchase her cosmetics. The first time Will had served her his heart had been in his mouth in case she recognised him from that night at the Sickle Moon. But he need not have worried for not even his late mother would have known him. Although his hair had grown back he still looked like a beggar's brat and Mistress Blister dealt with him in the same vulgar way that she did with any of the apprentices in the city.

Her sharp little eyes peeked out from her painted doll face and she managed to bare her mottled teeth, in that parody of a smile, without any of her garish mask cracking. 'Good day to you, Apothecary,' she said, but with difficulty for it was hard to say 'apothecary' without moving her lips.

Doctor Spittle nodded at her and moved away slightly. 'And what are you doing here, mistress?' he enquired politely.

Peg tossed her dyed ringlets and wagged her finger at him. 'I come for my spices,' she told him. 'I done got me a licence to sell London Treacle.'

'The preventative against the plague?'

'That's right. I don't want to take no chances, especially now my circumstances have changed. Besides if folk sees me taking the stuff, and if I've still got enough wind in me to bawl at them, then they'd surely buy some – that's what I reckoned anyway.'

The old man held up his hand to halt her prattling. 'Forgive me,' he said, 'I appear to be behind the times somewhat. Tell me good woman, what are you talking about – what are these changes of circumstance?'

'Ain't you 'eard?' she cooed. 'My alehouse is

shuttered up. It were the stable lad. Found 'im a retchin' an' a vomitin' they did – and covered with the sores. Thank God I were out when it 'appened or I'd 'ave been sealed in there an' all. Forty days the quarantine lasts – can yer think of it? All that time locked in with the sickness, not able to get out and with guards on the door to make sure you don't escape. No thank you. Plum 'orrid it is.'

Doctor Spittle moved even further away from her. 'How fortunate for you indeed that you were absent at the time,' he said fighting the urge to flee from her presence.

Peg nodded vigorously. 'Not 'alf. Still I got me a better paid job. Fourpence a body I gets now.'

'Fourpence a what?' he squealed.

'A body,' she repeated. ' "Honest and discreet matrons" is what they wanted, and if that ain't me to a shillin' I don't know who else.'

The alchemist clutched at his throat and swiped a nosegay from the counter. Shoving it under his own hooked nose and trying not to breathe too deeply, he asked in a choking voice, 'So what is it you do?'

'Searches them, o' course!' she replied. 'Well, they needs to know who died o' what don't they? Not everyone drops down with the plague you know and them death bills have to be as accurate as they can make 'em.' She patted her curls proudly and fluttered her lashes. 'If it's not certain how a particular person has snuffed it, us nurses have a good look and find out. Coining it in I am – 'bout time too, if you ask me. This plague has been the best thing that's come my way since the day them naughty cavaliers drank at the alehouse.'

'I . . . I'm pleased for you,' Doctor Spittle croaked. He jabbed a desperate finger at Will and rasped, 'Attend to this customer's needs at once.'

'Course,' Peg continued, 'it takes a strong nerve to go ferretin' through the dead. Take this very morning, now if that wasn't a sad an' sorry spectacle. Cried my eyes out I did.' As her make-up was undamaged this was patently a shocking lie. 'Makes yer think it does, there's *them* – poor as aught – an' then there *he* was. Yes, it makes yer think.'

The old man twitched his eyebrows in an effort to tell Will to hurry up, then he realised that Peg was waiting for him to comment. 'Hmm?' he mumbled through a fence of dried flowers and herbs.

'I was tellin' yer about those I searched this mornin',' she said with relish, 'side by side they were, bless 'em. Lived on the corner of Throgmorton Street – in the raghouse there.'

'Not the Gobtrots?' gasped the alchemist lowering his aromatic defence in astonishment.

'That's them,' she replied. 'Took me a while to find 'em too in that place, specially as some mutt of a terrier kept snappin' at me. Oh, but when I did – it fair broke my heart to disturb 'em. Ever so peaceful they looked, a-lying next to one another, like an old pair o' well worn slippers. They were hand in hand an' such sweet smiles on both their faces. When I go that's the way I'd choose.'

'Was it the plague?'

'Lor' bless you yes, but it weren't easy to discover, I can tell you. Not with that perishin' little dog yappin' and bitin' at my heels. Still, he won't be barkin' any more.'

'Why not?' This question was from Will.

'You got ears ain'tcha?' she snorted. 'What d'you think all the racket's been about this day? They're killin' all the dogs an' cats they can find – in case it's them what're spreadin' the disease. Givin' 'em a good wallopin' they are. Hoo, hoo, there'll be some nice furry mittens to be 'ad by the end o' the week I can tell you.'

'That's horrible.'

'Not as 'orrible as what I 'ad to deal with after I'd done wi' the Gobtrots. Ooh, what a stink and what a sight! Would you believe it – there's all these folk droppin' like flies wi' the plague and he goes an' swigs venom just like that.'

She put her hands on her hips and advanced towards Doctor Spittle. The old man took a few steps backwards and banged his head against the wall. Peg came closer and he waved the nosegay to and fro until it fell to pieces.

'Imagine it,' she said, her scarlet lips almost smiling at the gruesome memory, 'all that time locked away and no one knowing he was dead. Must've been there for months by the state of him. Never 'ave I seen a corpse like it an' I hope never to again. He should've been in the ground a long time ago. When I pulled back his bedcurtains I nearly died meself and almost fell on top of him. There he was, all laid out regal like, his clothes were still lovely – must have had a bit of money from the feel of 'em. An' all around him were heaps o' other fine clothes. I tell you it was as different from the other place I'd been to as it's possible to be. There were golden silks, wine-red velvets, silver lace, boots of the best Spanish leather – coo, I wish I'd known him when he was alive.'

'No doubt,' interrupted Doctor Spittle. 'Now I must bid you good day, mistress, we have much to do.' He ducked out of her reach and busied himself at the counter.

Peggy Blister shrugged. 'Took poison he did,' she concluded. 'There was a bottle of the stuff on the table by the bed. Still, maybe it's a good thing I didn't know him. If we'd have wed I'd 'ave been Peggy Lingley – sounds like a pig being sick, dunnit?'

Will held his breath and Doctor Spittle stood stock still. 'What did you say?' muttered the old man. 'Who took the poison?'

'Feller called Lingley,' she replied. 'Only someone told me he'd been a Lord or summat once.'

'Then he's dead!' cried the alchemist in disbelief.

'Was when I left him,' Peg laughed.

The significance of this was not lost upon the old man. If Francis was not disguised as a plague doctor – then who or what *was*? With a wail he ran from the shop and raced to the attic.

'What's ailed him then?' asked Peg.

Doctor Spittle flung the crimson door wide open and pelted inside. 'You're right!' he shouted, snatching the bottle from the shelf. 'I am doomed – Death has set a watch upon me. One night soon he will drag me away!'

'Death comes to most of us in the end,' returned the spirit.

'What do you mean, *most*?' shrieked the alchemist. 'All must perish at some time – but I had thought I could stave off that day for a while longer.'

The blue light welled up and the face of Magnus

Zachaire took on a cunning and crafty look. 'I meant what I said,' he told him, 'there is a way to cheat Death.'

The old man ceased his frantic babblings. 'What do you mean?' he asked.

'There is only one way thou canst spare thyself from the Black Death, Elias.'

'Is this a trick?' Doctor Spittle howled. 'How can you mock me so?'

'I speak only the truth,' assured the spirit. 'Hast thou never heard of the elixir of life?'

'It is an alchemical myth!'

'Was the Philosopher's Stone also a myth?'

'Can it be true then?' breathed the alchemist.

'Verily. Discover the elixir and thou wilt be saved.'

Doctor Spittle slumped into his chair and cradled his head in his hands. 'But how am I to find it?' he wept. 'All my life I have pursued the Stone and given no thought to the elixir. A man can only devote his time on this earth to one dream.'

'Exactly,' returned Magnus craftily. 'Thou wert foolish to chase the Stone. I was wiser, however.'

The alchemist took his hands from his face. 'You?' he stammered. 'Are you saying that you discovered it – but you died?'

'I died in water,' the spirit told him. 'The elixir is made from the elements of fire and water – and as such either of these retain the power to kill.'

'Tell me more!' insisted the old man.

By the hearth, Imelza stared at the door which Doctor Spittle had neglected to close. For the first time since her arrival she saw a chance to escape. She tensed her muscles and glanced quickly at the alchemist – he was too engrossed to notice her.

At her side Dab felt her mother stiffen. Curiously she raised her head. 'What is it?' she asked.

'Look, child!' Imelza hissed. 'The way is open to us now.'

The tortoiseshell stared at the door then turned back to her mother. 'What . . . what do you mean?' she murmured.

'Escape, child,' returned the ginger cat. 'We can flee from this place and follow the wild way. You can be a hunter at last.'

Dab's heart sank; this was the time she had been dreading. The attic was the only place she knew.

Imelza pushed her with the tip of her nose and urgently whispered, 'Tell your brothers. We leave at once, before the human can lock us in again.'

Dab stared at her unhappily. 'Must we go, Mother?' she asked. 'Are we not safe here? Are we not fed?'

Imelza snarled and her eyes shone fiercely. 'Hearken to me, daughter,' she spat, 'if I have to spend another night in this foul den then I shall go mad. It is bad enough that I am penned in, but that rat up there tortures me to the brink of despair.' A shudder passed through her and her tail switched back and forward. 'Would you see me driven insane, child?' she cried. 'You have never seen a hunter lose control. I have; he is not responsible for his actions. He kills wantonly and without thought.' She lowered her eyes and in a strained voice sobbed, 'If it were to happen to me then I would surely murder anything my claws could rip apart – even you, child, though it would rack me with remorse. There is no reason in madness. Now, do as I say – tell your brothers.'

Dab hurried away; she was too terrified to disobey. Jupiter was sitting by the alchemist's feet and she swerved round the old human to call to him.

'What is it?' her brother grumbled when he heard his name. 'What do you want?'

The tortoiseshell wiped her nose with her paw and sniffed. 'Get ready to leave,' she told him. 'Mother says we're to escape.'

Jupiter flicked his ears. 'I'm not going,' he said. 'There's too much for me to learn in here; the outside world cannot teach me the things I want to know.'

'But you must come!' she insisted. 'We can't split up.'

'I will not leave my master,' he said flatly. 'Now go while you have the chance.'

Dab shook her head; she hardly knew Jupiter any more. If he did not want to come then she could not force him. Reluctantly she left and ran to the far corner of the room.

'Leech!' she called into the shadows.

A pair of livid green eyes appeared in the depths of the gloom.

'Come quickly,' she cried, 'Mother and I are leaving.'

The eyes widened then became narrow. 'Is Jupiter going?' the sneering voice asked.

'No,' returned his sister.

'Then neither am I.'

'But why? I thought you would be glad to get away from him.'

'I will not leave him to discover more of the magic arts,' the runt replied. 'Those secrets should be mine. No, I remain here.'

Large tears tricked down Dab's lovely face. 'Please,' she begged.

'Hurry, sister,' Leech warned, 'the human has noticed his error. I see him take the door key from his pocket – your escape will be shortlived indeed.'

Dab spun round. Sure enough Doctor Spittle was rising from the chair and a key was in his hand.

'Mother!' she cried.

Imelza glanced up as the old man ran to the exit. Swiftly she leapt to her feet and sprang for the door.

'No you don't!' bawled the alchemist as he gave the door an almighty kick.

But she was too quick and was already racing down the stairs.

'Wait!' shouted Dab hurtling forward.

The door smashed into its frame then bounced out again. Doctor Spittle cursed and thrust it home. A shrill scream issued from the tortoiseshell as it trapped her back legs and held her firm.

'Another one who'd like to run?' squawked the old man furiously. He stooped down to drag the cat back inside.

'Help!' cried Dab as the strong hands gripped her.

From his place by the chair, Jupiter dashed forward and wasted no time – he could not let anything happen to his sister. Heedless of the consequences he ran headlong into the alchemist's legs. Doctor Spittle yowled and toppled backwards.

Dab was free; without pausing to thank her brother she pelted after Imelza as fast as she could.

Peggy Blister handed Will the money for the spices she had bought and he counted it carefully – it was a penny short.

The woman sucked the air between her clenched teeth and gave it to him grudgingly. 'Oh well,' she said huffily, 'I've a whole family in Fish Street to see next. With any luck they'll all be dead and I'll get pots o' money.'

She sauntered to the entrance and, with a toss of her head, opened the door.

At once two streaks hurtled over the floor and darted between her legs.

'Eeeee!' screeched Peg, her face cracking and falling in powdery fragments to the ground. 'What was that?'

Will hastened to the door and looked down the alley. 'Our cats,' he cried. 'They were two of our cats.'

Peg let loose a raucous laugh. 'Well they'll not last long out there!' she hooted. 'Not today they won't.'

Imelza ran like the wind; out into the great wild world she bolted. The warm sunshine burned on her back and the humid air of the city streamed through her fur. Down the lanes she sped – a blur of orange tearing over the cobbles. It was wonderful to be free. She could hardly believe it. After all those months of imprisonment her head became giddy with the joy of it all and she threw back her head in rapture.

Some distance behind, Dab chased after. The tortoiseshell had never run anywhere before and she enjoyed the new sensation. She bounded along, stretching her legs as much as she could, and gazing about her with interest. The noise of the city filled her ears. So this was what the outside was like, she marvelled. From the small window of the attic she had often looked down upon the rooftops of London. From that lofty position it had all seemed smaller somehow. Now those same buildings reared up on either side and the maze of roads and streets opened before her.

Imelza was just a tail that bobbed ever further away and Dab began to be afraid. If she lost sight of her mother then she would never find her again in this strange warren of a place. Her limbs began to tire and the breath rattled in her throat.

'Wait!' she called, panic-stricken. 'Mother, please!'

But the marmalade cat was caught up in the excitement that her new-found freedom had brought. Nothing filled her mind except the need to be as far from the apothecary shop as possible. Under carts, over barrels and through the people she raced. It was exhilarating and she gave no thought to her daughter who was now far behind.

'Cat!' bellowed an ugly brute of a man. In his hand he carried a spade and as Imelza rushed towards him he brought it crashing down. Sparks flew off the road as the blade struck the stones but the cat was too quick.

She zig-zagged round, darting out before an approaching coach, weaving between the iron-shod hooves and charging between the clattering wheels.

The horse whinnied in fright and reared up, tossing its head and kicking the air. The driver cursed, the whip cracked, and the passenger within went sprawling from the seat, fell out of the door and spilled on to the road.

Imelza did not turn back to see the chaos she had caused. The uproar blared in her ears but on she went.

Nothing could stop her now; all her old instincts were returning and the wildness burned in her blood, spurring her on. Liberty was hers at last – she could stalk through the night and hunt as before. She yelled with delight and rocketed round a corner.

Too late did she see the danger. Too late did she see the crowd of people with sticks in their hands and murder in their eyes, and too late did she think to turn back.

Her claws clattered and scraped on the ground as she scrabbled and skidded to a halt.

'Get it!' screeched a harsh voice.

Imelza whirled about, but the way back was cut off. More of the creatures closed in and she hissed with dismay as their shadows fell upon her.

A savage kick thrust her into the centre of the mob. She was completely trapped and, as the sticks and cudgels were raised, she knew all hope was gone. With a final mew of despair the light of the sun was denied to her and countless, grim faces towered above.

The people guffawed as they carried out their deadly work and Imelza's terrified screams were lost amid their clamorous voices.

Breathlessly Dab hurried past the horse as it stamped and blew. Just as the coachman had pacified both it and his bruised passenger, the sweating beast saw the tortoiseshell race by and it reared up again.

Dab turned the blind corner and stumbled to a standstill. It was a ghastly sight that she beheld.

The thronging mass of people were cheering and throwing their weapons into the air and to Dab's undying horror something else was being flung up with them.

'Mother!' she cried. 'Mother!'

Like some pathetic rag-doll, Imelza's broken body was tossed over the heads of the mob with as little regard as they might show to an old hat.

Dab was rooted to the spot and could not avert her eyes. A violent, terrible shudder racked her and she almost burst with grief.

A numb chill washed over the tortoiseshell as she gaped and stared. It was the most hideous moment of her young life but she was too petrified to escape from it.

'Another 'un!' shouted one of the vicious crowd. All the ugly faces turned to look at her and Dab quailed.

'Grind it into the dust!' the people shrieked.

Finally the bonds of fear fell from Dab's muscles and she shook herself.

'Here's a lovely,' said a voice behind her.

She spun on her heel but it was no use. A strong hand grabbed the scruff of her neck and she was roughly plucked from the ground.

A spindly man with a dirty beard and no shoes upon his feet held the squirming cat aloft and swung it round his head. 'Here it is!' he called to the others. 'A lovely bit o' trimmin' you could get off it too – if the skin's still in one piece at the finish.'

Dab wailed piteously and her claws raked the wind. The man's grip pinched her and the world lurched round sickeningly. Her beautiful amber eyes were wide with horror as the mob advanced.

'Chuck her over!' they shouted.

The man crowed with black mirth and he threw the cat to the waiting executioners. 'Off to the slaughter with you!' he cackled.

The tortoiseshell tumbled through the air, her tail fluttering behind like that of a kite. With a roar from the crowd she fell in their midst and they waved their sticks once more.

Dab whined with pain; she had landed awkwardly and her leg hurt. A stout stick came splintering down beside her and she leapt back in fright as another bludgeoned the ground.

'Kill it!' the call rippled through the people. 'It's us or them! Kill the cursed moggy!'

A hundred clubs and cudgels pounded around the shivering animal, the deafening racket rang in her ears and the street trembled at the violence. And then the first of them struck her and everything went black as Dab collapsed in the dirt.

'Stop!' came a stern, commanding voice.

A hush descended over the crowd as they turned to see who had dared speak against them. But then a murmur of surprise and apprehension issued from their lips.

'A plague doctor!' they whispered. 'What do he want?'

The sinister figure pushed its way through with ease, for no one was brave enough to withstand the glance of those round glass eyes, and the long beak seemed to scythe through them. Hastily they pulled back and a clear path opened for the newcomer who strode purposefully to the centre of the malicious gathering.

'Deliver the poor animal to me!' the muffled voice demanded.

A sneering youth with a squint eyed the tortoiseshell angrily. His stick was poised to deliver a crushing blow and he resented this interference. He wanted blood; he had already killed five dogs and three cats that day and no one was going to stop him doing the same to this one. He stared defiantly into the large glass eyes that covered the plague doctor's face – it didn't frighten him. With a venomous growl rumbling in his throat the lad spat at the stranger's booted feet. 'Nark it!' he cried and brought the stick swinging down.

A black gauntlet flashed out and caught the youth on his chin. Before he knew what had happened the stick was knocked from his grasp and he went sprawling on his back. The black figure of the plague doctor stepped over him and from the sharp beak the voice said, 'Have a care, boy. I have the authority to drag you into the pest-house with me if I wish. So do not provoke me or I shall surely leave you there and the pestilence will take you.'

There was no answer to that. The blustering courage had drained out of the youth and he clicked his jaw back into position, then scarpered.

The plague doctor knelt down and, with one deft movement, scooped up the limp and motionless body of Dab. Then stepping through the silent crowd, the striking figure marched out of sight, dissolving into the shimmering summer haze.

10

The Plague Doctor

Will hurried along Cheapside, Peggy Blister's shrill laughter echoing in his ears. He had to find the cats before something dreadful happened to them. It was not difficult to follow the trail for the traders were still muttering in their wake and a coachman struggled with his whinnying horse. The boy turned down Fryday Street and thus came upon the mob.

They were mooning around and grumbling against the plague doctor who had spoiled their fun. They dragged their feet through the dust and their weapons trailed behind. Only one stick was held aloft and from its sharpened point a limp ginger body dangled.

Will uttered a cry of dismay.

The crowd took no notice of the boy; they were shuffling about – not sure what to do next. Now that their quarry had been taken they were aimless and bereft of purpose. As they ambled past him Will peered amongst them, but there was no sign of Dab.

'Excuse me,' he said to a sharp-featured woman, 'was there another cat with that one? A tortoiseshell?'

The ferret face glared at him. 'What if there were?' she snapped, turning her back and plodding away.

'Lovely skin on it that one had,' another voice began.

Will looked up; the bearded man who had thrown Dab into the crowd was stroking his whiskers and regarding him suspiciously.

'What happened to her?' the boy asked.

The man kicked the dirt with his bare toes. 'Plague doctor snatched it,' he blurted with indignation. 'Things have come pretty low if'n folk can't have a jest or two.'

'Which way did he take her?'

A grubby finger pointed down the street. 'Over there, somewhere – were too hazy to be sure. But don't you go after, lad, I done heard unsettlin' tales o' them doctors.' But the boy was already running and did not hear him.

Swiftly Will hurried down the sun-baked streets, drawing ever closer to the wide Thames.

Trinity Lane was a narrow, dismal place. The houses on either side leaned out over the road so much that the windows of their second storeys were only a few feet apart. Only a slender ribbon of light ever touched the ground between those misshapen buildings and even in the fierce brightness of high summer the cramped way looked dark and chill.

Will came running into the lane just in time to see

the plague doctor march up to a low doorway. The boy nipped behind a rain barrel as the alarming, beaked face turned left and right to see if anyone was watching. The glassy eyes peered into the surrounding gloom then pushed the door open. Will raised his head as the nightmare figure entered and, there in the gauntleted hands, he saw a snatch of tortoiseshell fur. The plague doctor passed within and the door was closed behind.

Minutes crept by and Will tried to form some kind of a plan. What if he were to dash inside, take Dab from her abductor and race back to the apothecary? 'No,' he murmured to himself, 'that won't work. The plague doctor'll be stronger than I am. Besides, as soon as he hears the door open he'll come to see who's there.'

But then a latch rattled and when he peeked over the barrel he saw the figure emerge from the building, walk down the lane and vanish round a corner. Dab was nowhere to be seen.

'She must still be inside,' Will told himself. He took one more look at the empty street then dashed out of hiding.

The door was frail: one good kick and the lock would splinter away from the wood. Will forced it open and, with a groaning shudder, it swung on its rusty hinges.

A long, dreary hall stretched before him, at the far end of which was another doorway. The boy hesitated for a moment, as his nostrils met the stuffy air – it smelled of dry decay. The panelling of the hall was rotten with age and beetles burrowed into the grain, chewing the wood and spitting out sawdust. The tunnels and bore-holes branched through the panels like arteries and Will had the impression that he was gazing down the throat of some enormous forest spirit.

Taking a deep breath he entered. Great flakes and splinters littered the floor round his feet and the relentless scurrying of hungry, destructive insects moved through the soft heaps.

Down the passage he hurried and when he came to the far door, he found to his relief that it was unlocked. Slowly he turned the handle and pushed it open.

The room beyond was filled with light; the rear wall housed a large window and through this the sun dazzled and blinded, glittering over the floating dust particles in a wide, brilliant sweep. Squinting, Will gazed round – the chamber reminded him of the alchemist's workroom. Bottles and jars filled shelves and covered tables, books were neatly stacked in a long row and curious instruments gleamed in the sunlight. But this place had a more wholesome feel to it; here there was an order unknown in Doctor Spittle's attic – everything was arranged with a deliberate tidiness, even the floor had been scrubbed clean.

As Will entered, it was like leaving one world and passing into another. The room contrasted violently with the outer hall; he could not imagine any beetle daring to invade this territory. Even the air was sweeter here – a faint fragrance of flowers and perfumed herbs scented the atmosphere.

Then Will saw what he had come for. Dab was lying on a high table in the full glare of the sunshine. The warm rays picked out the honey-coloured speckles in her fur and set them blazing like veins of gold. By her head a saucer of milk had been placed and a bandage bound her leg – but the cat was motionless.

Will rushed over and lightly touched her head. A beautiful, amber eye flickered open and the tortoiseshell managed a pitiful mew.

'There now,' the boy said soothingly, 'don't you worry. I'll take you back to your brothers.'

Shakily, Dab raised her head and stared about her. She was confused and bewildered. Then, in a sickening rush, it all came back. 'Mother!' she cried.

Will felt her anguish and the cat began to tremble as the awful memory returned. She beheld the savage weapons beating her mother into the ground and the screams of Imelza rose once more to torment her.

The boy saw her wince and was saddened to see great tears spring from her eyes. 'Come on now,' he comforted, 'shush. Everything's going to be fine.' Will slipped his hand under her stomach and gently lifted her into his arms. 'Let's leave,' he said briskly, 'before—'

'Before I return?' snapped a stern voice.

Will whipped round and there, barring the door, was the plague doctor.

Dab hissed when she saw the nightmarish face and wriggled to be set free. Will could only stammer before the terrifying figure; the eyes behind the glass lenses were magnified to a horrible size and they glared at him accusingly. His courage disappeared as the door was closed and the key turned in the lock.

Will's heart pounded; what would become of him now?

The plague doctor seemed to be studying him. Seconds ticked by as those hideously large pupils pinned him to the spot like some puny insect beneath a microscope. The tension crackled through the air and it seemed to Will that the whole world had become silent, listening and waiting for the outcome of this meeting. It was so quiet that he could hear his own heart thumping in his chest and the slight breathing of the plague doctor through the herb-filled beak.

And then, the tension was relaxed, diffused with one shrug of the sinister figure's shoulders. 'Enough,' it said. 'The time has come for you to know the truth.'

The plague doctor bent its head and unlaced the hideous mask. With sweating palms Will watched as the beak was thrown on to the table, followed by the lenses. Then, with a toss of the head the heavy cowl was removed and a mass of golden curls was shaken free.

The boy stared blankly, too astonished to utter a word.

'Aren't you going to say hello, then?' asked the plague doctor with a wide grin.

'Molly!' he gasped eventually.

The pretty young woman laughed to see Will so confounded. 'You should see your face,' she told him.

'But . . . why?' he spluttered. 'What is the disguise for?'

'It is no disguise, Will,' she said pulling the gauntlets from her small white hands, 'but it does conceal my sex. How else would I be allowed to help those suffering from the pestilence? At least as a plague doctor I can give them some comforts. You know that I have a knowledge of medicines; I have always been interested in the healing virtues of certain herbs. In some small way I can give aid to those in need, but I am compelled to hide the fact that I am a woman to do so.' She shook her head bitterly. 'We are only fit for serving our lords and masters and looking decorative. An intelligent woman is a freak of nature and a dangerous threat to civilisation, Will.'

The boy said nothing; he was thinking of the alchemist and what he had seen from the attic window. 'Have you been watching old Spittle?' he asked suddenly.

Molly nodded as she took Dab from his arms and set her upon the table once more. 'I think her leg is broken,' she said. 'The creature must be in great distress. I was too late to save the mother and nearly didn't rescue this one in time. Is it not alarming how brutal people can be? Did you mark the faces of the mob back there? They were almost animals themselves. Fear does that, Will, and fear is born of ignorance – remember that.'

'But why were you watching the old man?' he persisted.

The golden head remained bent over the tortoiseshell as she struggled to find a way of explaining it all. Then Molly looked steadily into his eyes. 'Do you remember the last time we met?' she asked quietly.

'I could hardly forget,' he replied. 'You changed and became – horrible.'

Molly pursed her lips. 'Forgive me that,' she said, 'but you see, I had suffered a tremendous shock – John Balker was my father.'

There was a painful silence in which neither said anything. Then Will frowned. 'So you're really Molly

Balker,' he muttered slowly, 'but why did he never mention you?'

She sighed and sat on the table. 'My true name is Margaret Balker,' she said. 'I took the name Molly to hide from him. It was a long time ago now, you would have been a baby when I left. After the death of my mother, Father turned in upon himself, blaming everyone for her loss. He was a strict Puritan in those days, and my life – well it was not the happiest. His grief and loneliness was like a canker that ate him away. Many times I suffered at his bitter hands.'

She paused and her face clouded over at the memory of it. 'In the end I could bear it no longer and fled from Adcombe and my father. London seemed a goodly-sized place where a maid might hide herself and not be discovered, so I journeyed here.'

'And you never saw him since?'

'Only once,' she murmured. 'About five years ago he found me and tried to drag me back to the village. He was a pig-headed man in some ways you know. Fortunately the gentleman I was with at the time saw him off. I can still hear my father cursing and damning me; he said then that I was no longer his daughter and he would never return – I was . . . dead to him.' She fell silent and lowered her moist eyes.

'But he did return,' Will put in. 'He did come back for you and when he died your name was on his lips.'

'Was it?' she asked in a husky voice.

'Yes,' assured Will, 'and I remember that in the tavern when he mentioned you it was with regret and remorse.'

Molly wiped her eyes. 'Then maybe he had changed. Perhaps this time, if he had asked instead of demanding, I would have returned with him. I certainly have nothing to hold me here. I am not proud of the life I have been leading, Will, but I do what I can to relieve the misery of others. At least I have my wits and am not afraid to use them; there are doxies enough with only fluff in their skulls.

'When you told me that my father was dead, I knew that I was responsible for he would not have come if I were not here. Ever since that morning when I treated you harshly and demanded to know everything about that fatal night, I have taken it upon myself to find his murderers.'

'Jessel and Carver?'

'Yes – although it was not easy at first. Questions are never welcome amongst thieves and knaves. I met with many a sharp rebuke and on one occasion I feel sure that had I been a man I would have had my throat cut. Jack Carver and the one called Jessel went to ground once they got word that someone was looking for them. It was as if they had never existed; no trace of them could I find and the folk of the streets would clam up tighter than a Tyburn noose when they saw me coming.'

'So you never found them?'

A curious light gleamed in her eyes. 'I despaired of ever bringing them to justice,' she replied, picking up the grotesque mask and turning it over in her hands. 'And then the sickness began,' she murmured. 'I took up the mantle of plague doctor merely to aid those stricken, but, wonder of wonders – I discovered that I could go anywhere, into any house without question or suspicion. Then, one night fortune smiled on me. There was a mean lodging house in Smithfield shut up with pestilence and I went to give them aid. Nine people there were locked in that building and, to my astonishment and delight, amongst their number was one of the men I sought.'

'Carver?' Will gasped.

'Jessel,' she corrected. 'He was close to death but in his ravings I gleaned what information I could.' Molly paused and nibbled her lip distractedly. 'It was not pleasant work, listening to his crazed rantings, but what I learned was worth the vigil.'

Will leaned forward, enthralled by her tale. 'So do you now know where Jack Carver is?' he asked.

The young woman shook her head. 'No, but Jessel told me that both he and Carver were in the pay of another – somebody had employed them to kill my father.'

The boy stared at her in disbelief. 'But why?' he cried. 'John Balker had no enemies; he was shrewd in business and liked his ale, but no one hated him enough to want him dead. It makes no sense.'

'I don't know *why*,' Molly replied, 'but I do know *who*.' She looked Will squarely in the face and said, 'Jessel informed me that an apothecary had paid them to do the deed.'

'Spittle?' Will whispered in surprise.

'Who else?'

'But that is not possible, he didn't even know John.'

Molly gave a weary sigh. 'This is a muddy business,' she said, 'and the more I find out the murkier it becomes. Yet in time I am certain all things shall become clear.'

'So that's why you've been watching him!' Will declared.

'Yes, once I knew he was involved I began to keep an eye on old Spittle. Remember when I told you that he would not harm you? Well I believe I was wrong in that judgement. I am only just learning about our precious apothecary and the knowledge is far from comfortable. You had better take care.'

The boy shifted uneasily. 'I can look after myself,' he mumbled.

Molly stared at his bruised lip and arched her eyebrows. 'Yes, I can see that,' she said, 'but hear me when I say that I believe you are in great danger if you remain at that shop.'

Will gave a grim laugh; if she only knew about the powers the man possessed. 'I have no choice but to stay there,' he said.

'If I could find Carver,' Molly muttered, 'I would certainly learn the truth then. Unfortunately there is still no word of his whereabouts. If I could only contrive a way of getting him to confess to the murder whilst incriminating Doctor Spittle. Then we could get the old monster arrested and brought before a Justice.'

Will shrugged doubtfully. 'He'd find a way out of that,' he said. 'You haven't seen him when he's angry; that wretch is as artful and as full of deceit as the first serpent. It would take more than prison bars to hold that one.'

A plaintive mew from the table interrupted him. Dab was lapping the milk from the saucer and Will watched her in silence – he had almost forgotten she was there.

'I must get back to the shop,' he said quickly. 'If I am missed, Spittle will make my life even more miserable than it is now.'

'Must you return?' asked Molly. 'He won't find you here – why go back to that terrible place?'

'I must. Trust me when I tell you that he has ways of finding me – he will search me out and once caught ... I daren't think what might happen.' Tenderly he took Dab in his arms and made for the door. 'Should you discover Jack Carver,' he said, 'I would like to know. Your father was a dear friend.'

Molly smiled. 'If I hear anything, I'll tell you,' she promised.

Will pulled at the door – it was still locked. Molly laughed and threw him the key, then he was gone.

Fortunately for Will the alchemist had not stepped out of the attic since Imelza and Dab had escaped, and for the first time his wrath had been vented on Jupiter.

'Turn against me, would you?' he screeched, hurling a book at his familiar. 'Well, I'll not stand for such rebellion.'

Jupiter howled in surprise as the toe of a boot struck him hard in the stomach and forced the breath from his lungs. He leapt away and hid under the table, quaking with shock.

The alchemist scowled and sat in the chair. 'This is the thanks I receive for saving their miserable lives,' he grumbled rubbing the back of his legs where Jupiter's claws had dug into him.

'Does it matter?' asked Magnus. 'Are there not other, weightier concerns to attend to now?'

Doctor Spittle glanced up. 'The elixir you mean?'

'Thou ought to commence thy labours at once, for the sickness shall surely find thee.'

'Yes,' the old man agreed, staring out of the window

as his old fears returned. 'I must begin – tell me what I should do.'

In the shadowy corner by the door Leech laughed to himself. He could see his brother cowering under the table and it gladdened his heart. 'Now you know how it feels, brother dear,' he gloated. 'What merry sport it was to see you running with his boot up your hind parts for a change.'

Jupiter heard the runt's scorn but took no notice. Leech could be dealt with later – when the old man had retired to his bedchamber.

A knock at the door broke into all their thoughts. Doctor Spittle looked up from his notes. 'What is it?' he barked tetchily.

'Tis only me sir,' said Will upon entering. 'I've brought this one back.' He held up Dab for the alchemist to see. The old man's brows bristled at the sight of the cat and Will knew he meant to punish her. Quickly he told him the lie that he had prepared.

'Nearly got out she did; I couldn't stop her mother but I managed to prevent this one. How dare she try to leave – after all we've done for her too. Did you hear the rumpus we had, sir? I was very cross with this scrawny little moggy, battered her I did – only maybe I went too far. She's broke her leg, see. I never meant for that to happen; still, I don't think she'll try it again.'

Doctor Spittle pursed his lips and regarded the boy for a long time. 'So, you bandaged her damaged limb,' he said drily.

'Yes,' assured Will, 'I did the best I could, though I fancy you could have done better.'

The alchemist reached out as if to inspect the

bindings more closely; instead he gave the injured leg a vicious squeeze and yanked it hard.

Dab screamed in agony, leapt from Will's arms and hobbled over to Leech.

A satisfied smile crossed the old man's face. 'Merely testing your story,' he said, 'and I see that that much is true. She has indeed suffered a grievous blow. I did not realise you had such cruelty in you, my young dog.' His tone was sarcastic but he waved aside his doubts. 'At least she did not venture outside,' he muttered, 'for I would never have allowed her back had she done so. Now hearken to me, dog, if the mother returns then you are to deny her entry. She must not be permitted to bring the contagion into this place. Kill her if need be but she must not come in.'

Will nodded. 'Have no fears, sir,' he answered with a curious certainty, 'she will not be coming back.'

The alchemist dismissed him and the boy bowed, closed the door behind him and went down to the shop, pleased that he had saved Dab a further beating.

Doctor Spittle stared at the tortoiseshell and his eyes narrowed. 'And yet,' he murmured, 'I should dearly like to know where the lad learnt to bandage and splint an injury so expertly, for I did not teach him.' With a twitching brow he bent over his papers and resumed work.

Dab drew close to her brother, her eyes brimming with tears.

Leech stepped slightly away. 'Are all humans cruel then?' he asked. 'Would that I could claw both young and old to shreds.'

Through a series of sobs, Dab told him the truth. 'It was not the boy who did this,' she choked, 'he said that to spare me the old one's anger. You see Leech, I *did* escape into the wide world – but it was a horrific nightmare.' And she relapsed into a further fit of weeping.

'Then what really happened to you?' the runt asked.

Dab sniffed and rubbed her raw eyes. 'It was the people,' she said. 'A great crowd of them tried to kill me. They had sticks and were mad with the lust for murder.' She hesitated, searching for the words in which to tell him the terrible news. 'I . . . I was not the first to suffer at their hands,' she uttered in a small voice.

Leech stared at his sister, until his sly green eyes widened as he guessed what had happened. 'Where is Mother?' he cried in alarm. 'Where is she?'

The tortoiseshell took his paw and her tears fell upon it. 'Mother is . . . dead,' she breathed. 'The humans seized her and beat the life from her body.'

'No!' came a strangled shriek.

They both turned and there was Jupiter. He had heard everything that had been said. 'It cannot be!' he shouted. 'You lie, sister – Mother lives, tell me that is so!'

'It is no lie,' Dab said bitterly. 'I saw them toss her into the air like you would a mouse.'

Jupiter crawled away, too shocked to say any more.

Leech sneered. 'What does he feel the most I wonder?' he muttered. 'The loss of our mother, or dismay at the behaviour of his beloved humans? Our brother disgusts me.'

'We should not quarrel at a time like this,' Dab said sadly. 'We ought to support one another. We have only ourselves now; we are alone in the world, three orphans.' And she cried into her paw.

The shining green eyes of Leech glowed with menace. 'One day,' he growled, 'I shall avenge you, Mother, and all humankind will pay – this I swear.'

In the following weeks the plague continued to rage. All the dogs and cats were destroyed and the loss of their voices left the night woefully silent. Only the death bells spoke in the hollow darkness now.

July came and with it Will's twelfth birthday, but the occasion passed without any celebration and Will stared sorrowfully at the gloves he had received the previous year from his late mother.

Under the guidance of Magnus Zachaire, Doctor Spittle worked unceasingly on his experiments. A dreadful sense of doom and foreboding had fallen on the alchemist and he felt that time was running out. To his astonishment, preparing the elixir was comparatively easy and, at the end of the third week since he had begun, all was ready.

Another blazing hot day scorched London. It was not an uncommon sight to see the abandoned carcass of a pig or horse lie neglected in the road. Eventually they swelled and burst in the blistering heat and the stink rose into the clear heavens.

In his workroom Doctor Spittle poured a golden liquid into a jar and watched the steam rise off it. Sitting in the chair, he rested his chin in his hands and a look of wonder resided on his features.

'Can this truly be the elixir of life?' he breathed with reverence. 'Does this jar now contain the essence of eternity? To think that the dream of the ancients is now before me. This is a most holy moment, my familiar.'

Jupiter sat at the old man's feet. Since the day of Imelza's escape, the love between the alchemist and his cat had been cooler than before. But in the end, due to his yearning for knowledge, Jupiter had swallowed his pride and fawned once more to his master.

'Verily this shall protect thee from the pestilence without,' came the spirit's voice. 'Thy span of life shall be increased a thousand-fold. Through the long ages yet to come thy feet shall tread and miracles undreamed of will unfold before thee.'

A delighted gurgle, like that of an amused child, erupted from the alchemist. He clapped his hands together and nodded joyously.

'How much longer till it is ready?' he asked impatiently.

'The time is now, Elias,' whispered Magnus. 'Drink of that nectar and become immortal. There is naught thou canst not achieve – the world shalt be thine.'

Doctor Spittle held out a quivering hand. The jar trembled when he took it and a precious drop spilled on to the table. The light that streamed through the small attic window flooded through the golden liquid and played upon the alchemist's face. It was a tremendous moment; he would rise above everyone, nothing would he fear and anything he desired would be his. The old man's lips were dry as the jar drew close to his mouth. The fulfilment of his heart was nigh and all his senses were tuned to this one action.

'Drink, Elias,' urged the spirit.

The alchemist tilted the jar to let the miraculous solution disappear down his throat. As the elixir seeped over his lips, a faint chuckle sounded from Magnus.

Doctor Spittle's half closed eyes snapped open. He saw the eager smile on the spirit's face and suspicion engulfed his mind.

The jar slammed on to the table and the old man spat on to the floor then wiped his mouth on his sleeve.

'Whatever is wrong, Elias?' asked Magnus innocently. 'Can it be thou hast no faith in me?'

The alchemist opened his mouth and aired his tongue – there was something faintly bitter on his lips and they began to sting.

He grasped the spirit bottle and shook it violently. 'Have you betrayed me?' he cried. 'Would you murder me with poison, you untrustworthy soul?'

But Magnus replied, 'Peace Elias, thou knowest that to achieve immortality thou must endure an ordeal. Perfection is only attainable by taking great risks – the blackened beast will only be filled by the scarlet hue of life everlasting after severe hardship.'

'I know that!' screamed Doctor Spittle kicking back the chair and jumping to his feet. 'But I doubt if one is meant to be poisoned first. Death is a strange route to immortality.'

'Thy lack of faith wounds me, Elias.'

'I am only cautious,' the alchemist replied. 'There have been many times when my circumspection has saved me.' A cunning grin stole over him and he glanced up at the two rat cages. 'You must not grudge me my eccentricities, Magnus,' he said. 'Indulge me in this, I crave.'

He crossed to a cupboard and took out a strip of dried meat. This he dipped into the elixir and, standing on tiptoe, threw it into one of the cages.

Heliodorus was half asleep and dreaming of his exotic youth. A tropical sun shone down on him and his snout was filled with the aromatic scent of eastern spices. The timbers of his ship creaked and groaned on the foaming waves and the sea sparkled all around like silver fire.

He grunted contentedly, enjoying the lurch and swell of the vessel beneath him. This was the life, the only real vocation for a rat: to sail the high seas, journey to uncharted lands and taste undiscovered fruits.

In his slumber the black rat dived into a ripe melon and burrowed into its juicy heart, devouring the delicious flesh and spitting out the seeds. With shoals of tiny darting fish he swam and basked on baking white shores. As he lay there, breadcrumbed with the sand, a great fish rose out of the sea and launched itself at him.

With a startled yelp Heliodorus awoke.

The piece of dried meat landed with a bump on the floor of his cage. For a brief second he thought he was still asleep and shuffled backwards in case it really was a sea monster. But the turgid waves of his dream rippled and ebbed away as he slapped his face to gather his wits.

'What is this?' he chirruped, snouting the air and glaring at the morsel before him. 'Has it nibblesomeness and is it crunchmaking?' he asked, giving the object a tentative prod. Heliodorus looked across to the other cage and called to the brown rat within.

'Hoy, English!' he shouted. 'It is time for victuals – yes?'

Beckett stared dolefully back at him. 'Not fer me it ain't,' he whinged. 'There's you wi' that girt dollop o' stuff and here I am wi' me guts aching an' me belly grumblin'. 'Tain't fair it's not. Why ain't there none fer me?'

The black rat clicked his fingers. 'Hah!' he chortled. 'Heliodorus not eat all. He know how to share even split; on ship he learn this. Tit for tat and sharey share. I save some for you – oh yes.'

Beckett smacked his lips and clutched the bars of his cage in anticipation. For a rat, Heliodorus was really very generous.

The wanderer grabbed the dried meat in both his claws and sank his teeth into it. 'Eats very good,' he mumbled, 'nice and tasty – you will like this English, I think.'

'Don't forget to leave some then,' piped up Beckett anxiously.

Heliodorus ground his jaws together as he champed and chewed. A fair-sized chunk remained and he prepared to throw it to his jailed comrade.

But at once the meat fell from his grasp and a fierce shudder jolted down his spine.

Beckett peered at the meat longingly; was the other rat teasing him? One look at Heliodorus, however, and all thought of food vanished.

The black rat was choking. His claws flew to his throat and a horrible squeal issued from his mouth.

His entire body shook and his tail thrashed madly about the cage.

'AAARRGGHH!' he yelled. 'It blisters, it slices, it tears at me! AAARRGGHH!'

His bright, black eyes bulged hideously from their sockets and he hopped about the cage convulsed in some terrible agony. Then, to his anguish, every single hair on his body popped out of his skin and fell to the floor. A dense, dark cloud of fur drifted down from the cage as he rampaged and yelled.

Beckett drew back in fright; he had never seen him do that before. ''Ere,' he cried, 'what's got into yer?'

'Treachery! Murder! Assassins!' Heliodorus shrieked. He flung himself against the bars like a mad thing then collapsed, naked and shivering. Foam frothed from his jaws and he gibbered idiotically. 'Grogged up and land ahoy!' he croaked. 'Sail on, you laggards, there's islands to see and stars to steer by.' With his last strength he raised a feeble arm and pointed at the ceiling. The bulging eyes opened even wider as his dying breath rattled in his throat. 'Hobb!' he gasped. 'Hobb is come!' and with that Heliodorus perished.

Doctor Spittle screeched with fury. But for his caution that fate would have been his. He snatched up the spirit bottle and the blue light blazed through his fingers.

'Ha, Spittle!' scoffed Magnus. 'Didst thou really believe I would reveal unto thee the secret of the elixir? Oh foolish, credulous mortal – I scorn thee utterly!'

The alchemist was filled with wrath. 'Father of lies!' he roared. 'You shall never be released. In that bottle your felonious soul will forever be imprisoned. With

or without your help I shall cheat Death.' He thrust the bottle on to a shelf and stormed downstairs.

Beckett sniffed; the body of proud Heliodorus was already shrivelling. The venom had been potent indeed and his corpse withered swiftly.

Horrified, the brown rat watched as the skin wrinkled and shrank over the bones. He would miss the defiant traveller. 'Wot'll become of me?' he whined. 'There's just me an' them cats down there now, I'll get etted fer sure.' He wriggled uncomfortably then rubbed his shoulder against one of the bars. 'Crikey,' he mumbled, scratching himself all over, 'why fer does I itch all of a sudden?'

The last of the fleas that had fallen from Heliodorus's body leapt across the gulf between the two cages and dived into Beckett's fur.

11

At the Southwarke Mission

L eech scurried under a heap of parchments, but it was no protection, as he soon discovered. Three sharp pains pierced his tail and he squawked, tearing out from his cover and scrabbling over a brass telescope which toppled from its stand and spun across the floor.

The attic was dark; only the embers glowed in the fireplace and their radiance was too weak to reach the far wall. Under the low, sloping beams Leech frantically picked his way, stepping from one precarious foothold to another. A ghastly, bloated image reared in front of him, but it was only his reflection in the mirrored globe.

A mischievous chuckle sounded from below. 'You can't escape up there, Leech,' Jupiter told him.

The runt chanced to look behind and, sure enough,

the instruments of torture were closing fast.

They were long, sharp pins with pearl heads. Relentlessly they tapped and spiked their way forward, dancing over the obstacles with ease – their eager points gleaming ruddily.

Leech moaned and pushed on, squeezing on to the ornate shelf that held the large grinning skull.

Jupiter was practising his magic once again. This time he had cast a simple spell over the pins and the enchantment guided them with cruel intent. To jab and needle was their spiteful purpose and the runt's posterior their ultimate goal.

'The charm will pursue you until the task has been achieved,' giggled Jupiter. 'You might as well let them catch you for they will eventually. I want to see what a feline pin-cushion looks like.'

His brother whimpered, trying to squirm past the skull. But there was nowhere else to go.

Tap-tap-tap.

The pins came on, jumping with excited skips as they neared the frightened cat.

Leech's claws slid out and he struck at the oncoming menace. But the blow was feeble and went wide of the mark; he almost lost his balance and for desperate seconds teetered on the edge of the shelf.

The glinting points clattered feverishly as though in mockery of his puny efforts.

On the floor below, Jupiter watched, delighted at the amusement this spell was giving him.

'Not long now, Leech,' he sniggered. 'Two more hops and they'll have you stuck good and proper.'

'Jupiter!' scolded Dab abruptly. 'Stop it at once!' The tortoiseshell rose from her place at the hearth where she had been sleeping and darted over to him. Her hind leg had not mended properly and she now walked with a pronounced limp. 'You mustn't torment Leech!' she cried.

Her brother frowned at her. 'But it's such fun!' he laughed, 'and he deserves it – he really is horrid. Does it matter if he gets jabbed and pricked just a little bit?'

'Don't be cruel!' she said, appalled. 'What would Mother say if she were to hear you? It isn't fair to use your powers to tease him. He isn't strong you know; stop it at once.'

Jupiter stuck out his bottom lip. 'Just as the game was getting interesting too,' he grumbled. Making a sign in the air with his paw he muttered some words and cancelled the spell.

The pins above jerked and twitched as the enchantment left them and they toppled to the ground.

Dab and Jupiter leapt aside as, one by one, they fell, skewering the floorboards and quivering from the impact.

Leech stared down, his eyes burning like two green lamps that glared at Jupiter angrily.

The ginger cat padded after his sister. 'I'm sorry, Dab,' he apologised, 'I was only testing a new spell I found. I never meant anything by it – it was only a joke, honest.'

Dab went lamely to the hearth where she sat and curled her tail around her. 'It isn't me you should apologise to,' she said, 'and I doubt if Leech found the joke very amusing.'

'Who cares . . .' Jupiter began but he checked himself; he knew that his mother would. He looked at the empty place beside his sister. 'It's difficult to believe that she's really gone from us,' he murmured.

'You don't have to tell me that,' Dab responded. 'Not one moment goes by when I don't think of her. If only she could have been content to remain here.'

Jupiter held her paw in his. 'Tears won't bring her back,' he said gently.

'I know,' she agreed, 'but I don't seem to be able to stop myself. There are times when I hear those awful screams and I can't shut them out.'

Her brother hugged her tightly. 'Don't go upsetting yourself,' he said. 'She wouldn't want that now, would she? At least she died out there, free in the wild. That's better, dry your eyes and I promise to keep a tighter rein on my magic.'

'You won't torment Leech?'

'No.'

'Thank you, that is a weight off my mind. You two should try and be friends.'

Jupiter snorted. 'But he's so sneaky and sly – I don't want to be friends with him.'

'He's your brother!' Dab shook her head exasperated. 'I'm weary of you both,' she sighed, settling down to rest. 'No wonder Mother was desperate to escape. Ever since I returned I've come to realise just how much she had to keep you two apart. Sometimes I wish I had never come back the way you carry on.'

Jupiter saw the lines of care and sorrow that were already faintly traced upon her brow. Had he really put them there – was he such a trial and a worry to her? Perhaps she was right, maybe he and Leech had contributed to their mother's unease in the attic. He stared at the floor, abashed and ashamed. Tonight he abandoned his usual place on the alchemist's chair and stretched out beside his sister.

'I will try not to bully Leech,' he muttered.

'Mmm?' returned Dab as she drifted off to sleep.

A soft hissing came down from above. The livid emeralds of Leech's eyes pierced the darkness. Jupiter saw him, still balanced on the shelf near the skull. It was an opportunity too good to miss. 'I can always start being nice to him tomorrow,' Jupiter told himself, and he closed his eyes and recited an incantation.

'With all my heart I hate you!' Leech seethed softly. 'I despise you with every ounce of my being. Let darkness everlasting consume my soul and fill me with evil power that I might be revenged upon you.' His eyes shone with the malevolence that governed him and so intense was his hatred that he failed to see what was happening behind.

The large skull shuddered as the magic of Jupiter wove around it and seized control. Very slowly, the wide jaws started to open. A loose tooth rattled from the bone and bounced off the shelf. The noise disturbed Leech's concentration and he sniffed curiously. 'What was that?' he muttered. Then he became aware of the shape that loomed over his shoulder and, with dismay, he wheeled round until he was staring into the cavernous jaws.

The animal skull lifted into the air and the teeth snapped together, narrowly missing Leech's nose. He wailed and with that lost his footing. Like a shrivelled slug he dropped to the ground and landed with a crash.

Dab awoke with a start. She looked about her and guessed what Jupiter had done. The ginger cat smiled sheepishly. She threw him a despairing glance. 'Can you never stop?' she said accusingly. 'You drive me to despair; if it were possible for me to leave I surely would. You two can battle it out on your own – I've had enough.' And she hobbled into a quiet corner and settled back to sleep again.

Leech licked his bruises and crept out of sight to nurture his malignancy in the darkness.

The night clawed by, silent and brooding.

Dab slept fitfully, troubled by dark dreams and visions of Imelza. Her mind fluttered on the very edge of slumber and she uttered forlorn and fretful mews.

A distant noise wrenched her further into the waking world. Dull sounds clumped about below and on the stairs a board creaked. One of Dab's ears flicked with irritation. Slowly the key clicked in the crimson door and the handle gently turned.

Dab stirred and her eyes blinked with drowsiness; the lids were heavy but she forced them to stay open.

There, silhouetted in the doorway, was the tall figure of Doctor Spittle. He was still dressed and the smell of chemicals clung about his clothes, pervading the air with acrid fumes. The old man's face was cold and hard, but something about his eyes made Dab shake her head and stumble to her feet.

'Are you awake – my beautiful, variegated maiden?' crackled his whispering voice.

She swallowed and edged away – the deliberate menace of his tone was unmistakable.

The alchemist moved forward and his steps were stealthy and silent. 'Would you not like to help me in my experiments?' he breathed quietly.

Fear overwhelmed Dab as his shadow fell on her. She reached out to wake Jupiter but Doctor Spittle stooped to catch her.

'Help!' she cried, shuffling backward to escape the hands that came groping for her.

In his cage Beckett yawned and peered blearily down to see what had disturbed him. Immediately he sensed the terror in the air and he hid his face in his claws.

'Help!' Dab called again, but the strong hands grabbed her and closed over her mouth so she could cry out no more.

Kicking and struggling, the tortoiseshell gazed wildly at Jupiter, but he was still fast asleep. The alchemist pressed her close to his chest and, whimpering, Dab was borne from the attic.

Neither of her brothers ever heard her sweet voice again.

In the morning Jupiter awoke and for the first time in many months felt cold, for an unknown chill reached in and touched him.

'Dab!' he called, wondering where his sister had got to. There was no answer and he chewed his lip with concern. A draught ruffled his fur and he looked to see where it came from. The small attic window was open. He ran to it, filled with anxiety; she must have decided to leave after all. 'Dab!' he called again, peering over the sill – but it was no use, there was no sign of her. Jupiter groaned and a tear ran down his cheek. 'She's left us,' he said sorrowfully. 'It was all too much for her and it's my doing. She said she would go and by my pride and bullying I've driven her away, just like I did Mother.' Filled with remorse he slunk away to where Leech hid in the shadows.

'Brother,' he said woefully, 'our sister is gone.'

Leech's eyes flickered open and at once he was watchful and wary. 'Then you and I are alone now,' he hissed. 'One by one it seems our family diminishes – who shall be the next to depart?' And he purred threateningly.

'Let us fight no more,' beseeched Jupiter, 'for Dab's sake can we not be friends? For my part I am sorry for the hurts I have inflicted on you and swear never to taunt you again.'

But Leech scorned his offer of peace. 'Never will I find room in my heart for you – vile and treacherous lover of humankind. Go to your master and serve him your platitudes, I desire none of them. For the loss of my sister I shall not grieve, if she is indeed free then I envy her. Never can I depart whilst you remain alive, usurping my rightful power and place.'

So the rift between the two brothers was not healed and although Jupiter kept to his oath and never again afflicted Leech with his magic, the runt loathed him all the more.

The months wheeled by but Dab did not return. In the city anarchy reigned and those who tried to leave and flee to the country were met by frightened villagers who pelted them with stones. The churchyards of London were gorged with bodies and the gravediggers could not keep up with the burials. Over the doors of the capital the red crosses spread, until they covered the buildings like a dreadful rash.

The autumn came and winter duly followed. On a

night of November a furtive tap sounded on the window of the apothecary shop.

Will was not yet asleep and he ran to see who it was. There, peeking through the leaded panes, was Molly.

Quickly Will opened the door to let her in but she refused and remained standing in the dark alley.

'I cannot stop,' she told him breathlessly. 'I have come to bring you news, that is all.' She paused and he caught her excitement. 'I know where Jack Carver is!' she announced.

'Where?' cried Will. 'Did he tell you why they . . .?'

She waved him into silence. 'Wait,' she laughed, 'I have not yet spoken with the man. I only discovered his whereabouts this evening.' From the inside of her plague doctor's coat she took a scroll of paper and showed it to the boy.

Will scowled at it; a firm, flowing script covered the page, but he shrugged. 'I cannot read,' he admitted with embarrassment.

Molly tutted. 'Never mind, I'll tell you what it says. I wrote it some time ago – not long after my meeting with Jessel. It is a confession. It accuses old Spittle of paying those two villains to murder my father. If I can persuade Carver to sign it or make his mark then I have something to take before a Justice. I'd dearly like to see that wretched apothecary dance from the gallows.'

'But what if Carver refuses to sign? Why should he? – that confession will hang him too.'

The young woman flicked back her golden hair. 'He'll sign all right,' she said sombrely. 'Hanging'll be too late for him. By the time the assizes come round he'll have already answered to another judge.'

Will scratched his head in puzzlement, then he understood. 'Your costume,' he said. 'Then Jack Carver has the plague?'

Molly nodded grimly. 'That he has and he'll not be long in this world by what I've heard.' She tucked the scroll back inside her coat and gave Will her farewells. 'I must go now,' she told him. 'I never heard of a corpse signing anything.'

'Wait!' called Will as she turned to leave. 'Let me come too!'

The woman stared at him then shook her head. 'Don't be foolish,' she said.

But the boy's mind was resolved. 'I'm coming with you,' he told her flatly and there was no room in his tone for argument. 'This matter touches me closely,' he said. 'If we succeed then my life of servitude could be ended forever. Besides, I am not going to stay here whilst you confront Jack Carver. He is an evil rogue!'

'But Will,' she protested, 'you can't go into a pest-house. Think of the danger.'

'You venture inside those places.'

'Only wearing these clothes,' she countered. 'If you were to go without such protection you would surely die! A pest-house is not a small place, it can hold many people; all the vagabonds and poor folk are taken there.'

Will did not reply but ran back into the shop and within a few minutes he returned. Over his face he had placed a flour sack, into which he had cut two holes for his eyes. With his gloves on his hands, he was busily trying to stuff a collection of herbs taken from a nosegay into a cone of paper.

Molly laughed when she saw him and relented. 'Very well,' she said, 'tonight you can be an apprentice plague doctor.' She helped him put a string through the paper and tied it around his head.

Will made to shut the door but he looked at Molly's heavy coat and a sudden idea came to him.

'Stay a moment,' his voice mumbled through the mask, and he nipped inside once more.

'Hurry, Will!' Molly called after him. 'We do not have time to tarry here.' Her voice faltered as the boy returned bearing a large red bundle. 'What have you there?' she asked.

'Spittle's posh robe,' he replied. 'He left it in the shop this afternoon. It should serve as an excellent top coat. Why, I could wrap it round me three times over.' He closed the door and they passed quickly down the alley.

'Where is this pest-house?' he inquired, struggling into the velvet garment.

'Southwarke,' she answered, lacing up her own mask. 'I have not visited it before. It is on the far side of the river. We shall have to cross by the bridge for no watermen will bear us.'

Into the melancholy night they went. Cheapside was a sad and dreary place; on every corner a small fire burned and, huddled around the flames, was a woebegone collection of people: those whose livelihoods had disappeared since the arrival of the pestilence, or who had been absent when their homes had been boarded up and now had nowhere to live.

'Mercy on us,' came their heartwrenching pleas when they saw the two plague doctors go by.

Molly put her arm round Will's shoulder. 'The tale of grief is vast,' she said gravely. 'Innumerable tears has this city shed since the plague began – enough to fill the Thames and wash it clean.'

Will said nothing, for at last they had come to the river itself and the bridge stretched before them.

There was only one crossing over the Thames and London Bridge was a mighty thoroughfare. It was lined with tall buildings and shops that sold everything, from vegetables to shoes. This was the only way into the city from the south and it had spanned the river for many years. In the day it was congested with traffic and bustled as if the sickness had never been heard of. But at night all was quiet and still.

The few lights that shone in the high, latticed windows were reflected in the dark, rippling water below and all seemed calm and peaceful.

Molly took Will's hand and through the avenue of half-timbered buildings they went, the gurgling river swirling beneath them.

When they were only half-way across a different sound came to them. The young woman paused and pulled Will next to her.

'What is it?' he asked straining to listen through the thick sackcloth and trying to peer out of the ragged eyeholes.

'A pest-cart approaches,' she whispered. 'Keep by me.'

Presently Will too heard the clatter of wheels and the slow plod of a horse's hooves.

'Bring out yer dead,' rang out a lusty voice.

Will had never come this close to one of the death

waggons before and his heart beat quickly. To his surprise he found that he was apprehensive – afraid even. Here, on the bridge, there was no way to avoid this grisly meeting. Molly squeezed his hand and he automatically drew close to her.

'With luck the cart will be empty,' she prayed for the boy's sake.

A slurred voice hailed them as the dreaded waggon came nearer.

'What'sh thish then? Two plaguey doctorsh? Well, one and a half – hoo, hoo!' The bearer on the cart swayed like a reed in the breeze as he hooted at his little joke. He was a dirty, squalid-looking man with an uncouth leer on his face and a tall hat pitched rakishly over his bloodshot eyes.

A stream of slobber poured from his mouth as he pointed at Will and continued. 'I'd heard they were short o' physicians,' he hiccuped, 'but I didn't know the physicians were short as well!' He slapped his knees as he drew level with them and then pulled on the reins. 'Whoa!' he shouted. 'Halt there, you knackered old fleabag!'

The horse was a sorry, dishevelled beast; a shambling array of bones loosely covered by a threadbare hide. It rolled its scabby eyes and came to a standstill, then hung its head wearily.

The bearer leaned forward in an awkward motion as he tried to focus on the two figures at the roadside. 'Ain't never heard o' no dwarf doctorsh,' he declared.

Molly glanced fearfully at the open cart behind him and stood between it and Will. 'You're drunk!' she told the man in as gruff a tone as she could manage.

'Get about your business, fellow, and let us attend to ours!'

'Drunk he says!' tittered the man. 'What if I was says I?' From under his cloak he brought out a large jug and took a great swig from it. 'Arr!' he belched, blowing a bubble of ale and saliva from his mouth. 'Do you know summfin, my fine, fanshy gentlemen? I do believe you shpeak the truth – old Ned Bunkit's as sloshed as a bog-hole beetle.' And he broke into a throaty, gargling laugh.

'Come, Will,' said Molly quickly. She pushed the boy behind her to screen him from the grisly mound that the cart carried and made to walk off. But the bearer cracked his whip and shouted after them.

'Oh, how they sidle by. Ain'tcha gonna have a drink wi' Ned then? Too good for him are you?' He tottered to his feet and jabbed a finger at the jug in his hand. 'I'd like to shee you do this job without my friend here fer company! Aah, a pox on you both saysh I. When this plague's done there'll be no more scrapin' to the likes o' you, for there won't be no gentry left. Many a gallant, dashing and dandy, I've carted off to the pits.' Clumsily, he stepped into the cart and gestured to its silent passengers, 'And *they* don't want to sup wi' me either,' he caroused. 'Hoo, hoo!'

Molly urged Will onward. 'Don't look back,' she warned. 'Don't see what he carries this night.'

Will pulled the robe tightly about him, but the desire to take one glimpse of the ghastly cargo was too much. Quickly he glanced over his shoulder and his stomach churned over.

The drunken man was staggering through a heap of bodies and to Will's disgust he stooped and held up a tiny figure. Then the bearer roared in his stupor, 'Kindling, get yer kindling 'ere – five for sixpence! Ha ha!'

The two plague doctors rushed over London Bridge and passed into Southwarke. Only when they were under the shadow of St Saviour's did they pause for breath and the sweat of horror trickled down Will's neck.

Molly leaned against a wall as she calmed herself. 'What evil dwells in man's soul to drag him into such baseness?' she muttered. 'I tell you, Will, the sights I have witnessed this past year would make the most hardened sinner blanch.'

'Your father said the Devil stalked the streets of London,' he panted.

'I'll not gainsay him in that!' she agreed. 'It would seem the Almighty has abandoned this city.' With a shudder she pulled herself together. 'Even so,' she said firmly, 'it is up to us to do what we can. Come, we go to call on Jack Carver. Let us hope we arrive before the Reaper harvests him.'

As they hurried down the gloomy lanes a worrying thought came to Will. 'What if the Justices won't take any notice once the confession is signed?' he asked.

'Then I shall take the matter to a higher authority,' she replied. 'A friend of mine was an orange seller in one of the theatres, before they closed them down. She was on intimate terms with His Majesty. If need be I shall go to court and lay the evidence before him. But look – this is the place.'

They had come to a low, rambling building whose windows were nailed shut, and from the heavy oak doors hung an iron padlock. A guard stood outside the barred entrance and he eyed Will suspiciously.

'Let us pass,' Molly commanded.

The warden gave Will one last, dubious look then took out his clinking bunch of keys and released the padlock. It was not for him to question the comings and goings of plague doctors.

Will stared at the arch above the doors; the familiar red cross had been painted there and at the sight of it all his courage drained away.

The guard placed a cloth over his mouth and gave one of the doors a shove. It opened with a creak and Molly stepped across the threshold. Will hung back but the man was anxious to seal the building again and he stamped impatiently. Nervously the boy followed Molly inside – had it been the gateway to Hell itself he could not have been more afraid.

He stared out of his makeshift mask; they were in a dim passage, lit by a single tallow candle. The boy coughed; even through the sweet-smelling herbs the reek of the sickness assaulted his senses and he gagged at the cloying vileness.

The guard did not come after them; instead he hastily removed the cloth from his mouth and called out, 'Mother Myrtle! Ye have visitors. The doctors are come!' Then he pulled the door shut and it closed with an ominous thud that vibrated through the floor.

Behind the thick barrier of oak Will heard the padlock snap together and he caught his breath; he and Molly were now locked inside the pest-house.

'What now?' he whispered in a wavering voice.

'We wait for the nurse in charge,' she replied. 'She will take us to Jack Carver.'

As soon as she had spoken they heard a light

footstep. Beyond the candle a curtain was drawn aside and from it emerged Mother Myrtle.

She squinted at the newcomers and heaved a sigh of relief. 'At last,' she called in a frail voice. 'We have not had masters of physic here for five days. Welcome gentlemen.' Carefully she shuffled up the hallway to greet them and in doing so entered the small circle of candlelight.

Mother Myrtle was a small, elderly woman, whose back was bowed with age and whose hands were knobbled and swollen by the same cause. She wore no protective garments, just a simple dress of puritan black and the customary white starched collar about her neck. As she passed beneath the flame it glinted over her hair, which was white and fine as cobwebs on a frosty morning. She blinked in the yellow glare and a warm smile spread over her care-lined face.

'A most heartfelt welcome to you both,' she said, brightly dismissing Will's lack of height with a special grin meant for him alone. 'This is indeed a most happy answer to my prayers. But for you to have come so speedily – why I had only just finished asking the Lord for help when I heard the guard call my name.'

As she beamed at the pair of them Will drew strength from her steady gaze. In the depths of her pale, wrinkle-besieged eyes there was no trace of age; only a pure, almost saintly light shone there. He found himself liking her immediately.

Her twinkling smile faltered for a moment. 'I'm afraid there is little coin to pay for your services,' she murmured apologetically. 'All we had left was spent on food and medicines.' She wrung her arthritic hands together and her fingers closed about a golden ring. 'This belonged to my beloved mother,' she said trying to twist it over her knuckles. 'She gave it to me when I was a mere nursling, but please take it as payment. Oh, if only the nuisance would come off.'

Molly declined the offered ring and said, 'If we can give aid then that is reward enough.'

'Bless you!' Mother Myrtle wept, taking hold of Molly's gauntleted hand and kissing it gratefully. 'I know the Lord shall keep you from harm. Now, come if you will. Let me show you my charges; the sight of two physicians such as you will surely ease their burdens.'

'How many sick do you have in this house?' Molly inquired.

'This morning there were eighty-seven,' she replied. 'Now, alas, only sixty-five remain and I am the only one left to tend them.'

Molly stared at her incredulously. 'Sixty-five? Can more help not be provided?'

The old lady smiled, 'If this were a city pest-house no doubt – but we are a private mission. You see, when the pestilence first began we opened our doors and took in those stricken.'

'You mean that you invited the plague in willingly?' gasped Molly.

'What else should I have done? The Good Book makes our duty plain.'

'But are you not afraid for yourself? You ought at least to protect yourself in some way.'

Mother Myrtle shrugged. 'Swaddling clothes are for babes,' she said, her eye briefly alighting on Will, 'and I am far from that. I do but trust in the Lord, and when He decides that my work is done I am content to abide by His judgement.'

She turned and led them to the curtained doorway. 'Herein lie my patients,' she whispered. 'Do what you can for them. But please, no blood-letting; I will not permit such a barbarous practice. I had to expel the last physician by the scruff of the neck because he tried to do that to one of them. My, but he was a foul-mouthed doctor.'

The partition was pulled back and Will staggered, reeling from the wave of nausea that seemed to strike him. This was where the reek originated. His stomach rebelled at the stench and he struggled to keep from fainting.

The room beyond was long, narrow and dark. The only light came from a lantern hanging on a nail by the door and Molly recoiled from what she saw in there.

Row upon row of plague-riddled people covered the floor. All were in various degrees of death. Their groans and shrieks were enough to turn one mad and the clamour put a shadow over Will that stayed with him for the rest of his life.

Mother Myrtle smiled at all the pale, twisted faces as though she were viewing a room of small children rather than a place filled with despair. 'See my friends,' she told them, 'help has come as I knew it would.' She turned to Molly and motioned towards the lamp. 'Could you take up the light, sir?' she asked politely. 'Its brightness hurts mine eyes.'

Molly hesitated before answering. 'Of course,' she said quickly. So, holding the lamp aloft, she and Will were escorted by the old lady into the terrible room.

Surrounded by the soft glow of the lantern they trod

carefully amongst the sick and dying and Will stared, horrified, about him.

An emaciated man lay wrapped in a filthy blanket; beside him shivered a woman not much older than Molly and the light shone in her dark, staring eyes. At her side someone crouched in a ball and gibbered to himself; the next person was dead. Thus the awful spectacle unfolded until one of the patients let out a blood-curling howl as they passed and it frightened Will so much that he stumbled and fell against Molly. For a while the lantern swung uncontrollably and horrible shadows flew like giant bats over the walls.

'Take care,' Molly told him. Then she knelt beside the patient and tried to calm him. 'Have you clean water?' she asked Mother Myrtle. 'I can do nothing without it.'

The old woman nodded. 'I will fetch it,' she said.

'One moment,' put in Molly. 'Have you one here by the name of Carver?'

'Carver?' the other repeated. 'I don't think we do.'

Molly's hope sank – Jack was probably in the plaguepit by now.

Will pushed forward. 'Are you certain?' he asked. 'He has a big scar down his face.'

The old lady's doubtful expression cleared at once. 'Oh, Jacky boy!' she chirped. 'Why did you not say so before? He lies in the far corner – a friend of yours is he? Well that is nice; he's a bit of a scoundrel you know, but if he has someone like you two to care about him then he can't be all bad, can he? You go see him and I'll fetch the water you wanted.'

'And make it hot if possible,' Molly called after her retreating figure.

When she had gone, they hurried between the prostrate forms around them until they reached the farthest corner.

Jack Carver lay on a mattress of straw. A rat scurried over his legs as the lantern was raised and the light fell on his face.

The plague had worked a dramatic change on him; he was a wasted shadow of his former self. The muscles which had once thrown Will to the ground were now shrunken and weak. His face was beaded with sweat and festering sores pitted his skin. If it had not been for the livid scar on his cheek Will would not have recognised the man and he actually pitied him. Carver's days of evil were over and Death seemed to lurk in the shadows nearby, waiting to drag the soul from his failing body.

'Jack Carver?' said Molly impassively. 'Is that your name?'

At first he did not seem to see the two plague doctors standing over him. Then his staring eyes swivelled round and fixed upon Molly's mask.

'NOO!' he shrieked. 'He has come! He has come for me!'

The man was terrified. He flailed and thrashed his arms until Molly feared he would injure himself. Nothing she could do would calm him. 'It's no use,' she said to Will, 'the man is crazed – the mask frightens him.'

'What are we going to do?' the boy asked. 'We'll never discover anything with him screeching like that.'

'There is only one thing we can do,' she said grimly, and she reached up and began to unlace her mask.

'Stop!' cried Will. 'You mustn't remove it.'

But she took no heed. The beak and lenses fell away and the cowl was swept from her head.

The sudden revelation of Molly's beauty in that dark and dreadful place was like the sun appearing from behind black storm clouds. The lamplight gleamed in her golden hair and the gentle beams became enmeshed there, until it seemed that it shone with a radiance all its own and a glimmering halo surrounded her.

All about them, from the dismal sea of human suffering, came gasps of amazement and some muttered that an angel had come amongst them.

Molly crouched beside Jack Carver who gawped and goggled at her. 'What's this?' he spluttered, ceasing his violent twitchings. 'Am I to go upwards? Ha! I did think a hotter clime waited fer me.'

'Tell me your name,' said Molly.

'Jack I was,' he uttered, mesmerised by her loveliness, 'but Jack no more. It's the pits I'll be going to soon; one last ride and in they'll tip me.'

'My name is Margaret Balker,' she told him, 'does that mean anything to you?'

A fit of shivering and retching convulsed him but when it passed he gazed at her. 'Balker?' he mumbled trying to remember. 'No, it's gone.'

But Molly was insistent. 'Have you forgotten Johnathon Balker – miller of Adcombe, whom you slew?'

Carver's expression changed and a stillness crept over him as her words sliced through his plague-clouded mind. 'The fat miller,' he breathed.

'He was my father,' she said quietly.

The dark eyes closed. 'Then you must take after your mother,' he murmured with a black chuckle.

'Why did you kill him?'

'Let me rest . . . give me a moment's peace here at the end.'

'What peace did you give to him?'

The man passed a hand over his sopping brow. 'Very well,' he rasped. 'Jessel an' me were in the pay of another.'

'Who?'

'Some apothecary.'

'Which?'

'I can't recall.'

'Was his name Spittle?'

'Yes, that were it, now let me be.'

Molly took the confession from her coat. 'This is an admission of guilt,' she told him, 'yet it also accuses the apothecary of hiring you to murder my father. Sign it and I will let you alone.'

Carver managed a faint laugh, but it led to a bout of coughing and when it was over his breath wheezed in his throat. 'Why not?' he muttered. 'I'm not going to linger in this world much longer. It might even do me a bit o' good in the next.' He stared at the young woman and a gleam kindled in his eyes. Then he took the paper from her and said, 'But it weren't specifically yer father we were paid to dispatch.'

'I don't understand,' she whispered, taken aback.

' "Wait in the Sickle Moon and butcher whosoever you find with the boy" were our orders,' said Carver, repeating the words that Doctor Spittle had uttered a year ago. 'Then he says, "Once you're rid of him chase the lad towards my shop." '

'What!' exclaimed Will in surprise. And before Molly could prevent him he yanked his mask off also.

Jack peered at him and the ghost of a smile appeared at the corners of his mouth. 'So, it's you is it?' he croaked. 'A fine dance you led us that night, lad – good job fer you an' all. I was gonna cut your throat no matter what he told us.'

'But why did Spittle want me?' asked Will in disbelief.

'I never asked, just got me money and did the job.' He coughed again, but this time the attack did not pass. Will backed away as the man balked and choked. Carver clutched his chest and strangled groans whistled from his windpipe. Then, even as they watched, it was all over. A shuddering spasm rifled through him and Jack Carver collapsed. The shadow of Death deepened in that place as Carver's soul departed from his body going whither it was bound.

'No!' cried Molly in dismay. 'The confession – he never signed it!' She tore the paper from the dead man's hand and scrunched it into a ball. 'All for nothing,' she wept. 'It's been all for nothing.'

'Here we are, my fine gentleman,' Mother Myrtle sang breezily as she entered carrying a steaming basin. She pattered over to them, her eyes fixed upon the water in case she spilled any. 'Now, where would you care to begin, sir?' she began.

Molly turned and the old lady let out a coo of delight. 'Why, what a lovely sweet face you have, my dear,' she said not in the least bit surprised, 'and should you not be abed, young man?' she asked Will.

They were both too stunned by Jack's death to say anything.

'Oh, my dears,' she tutted, 'Jacky boy's gone has he? I didn't think he would see the night out. He must have been very special to you to affect you so.'

'Not "special",' answered Molly, 'but important, yes.'

The old lady patted her arm. 'Don't you worry yourself now, we are all earth when all is said and done. It is not this world that matters, but the next. If I did not believe in the kingdom of Heaven then I would have given up long ago. Without that there would be no point to it all, would there? My faith in the Lord is the only thing that keeps me going.'

'I wish I had your faith,' muttered Molly. 'I can see no reason for anything that happens.'

'Oh the reasons are there,' chuckled Mother Myrtle, 'we're just not wise enough to see or understand them. Now, do you think you could help me with this basin, it is rather heavy?'

'Here,' Molly apologised, 'I'll take that, you rest for a while. I cannot cure these people but I can make their remaining hours more comfortable.'

'Rest?' repeated the elderly nurse. 'I don't think I've had any rest for, ooh I can't remember when. No, I'll help you, dear, if you don't mind.' She rolled up her sleeves and her bare arms entered the light of the lantern.

'Your arms!' cried Molly suddenly. 'Look at them!'

The old lady clucked dismissively. 'Not very pretty is it?' she said. 'But what can you expect, working here?'

Will leaned forward and there on the exposed flesh were the symptoms of the plague. Painful red boils covered Mother Myrtle's arms entircly. His heart bled for her; she would shortly die.

'Sit down,' Molly told her, 'you must be in agony. How long have you been liked this?'

'The sores appeared on the second day we opened our doors,' she said slowly. 'That would make it about seven months ago now.'

Molly shook her head. 'That isn't possible,' she breathed. 'No one survives that long.'

'Did I not tell you I trusted in the Lord? When He is sure my work here is done no doubt He will permit me to leave. Until then I am needed; that is why He has sustained me, and why He will sustain you also.'

Molly stared, then flung her arms about the old lady's neck as she understood. 'You make me feel ashamed!' she cried. 'Let us set about caring for these poor folk.' Then she turned to Will and told him to leave the place and go to her room in Trinity Lane.

'I can't,' he protested. 'Now that our hopes have failed I must return to the apothecary shop.'

'But after all you heard from Carver?'

'Even so,' he shrugged, 'I have to go back.'

'Then be careful,' she said. 'Whatever purpose that old sinner had in catching you, he hasn't revealed it yet. He wouldn't lay such elaborate plans just to get a lad to work for him. Be forever on your guard.'

Will nodded, 'I shall.'

'Then go now,' she told him. 'I doubt if we shall ever see each other again. It would seem that I am to stay here, and after all the things I have done in the past, this is no bad way to end. Goodbye, Will.'

'Goodbye – Margaret.'

And so they parted; and, as he ducked under the curtain, the last sight he had of Molly was her tending the sick, her hair burning like a golden flame and at her side Mother Myrtle doing all she could to assist her.

Yet through his misery and desolation one perplexing question rose and dominated his thoughts – how did Doctor Spittle know that he was coming to London in the first place?

12

The Fall of Adonis

A nother cheerless Christmas passed and the winter faded into spring. The plague decreased in the cold months but when the warm weather returned it flared up again. Doctor Spittle continued with his work however and if he noticed Will's unease during this time he did not refer to it.

Beckett gazed glumly from his cage; below him the alchemist was pacing about the attic and stirring a colourless solution with a long glass rod. Jupiter sat on the chair and watched all that was done. The rat scratched himself unhappily – he knew what was coming. It was going to be a most miserable night.

'Oh beggar me,' he whined. ' 'Tain't right an' natural it's not. Glad my old mum can't see me now – she'd thwack me round the chops and give me what fer she would. Oh the shame of it.' He peered down at his body and shivered; perhaps this time he could die like Heliodorus had done – that would be better than this. At least he went out with a bang.

'Pink!' he blubbered forlornly. 'Who ever 'eard of a pink rat? Oh I wish I could drop down dead!' And he buried his snout in his claws dreading what was to come.

With no help from the spirit of Magnus Zachaire, Doctor Spittle had pursued the elixir of life unceasingly. There had been many times he thought he had succeeded, but each new concoction had been fed to Beckett with exceedingly strange results. The first time the brown rat had been forced to digest a potion, he immediately began to bark like a dog and growled at Jupiter and Leech. After a second formula had been prepared and given to him, his ears grew to an incredible length and trailed across the floor of the cage, tripping him up whenever he tried to move. The effects of that potion had not lasted very long, thank goodness; but since then he had been purple, a sickly green, black with livid yellow freckles and now, to his disgrace, his fur was a beautifully delicate shade of pink.

It embarrassed him no end and, to his distress, it had so far shown no sign of wearing off. The others had only lasted a week or two at the most, but he had been pink for three months now. All through the summer of 1666 he had been forced to endure the jibes and rude comments of the cats below and, although he was not a brave or conceited rat, it stung his pride nonetheless.

Doctor Spittle tapped the glass rod on the side of the jar that contained this latest experiment and looked up at the cage. 'Are you ready my little rosy rodent?' he chortled. 'Let us see what effect this mixture has upon you.' He raised the rod and thrust it through the bars.

Beckett clapped his mouth tight shut; no way was he going to taste it this time. He folded his arms resolutely and shook his head, defying the drops that ran down the glass towards him.

'Don't be churlish, my blushing beauty,' coaxed Doctor Spittle, 'there's nothing to fear – you won't feel a thing.'

But for once in his timid life Beckett refused to obey and he covered his mouth with his claws.

The alchemist glared at the rat angrily and shoved the rod in even further until it poked Beckett in the eye. He smacked it away from him and took some steps backwards.

'Abandon hope, Elias,' came Magnus's gloating laugh, 'thou art a bungling amateur. Why even the rats of thy laboratory have no faith in thee. Return to thy pills and paltry remedies. The Hermetic Art is beyond thy cloddish wits.'

Doctor Spittle scowled. 'Be silent,' he snapped. 'Perhaps this time I have discovered the elixir.'

'But how canst thou be certain?' scoffed the spirit. 'Why not sample what thou hast made thyself?'

The alchemist ignored him but his black brows twitched craftily. Returning his attention to the pink rat he prodded it once more. Beckett waddled a little further away until he pressed himself against the bars of the cage and his tail dangled down.

A smirk flickered over Doctor Spittle's face. In a trice, his free hand snaked out and he gave the tail a fierce tug. Beckett threw back his head and yelled. At once three drops fell from the tip of the glass rod and vanished down his gullet. The old man roared with laughter and rubbed his hands together to see what would happen.

Beckett kissed his bruised tail and patted it gently. 'Dirty, rotten trickster,' he complained with a grumble, 'now that just ain't fair – cheatin' I calls it.' He turned his back on the alchemist and pouted peevishly.

Before long a tingling sensation began to prickle the back of his neck. 'Ere we go again,' he whined.

His pink fur stirred as though invisible snakes were slithering through it, then all the hairs writhed and the fleas had to cling to his skin to remain on his body.

The pale rose colour deepened, slowly at first and then the change increased in speed. Beckett howled as the potion took control of him and he was lifted into the air. Desperately he clutched at the bars to stop himself hitting the roof of the cage. Then he clenched his teeth and it seemed that the room was filled with all the colours of the rainbow. Sparks flew from his fur, spitting green and blue stars at the astonished alchemist.

Beckett's howl soared to a piercing shriek as the brilliant hues stampeded over him, and then it was over. He slid to the floor with a groan and put a trembling claw to his dizzy head. Cautiously he opened one eye to see what disaster had befallen him this time.

To his surprise, the effect wasn't bad at all – in fact he thought it was rather dashing. 'Lumme,' he mumbled, 'I does look a dandy.'

The rat was now a delicious orange, not a florid, citrus shade, but a rich warm apricot that contained tints of copper and was covered by a wonderful, lustrous sheen. Delighted, he stumbled to his feet and combed his claws through the lush new coat. 'I fink I could get used to this,' he said admiringly.

Doctor Spittle studied him carefully, then pulled a sour expression.

'Another failure,' Magnus told him. 'The elixir of life does not alter the colour of thy hair.'

The alchemist snarled and was about to say something in return when he blinked and a wide grin split his face. 'Oh no, Magnus,' he whispered, 'I have not failed at all. In fact I rejoice.' He poured the remaining mixture into a pewter bowl then unlocked the attic door. 'It is time for me to retire,' he said. 'Goodnight Jupiter, and goodnight to you my little rodent friend.' With that he left the room and descended to his bedchamber, taking the bowl with him.

Jupiter stared up at Beckett and frowned; why was his master so pleased? he wondered. He pulled a book from the table and opened it at the page he desired. The alchemist's familiar had learned many things over the past year and a half and Doctor Spittle was extremely pleased at his progress. Yet he did not realise just how knowledgeable Jupiter had become, and the ginger cat chose not to demonstrate to him how powerful he really was.

Stifling a yawn, Jupiter curled up with the book and started to read.

Leech kept his ears pressed against the floor. When he was certain that the old man had gone to bed he crawled out of hiding and crept to the shelf where the spirit bottle was kept.

'And how art thou?' asked Magnus as the runt approached. 'Does the hatred for all living creatures still burn inside thee?'

Leech did not reply; sullenly he twisted his ugly head and glowered at Jupiter. Then he turned to the bottle and said, 'What is the lesson tonight? What mysteries of the unexplored arts will you teach me now?'

For some time now, after Doctor Spittle had gone to bed, Leech and the spirit had talked together in the darkness. The runt had learned many secrets from the tormented soul, yet all the knowledge was useless, for only his brother was capable of wielding magic.

Magnus Zachaire's face glimmered through the dark glass of the bottle. A peculiar expression formed over the ghostly features and a smile appeared amid the neat little beard. 'The time draws closer, Leech,' he said in a solemn voice. 'The trap is set and soon I shall have my freedom. Once Elias is dead his enchantment shall no longer imprison me and I can return to the oblivion of the cold void.'

Will rubbed the sleep from his eyes and unlocked the shop. The cries of the street traders were already clamouring in Cheapside. At least the sickness had decreased enough to permit some measure of normal life. He gazed wistfully out of the window and remembered that night, nearly a year ago now, when he had said goodbye to Molly. He had not heard from her since and he presumed that meant she was no more, her bright young life must have burned itself out in the dark Southwarke pest-house.

'A merry morning, my young dog,' came the cheery voice of Doctor Spittle.

Will looked round and then his eyes widened.

The alchemist airily waved his fingers at him and twirled about on tiptoe as if he were a dancer at court. 'Am I not elegant and dignified?' he announced, delirious with glee. 'See how the sunlight picks out the glints of red. Who needs an elixir when you are as handsome as I?'

Will struggled to keep from laughing out loud. Upon the old man's head there was now a thick growth of auburn hair. It flowed over his shoulders in luxuriant tresses and he ran his fingers through it adoringly – he looked ridiculous.

'Am I not the most ravishing spectacle?' he cried. 'I make Narcissus seem toadish by comparison.' He raised his left hand and for the first time Will noticed that he held Beckett in his grasp.

'Oh noble, brave and faithful rodent,' the alchemist crowed, 'a trusty, dependable creature you have been to me. Without you I might never have discovered this most marvellous mixture. Who can gaze at me and not be consumed with envy? No periwigs do I need, for my crowning glory outshines all others.'

The orange rat wriggled in his grasp and squirmed wildly. It had been a long time since he had been out of the cage in the attic and the sights and smells of the shop were strange and unfamiliar.

Doctor Spittle squeezed him tightly and Beckett gasped, fighting for breath. 'Never let it be said that Elias Theophrastus Spittle is ungrateful,' he said, hugging the rat against his cheek. To Will's disgust, and to Beckett's dismay, the old man puckered his lips and gave the rodent a big kiss.

'Yeuch!' spluttered Beckett wiping his face.

With a light, silvery laugh, the alchemist crossed to the door and opened it wide. 'Here we are,' he told the rat, 'this is the greatest reward I can bestow upon you. In return for your invaluable assistance I give to you your freedom.' He set the rat on the ground and let him go.

Beckett sniffed the air of the alley suspiciously. 'What be this then?' he muttered. 'Some nasty trick is it?'

'Go on,' urged Doctor Spittle, nudging him with his toe.

The rat gave one last scratch, then dashed over to a pile of weeds, darted through them and disappeared into the city.

The alchemist hummed a merry tune to himself – it pleased him to be benevolent occasionally. 'And now,' he said addressing Will, 'I shall take the air of this fine, first September morning and stroll through the streets.'

'You're going out there?' stammered Will. 'But you haven't stepped outside the shop since the plague began.'

The old man chuckled and tossed his head. 'Yet I hear that the sickness has decreased and now only a small number die of the pestilence each week. It will do me good to breathe the fresh air once more. I have been cooped up for far too long, I might even partake of something sweet in a coffee house to celebrate the return of my Samson-like mane.'

He swept the hair from his face and strode down

the alley. Will watched him go; the vanity of the old man knew no bounds – it had even overpowered his dread of the Black Death. The boy laughed at the idiotic sight then set to work.

Through the traders and purveyors of fancy goods Doctor Spittle wound his way and wherever he went conversations ceased as folk gawked at him. A man selling apples tipped the entire tray on the ground when the alchemist sailed by, whilst the ragamuffins and street urchins pointed and called rude names after him. With his pale, greenish-white face framed by the violent orange locks, he looked like some horrendous apparition that had broken out of a tomb, and no one knew whether to laugh or be afraid.

Yet Doctor Spittle was blind to the ridicule and yelps of fright. He was so enamoured of his luscious hair that he actually believed they were all staring at him in admiration. Holding his head up high, he strutted along graciously waving to the startled populace as though he were a visiting king. Not one inkling did he have of the fool he was making of himself; he was truly an eyesore. But in his delusion, he was convinced that the splendour of his hair lent him a statuesque symmetry and it was only right and proper that the world should behold him.

Quite a crowd followed him through the streets, sniggering and elbowing one another and giggling at the old, misguided buffoon.

And then a chink appeared in the glory of his self-deception. As he pranced down towards St Paul's, with the vulgar laughter rising like a swift tide behind him, his flesh began to creep and he itched terribly. Absently he rubbed the side of his face where his skin irritated and stung, then he scratched the top of his head, then his leg.

It was not long before he was scratching himself all over and the crowd hooted to see him doing this insane jig.

'Lo!' they jeered. 'St Vitus has come amongst us.'

A tinker with a flute struck up a wild tune to accompany the alchemist's jerks and frantic movements and all roared at his expense.

Doctor Spittle raked his fingers through his hair and clawed at his cheeks. His very blood seemed on fire and the raucous laughter resounded all around until he was caught in a storm of derision and mockery.

'What are you laughing at?' he bawled, wheeling round to confront his tormentors.

All he saw was a sea of leering faces and mouths that were wide with scornful mirth. Then the sun became brighter, for it dazzled his eyes and almost blinded him. He held up his hands to shield himself from the painful rays and at once the laughter stopped.

The faces of the mob took on terrified aspects and those at the front began to scream.

'The plague!' they screeched. 'He has the plague!'

Doctor Spittle lowered his arms and he squinted in horror at the back of his hands. Already the marks of the Black Death were blotching his skin with ugly red weals.

'No!' he whimpered. 'It cannot be – not now!'

The crowd pushed and jostled one another to escape from the old man and soon he was left standing alone in the middle of the street where he threw back his head and wailed.

An earthenware pot fell from Will's hands as the shop door burst open and Doctor Spittle charged inside.

'The plague!' he shrieked holding up his hands for the boy to see. 'I have the plague!'

Distraught, he raced upstairs sobbing and shaking his fists heavenward.

Will stood as one frozen and amazed, but the possibilities of the situation slowly started to unravel and a desperate glimmer of hope lifted his spirits. The alchemist was going to die – at last he would be free to return home.

Above the anguished cries of the doomed man he heard the attic door slam shut and he became troubled. Was his liberty worth the loss of a life – even one as vile and wicked as Doctor Spittle's? It was a dilemma he had faced once before, when Sir Francis Lingley had tried to kill the old man. He had been spared the decision then but what would happen this time? Will sat on the counter. He had prayed unceasingly for his freedom; in doing so had he brought this awful fate down upon his captor?

At the top of the building the alchemist rushed over to his chair and flung himself into it. 'Is this the end of Elias Theophrastus Spittle?' he murmured, tears welling up in his eyes. 'Does my existence truly terminate here? Will all that I am, all that I have learned – all my genius be snuffed out for eternity?'

The room was filled by a cold blue light and the voice of Magnus Zachaire chuckled from the spirit bottle. 'Ha! Vainglorious wretch!' he trumpeted. 'Taste now the bitter bliss of death. Thy folly and conceit hath fashioned thine own demise. How much more bitter is that draught when it is drunk from a cup of thine own making?'

'What do you mean?' stammered Doctor Spittle in confusion. 'How have I brought this upon myself?'

The spirit's face glowed with triumph as it peered out of the bottle at him. 'Beckett, thine orange rat!' he declared. 'Knowest thou now that the pestilence is carried by the fleas which such creatures bear. When thou didst hold him to thy bosom the trap was sprung and thy days were numbered. But what an excruciatingly painful end Elias – it gladdens me that thou shalt perish in a torment equal to that thou hast forced me to endure. For such was my desire from the very beginning.'

Doctor Spittle was thunderstruck. 'Have you done this to me?' he whispered in a crushed, tragic voice.

'Indeed I have!' announced the spirit proudly. 'Ever have I guided and goaded thee into preparing the formulae which have been my design alone. Thou hast been working for me, Elias, and thou didst not suspect at any turn that it was I who led thee on and brought thee hither, condemned by thine own hand.'

The alchemist's face was a picture of bewilderment as he realised just how much of a fool he had been. Then the mood changed to anger which burst into fury.

'No!' he screeched, tearing the books off the shelves and hurling the table over in his wrath. He snatched up the spirit bottle and his fingers tightened around it until his knuckles turned white. 'I will not succumb to you,' he raged. 'I will conquer you yet, treacherous and baseborn phantom.'

Magnus laughed all the more. 'Proceed, Elias,' he

urged, 'crush the glass, release me even sooner than I did anticipate.'

'Oh no,' growled the alchemist, 'I cannot do that – not whilst I still have a use for you. You know the true formula for the elixir of life – only that can save me now.'

The spirit smirked, highly amused at this. 'Dost thou truly believe I would guide thee to the brink of death only to rescue thee now?' it mocked. 'Thou art a greater simpleton than I did envisage.'

But Doctor Spittle did not reply. He took up a candle, lit it, then snarled, 'Now I do what I should have done at the first.' He held up the bottle and placed it over the flame, turning it slowly until the glass became black with soot and scorching.

'AAIIEEE!' screamed Magnus from within. 'AAIIEEEEEEEEE!'

Now it was the alchemist's turn to laugh. 'Ho, Magnus,' he cackled grimly, 'does the heat burn? Does it shrivel and blast? Is this more painful than death, oh vile and deceitful wraith? Until I die of the sickness I am quite able to keep you in such torture – in fact it will hearten me and keep me in a merry humour till the end.'

The spirit squealed in despair. The searing pain was more than he could bear. 'Stop!' he pleaded. 'Stop – I beseech thee!'

'Tut, tut,' muttered Doctor Spittle, momentarily lifting the bottle from the flame, 'would you deprive me of my final amusement?' He lowered it once more and Magnus's shrill shrieks rang in his ears.

'I submit!' the spirit shouted. 'Spare me further suffering and the elixir is thine – I swear!'

Doctor Spittle kept the bottle in the flame for one lingering, sadistic moment, then he pulled it away – black and smoking. 'Now tell me you foul, unwholesome undine.'

Utterly defeated and tamed by the violence of the heat, Magnus Zachaire revealed his secrets at last and, within an hour, Doctor Spittle had a complete and precise formula written on three sheets of paper. 'Thank you,' he told him. 'See how your plans have brought me not to death but life everlasting.'

Magnus wept to himself; his defiant spirit vanquished, the blue light dwindled and was extinguished.

For the rest of the day Doctor Spittle set about making the elixir. Time was his enemy now – he reckoned that he had only a few hours before the Black Death robbed him of his wits and so he hastened to complete what was needed.

Jupiter assisted his master as much as he could, watching over the seething crucibles and giving help when required.

'I shall be victorious,' the old man informed his familiar. 'Death shall never garner me to his cold realm – I have too much to live for.'

And Jupiter hoped that he was right. He did not want to see the alchemist perish, though it was not really affection that he felt for him – rather the respect that one might show to an aged tutor. Besides there was still so much to learn and without Doctor Spittle the ginger cat doubted if he would be allowed to continue.

Endlessly they toiled over the broiling pots, but every now and again the alchemist would pause and stare at the boils which festered over him. 'More speed,' he would cry. 'The sands of time run out too quickly.'

Leech crawled out of the shadows, fascinated by this macabre turn of events. Stealthily he crept over to the spirit bottle and whispered to the soul inside.

'Magnus,' he wheedled, 'will the old human die? I should like to see him race into the darkness. I hear the plague is an agonising way to go – how long before he starts to shiver and sweat and when do the ravings fog his mind?'

There was no response from the spirit so Leech wiped the soot from the glass to peer inside.

'Leave me,' moaned Magnus feebly. 'I have failed. All too soon Elias will be immortal and my real torment shall only commence. What have I done?'

Leech's jaw dropped open and he let out a pitiful whine. 'Then no doubt Jupiter shall also drink of the elixir,' he muttered. 'My brother will endure beyond me – I too am lost.'

The faintest glimmer began to pulse from the bottle, and a cunning look stole over the spirit's face.

'And yet who can tell?' he murmured. 'There may still be a way for my vengeance to succeed.'

As the shades of evening deepened outside the attic window Doctor Spittle wavered in the yellow smoke that filled the room. 'The two-headed dragon,' he whispered pouring five silver drops from a small jar into the bubbling mixture. He swayed and put his hand to his brow in an attempt to steady himself.

'Jupiter,' he mumbled, 'are you there?' The billowing clouds of sulphur gathered thickly about him and it seemed that they entered his mind. A dark mist closed over his eyes and he felt all his energies

trickle swiftly away. A blackness crept over him and the alchemist gibbered woefully, 'I . . . I fear I am too . . . too late.' Even as he spoke, his legs went from under him and the old man fell to the floor.

Jupiter dashed to his side and mewed frantically.

Doctor Spittle shivered and beads of sweat appeared on his forehead. 'I cannot continue,' he muttered. 'I was too late – the grim gentleman has won after all.' He reached out a shaking hand and patted his familiar on the head. 'And we . . . we had it . . . almost within our grasp,' he said bitterly, 'so . . . close . . .' The alchemist closed his eyes and surrendered to the plague fever.

From the shelf Leech stared through the curling smoke and his hope soared. 'It would seem my brother is denied immortality,' he chuckled.

But Magnus Zachaire was not so confident. 'Do not underestimate the power of Jupiter,' he warned. 'Did I not tell thee that he shall grow very great and his name will live on beyond the lives of men? Look now and witness the beginnings of his destiny.'

Jupiter gazed wildly about him – the elixir was so close to being completed. Just a few hours more and it would be ready, yet it was impossible to see to it alone. Then his golden eyes widened and the solution came to him. 'The boy!' he said. 'He can help me.'

In one tremendous leap he bolted over Doctor Spittle and ran out of the door. Taking four steps at a time he tore downstairs and charged into the shop.

Will had been pondering over what he should do; really the shop ought to be shut up and a quarantine period begin. But if that happened then he might catch the plague as well as the alchemist. He had just made up his mind to sneak out, telling no one, when Jupiter rampaged from the attic and came skidding to a halt at his feet.

He stared at the ginger cat, startled by its frantic and sudden entry. 'Hello,' he said in surprise, 'what are you doing down here?'

Then Jupiter revealed for the first time his power. He glared at the boy and, taking a deep breath, spoke in a hissing parody of a human voice.

'Quickly,' he said in a commanding tone, 'my master is ill. If we are to save him you must do all that I say.'

Will fell off the counter.

He gaped at the cat then shook his head. 'I'm going mad,' he breathed. 'The plague must have touched me as well – my brains are addled.'

'Listen to me, boy!' shouted Jupiter forcefully, and such was the authority of his voice that Will had no choice but to obey.

'Upstairs Doctor Spittle lies dying,' Jupiter told him. 'Come with me now.'

Still astounded and amazed at the familiar's gift of speech, the boy followed him back to the attic.

'See,' the familiar cried, 'my master is in a deadly swoon, he was overcome by the pestilence.'

Through the choking yellow fog Will gazed down at the alchemist. The Black Death was devouring him completely; not one inch of skin was left uncovered by the sores that almost glowed with a greedy, red malevolence. Not even Jack Carver had looked so awful, but in the boy's heart he felt neither pity nor remorse. 'What do you expect me to do?' he asked coldly. 'I cannot save him.'

'No, but I can,' Jupiter replied. 'Shortly the elixir of life will be ready, it can restore him to health and all will be well.'

'Not for me,' returned Will.

'Are you going to help me or not?'

The boy coughed amid the thick smoke and shrugged. 'Well, this atmosphere won't be doing him much good,' he said. 'I'll take him to his bedchamber.'

Scrunching up his face, to block out the sight of the alchemist at such close quarters, Will put his hands under the old man's arms and began to drag him out of the attic. 'Well you've done it now, William Godwin,' he told himself, 'the plague'll get you for sure.'

It took fifteen awkward and uncomfortable minutes to lift and pull the alchemist down the small flight of stairs to his own room. Once Will had heaved him across the floor he hauled him on to the bed and the old man fell against the pillows. He was totally unaware of what was going on around him and, in his delirium, he groaned and mumbled unintelligibly.

Jupiter jumped on to the bed and looked at Doctor Spittle's face. 'We do not have much time left,' he said. 'Come, we can do nothing down here.' He leapt to the floor but turned when he realised Will was not following him.

'Why do you stay?' the cat asked. 'Is not the need for urgency plain?'

The boy was staring at the alchemist and he fought with the emotions that heaved in his breast. 'His life depends on me,' he murmured, more to himself than Jupiter. 'Should I save him?' He thought of all the misery he had been forced to endure because of this vicious old man; John Balker – Molly's father – had been murdered on his instructions and she had died in a pest-house in trying to learn the truth. The months of his own hard toil and cruel starvation filled Will's mind and his face hardened.

'I won't do it,' he spat. 'Let the monster die!'

Jupiter moved forward and pawed at the boy's leg.

'I know little of what my master has done to you, human child,' he said softly, 'but whatever the evils he may have inflicted upon you is it right that you should now destroy him? Does that not make you even as he?' His golden eyes gleamed and Will could not withstand their intense stare.

'You're right,' he whispered. 'If I stand by and do nothing I become like him. Whatever happens to me, I'll not be dragged unto his depravity. No matter what he does to me I could never be so cruel to him – or anyone.'

'Then come,' said the cat kindly, 'let us rescue the old villain, and I think your life will be sweeter once we are done.'

Into the night the two of them worked together, for the task took longer than Jupiter had anticipated. The smoke burned in their eyes and changed colour a thousand times before it was done. But, just as the hour struck two in the morning, the elixir of life was ready.

13

The Depths of His Black Heart

William rubbed his tired eyes and gazed at the glass jar in his hand. A clear liquid filled it and the candlelight rejoiced in sparkling over its shimmering surface. 'Is this really it?' he asked wondrously.

The cat nodded. 'It is. Come – not a second have we to spare.' He ran to the door and hurried downstairs.

Doctor Spittle lay still; the ravages of the pestilence had left his face cratered and swollen, but the skin had lost its livid glare and a blueish pallor now bloomed in his cheeks with a ghastly luminescence.

Jupiter leapt on to the bed and a frown furrowed his brow. 'Master,' he began. 'Master, it is I, Jupiter, come to save you.'

The old man did not stir and the familiar's lips trembled. Quickly he put his ear to the alchemist's chest and listened. All was silent; no faint pit-a-pat fluttered and not one breath issued from Doctor Spittle's lungs.

Jupiter staggered back. 'I am too late!' he cried. 'He is dead!'

Bearing the elixir, Will came into the bedchamber. The ginger cat shook his head tearfully. 'Alas,' he sobbed, 'all our labours were for nothing, the old one is no more.'

'Are you certain?' Will murmured. 'Perhaps he is only in the black swoon.'

But Jupiter stared at the alchemist and sighed, 'No, he is gone, and beyond recalling.'

Will looked at the dead man and a lump stuck in his throat. 'Strange,' he thought, 'but I believe I shall miss him. For the last two years that miserable old sinner has been the only constant person in my life.' He lifted his eyes and gazed sorrowfully at Jupiter – the cat was feeling this most of all.

And then a bizarre impulse drove Will to the bedside and he brought the jar to the corpse's white lips.

'What are you doing?' asked Jupiter.

The boy shrugged. 'This took long enough to make,' he answered. 'I'm not going to waste it now. Who knows, maybe it's strong enough to actually bring him back to life.'

'I do not think so,' said Jupiter doubtfully.

But Will ignored him and tipped some of the liquid into the alchemist's mouth.

'You're spilling it,' the cat told him. 'Be careful.'

'It's this jar,' Will muttered.

'Then pour it into another vessel first.'

The boy cast around for something else. On the

floor by the bed there were two pewter bowls; one contained what looked like water, the other was empty. Picking up the latter he filled it with some of the elixir then put it to the old man's lips.

'That's better,' he said, 'it's all going in now. How much do you think we should give him?'

'It does not matter,' replied Jupiter, 'it will do no good.'

At that instant the bowl was knocked from Will's hands and Doctor Spittle spluttered into life.

'AARRGHH!' he groaned, sitting up and coughing. 'The void spins around me.'

Then his head wobbled and he collapsed on to the pillows once more, the nostrils of his hooked nose flaring and his breath rattling in his throat – but at least he was alive.

Jupiter stared at him incredulously. 'You did it!' he exclaimed. 'My master lives!'

Will filled the bowl a second time but the old man would drink no more – he pushed him away and rolled on to his side.

'It is the plague,' Jupiter announced. 'He still suffers from it. We have brought him back from death but the elixir has not yet cured him of the sickness. His agony is renewed.'

'What are we to do?' asked the boy.

'Remain at his side,' muttered the familiar, 'for his pain and suffering will be beyond the understanding of we mortals. Doctor Spittle has life everlasting now and must endure the pestilence until it passes. Not for him is the blissful release of death; he cannot escape his burdens any more. He must withstand the fever and vanquish it.'

Will sat back then murmured, 'Have we really toiled all night?'

'It is but a little after two of the clock,' Jupiter informed him. 'Why do you ask?'

The boy rose and wandered over to the window saying, 'Then if it is not the dawn that glows in the sky, what is it?'

A ruddy glare had risen over the rooftops. It lit the black heavens with a vivid scarlet that was too harsh and bloody for any sunrise.

Jupiter gazed at it bewildered. 'I shall ascend the stairs and see if I can espy more from there,' he said. 'Stay here and watch over my master.'

Leech was sitting on the sill of the attic window when he arrived. The ginger cat leapt up beside him but the runt hissed and backed away.

'Peace, brother,' said Jupiter sternly, 'I come only to discover the source of the light in the sky.'

Leech sneered and sniggered out of the corner of his mouth. 'Then behold!' he cried. 'That is the sign of a great burning – buildings are ablaze and, it is to be hoped, humans are dying.'

Jupiter stared over the mass of chimneys, steeples and bell towers. In the distance a huge fire blazed and tongues of flame soared into the night.

'What a lovely sight it is,' breathed Leech. 'See how it makes the darkness red, staining it with its violence.'

Jupiter dragged his eyes from the spectacle. 'It must be over a mile away,' he said, satisfied they were in no danger. 'I must return to my duties.'

Leech stayed him with a paw. 'The old human,' he began with a leer, 'how does he fare? Has the sickness taken him? I heard you cry that he was dead – is that true?'

'It was,' the familiar replied, 'but not any more; the elixir has brought him back from death. My master will soon recover and be the greatest man that has ever lived.'

A twisted snarl curled over the runt's foul mouth but Jupiter paid no attention to him. With a light heart he ran out of the attic to see to the alchemist's needs.

Alone, Leech made a horrible whining sound as he realised how miserable his life would be from now on. 'I shall never gain power,' he snivelled. 'All my patience has been in vain.'

From the spirit bottle a teasing voice answered, 'Maybe not, my disheartened runt. There is yet a slender ray of hope for both of us.'

Leech slunk over to where the face of Magnus Zachaire shone out at him. 'What do you mean?' he asked, and then his expression changed. 'You are still trapped!' he declared. 'But did I not hear that the old human had perished before the elixir revived him? Why did you not escape then when all his enchantments had failed?'

A cunning and vengeful look blazed in the spirit's eyes. 'My desires have altered since Elias tortured me in the flame,' he growled. 'My freedom I still hold dear, yet it is liberty of a different sort I seek now. To return to the empty, freezing void is not my wish. I, Magnus Zachaire, want to live again!'

'But . . . but is that possible?' spluttered Leech incredulously.

'Elias hath achieved it.'

'Yes, but he had only been gone a short while –

you departed many years ago. Your remains are buried deep in the earth, corrupt and rotted with age.'

'That is why I made certain the formula I gave him was of the utmost power and strength, and why I did stay here when I might have escaped. To supervise and oversee my rebirth is now my goal. Presently I shall breathe the air of mortal lands once more.' His voice lowered to a conspiratorial whisper as he murmured, 'And that is why I need thy help, friend Leech.'

'What can I do?' asked the runt. 'You know that I have no magic.'

'The magic is in the elixir. Dost thou remember thy birthplace?'

Leech nodded, 'The graveyard, yes.'

'Then take thither a quantity of the precious liquid and pour it over my grave.'

The runt scowled uncertainly. 'But how will that help *me*?' he complained. 'Besides, the elixir is in the bedchamber downstairs – how am I to steal some with Jupiter and that boy standing guard?'

'Use the sly craft that was in thee from the beginning,' Magnus told him, 'and have no fear, I shall reward thee for thy service.'

Doctor Spittle moaned and stirred in the dark faint that gripped him. With a wet handkerchief Will wiped the beads of sweat from the old man's pustule-covered brow and tutted.

'It's taking a long time,' he said. 'The boils still increase and the shivering won't cease.'

Jupiter nodded wisely. 'All will be well,' he answered. 'Even now the elixir is battling with the sickness inside my master's body – he shall win through.'

The alchemist muttered under his breath but they could not catch the words.

'Pear tarts!' he squealed suddenly. 'Marmalades, syllabubs, jellied milk, apple mousses, marzipan and cheesecakes – come to me you divine dainties. Let me guzzle you down. Ahhh, how delightful!'

'He is raving,' commented Jupiter. 'The fever shall make him ramble incoherently from now on. No doubt we shall both tire of his rantings before he is cured.'

'Keep your Dutch Pudding!' gabbled Doctor Spittle. 'Where are all the spice cakes gone?'

Will grinned but it quickly turned into a yawn and the ginger cat eyed him kindly. 'Why do you not get some rest?' he asked. 'I can see to the old one now. You have done your part and there is little point in staying awake.'

'You're right,' the boy agreed, 'I really am very tired. I'll go to bed but if you need anything, wake me.'

'I shall,' returned Jupiter, 'and thank you.'

Will smiled. 'I still can't believe that you can really talk,' he chuckled. 'Maybe I'll wake up and find this has been a dream.'

'WILLIAM GODWIN!'

The scream had come from Doctor Spittle. He let out a long, wailing shriek and his hands clawed the air.

Will hesitated at the doorway; Jupiter turned to him. 'It is the fever that speaks,' he said. 'It means nothing.'

But Will was not so sure. 'I've never told him my full name,' he muttered.

'No!' babbled the alchemist. 'You cannot do that – yet why not? What was his should be mine. It is my right, I am the rightful heir of the house.'

Will knelt by the bedside. Doctor Spittle was evidently reliving some past moment when his mind had been in some great turmoil.

'Take the land,' gusted the alchemist's shrill voice. 'Sell it – think of the gold, man! Why all these qualms? – you've never had them before now.' He huddled himself into a ball and his fingers pressed against his full lips as he hushed himself to a hoarse whisper. 'But I have,' he rattled on in this demented fashion. 'Remember the child – and this one is the same. What are you to do with him?' His face hardened and the answer came snapping back. 'Death!' he seethed. 'Slay him swiftly, let none remain that have a claim on the land. Rectify the blunder you made back then.'

Will and Jupiter looked at one another, confused and astonished. 'It is as if two people are speaking,' remarked the cat.

'No,' corrected Will, 'more like Doctor Spittle's conscience arguing with the evil side of his nature.'

'But what are they discussing?' asked Jupiter.

The boy did not reply – an awful suspicion was forming in his mind.

The alchemist wailed sadly in his delirium and the bizarre conversation continued. 'No,' he pleaded, 'not death for one so young, can we not keep him under our watchful eye yet let the world think he has perished?'

The dark half of his personality spat and the old

man bared his teeth. 'A curse on your yellow liver,' he grumbled. 'Very well, but I like it not. Do not expect me to be kind to the lad; he can rot in my service for all I care – yet I would rather he was dead.'

'Even though he is of our blood?'

'Silence! Long ago I broke free of such shackles. I have no kin now. My name is Elias Theophrastus Spittle – I do not recognise that former life. I have ceased to be Samuel Godwin!'

Will cried in alarm as the answers to all his questions flooded into his mind. 'Lord in heaven!' he gasped, staggering to his feet and stumbling away from the bed.

'What is the matter?' asked Jupiter, not understanding the significance of what had been said.

The boy raised a quivering finger of accusation and pointed it, aghast, at the old man. In a faint and stricken voice he stammered, 'He . . . he is my uncle.'

A wicked and disdainful expression darkened the alchemist's face as his evil aspect conquered his weaker, timid conscience. And, as if the outcome of this turbulent, inner conflict was the awaited catalyst, the elixir of life finally triumphed over the Black Death. Very slowly, the plague boils began to shrink and disappear.

Jupiter noticed the reaction but he was more concerned for Will. 'Tell me what is wrong,' he asked. 'I know nothing of this matter.'

The boy gazed fearfully at the rapidly recovering old man then turned a pale, drained face to the cat. 'I was brought to London by an invitation from an uncle I had never seen,' he explained. 'Now I discover that the black-hearted rogue who has made me slave for him is none other than he.'

Jupiter listened attentively as Will related the story of how he came to London with Mr Balker. Neither saw a dark shape slither through the doorway and creep towards the bed.

Leech stole forward, his emerald eyes warily glinting and shining as they searched for the elixir. Then he saw it; the large glass jar was on the low bedtable. Slinking between piles of old clothes he crept closer. Stalactites of ancient candle grease were glued down the table legs and Leech regarded the sticky streaks contemptuously.

'I could never get my claws to hook into that slippery mess,' he told himself. 'How then am I to climb up?'

He gave his brother and the boy a sideways glance; if he jumped up on to the pillows and reached over to the jar then they would surely spot him. Then his green eyes fell on the two pewter bowls that Will had shoved under the bed. Both contained a clear liquid and he twitched his whiskers over each of them in turn.

'One of these is definitely the elixir,' he muttered, 'yet which one I cannot tell.' He sniffed them again but still he could not decide – both smelled strange but the chemical fumes confounded his senses.

'If I were to drag one bowl to the graveside then it might be the wrong one,' he told himself, 'and I would be sure to spill most of it getting there.'

Faced with this problem Leech did the only thing he could. Going to each bowl in turn, he sucked up an equal amount of both liquids then darted for the door, his full cheeks swollen into distorted balls of black fur that threatened to burst at any moment.

Down the stairs he galloped, like a hideous four-legged spider scurrying after its prey. Then across the floor of the shop he dashed and snaked out through the open doorway.

A pall of choking smoke rose into the sky and blotted out the stars. The London streets were filled by the clamour of voices as curious people left their beds to see the fire. Wrapped in dressing-gowns and tripping over the cobbles in their slippers they pattered towards Pudding Lane where the King's bakehouse was ablaze. The capital was agog with wonder and speculation as to how it had started.

' 'Tis a popish plot,' some of the citizens muttered. 'The Bishop of Rome is behind this I'll warrant.'

But no one truly felt threatened by this new calamity that crackled on into Fish Street – London had seen many fires in the past and they all believed this one would burn itself out and cause no great harm.

Like an angry demon, Leech sped between the inquisitive sensation-seekers and hurtled down Cheapside towards the church of St Anne's.

The tall tower rose starkly against the infernal heavens, a brooding, black shape whose stained-glass windows reflected the glare of the fire-like jewels. In the dark, lofty heights of the belfry, the bats took counsel with one another and they flitted about the church, anxious to leave, yet yearning to stay and see what had been foretold.

Leech slipped through the cemetery gates, invisible in the shadows, and passed into the wild tangle of bushes and thickets beyond.

His face ached with the strain of carrying the liquid in his mouth and twice on his journey he had almost swallowed it by accident. Prowling through the weeds and knotted undergrowth he hunted for the grave of Magnus Zachaire. He knew it was here somewhere, all his instincts told him that, yet in the two years since Imelza had given birth to him the graveyard had changed dramatically.

It was an impenetrable jungle of briar and hawthorn. The Goddess had not been idle and her ancient and perilous might had focused on this one area of neglect. Alone in all London she made her abode there, silent and cold, threatening the order of civilisation and reason with her tendrils of nightmare – a remote vision of how England would look without the hand of man to till the soil and keep her wildness in check.

Leech was aware of her, yet he sneered. Such primeval powers were on the wane, he thought to himself. The time of the old gods was drawing to an end; soon they would be a fanciful memory and only the places where they had been worshipped would mourn them. Now a new age was sweeping aside all past allegiances to sacred hilltops and woodland groves. It was a time for order and control, for nature to be subdued and tamed and the wildness removed from the land.

The branches rustled over the runt's head as he passed beneath, searching and prying for his birthplace. Squeezing between the brambles that tried to bar his way, he pushed by crumbling tombs and then he found it.

There was the ornate carving of the dragon, twisting

and curling about the headstone, its scales encrusted with moss and a noose of ivy strangling the roaring throat.

With relief Leech crept forward, then lowered his head. His lips parted and the liquid he had carried so far spilled on to the ground and seeped into the soil.

The cat gave a grunt of satisfaction. 'At last,' he smirked taking a deep breath. 'Now we shall see who will succeed, brother dear.'

A faint sizzling sound rumbled in the earth and Leech settled down to see what would happen. Soon it would be over; Magnus would live again and reward him handsomely. Licking his wet chin he began to purr, but it was a vile, malicious noise. Then he swallowed and the bats high above wheeled excitedly in the sky and were content to leave.

Will peered under the bed and fumbled around with his hands. 'What are you looking for?' ventured Jupiter curiously.

'I'm not sure,' the boy replied, 'but there must be something that . . .' He stared at the large wardrobe which dominated the room and crossed to it. The single door opened with a creak and he held up a candle to see what lay inside.

A musty, damp smell flowed from the wooden interior and when the glow fell upon its contents Will wrinkled his nose. The wardrobe was filled with old clothes. Everything Doctor Spittle had ever worn was stashed and hoarded in there – he never threw anything away even if it was frayed and full of holes.

The garments were spotted with black mould and Will was about to close the door again when he noticed the corner of some bulky shape protruding out of a tatty and grime-stained shirt.

He pushed the filthy material out of the way and revealed a small wooden chest. Will placed the candle on the floor and lifted the box out of the mouldering heap. It was very heavy and, by the sound of it, filled with coins.

Hastily he knelt down and Jupiter came to sit next to him.

The chest was painted black and strong iron bands sealed it firmly, yet it was plain that the hinges had been oiled only recently. The boy fiddled with the lid but the lock was too strong. 'It's impossible to open without the key,' he said. 'Where would old Spittle keep that?'

'No key is necessary,' put in Jupiter. 'There are many spells concerned with breaking and releasing. I could easily open the chest for you and seal it again when you have done. My master need never know.'

'But why should you help me?' asked Will.

'You have been wronged,' the ginger cat said simply, 'and you helped me when I needed you. This is but a debt repaid.'

'Very well,' Will declared, 'open it.'

Jupiter closed his eyes and pressed his paws together. The wooden box began to tremble and then, with a snap, the hasps sprang apart.

Gently, Will lifted the lid and his face was lit by a rich, golden radiance.

The chest was filled with sovereigns and he gazed at the fortune, speechless.

Jupiter peered at the contents impassively – money

had no dominion over him. There was however something else inside the box.

'What is that?' he asked, pointing to a scroll of parchment half buried amid the treasure.

Will took out the document and unfurled it. 'I do not understand what is written,' he told the cat.

'Then show it to me,' said the familiar, 'I shall read what it says.'

Jupiter narrowed his eyes and commenced reading. 'It is a deed of sale,' he murmured quietly, 'between my master and an agent in a place called Adcombe.'

Will started. 'What has Spittle bought there?' he cried.

'Nothing,' returned Jupiter, 'but he has sold a farm, plus its livestock and all its lands.'

'Not the Godwin estate?'

'The very same; it would seem this is the money from that transaction. Is it important?'

'My father laboured all his life on that land,' the boy sadly answered, 'building it up with his blood and sweat. Spittle had no claim to it – the farm was mine, this is my inheritance. Is that what he wanted then? Has all this misery and murder been brought about merely by greed? Does he think of nothing but gold?'

'Oh yes,' whispered a familiar voice.

Both of them whirled around and there, standing behind them, tall and forbidding – was Doctor Spittle.

The candlelight flickered over the old man's face. Not a trace of the plague remained; he was fully recovered and a sinister, evil gleam shone in his eyes.

'I have learned that there are many cravings more satisfying than wealth,' he hissed in a silken,

menacing tone. 'Since your arrival, my young dog, you have taught me much.' He stepped forward, the flame illuminating his face from below, sending up deep shadows, like two horns spiking from his eyebrows. 'I see in you all the weaknesses of Daniel my hated brother. He was a fool also – gullible and ignorant – yet our father made the estate over to him instead of me – the elder son.' The alchemist's face was terrible to look on and Will shrank away from him, horribly afraid.

'If I had succeeded all those years ago my life would have been very different,' the old man continued. 'I ought never to have stayed my hand. Daniel would have been easy to kill.'

His voice trailed off as that remote and distant night unfolded before his eyes once more. The long years fell away and he raised his hand just as he had done then. His younger self crept up behind his infant brother and the knife glinted in his grasp, poised to cut the baby's throat. He shuddered and snapped back to the present.

'I should have done it then!' he snarled through gritted teeth. 'All my life his very existence has infected me with weakness – I even changed my name to escape the bonds of his innocence and purity. But still the thought of him, living and breathing, hounded and persecuted me – never whole, never complete, always thinking of him! I have been crippled and thwarted in all my designs just because he was out there!'

He slammed the wardrobe shut and his lips pulled back in a hideous grin. 'And then he died,' he cackled. 'I felt it the instant he perished. At last, I thought, I can be free and what was mine by right shall be so again. Then I sensed your wretched presence – dog! Not only would you claim the estate but you were just like your devout father and I could almost taste the reek of your piety.'

'You're mad!' stammered Will in fright.

'Oh no,' returned the alchemist softly, 'but I was. The elixir is a miraculous compound in many ways; finally I can think clearly and my mind is no longer divided between hatred and guilt – I have been purged of all distractions forever. Now it is time to begin my new everlasting life, but unfortunately for you, you shall not be a part of it.'

His hand grabbed Will by the hair and dragged him to his feet. 'How fitting that your life will end just as mine starts afresh,' he muttered coldly. 'The Godwin line shall finish here!' and he brought his fist swiftly down, hitting Will on the jaw and sending him flying across the bedchamber.

Jupiter watched all this in fear. What was he to do? He did not dare to turn against his master.

The alchemist opened his hand and the tufts of hair that had been wrenched from the boy's head fell to the floor.

Will groaned as he raised his pounding head. Blood dribbled from his mouth and he spat out a tooth as he propped himself upon his elbows.

'You want more?' sniggered Doctor Spittle slowly advancing, his fists clenching in readiness.

Will tried to stand but the blow had weakened him and the old man laughed.

Confused, Jupiter ran forward and stood between Doctor Spittle and the boy. 'Master!' he cried. 'The child saved your life – you would not have returned were it not for him.'

The alchemist glared at the cat. 'It gratifies me to see how mighty you have become, my familiar,' he growled, 'although how much more pleasing it would have been if you had deigned to speak to me first of all. Out of my way, if you want to remain here and learn from my genius!'

Jupiter knew that he could not withstand the powers of his master so, reluctantly, he stepped aside.

'Save my life did you?' cackled Doctor Spittle to Will. 'A most pretty irony – still, we must not let Death leave empty-handed must we? A life he came for and a life he shall receive!'

But the intervention of Jupiter had been long enough for Will to regain his strength. He shot to his feet and fled down the stairs.

The alchemist thundered with rage and sped after him.

In the apothecary shop Will tore towards the door, but before he reached it, it closed of its own accord and invisible fingers threw the bolt home.

'No!' he yelled, fighting with the unseen force as he struggled to escape.

A soft, mocking laugh hissed behind him. 'You cannot leave that way,' Doctor Spittle murmured, 'I have laid spells upon it.'

Will abandoned the attempt and pressed himself against the wall. 'Keep away from me!' he shouted.

The old man raised his eyebrows wickedly. 'How shall I murder you?' he mused in a calm, dispassionate voice.

He clicked his fingers and a stool rose from the

ground. For a moment it hovered in the air then, with one nod from Doctor Spittle, hurled itself straight at the frightened boy.

Will ducked and the stool crashed into the wall then tumbled to the ground, scattering pots from a shelf in its downfall. The vessels smashed and exploded all around him, showering the shop with splinters of ceramic and splattering their contents over the floor.

The alchemist clapped his hands with amusement and Will grabbed his chance. He seized the stool and threw it at the window. The diamond panes shivered away from the lead and the boy kicked a hole through what remained.

'Oh no!' bellowed the old man striding forward. 'You must stay here!' Just as Will was scrambling out the alchemist snatched at him and dragged the boy back inside.

'I always thought magic was too antiseptic a method!' he shrieked, flinging the lad against the counter. 'The personal touch is far more enjoyable.' And he punched Will fiercely in the ribs.

The boy doubled up; with the elixir of life coursing in Doctor Spittle's veins his strength was that of a hundred men. The back of his hand dealt Will one vicious and brutal blow after another.

'Down!' he commanded, beating the boy to the ground. 'Grovel at my feet, scion of Daniel!'

Will's legs buckled under him and, as the punches continued to hammer and bludgeon, his eyes rolled upwards until only the whites showed. With a lurch, he sprawled on to the floor – unconscious. Then he knew no more.

Doctor Spittle gave him a malicious kick and brayed like a donkey. 'No more purity to infect me,' he muttered, 'but just to make sure . . . ' He marched over to a high shelf and reached up to take down a bottle of dark blue glass.

'What are you going to do with him?' asked Jupiter suddenly.

The alchemist spun on his heel and clutched the bottle to his chest. 'What business is it of yours?' he barked.

The familiar stood in the doorway by the stairs, his golden eyes looking appealingly up at his master.

'Can you not let the boy go free?' he pleaded. 'Has he not suffered enough at your hands?'

Doctor Spittle drew himself up to his full height and he stared down at the ginger cat indignantly.

'How dare you speak to me like that!' he cried. 'Do not meddle in your master's affairs, my pet – you cannot begin to understand the subtle workings of his mind.'

'Are you going to kill the child?' Jupiter persisted.

'Indeed I am!' raged the alchemist angrily. 'I hold here a most lethal poison! Enough to slaughter an entire herd of elephants. One drop of it and the young dog will wither away and corrode from within. I believe it is the only death I can contrive which is more horrible than the plague. Now go away and let me savour this moment in peace.'

Jupiter wavered. His heart went out to the boy; he was the only human that had ever really been kind to him and his family. If it were not for Will they would have all died in the graveyard. The cat scowled but the old man was insistent.

'Begone!' he shrieked. 'Before I use this on your miserable skin!'

With one last glance at Will, Jupiter turned and ran upstairs.

Doctor Spittle sucked the air in through his teeth.

'My familiar grows above himself,' he murmured. 'There is no longer room for him at my side. Some accident shall have to be contrived for him also.'

Grasping the bottle of poison he raised it over his head and let out a harsh, cruel laugh. Then he bent over Will's senseless body and his hands reached out menacingly.

As the alchemist turned the lad over, an ugly, black head peered over the glass-strewn window-ledge. Leech's green eyes glowed between the damaged lattices and he gazed fearfully at the stooping figure of Doctor Spittle. Then, when he was certain the old man could not observe him, the runt leapt through the wreckage and darted upstairs.

In the attic Jupiter sat on the chair, feeling dismal and dejected. Outside, the great fire appeared to have diminished and the aura of scarlet was fainter in the sky.

Leech pelted into the cluttered room, but when he saw his brother his pace slowed and he sneaked over to the shelf where Magnus Zachaire waited for him.

'I am indeed glad to see thee, friend runt,' said the spirit eagerly, 'and what tidings hast thou brought for me?'

The black cat shuffled and twitched uneasily.

'Little news,' he answered.

Magnus's face grew stern. 'What sayest thou?' he rumbled. 'Did the ground not open and my restored body not come forth, awaiting only the return of my soul?'

'No,' muttered Leech, 'believe me I waited and waited but nothing happened, except . . .'

'Except what?'

The runt looked bemused. 'The grass turned orange,' he spluttered, 'though why it should do so I have no idea.'

'Fool!' shouted the spirit and his ghostly light blazed cold and fiercely. 'Thou didst take the wrong potion to my grave – that was the hair restorer!'

Leech looked down shamefully. 'But I was confounded,' he whined self-pityingly. 'There were two bowls, and I was so afraid I would be caught that I did not have time to discover which contained the elixir. So I took some of each – I did not think it would matter.'

The spirit pressed its hands against the bottle and glowered at him. 'Then the strength of the elixir was diluted!' he cried. 'I cannot guess what will be the outcome of such folly. Thou hast torn my plans to shreds, perfidious and dunderheaded creature that thou art!' He drew away from the glass and considered this disastrous turn of events. 'Only one road lies open to me now,' he whispered. 'Leech – call thy brother over to me.'

'What do you want him for?' asked the runt sullenly.

'Just do as I say!'

Leech sulked but he crept from the shelf and scuttled over to the alchemist's chair. 'Brother,' he called in an unpleasant voice.

Jupiter roused from his troubled thoughts and he

stared down at Leech in surprise. 'What is it?' he asked. 'What do you want?'

'It is not I who requests your company,' Leech snapped crossly, 'but the soul in yonder bottle. He would like to talk with you.'

The ginger cat flicked back his ears in astonishment. 'Magnus wishes to speak with me?' he said. 'But why?'

He received no answer for Leech had given an annoyed lash with his tail and strutted away. Jupiter jumped from the chair and wandered over to the shelf where the bottle pulsed and throbbed with icy light.

In the shadows Leech was listening, furious with jealousy and his pride rankling by his curt dismissal. It seemed that even the spirit had abandoned him in favour of his brother.

'Hail Jupiter – Lord of All,' greeted Magnus humbly.

'Why do you call me by that title?' Jupiter asked.

'I speak only of that which assuredly shall come to pass,' returned Magnus. 'Thy realm will last for hundreds of years and thy powers shall extend over the whole earth and finally beyond.'

Jupiter stared intently at the tiny form that bowed within the bottle. 'Why do you say this now?' he inquired. 'When you have never spoken one word to me before.'

'I need thy help,' answered Magnus, 'for art thou not deep in wisdom and mighty in all sorceries?'

The familiar was tired of all this flattery. 'Come to the point,' he said. 'What is it you want me to do and why can't you do it? Were you not learned in the secret arts yourself?'

'Yea, and thrice times more noble than thy detestable master!' the spirit proclaimed. 'Yet in this my skill may not be used; to recall one's own bones from the cold grave is forbidden.'

'Your bones!' exclaimed Jupiter. 'Why should I do that?'

'To give aid where it is requested,' came the swift reply. 'This is now my only chance – if I could but bind my soul about those mortal remains I could kindle the power of the weakened elixir which thy foolish brother poured into the grave. Flesh and sinew would creep over the rotted cadaver and new blood would pump round the body, imbuing it with life. I would live again!'

'You want me to recite a spell that will animate your corpse and bring it here?' muttered Jupiter in horror. 'I won't do it – the notion is obscene.'

'Just give it the slightest spark,' pleaded Magnus, 'enough for it to crawl from the ground, after that I can bend my will upon it and guide it hither myself. I beg thee!'

But Jupiter turned away disgusted. 'Never!' he said. 'I perceive your true purpose Magnus Zachaire! Two things you crave – one is your freedom but the other is the destruction of my master. I will have no hand in that.'

'Thy master!' shrieked the spirit with scorn. 'Listen to thy words, most gullible of felines. Dost thou not realise the extent of Elias's iniquity? Knowest thou of all his evil wickedness? Is it wrong to turn against him who hath no pity in his foul heart?'

Jupiter was about to leave this bothersome sprite but he faltered as the words rang true. He thought of the scene in the apothecary shop, of the boy beaten to the ground and of the poison in the alchemist's hand.

'Thou knowest I speak justly,' goaded Magnus. 'Why keep faith with one who understands nothing of loyalty and virtue? Even now Elias is uncorking the poison; shall that child's death be on thy conscience for ever, Jupiter?'

A pained expression crossed the familiar's face as he thought of Will lying helpless with an agonising death being prepared for him by Doctor Spittle. Yet if he intervened and the old man was overcome, how would he ever be able to learn anything more?

Jupiter cast his eyes down and uttered, 'I must not meddle in the affairs of mankind, their troubles are their own.'

The phantom light flared up and Magnus screamed. 'Are they indeed?' he shrieked. 'Then I say unto thee Jupiter, go to the cupboard which Elias keeps locked and tell me again that thou canst not interfere!'

Puzzled by the earnestness of this command, the cat padded over to a small cupboard. It was partially hidden by books and papers. He looked round at the spirit bottle and Magnus urged him on. Jupiter cleared the mess from one of the doors and tugged at the handle.

'It is locked,' he said.

'Then open it!' hissed Magnus furiously.

Just as he had done before, Jupiter put his paws together and closed his eyes. The cabinet rattled and, with a click, the lock turned. Both doors opened a chink.

Jupiter hesitated. He did not know why but for

some reason he was afraid to look inside and he glanced at the spirit nervously.

'Proceed,' spurred Magnus. 'See now the cruel nature of thy beloved master!'

The cat took hold of the brass handles and cautiously pulled one of the doors fully open.

The cupboard was full of sealed glass jars – the results of Doctor Spittle's half-hearted studies in anatomy. Each vessel contained a yellowish liquid and immersed in this was a sorry collection of serpents and other small creatures in various states of dissection. Jupiter shuddered, for in the nearest jar was the shrivelled body of Heliodorus.

The rat floated in the preserving alcohol forlornly, his once proud head submerged just below the surface. It was a nauseating sight. The eyes of Heliodorus were open, the lids fixed back by pins; his mouth gaped wide as though frozen in a perpetual scream and all the way down his chest to his navel ran a long and jagged scar. Doctor Spittle's curiosity had been too much – he had desired to peek inside and see how the false elixir which had killed the rat had worked. But his skill as a surgeon was minimal and the botched job he had made of the operation had forced him to consign the hacked-up body to his anatomy cupboard, there to be discarded and forgotten – pickled for eternity.

'Poor wretch,' mumbled Jupiter sadly, 'no one deserves such callous treatment. Not even a rat.'

'Wholeheartedly do I agree,' breathed the spirit, 'yet thou hast not opened the other door – discover what the remaining half contains.' And as he said it he could not conceal the anticipation in his voice.

With a queasy stomach Jupiter obeyed. The shadows retreated as the door was opened and the light of the candles gradually filled the interior. The cat's heart pounded in his chest as a larger jar was slowly revealed and his breath came in rapid gulps.

And then he saw.

'NOOO!' he screamed. 'NOOOO!'

Drowned in the liquid were the remains of a cat.

Jupiter's staring eyes fell upon the scraps of tortoiseshell fur that still clung to the preserved pieces and he screeched hideously.

'DAB! DAB!'

'Now thou knowest the full depths of thy master's black heart!' said Magnus grimly. 'Wilt thou still deny me my revenge?'

Jupiter staggered back, his face an awful mask of horror and despair. 'Dab!' he howled, and then his countenance became terrible, filled with anger and hatred for the man who had murdered his sweet and gentle sister. 'Spittle!' he roared. 'Your time is over!'

'The incantation!' Magnus shouted. 'Thou must summon my bones from the grave!'

But the cat was too inflamed with wrath to listen. Exploding with rage, he tore down the stairs, shrieking at the top of his voice, possessed by hatred and revenge.

'Come back!' cried the spirit. 'The spell!'

Leech crawled out of the shadows and gazed at the body of his sister. No emotion betrayed his thoughts and his green eyes were dry and free of tears.

'Fetch Jupiter back!' commanded Magnus. 'Or all will be lost.'

The runt blinked and turned his ugly head. 'No,'

he whispered, 'I obey none but myself.' He glanced back at the cupboard and muttered, 'I saw him take her you know. I saw his hands cover her mouth as she called to my brother for help. Her pretty voice was still whimpering as the door was closed and I heard it slowly fade away as she was taken downstairs.'

The spirit looked at him bewildered. 'Then why didst thou not help her?' he asked.

'My name is not Jupiter!' snapped Leech. 'My sister did not call out to me – oh no, only my grand and noble brother filled her mind. When it mattered most she forgot I was there! Nobody thinks of Leech!'

'And so thou didst let her die?' gasped Magnus. 'Then I curse thee Leech, for thou art a misshapen abomination!'

The runt gloated under his breath. 'What do I care for your curses?' he mocked. 'You have no power to enforce them. Your hope has ended. My brother can never overcome the old one: he has gone haring to his doom.' And he laughed like one gone mad.

14

Of Reckoning and Destiny

Jupiter hurtled down the stairs, but when he reached the small landing he halted and charged into the alchemist's bedchamber.

On to the pillows he jumped and from there reached over to the jar which held the elixir. Grasping it with both paws, Jupiter thrust his head inside and drank deeply.

The cat gulped down as much as he could, and when he reared up and vigorously shook his whiskers he saw that he had drained it to the dregs.

His fur dripping with the water of life, Jupiter bounded from the bed and stormed down the stairs. He was strong now; filled as he was with the power of the elixir, he roared like a tiger and the hatred of his cruel master burned into his mind, consuming all other thoughts.

Doctor Spittle had slid a glass rod into the neck of the bottle and was just drawing it out. The poison was green and thick, oozing and trickling down the rod until it formed a large, quivering droplet.

Sniggering, he crouched down and dangled it over Will's mouth. 'At last,' he breathed, 'the last of the Godwins are gone.'

'SPITTLE!'

The alchemist shivered at the force of that voice. The glistening venom flew from the tip of the rod but it missed Will's mouth and where it hit the ground the very stone foamed up and a thread of black smoke steamed into the air.

Doctor Spittle twitched with anger; stiffly he rose and turned upon the intruder.

Jupiter stood in the doorway, tall shadows tapered behind him and he appeared immovable as a mountain. His boiling temper seethed within him, threatening to erupt at any moment like a restless volcano.

'Get away from the boy!' the cat demanded.

The alchemist regarded his familiar warily; a perilous light blazed in those golden eyes and righteous fire shone from the slits of his pupils. Doctor Spittle guessed what he had found.

'I assume you've seen your sister,' he said, then added with a cold chuckle, 'Well, some of her.'

Jupiter roared and the building quaked from the might of his fury.

But Doctor Spittle was not impressed and he showed no trace of fear. 'I told you not to meddle in my affairs,' he said. 'Begone before I make you suffer.'

'Suffer?' yelled Jupiter. 'There is nothing you could

do now that would make my torment any greater.'

The old man tutted. 'Many griefs there are greater than the loss of family. Now leave while you may.'

But the cat grinned, revealing his sharp teeth. 'You are mistaken, Spittle!' he cried. 'No longer am I bound to you – I have come not as your familiar, but your executioner!'

At this the alchemist laughed. 'Are you crazed?' he asked with derision. 'I am not afraid of a mangy cat – however educated it presumes itself to be.'

'Have a care, Spittle. Do not underestimate my powers.'

'Pah!' scoffed the old man. 'What do I who have drunken of the elixir need to fear from the likes of you?'

Then Jupiter threw back his head and laughed. 'Then gaze upon your doom, Elias Theophrastus Spittle! For I, Jupiter, have also drunk of the water of life and my strength increases with every passing second.'

His claws sprang out and they gouged deeply into the floor, ripping through the stone as easily as if it were butter. Then Jupiter muttered under his breath and at once the ground trembled. With a terrible splitting sound, a great fissure opened, running between his paws and Doctor Spittle's feet. The challenge was unmistakable.

The alchemist glanced calmly at the gaping chasm that yawned before him. 'A contest?' he asked in a confident and casual manner.

'No contest,' Jupiter boomed, 'but a battle to the death!' He stamped his feet twice and called upon his secret arts. Sudden bolts of lightning crashed about him, walling him round with a fence of dazzling, jagged energy.

Doctor Spittle shielded his eyes from the blinding spectacle. He was impressed by the cat's powers but had studied the black mysteries for too long to feel threatened by a jumped-up familiar.

'This is a waste of time,' he said undaunted. 'Since we have both drunk of the elixir there can be no victor.'

'Are you indeed so confident?' hissed Jupiter, his voice filled with menace. 'Then this will do you no damage!'

He pressed himself flat against the floor, inhaling deeply. Then, with a rush he blew his breath upon his sister's murderer and the shop was filled with scarlet flame as fire gusted from the cat's gullet.

The alchemist raised his hand, an unconcerned smile flickering on his lips as the torrent of flame burst towards him.

And then it happened: the fingers of his hand passed within the jet of fire and pain rifled down his arm as they blackened and burned.

'AAHH!' squealed the old man wrenching his hand quickly away and staring dumbfounded at the grinning cat. 'My hand!' he yelped. 'My hand – it is scorched! The pain is unbearable!'

'Did you not listen to the words of Magnus Zachaire?' Jupiter chuckled. 'Were you so eager for success that you heeded nothing of his warning?'

Doctor Spittle blew on his smoking palm and whimpered, 'What warning?'

'Fire and water!' exclaimed Jupiter gleefully. 'The two elements from which the elixir was made.

Only they can destroy its effects and undo the life it has given.'

Finally the alchemist became aware of his danger and he realised that his immortality was truly under threat. He had never been valiant and now, in his alarm, stood like one bereft of thought and will. He was plunged into a fit of doubt and fear, and with increasing terror he saw the blazing coals of the cat's eyes as he prepared for another strike.

Hurriedly Doctor Spittle gathered his shredded wits and groped in his memory for a spell to counter with. Clenching his teeth he drew himself up and began uttering a deadly incantation. But before he could complete it Jupiter had lowered his head once more and a second stream of flame poured from his mouth.

Abandoning the unfinished spell, the alchemist hastily threw up a wall of defence. All about him the air shimmered as a magical shield snapped into existence, and not a second too soon.

With a deafening squall of fury, the heats of Jupiter's fire smashed into it, and the violence of the attack made the old man jump back in fright. Already his defence was buckling as the inferno battered and blasted and Doctor Spittle was forced to squander valuable time keeping the blistering wall in place.

'Do you know fear now?' asked Jupiter, flames dripping from his lips. 'Are the thoughts which run through your mind the same as those my sister had? I think not – for your brain is sick and twisted, whereas hers was kind and trusting. Go now to the abyss which awaits you!'

The cat began to purr but it was not the soft sound of ordinary felines, this was a jarring rumble that cracked the plastered walls and sent splinters flying from the oak beams. Steadily it rose, piercing the ears of Doctor Spittle until he thought his head would burst. The entire building shook and tiles clattered from the roof, smashing in the alley below. Then a change came over the ginger cat.

As his voice grew louder, so he increased in size. His fur bristled and his taut muscles quivered. The lightning which surrounded him leapt upon his brow and he was crowned like a dreadful lord of destiny and doom. Beneath his skin the bones of his body creaked and stretched as the awful power of the elixir inflamed him. Doctor Spittle could only gawp as the cat swelled and grew to horrible dimensions, filling that corner of the shop where he glared down at his cruel master. Larger than the mightiest lion Jupiter became – his back touched the ceiling and his tail reached out of the door and up the stairs.

The alchemist was terrified; never had he encountered a more deadly foe, with powers that seemed to outstrip his own.

Jupiter's eyes stabbed with baleful light and the shop was lit by their unwavering and glittering stare. The huge maw of his mouth fell open and the vapour of his breath smote the old man like a barrage of bitter darts.

'Lord of All I shall be!' Jupiter told him. 'But you shall never witness my full glory. Breathe your last, Spittle – your petty life is ended.'

The fiery tempest tore through the shop and beat upon the magical shield of the alchemist. But Doctor

Spittle was not beaten yet; Jupiter had shown his hand, fire was his selected weapon – now it was the alchemist's turn. Standing like a pinnacle of stone amid the turmoil of the final storm, the old man raised one hand and declared, 'Two elements there are you say that are fatal to we both; then I shall wield what is left to me!'

With a pass of his hand a faint glimmer of cold light began to swirl in the air. Rapidly it became a whirlpool of icy stars that churned and spun above his head. 'Ignorant fool!' he shouted. 'If you dare to turn against your betters, be prepared to endure their punishment. You have overreached yourself, my reckless familiar, vaunting your skill like a boastful and bragging idiot. Too rash were you; fires are indeed spectacular, but what can they do other than char and burn? Brash and brazen are they, yet he who is wise knows that heats can be quenched. Water is a more amenable element, having many forms and uses.'

He pointed at Jupiter and at once the glittering host of stars raged forward.

The immense cat sent a ball of flame to meet them and it shot through the crackling air, pulsating with lethal force. A thunderous explosion sent Doctor Spittle staggering back but when he recovered he saw that his magic had prevailed. The icy stars had speared the fireball and utterly destroyed it. Now they raced towards Jupiter – spitting frost and deadly cold at him.

The cat braced himself for the attack, having no time to protect himself. The ice hailed down, bombarding his huge face and biting deep into his flesh. Jupiter cried out as the fierce blue stars drove into his fur, slicing him like razors.

Cackling, Doctor Spittle held up his hand and snatched a long, sharp icicle out of the air. 'The choice you made was the wrong one!' he declared. Then he hurled the bitter spear straight at Jupiter. It shot through the cat's leg, skewering and pinning him to the floor. His anguished screams rang into the troubled night and, twisting up the stairs, the enormous tail thrashed about in his agony and the banister buckled beneath it.

Then, conquering his pain, Jupiter lifted a claw and a circle of flame sprang up around the alchemist. The old man laughed scornfully and at once a downpour of cool rain flooded from the ceiling. Clouds of steam hissed and engulfed the shop as the two magical forces collided – and at last Doctor Spittle had the mastery.

The fires of Jupiter were extinguished and the old man advanced purposefully. 'With the waters of Death I vanquish you,' he intoned, 'and by the powers in me I have beaten your insolence.' As he spoke the rain turned into a blizzard of driving snow that focused on the giant cat, beating him to the ground and covering him with a hoary white frost. Jupiter shivered and the crown of lightning dwindled from his brow as he tried to kindle the flames once more. But it was no use; freezing mists clung to him, locking his joints so that he could not move. The tears of pain that streamed from his glimmering eyes hardened and slid from his cheeks like tiny glaciers; he could not speak for his jaw had grown numb and a white beard of arctic rime dripped from his chin. Doctor Spittle had won.

The great fissure in the floor became filled with water as proof of the outcome and the old man raised his arms in exultation.

As Jupiter felt the unending, wintry cold of the bleak void bite him, he yielded at last. A final flicker of flame trailed from his nostrils and the battle was over. Now both elements were at the alchemist's command and he seized the prize triumphantly.

'Now shall I taunt you with them both,' he sniggered.

From the cat's fur there sprang tongues of blue fire and Jupiter screeched in torment as both heat and cold racked him. The powers of the elixir waned within his body and, like a candle melting before the fire, he began to shrink. Back to his normal size he wilted and Doctor Spittle strode harshly up to his small, spent figure.

'Did I not tell you that I was the master here?' he asked. 'From now on no one shall stand in my way!'

He raised his hand to deal the cat the final blow. Bitter stars gleamed and danced around his fingers and Jupiter, lifting up his exhausted and failing eyes, beheld them fearfully.

But he was not dead yet – using his last energies, he snapped the icicle which held him down and scrambled to the door.

'There is no escape,' sneered the old man but Jupiter dragged himself away and ran up the stairs.

Leech was hiding when Jupiter staggered into the attic. The ferocity of the contest had frightened the runt; he thought that the building would come crashing down, so had dived under the table for shelter.

And now, emerald eyes shining, he saw his battered brother stumble in through the door and collapse – gasping on the floorboards. Blue smoke still drifted from his frozen fur and fizzing stars of ice burned into his skin.

'Jupiter!' cried a frantic voice. 'Thou livest still. Quickly – recite the spell I need!'

The weak cat raised its head and saw the face of Magnus Zachaire staring desperately out of the bottle. As the frost bit and pinched him, he realised that one slender chance still remained.

With the breath wheezing in his icy lungs Jupiter summoned the few tatters of magic that he still possessed.

'Arhiel dor lievel adrasto Rameth – akad zerphiel Bellonar!' he uttered in a feeble voice. 'Come forth – come forth!' And then he fainted and his head hit the floor, scattering shards of ice everywhere.

The spirit's face split into a glorious smile and his laughter echoed from the bottle and resounded through the attic.

'My thanks Jupiter!' he crowed. 'Now I am freed. Even as I speak I feel my bones claw away the soil and escape the silent grave.' His phantom light shone like a beacon in his joy. 'Come my corpse,' he shouted, 'come unto me!'

Leech crept from the shadows beneath the table. His eyes were fixed upon his stricken brother and darkness ruled his mind.

'So vulnerable,' he whined to himself, 'there he lies – close to the precipice of Death. How simple to push him over the brink and claim the power which he denied me.'

The runt crawled forward, consumed by evil and malice. His claws slid out and he hunched his shoulders as he prepared to spring – then he pounced.

His teeth went straight for the exposed throat. But some trace of the elixir still lingered in the familiar's body for he awoke instantly and lashed out at his attacker, catching the runt on the side of the face and tearing great gashes into his cheek.

Wailing, Leech leapt aside; he had aroused Jupiter's wrath and fearfully he saw him struggle to his feet. The hackles on both cats rose and their backs arched as they paced round one another – their tails rigid.

'The time has come,' spat the runt, 'the time of reckoning and destiny. Only one of us will leave this place alive!'

Jupiter hissed back at him and his ears flattened against his skull. 'If that is what you wish, brother – so be it. I have been patient with you but now I agree. One of us must die!'

'Remember the oath that you swore,' snarled Leech. 'You promised never to use your magic against me! Tooth and claw only.'

'I need no enchantment to kill you!' replied his brother.

'Then make the sign of the Hunter!'

Jupiter lifted a paw in honour of the wild night and at that moment Leech flew at him.

The two cats rolled across the attic, biting and clawing one another. They were a blur of sable and ginger and their tails lashed furiously about them.

Into a pile of books they cannoned and their savage mewling filled the air.

All the spite and misery of his wretched life gave strength to Leech's scrawny limbs. Bitterly he wrestled, clutching and throttling, tearing and snapping. Using his hind legs to thrust the ginger cat against the wall, he directed his attention to the wound gouged by the ice spear and sank his fangs into it.

Jupiter shrieked and he shoved Leech away. The runt tumbled head over heels, his brother's blood dripping from his jaws. His somersaults ended when his head struck the leg of the table and for a moment he was dazed. Shaking his head he wiped his mouth and smacked his lips, but his courage fled when he saw the look on Jupiter's face.

The familiar growled and darted forward. With a frightened yell Leech jumped on to the chair then pelted over the shelves for dear life. To murder Jupiter as he lay prone and weak had been his plan, not meet him in mortal combat.

Books, scientific instruments, jars, scrolls, and everything else that the shelves held were thrown aside and they crashed to the floor as Jupiter raged after the gangling coward.

Amongst this uproar one other object toppled from the shelf and landed amid the wreckage. It was a small glass bottle and, from its depths, the face of Magnus Zachaire peered out at the deadly cat fight which rampaged round the room.

'So it is written,' he whispered. Then he closed his eyes and began to concentrate. With a jerk and a hop, the bottle started to roll across the attic floor and bounced through the doorway.

Doctor Spittle brushed the auburn locks away from his face and preened himself. A pale light was edging into the alley outside the apothecary shop as the grey morning of the second of September gradually dawned.

The alchemist gazed round – the place was ruined beyond repair; the walls were blackened and charred, the beams had split and plaster flaked from the ceiling. Not one pot was left intact and the floor was thick with the spilt contents. Through a mire of treacle, oil, pitch and spices he waded and the foundations of the building creaked and complained. Yet amid this devastation the old man smiled – none of this mattered any more, he needed the shop no longer.

'Elias Theophrastus Spittle,' he murmured softly, 'you are almost a god.'

Then his eye fell upon Will's unconscious body. During the battle with Jupiter the alchemist had forgotten all about him. Quickly he strode over to where the boy lay, covered by dust and soot. He was unharmed. It was as if the familiar's magic had purposefully avoided him.

Doctor Spittle leered and gave the lad a swift and malicious kick. Will stirred and groaned.

'Now I can dispatch you at my leisure,' said the old man, but a fierce noise from above made him look up sharply. Vicious squeals and shrieks floated down the stairs from the attic and he glowered irritably. 'How can I do anything with that caterwauling ringing in my ears?' he cried. 'I hope they slaughter each other!'

Suddenly the latch rattled and Doctor Spittle

whirled about. A dark figure was pressed against the door trying to get in.

'We are closed!' he shouted. 'And will be henceforth.'

The latch fell silent but the shadow outside did not move away. Instead a violent hammering commenced.

This was too much. 'How dare you!' the alchemist cried angrily, but before he could reach the door to let loose a tirade of abuse it shivered, splintering off its hinges, and burst open. A cloud of dust was flung into the air and as it settled Doctor Spittle whimpered in terror as the nightmare which filled the entrance was revealed.

'No!' he shrieked. 'Keep away!'

There on the threshold stood the mortal remains of Magnus Zachaire.

It was a ghastly apparition: a tall skeletal horror, with blank sockets for eyes and bones for fingers. A black shroud was wrapped loosely about its spindly limbs but the garment was ragged and the tattered wisps fluttered in the still air like shreds of mist caught in a wintry hedge of thorns.

The mouldering smell of the grave flowed out from the figure in waves of corruption and decay and the gruesome head twisted towards the alchemist. The hollow eyes fixed on him and the bottom jaw fell open.

'Begone!' cried the old man. 'By the powers of the underworld – return to your silent sleep.' Flapping his hands he desperately sought for a spell which would banish the awful monster.

The folds of the dark shroud rippled and the grinning cadaver stepped forward.

Doctor Spittle wailed in alarm as every enchantment he flung against it broke and was dispersed.

Slowly it stalked him; the arms of the skeleton were raised and the bony fingers groped the empty air relentlessly.

'What do you want?' squawked the old man. But it made no reply and as it prowled nearer its intent was plain.

Down the stairs a small shape tumbled and bounced. The spirit bottle landed at the bottom of the steps with a bump then rolled into the shop.

Doctor Spittle, however, was oblivious to it, for he was unable to drag his eyes from the animated collection of bones that continued to advance and so the bottle came spinning up behind him.

Swiftly it moved over the sticky floor, guided unerringly by Magnus's will until it came to an abrupt halt and a voice shouted, 'Behold Elias thy doom is nigh!'

The alchemist squirmed to see who had spoken and in doing so brought his boot crashing down directly on to the bottle.

Crushed by his weight the glass cracked and shattered.

With an almighty roar a fierce explosion rocked the shop and the front wall was blown into the alley.

Magnus Zachaire was free!

In a blinding flash his soul shot upwards and dazzling stars of sapphire trailed in his wake. Up through the ceiling he blasted, up through the alchemist's bedchamber, into the attic, then out – bursting from the roof like a rocket. He soared into the leaden sky and his rejoicing boomed over London.

Near the river the great fire crackled still. During the night it had claimed over three hundred houses and was now close to London Bridge. The buildings burned like kindling and a choking smoke rose steadily into the heavens. Luckily there was no wind to drive it into the city and all the people prayed it would soon be under control. The Thames was crowded with boats as folk tried to get a better view of the dramatic spectacle and the hungry flames were reflected in the glimmering water. It was almost a pretty sight and several jolly sightseers commented on this as they bobbed up and down in their little crafts, enjoying the display.

If anybody saw the blue radiance of Magnus's spirit as it glinted high above the rooftops, they assumed it was a morning star and turned their attention back to the burning. No one noticed the brilliant light plummet towards the flames, curving in a wide gleaming arc down to the incinerated buildings.

Out, over the blazing roofscape the spirit flew, swooping in amongst the fumes and infernal smokes that belched from the splitting tiles and exposed rafters. Like a whirlwind he whipped up the heats and fanned the leaping flames until the fires intensified and became an inferno. The very bricks began to crack and molten lead dripped from the gutters.

Enduring the agony of these furnaces, Magnus tore through the sheets of flame and bent them towards the city. With dreadful speed the fire jumped from one building to another and cries of dismay rang out from the assembled onlookers; to them it seemed that a great east wind had started to blow and all watched in dread as the fire grew until it seemed that the air itself was ablaze.

With the flames lashing about him and glowing cinders flying upwards, Magnus dived. His sparkling light outshone the livid glare all around and it streaked down to the alley where the apothecary shop lay.

In a thunderous rush the fire leaped after him, forming an enormous arch of flame from one part of the city to another. Through the broken front of the shop the terrible burning crashed and everything was engulfed in the blaze.

Will opened one eye and waited for the black specks that swirled before him to fade from view. His head thumped, feeling like a horseshoe that was being tempered by a blacksmith. Why was it so hot? he wondered. Gingerly, he opened a second eye and the awful vision became clear.

The whole shop was aflame; the rivers of oil and pitch that had oozed over the floor were fine fuel for its hunger and it tore over the ground ravenously. The boy came to his senses and he hauled himself to his feet, but he was trapped. A massive wall of fire separated him from the exit and the intolerable heat beat him back towards the stairs.

'Noo!' gurgled a frightened voice.

Will started and peered through the towering flames. At the centre of a fiery ring two figures struggled and fought with one another. One was unmistakably Doctor Spittle but the boy could not make out who his attacker was.

The alchemist let out a strangled shriek, for at that moment the skeleton hands found his throat and the bones pressed into the spare and baggy flesh, squeezing the breath out of him.

'You cannot harm me!' gasped the alchemist clutching at the shroud which disintegrated in his hand.

The dreadful skull drew close to his face and the breath of darkness and the stale dead blew upon him.

'AAAAGGHH!' he howled, and the hands tightened at his throat. His face had turned purple and no matter how much he kicked and wriggled the deadly grip grew ever stronger. He knew that the corpse could not throttle the life out of him but he glanced fretfully at the encroaching flames.

'Release me!' he demanded. 'Release me at once!'

But the grave-stained fingers clung tenaciously to him and Will could do nothing to help. The boy's face was burned and the violence of the blistering fire drove him up the stairs. The steps ignited even as he sprang up them and flames licked constantly at his heels.

Doctor Spittle clawed at the vice-like hands and, with a tremendous effort, snapped one of the fingers from around his throat. The cadaver wavered and, seizing his chance, the alchemist twisted his neck, loosened the grip of the others and thrust the skeleton away.

The ghastly figure stumbled backwards into the flames. Immediately the ragged shroud was consumed and the apparition was wreathed in fire, burning like a torch.

The old man fled; through the hellish walls of heat towards the doorway he ran. 'I must survive!' he gabbled, scurrying from the furnace that had once been his shop. 'I must!'

His hands covering his face, he charged for the entrance but before he reached it a cold voice rang in his ears.

'Oh no, Elias – thou must not leave yet.'

Doctor Spittle pulled his hands from his eyes and in front of him the tall spirit of Magnus Zachaire barred his escape.

'Dost thou not like the warm party I have thrown in thine honour?' the spirit asked. 'Stay awhile longer, I beg.'

'I cannot!' screamed the alchemist trying to push aside the glittering phantom. 'Out of my way!'

Magnus laughed. 'Thou wert always a most discourteous fellow, Elias,' he chuckled. 'Yet I must insist – this is one time thou shalt obey my command.'

He rose into the air and his radiance gathered about his crackling corpse, winding tightly round it, seeping into the long dead bones. As Doctor Spittle watched, a change came over the skeletal figure: through the trembling haze he saw skin cover the hands and lights gleam in the dark sockets forming two keen eyes; bristles sprouted from the chin as a neat beard appeared and the lips parted into a wide smile. Magnus Zachaire had life again.

He was a lean, imposing man with a grim face and, as the infernal tumult raged, he breathed for the first time in nearly a hundred years.

'Behold, Elias,' he cried, 'I am reborn! Didst thou expect this when thou didst summon my soul from the sleep of Death?'

'No,' stammered the old man, 'I . . . I never did.'

Magnus stretched his long arms. 'What rapture it is to be renewed!' he rejoiced.

347

Doctor Spittle stared about him; the withering heats were becoming more intense. 'Quickly!' he spluttered. 'Now that you are alive you must realise our danger – we could die in here. Let us flee from this place.'

Magnus nodded and the alchemist sighed with relief, glad that the man had seen sense. 'Whatever quarrels lie between us they can be dealt with later,' he said, 'now let me pass!'

But the man did not move. He stared at the alchemist strangely and a chill crept over him; even as the sea of fire lashed around them he turned cold.

'Am I truly in agreement with thee?' Magnus asked in astonishment. 'Whyfor did I seek to walk again under the sun? There was peace in the void, I could forget the woes of the waking world and fear no more the unending torment of existence.' He glared at the alchemist and his eyes shone like steel. 'The elixir of life is a curse, Elias!' he declared. 'For me the burden of increasing years was a perpetual agony – I was glad to be released of it. Have I now condemned myself to another interminable sentence?'

Doctor Spittle edged away as Magnus reeled from the shock of what he had done.

'A torment to you perhaps,' he said, 'but not for me. You cannot deny me now – I relish the thought of my immortality.'

Magnus's strong hands caught hold of his arm and wrenched him back. 'Thou art to blame, Elias!' he shouted. 'If it were not for thee I would be sleeping still!' He stared round at the fury that besieged them and a wild look lit his face. 'Now shall I embrace Death willingly,' he cried. 'Come! Let us both go to the emptiness that awaits us.' And clutching the old man fiercely he began to drag him into the heart of the flames.

'NOOOOOO!' screamed Doctor Spittle in terror. 'You're mad! Don't do this to me!' But his shrieks were lost amid the roars of the firestorm and though he bit and struggled he could not escape Magnus Zachaire's iron grasp.

The tall man strode straight into the inferno, his voice raised in laughter – hauling Doctor Spittle behind him.

'Hand in hand, Elias,' sang Magnus, 'we meet oblivion together!'

With a last screech of protest the alchemist was overcome and the flames swallowed him.

Will scrambled up feverishly. As he reached the small landing the entire stairway lurched, splitting away from the wall, and thick, spark-filled smoke gusted from the splintered crevice. Will staggered and the steps fell away, leaving him tottering on a high platform, unable to reach the attic.

'Jupiter!' he called miserably. 'Leech!' There was no response; perhaps the fumes had already got to them. The poor creatures would be roasted alive up there.

The edges of the landing smouldered and blackened – then it dropped an ominous three feet and swayed unsteadily. Any moment now it would give way and go crashing to the ground.

Will sprang forward, launching himself at the door to Doctor Spittle's bedchamber. As he tumbled inside the landing finally disappeared and a savage jet of flame shot up the stairwell.

Smoke was already curling between the floorboards in the alchemist's room and the wood was hot to the touch. Will's only escape was the window and he hurried over to it – fumbling with the catch. But it was rusted and would not budge.

Eager tips of yellow flame stabbed up through the scorching floor and the piles of clothes that were strewn carelessly about steamed and were set alight – combusting into raging bonfires.

The smoke billowed in more thickly and Will cast round for something to break the glass with. He saw the small chest which contained his inheritance and threw it against the latticed window. With a tinkling crash, the heavy box tore through the leaded panes and plunged to the alley below.

The black fumes that filled the room were sucked out of the jagged hole and the flames roared towards it, surrounding Will as he tried to make the gap large enough for him to crawl through. The sharp glass cut and sliced into his hands but in his despair he found a heap of material on the buckling floor and with it he was able to cover the cruel spikes that jabbed from the casement.

Will squeezed out of the narrow window and balanced on the meagre ledge outside. It was a horrible, high place; the alley fell away beneath him and the world seemed to spin as he braced himself for the jump. With a horrendous clamour the floor of the bedchamber collapsed behind him and the walls of the building shuddered alarmingly. Flames shot out of the window, burning Will's arms and legs and lapping up to the roof.

With his eyes clamped shut, the boy leaped from the ledge.

The attic burned furiously. The crimson paint blistered from the door and the mirrored globe exploded into a thousand twinkling fragments. The shelves fell from the cracking walls and the dried herbs which dangled from the rafters dripped fiery flowers. The ancient scrolls were consumed by the flames and the books which contained the secrets of alchemy and magic were reduced to ashes. In only five minutes, the lifetime's work of Doctor Spittle was utterly destroyed.

Amid this torrent of flame there was no sign of Jupiter or his brother.

As the smoke poured into the attic the two cats had continued to claw and bite one another. So locked in their deadly contest were they, that only when the flames licked under the door did they know of the danger.

The fight had ceased as both hunted for a way out. But the only exit they could find was through the fireplace and up the chimney. It was in that blackened, soot-filled passage they now climbed.

Leech had been the first to scramble into the cramped passage of brick but Jupiter was not far behind.

The air inside the chimney was hot and stuffy, it stung their eyes and parched their mouths, but it was the only way out. Several feet above, a circle of ruddy daylight lured them on, but each movement was slow and laboured. Both cats were already drained from their struggles against one another and they hauled themselves up as fast as they were able.

Jupiter's arms ached as he clung to the brickwork; the scorching smoke rose about him and far below he could hear the floor of the alchemist's bedchamber crash into ruin. The chimney quivered and Leech whined piteously as his claws lost their grip.

Desperately, the runt groped for a foothold but his panic was too great and he scraped away at the brickwork in vain. He looked down in despair and whimpered all the more. The chimney was on fire!

In the dim, smoke-swirling distance beneath him orange flames leapt upwards, drawing closer with every second.

Leech squealed as one of his claws snagged on a brick and was torn from his paw. Shrieking, he slithered down, dropping like a stone, and the fire rushed up to greet him.

Jupiter heard the mew of dismay; glancing upward he saw the dark shape of his brother come hurtling down. He hesitated then made up his mind – he could not bear to see his brother plunge to such a horrible death. Deftly he reached out and caught Leech's paw as he plummeted past.

'Hurry!' he told the runt. 'Find a ledge – I can't keep hold much longer.'

Leech did as he was instructed and his gasping breaths filled the narrow chimney until he was ready to set off once more.

All that time Jupiter supported him and the flames came ever nearer. The fur on both cats frazzled with the broiling heat and their whiskers were singed off their faces.

Of Reckoning and Destiny

As the ravening fire approached, Leech turned a bewildered head to his brother. 'Why did you save me?' he asked. 'It would have been easier for you to let me perish. You could have escaped by now.'

Jupiter shrugged. 'I realised just how selfish I have been,' he replied, coughing in the stifling atmosphere. 'Magic is not the answer. The secret arts ought to be left alone – problems are better dealt with on a humbler scale. After this day I swear never to use my powers again.' Through the clouds of reeking smoke he stared intently at Leech then said, 'Can you forgive me, brother, for all the hurts I have caused you? If we both escape this madness I promise we shall live happily together. The simple lives of hunters – no more spells for me.'

Leech grinned and he shook Jupiter's paw. 'Now do I forgive you,' he said gladly, 'but let us leave this terrible place.' With a glitter in his green eyes he clambered upwards and Jupiter followed.

The Great Fire rampaged through the city and nothing could stem its progress. Gunpowder was used to blow up houses in the fire's path but it bridged the gaps and spread more quickly than before.

The apothecary shop was almost totally destroyed. The first two storeys were already burnt out shells and the attic was in full flame. Only the roof remained intact but the tiles were falling away like autumn leaves and cinders were shooting up through the holes like fireworks.

The chimney stack of the building was tall and towered high above the sloping roof. Black smoke curled lovingly about it, like dark waves about the mast of a sunken galleon.

In the streets, all was confusion and chaos. People were salvaging what belongings they could before the flames reached their homes and bearing them through the razed lanes. The pigeons fluttered and wheeled over the city in fright and amazement and those that were foolish enough to dare the heats fell from the sky with burned wings.

Into this frightening, fire-brimming world came Leech. His ugly head reared over the top of the chimney stack and he hauled himself up to the precarious ledge. Putting a paw to his chest he fought for breath; the airs above London were hotter than those he had just escaped. He looked about him and wondered how to escape from this lofty height.

The roof was burning now and as he gazed round he saw the horrible devastation that the fire had already caused. The city would never be the same.

'Leech!' called Jupiter suddenly.

The runt turned and a charred, black paw came grasping over the edge of the chimney.

'Help me!' Jupiter cried. 'My strength is failing. I can't make it – please!'

Leech stared down. His brother's face was contorted in anguish, but an evil glow shone in the runt's eyes.

'If we both escape indeed!' he spat with scorn. 'Do you really think I want you to live, brother dear? Do you not understand that your precious gift should have been mine from the first?'

Jupiter looked at him beseechingly. 'My claws,' he cried, 'they're slipping – you must help me!'

Leech drew himself up, all the misery and hatred swelling inside. His loathing for his brother overwhelmed him and he hissed, 'I said I forgave you brother, and now I do indeed. This is my hour – when I shall take what is rightfully mine.'

Reaching down, he clutched Jupiter's paw and began to prise it from the edge.

'Stop!' shouted Jupiter. 'I'll fall!'

'I know,' his brother murmured as the last claw scraped down the mortar. 'Go to your doom – Lord of Nothing!' he exulted.

Jupiter fell.

Down into the fiery hell of the building he spun and the excited flames blasted up to receive him.

One final cry of surprise and dismay floated up to the runt's twitching ears.

'LEEEEEEEEEEEEEEECCCHH!' came the echoing call – and then the voice was silenced.

Leech threw back his head and crowed triumphantly. He had succeeded at last: the only member of his family left alive, the magic was his to command. But the laughter died in his throat for his lofty perch shivered and the bricks began to split.

The runt held on grimly as a tremor quaked through the chimney and a long crack snaked up it. He looked around but nowhere was safe, everything was burning about him and he realised that his brother had cheated him at the end.

His emerald eyes fixed straight ahead, Leech clung to the ledge as it slid and toppled towards the ground. His shrill screeches pierced the heavens as the smoking remains of the apothecary shop came crashing down. A mighty roar erupted in the alley as the chimney stack collapsed and the choking soot exploded in all directions. Leech's screams were drowned and the fire raged on.

The roads out of London were impassable. Thousands of displaced people thronged the road to Greenwich, their few belongings strapped to their backs or carried in their arms. The lucky few who had managed to rescue most of their possessions ploughed through the dismal masses in heavily-laden carts. It was a scene of biblical proportions; the flight from the burning city was awful to behold. An enormous tide of shambling, dispirited figures leaving the devastation behind them – not knowing where to go.

It was as though God had visited His wrath upon the whole of London, such was the fury of the flames, and so terrible was the burning that no one dared turn back to look on it in case they were transformed into salt.

On the horizon the fire still blazed. It had been rampaging out of control for three whole days now and the fumes blotted out the sun so that midday seemed like the blackest, bloodiest night. The massive bulk of St Paul's was a charred husk, its tower a funnel for the gushing smokes to issue from. Despair was in everyone's heart.

The flow of human sorrow trudged down the old Woolwich road. Even at this distance the glare of the burning threw their stark shadows before them and it was as though they walked in a river of darkness.

Young and old, rich and poor, all rubbed shoulders in that sorry expanse, sharing the misery and loss.

And there, dazed, shivering and covered in ash, was Will. Carried along by the forlorn masses he staggered and stumbled. In his arms he carried only two things – one was a small chest, the other a filthy bundle of material. He had no idea where he was heading; numbed with shock and pinched with hunger he just followed everyone else. His world was in ruins and the horror of his ordeals had laid a silence over his mind.

Not one word had he spoken since he had jumped from the window and if anyone tried to help him he would run off in fear, clutching his treasures to his breast.

As the multitude crossed the boundary of Deptford, a sweet voice cut through the desolation of Will's soul and he gazed around dumbly.

'Will!' cried the voice, and it seemed to him that he had heard the sound before. He stopped marching and the people roughly surged past him.

'Will!' It rang out again.

A gleaming, white swan seemed to be riding on the surface of the black river, and it was that which called to him. The boy shook his head giddily – it was no swan, but a milk-white arm raised above the bowed heads and it was waving frantically.

The figure pushed towards him, sobbing with joy beyond all hope.

'Oh, Will!' she cried flinging herself about his shoulders.

He backed away and peered at the vision that wept before him. She was beautiful; her cascading hair was like fine gold and he reached out to touch it to make sure she was real. Will's lips trembled as he recalled the word that went with this angel.

'M . . . Molly,' he whispered.

'That's right, my little darlin',' she said tearfully. 'Don't you worry now – Molly's here.'

He stared at her again and at last he was released from the pits of his despair. 'Molly!' he yelled. 'You're alive! But how? And where have you been?'

She laughed and hugged him tightly. 'All in good time,' she said, 'but first let's get clear.'

Out of the expanse of people they slowly made their way and she led him to a tavern situated at the roadside.

'It's a miracle I managed to get a room here,' she told him, 'and another that I was gazin' out of the window when I spotted you.'

They passed into a small, crowded parlour; everyone was looking for somewhere to stay and the buzzing talk was all of the fire. Molly bade the landlord bring food and drink then found a relatively quiet corner where Will collapsed into a soft chair. The chest fell from his grasp and landed with a jingling thud on the floor. He smiled at Molly's surprise then told her what had happened.

'He deserved that and more beside!' she declared when his tale was finished. 'But at least Spittle won't trouble you any longer. You won't find me grieving for him.'

Will had been clutching the dirty bundle of material close to his chest, now he laid it gently on his lap and asked, 'Where have you been all this time? Did you stay with Mother Myrtle in the pest-house?'

She lowered her eyes. 'Yes,' she murmured, 'I stayed and was spared – this whole year I have nursed and tended to the sick and dying.' She shuddered, then a faint smile lit her face. 'With the plague decreasing, come last Friday there was only one patient left and when she died there was nothing further for me to do there. I'm glad she passed peacefully; she said the Lord would take her when her work was done and He did.'

Just then the food arrived and Will fell on it hungrily. Molly waited whilst he ate his fill but her attention was increasingly drawn to the heap of cloth that he had placed on his knees. As he gulped down the last mouthful and was leaning back in his chair patting his stomach, she pointed at the curious bundle.

'Here's you letting fortunes drop to the ground,' she said, 'but what's so precious about that?'

Will took up the soot-covered velvet and began unfurling it. 'This,' he told her, 'is Spittle's posh robe – or rather it was. A sorry sight it is now, but it was the only thing I could find in the wreckage to wrap him in.'

'Him?' repeated Molly. 'If you've got the apothecary's head there I reckon we should stick it on a spike like they did to Cromwell.'

Carefully the boy lifted the last fold and there, huddled in a pathetic ball was a cat. It was charred and scorched, all the fur had been singed off its body and it was covered with terrible burns.

'Is it alive?' breathed Molly.

'I don't know,' he answered sorrowfully. 'When I found him there were signs, but no – if he isn't dead yet he soon will be.'

Molly asked the landlord for some milk and when it arrived she poured it on to a saucer. 'Lay it here, by the hearth,' she said gently. 'Does it have a name?'

'Yes,' Will replied, 'but I'm not certain if it's Leech

or Jupiter. The poor thing, it must have been terrified in that attic, I've never seen anything like that awful fire.'

The young woman said nothing but stared out of the window towards the smoking city. 'Maybe when it's rebuilt,' she muttered, 'the devil won't stalk through the streets any more. It's a new beginning.' Then she turned back to Will and, with a grin, said, 'I saw Peggy Blister yesterday – or rather Peggy Mortichuke as I should call her now. Only went and got married she did, and to a minister as well! Lord knows how she managed that.' They both laughed and Molly softly murmured, 'If Peggy Blister can do it I'm sure I can – the slate has been wiped clean now.'

Tenderly Will placed the limp and motionless cat by the hearth, but it was too weak to drink the milk. The sight of its sad, battered body was the last straw and the boy burst into tears.

'Come Will,' said Molly, 'let's see if we can get you a room here as well. You need a good night's rest. After that, who knows? Perhaps we can both return to Adcombe.'

'Maybe,' Will murmured, 'maybe.'

'You never know,' Molly gurgled, 'I might even open my own apothecary shop. Can you imagine Aunt Hannah's face?'

And laughing, they went up the stairs.

'The Blackened Beast'

The glow of the Great Fire was bright in the night sky; for another two days it would burn, savage and remorseless. The distant reports of gunpowder boomed out over the river and the crashing destruction of church spires as they toppled in ruin disturbed the sleep of those camped by the roadside or sheltering under friendly roofs.

Only Will slept soundly; no rumour of disaster could reach down into the depths of his comfortable slumber. For the first time in two years he lay on a genuine bed and his faint snores were peaceful and contented.

Down in the dim parlour nothing stirred, only a red glimmer played over the walls, echoing the dancing flames across the water.

By the cold hearth, on the embroidered robe of Magnus Zachaire, the breaths of the burned and withered cat rasped in its parched throat. A low, dismal moan issued from its mouth and an eye flickered open. Blearily the smoke-filled slit roved round and took in the unfamiliar surroundings.

The cat remembered nothing of the last three days, he recalled only his rescue from the smouldering rubble. After that all was dark and he had been lost in a pathless sleep ever since.

He was tired; every fibre of his body ached and the searing pain of his burns almost made him faint. Death was close at hand – he sensed his watchful presence waiting for him to yield. It was a tantalising prospect, to leave all the hurts and quench the fires that shrivelled his skin. But he clung on grimly; a fierce determination stronger than 'He who waits in the shadows' controlled him.

That gentleman would leave alone this time, he told himself, and one who had tasted the elixir would never have to fear his return. The eyelid fluttered shut and the cat fell into a tortuous swoon.

The night stretched by and it was so silent that when a small voice exclaimed, 'Lumme! By crikey, just have a goggle at all that grub! Har har!' the sound seemed much louder than it actually was.

Waddling footsteps pattered over the floor as a rat came into the room. He darted over to a pile of crumbs left over from somebody's supper and wolfed them down.

'Luvverly, luvverly,' he squeaked licking his lips. 'Now what other bit o' nosh is a waitin' fer me to guzzle it down?'

He turned, searching for more food, and then let out a frightened squawk. 'EEK!' he yammered, when he saw the cat lying on the robe.

The rat froze, not daring to move a muscle – but his teeth chattered and he had to bury his snout in his claws to silence them.

'I'm done fer now!' he blubbered. 'I'm tiger's meat fer sure!'

He closed his eyes, waiting for the cat to pounce, and his knees knocked in fear. Several minutes passed and the rat patted himself all over to make sure he was not dead. Then he peered over at the motionless terror and frowned. 'Ain't I good enough fer yer then?' he cried, grossly insulted.

There was no response.

'Hello, hello,' the rat muttered, 'hoy you, Fangface! Are you dead then?' He waited for a reply but none came. Taking heart at this lucky turn of events he plucked up the courage which had fallen about his heels and bowled right over to have a closer look.

The rat's whiskers twitched. 'Burned to a cinder,' he remarked, 'but who'd want to lug a duff dead moggy like that in 'ere?'

He raised his eyebrows and looked about him. This was an opportunity too good to waste. With utmost daring and valour he snapped his fingers right in the cat's face then blew a long, insolent raspberry.

'Ho, ho,' he chortled, 'I likes this.' Then he extended one single claw and gave the cat a hard prod.

At once the eye snapped open. The rat squeaked in horror and jumped into the air. 'Strike me!' he wailed. 'It's not deaded after all.' And he turned to scarper.

'Stay!' croaked a commanding voice. 'Do I not know you?'

The rodent spun round, and the eye stabbed at him with a harsh light. It flickered over his orange fur and the voice said, 'Your name is Beckett is it not?'

'Er . . . yes,' mumbled the rat in surprise, 'that be my name – how comes you knowed it?'

'Do you not recognise me?' teased the lulling reply.

Beckett scratched himself. ''Ere,' he declared, 'you be one o' them tigers wot prowled under my cage ain'tcha?'

'Most wise and wonderful rodent,' the cat purred silkily, 'how good it is to see you again.'

'Which one are you?' asked Beckett curiously. 'Be you that sickly runty one or that ginger tike who kept making fun at me when I was – ahem, pink?'

'Can you not tell?'

'You'm too mangled an' singed to know fer sure – you might be either.'

'Then what does it matter? Know only that I need your help.'

'Mine?' cried Beckett greatly flattered. 'How come?'

The cat coughed and the head lifted from the folds of the robe. 'I am weak,' he said, 'I need a place to heal myself, somewhere to hide – away from this harsh world of man. I have lived too long as their thrall. Help me to a place of safety and I shall reward you.'

Beckett sucked his teeth thoughtfully. 'Oh I don't knowed about that,' he burbled rubbing his ear, 'I doesn't see why I should trust you. But there is a place nearby, a chamber under the ground it be – right good fer you an' all, it bein' so dark like.'

'Excellent,' hissed the cat. 'Take me there.'

'Ooh no, I dursen't! It's for ratfolk only – they'd never let a moggy down there. I'd get bloody-boned if they found us! Nasty things there are in the tunnels down there, places that ain't nice an' what I steers clear of. The Three haunt there 'tis said. Oh no, I can't never take you!'

'Obey me!' spat the cat and both eyes snapped wide open. A fiery light shone from them and they glowed yellow and red. Beckett tried to step back but it was too late, he was snared in their power and could not move.

The cat laughed softly and smoke curled from his lips. 'Come,' he commanded, 'lead me to this place – petty rat gods hold no fear for me.' Slowly he rose from his bed of velvet and crept nearer to Beckett, wincing with every painful step.

The orange rat had no strength to disobey. 'Yes, sir,' he murmured.

Pausing, the cat stared down at his own blackened fur. Even as he looked the transformation was beginning and what had been sable was turning to ginger.

Leech sneered at the irony of it all, and yet perhaps it was better so. He had never been happy as the unloved son of Imelza whose brother was so mighty and noble. His jealousy had gnawed at him then, envying and desiring everything that Jupiter had. But now he was in possession of it all – save one thing only.

Rousing from his evil, brooding thoughts, Leech glared at Beckett and announced, 'Do not call me sir, I have a far more fitting title. For I am Jupiter!' he lied. 'Lord of All.'

And they stole away into the deep places under the ground and the cat crawled at last into the dark portal that awaited him.

THE DEPTFORD HISTORIES

Book Two: The Oaken Throne

Robin Jarvis

It is a time of magic and a time of darkness. The Starwife, leader of the black squirrels, lies dying, betrayed and poisoned. But as the bat army launches a devastating attack on her realm, she staggers to a window and summons aid . . .

These terrible events are to draw Vesper, the young bat, and Ysabelle, the squirrel maiden, into taking a fearsome journey – in a desperate attempt to save their lands from destruction.

THE DEPTFORD HISTORIES

Book Three: Thomas

Robin Jarvis

It is four years since the fall of Jupiter, but upon the Cutty Sark, all is far from well. Thomas Triton, a retired midshipmouse, is tormented by horrific visions of the past: of storm-lashed seas, ferocious battles, lost cities and terrifying heathen gods.

But worse still, now he knows the time has come to confront the most chilling memory of his youth and a dark, deeply dreadful secret . . .